I.D. RUSSELL

Demon in the Sack

First published by Ringo Jones Productions 2024

This novel is entirely a work of fiction. The names, characters and incidents portrayed in it are the work of the author's imagination. Any resemblance to actual persons, living or dead, events or localities is entirely coincidental.

Designations used by companies to distinguish their products are often claimed as trademarks. All brand names and product names used in this book and on its cover are trade names, service marks, trademarks and registered trademarks of their respective owners. The publishers and the book are not associated with any product or vendor mentioned in this book. None of the companies referenced within the book have endorsed the book.

First edition

ISBN: 9781988383361

This book was professionally typeset on Reedsy.
Find out more at reedsy.com

For RedLetterMedia, Game Sack, Cinemassacre,
MetalJesusRocks,
and any other YouTubers I've ever watched

PROLOGUE

C andles burned with the aroma of brimstone, casting flickering shadows along the cracked and peeling-paint brick walls. A ceremonial altar in the centre of the room, covered in thick red velvet, was encircled by a painted pentagram intricately drawn with the blood of sacrificial animals. Figures in crimson robes lined up just outside of the symbol, chanted in a slow murmuring hum. He walked down the dimly lit hallway, gingerly carrying the components of the ritual on a plush cushion. Candles ensconced in wall mounts glowed with an increased fierceness as he passed, then burnt out in a puff of smoke, leaving the area behind him smothered in stygian darkness. The chanting rose to guttural rumblings as he entered the room. The figures in the dark robes made way for him to pass. He paced around the pentagram counterclockwise three times, repeating the sacred phrases of power in a language long forgotten to civilized man, words from a distant past of superstition and prophecy.

The candles burned six inches high as he stopped at the head of the altar and raised the pillow upwards, crying out the final syllables.

The flames blared with impossible heat. He was sweating

beneath the robes. The room was awash in fire and flame. As he lowered the pillow, the blaze lowered in unison, until the candles were nearly extinguished. The pentagram on the floor began to pulse rhythmically, glowing a crimson red, as if in time to an inaudible heartbeat.

He took a deep breath. The next step would determine success or catastrophic failure. The pulsing symbol, imbued with demonic energy, would be his only protection. Should it fail, he would be incinerated.

Finish the ritual. Years of planning will bear fruit.

He lifted his leg. A slight gasp came from someone in the line. He shot them a dirty look. Faces were hidden behind cowls. He steeled himself and stepped to the floor beyond the pentagram.

The space within the circle was thirty degrees warmer than the rest of the room. He froze. Would his leg ignite? The room filled with nervous energy.

He stepped his other leg in, careful not to disturb the drawing on the floor. That would unleash the fires of hell onto the others.

Both feet were now inside the circle, and he felt an oppressive heaviness, thick, smoky air, as if he was in a sauna. Two more steps and he was at the altar. He laid the pillow down. Two objects rested on top. One, a curved blade, reflected his cowled face.

This is it. There is no turning back.

His hands closed around the cool metal hilt. He held it aloft as he spoke the rest of the archaic spell.

The candles burned high, the chanting rising to shrieks of fevered passion. He looked to the ceiling, only it was gone. The space within the circle was a wall of burning fire. He could no longer see the others.

"Oh, dark one, we beseech you to waken your servant. Ignite the flames of hatred. Set forth the path of destruction. Bring on the end times. This final sacrifice is proof of our devotion. Awaken the evil you have seeded. Awaken!"

He held the knife over the squirming form on the pillow. White, hairless, tiny hands reaching upwards curiously.

"I give this firstborn to you."

The flames around him seemed to coalesce into a mass of swirling darkness within the blazing heat. Was it just his imagination, or was there a presence? Part of the fire, watching, waiting, whispering in his head.

He would not back down.

"By the dark rites, a life for a life!"

He cast the blade down. The fires flared once in an intense white heat explosion. Blinded, he stumbled backwards. Heat enveloped him. The room seemed to immolate in a flash. The smack of concrete jarred him out of the impossible brightness that penetrated his closed eyes. Forms began to take shape, shadows looking down over him.

A hand grabbed his.

"Did the dark one hear?"

After-images of reddish glare vibrated around the speaker. The candles in the room were nearly depleted. The others were pressed up against the walls, nervously anticipating his response. He looked to the altar. The blade pressed into the tiny, blackened shape on the pillow, lifeless. He thought of the centuries' old ash forms of the victims of Pompeii.

He stood up. The pentagram was gone, the floor burnt clean. He slowly reached out to the blade. As his finger touched the hilt, the charcoal body beneath crumbled into dust.

"I'm not sure," he said as he stared at the ash that had once been a newborn. "I felt something watching me as I performed the ritual."

"You disappeared. It was like the entire area within the circle was nothing but darkness."

"I was in his realm, it was... disorienting."

"But—"

He touched the ash gently with his fingers. Still warm. There was no time to mourn, nor reason to. The ritual was complete. "It is done," he said calmly.

"Now we—"

"Watch what his servant will unleash."

CHAPTER ONE: THREE ROOMATES

"Welcome to another episode of Three Gamers. Tonight's stream is going to focus on Bond, James Bond, and we're going to start with a well-known classic that some of you may have heard of."

Joe Evans lifted a small grey cartridge with a faded sticker on the front. His thumb partially obscured the image of Pierce Brosnan holding the classic Walther PPK.

"Whoops." He realized he was blocking the image and moved his finger. The blinking red light of the camera looked back at him. "In case it's still not clear what I've got here, it's the pretty legendary Nintendo 64 game, *Goldeneye*."

He slowly moved the game towards the lens, hoping the auto focus was tracking properly.

"As soon as the rest of the guys get here, we'll get into it—" he began but was interrupted by a loud shout of:

"It's beer o'clock!"

Joe looked away from the camera to the now-open apartment door where Mike Baumer walked in, carrying a case of beer. He wore the brown shorts and button-up shirt of a UPS delivery driver. His dark hair was cut short, starting to show signs of thinning, with a few grey hairs near the ears.

His brow was prominent, his chin pointed, and his cheeks covered in a few days' stubble. He swung the door shut with his foot.

"Hang on," Joe said frantically, trying to spin the camera around to catch Mike entering.

Mike carried the beer over to the couch. "No artistic stuff, man, this is just beer."

Joe struggled to keep Mike in frame.

"You're late, I've already started the show," Joe said.

"Without the beer?"

Joe returned the viewpoint of the camera back to show the whole couch.

Mike sat on the right-hand side seat of the crimson sofa, his bulk flattening the cushion down. Next to him, two indents in the other cushions awaited the bodies that had created them.

"There's a schedule, you know." Joe took one last look to make sure he'd framed the couch right, before moving to sit back down in front of the large television. He mouthed 'sorry, guys' to the small camera recording them on the couch.

"Hold up, Evans, I had a brutal day. They made me pick up a pallet of heavy shit from Kyle's Refrigeration. I almost threw my freaking back out. Seventy-five-pound weight limit, my ass."

"What was it?"

"I don't look in the boxes, I just pick them up," Mike said, rolling his eyes to the camera.

"If it was Kyle's Refrigeration, I'm guessing it had something to do with refrigerators, right?"

"Google it if you care so much." Mike looked into the camera. "Anyone out there give a shit, look up Kyle's

Refrigeration in River City. For all your whatever-it-is-they-do needs."

"The first plug is free, folks, after that we have to charge," Joe said.

"There's no way I'm going to do tonight's show sober after all that, so I stopped on the way home to get something brown and intoxicating."

The camera took in the whole exchange from its impassive, fixed angle, but Mike was blocking the beer case.

"Tonight's stream is going to be brought to you by…" Joe paused, trying to read the beer label from through Mike's legs. "What beer did you get?"

Mike ripped the side of the box open with a practiced motion and slid a can out, flipping it over to Joe in one quick toss.

Joe turned the label outwards, showing it clearly to the camera.

"River City Brown. Same as last stream. If you guys were expecting a local craft beer, maybe something imported or exotic, you're not going to get it."

"What's wrong with River City Brown?"

"Leave any comments about his taste in beer and—"

"I don't give a fuck what you guys write," Mike said to the camera. He put the case of beer on the coffee table and turned it around, so the opening faced him. He took his shirt off and threw it over the couch with a layup shot.

"There's the shot…"

It hit a yellowed stain on the wall and slid down on the top of a pile of clothes.

"And a perfect swish."

"If you had that in the Three Gamers drinking game, take

a shot now," Joe said.

Mike wore a faded white undershirt that was beginning to turn yellow. He bent over and dropped his shorts to his ankles, stepping out of the brown fabric right in front of the camera and Joe.

"Ever think of doing that in your room and not in front of everyone watching?"

"Does this show have standards now?" Mike said as he kicked the shorts towards Joe's head. It took a quick head dodge to avoid getting hit in the face. The shorts hit another yellow spot on the wall behind him to slide down to land on a second pile of unwashed clothes.

"I don't want to have to put an age warning up," Joe said. "It'll limit our discoverability."

"This ratty old couch is limiting my discoverability right now," Mike said as he fished around underneath the cushions.

"Is Mike looking for loose change? Yesterday's pizza?" Joe said in his best sportscaster's voice.

Mike's eyes lit up. He pulled out a pair of dark navy workout shorts.

"Wrong on both counts," Joe said. "It's his favourite pair."

"I knew they were in there somewhere," Mike said as he slid the shorts on and sat down.

"Most people keep their stuff in a, uh, I don't know, dresser? Closet? Not Mike, he prefers the hidden alcove underneath the cushions."

"At least here I don't have to walk all the way over there," Mike said, pointing to the hallway behind him and his room beyond.

"A room too far," Joe said. "Drop your pants live on stream or walk twenty feet away."

Mike turned his head in a circle to get a kink out of his neck and scratched his shoulder just next to the frayed strap of his undershirt. Chest hair struggled to escape the low collar. "You know they get a kick out of seeing this stuff, Evans."

"What demographic?"

"All of them," Mike said. "I'm the one they come to see. Legs are a key part of why."

"The comments prove they aren't," Joe said sarcastically.

Mike slid in perfectly to the indent of his body on the couch, attached like velcro. "Someone out there has got to be into it, internet rule thirty-four."

"Don't give them any ideas."

Mike took a sip of his beer. "How many people are watching this right now anyway?"

Joe looked over to a laptop set up on the coffee table in front of the couch. The table was covered in crumbs and a massive tangle of wires from a dozen different game controllers. The huge jumbled-up ball of cords led back to the shelving unit upon which sat the massive television and all of their different video game systems. Consoles from the entire history of video gaming, from the Atari and Nintendo of the 70s and 80s to the PlayStation and Xbox of the modern era with every SEGA machine in between. On one wall of the apartment rested a titanically huge DVD shelf filled to the brim with movies and games. Some were loose, cartridges piled up vertically next to each other, while others were still in their original cases. The entire shelf represented thousands of dollars and years of their lives. The laptop displayed their streaming stats live as they happened. "It looks like we are currently rocking... four people."

This stream, "Three Gamers", aired four nights a week. A

live session where the three of them played and talked about their favourite games, riffed on movies, music, pop culture, memes, jokes they'd heard, the things that went on in their day-to-day lives. They attracted a small audience of people who liked the connection they shared and identified with the personalities they let show. They'd been doing it for years.

"Four people?" Mike said.

"Yup, there are four people watching," Joe said.

It was a far cry from their busiest nights where upwards of a few hundred people might be tuning in.

"You're worried that four people might have seen my gitch?"

"First of all, any people that have to see your gitch is too many and second of all, who the hell says gitch anymore? That's kindergarten shit."

Mike looked to the camera and rolled his eyes. "Hey, all four of you. If you were offended by my gitch, be sure to let us know in the comments section. And tell Joe Evans here that gitch is a perfectly normal thing to call your underwear. People of all ages do it. Okay? Thanks."

A soft ping sound came from the laptop. Mike and Joe peered towards the screen to see that someone had just posted in the *live comment* section of the stream window.

"Shit, there you go!" Mike said proudly. "YourNiNight420 says there's nothing wrong with dropping trow live." Mike leaned back, putting his hands behind his head in triumph. His armpit hair was fabulously thick, four inches long, rich and luxurious.

"Yeah, well, he or she, or whatever YourNiNight420 is, also says that it's pronounced gotch, not gitch, so there," Joe said.

"Come on, YourNiNight420, work with me here," Mike said as he cracked open another one of his beers and poured it into a clear glass marked with their Three Gamers logo.

"Look at that rich brown liquid," he said. "Lots of body, only a little head."

"Sounds like your last girlfriend," Joe said.

Mike stopped pouring as another ping sound emerged from the laptop. "Don't even say it."

"YourNiNight420 gave me a thumbs up."

"You're on your way to the banned list, YourNiNight420," Mike said grumpily.

He finished pouring and tilted the glass with the logo towards the camera. "Only the finest of licensed glasses for the finest of beers." He took one long sip, pounding back a third of the drink.

"We will not bow to any sponsors," Joe said. "Even our own merch. Available on Three Gamers Dot Com by the way."

"Nice plug. Real subtle."

"I pride myself on subtlety," Joe said.

"I hadn't noticed."

"Exactly!"

"You are such a dork."

"That's what my fans like," Joe said.

Mike finished the rest of the beer and belched. "And that's what my fans like."

They stared at each other in silence for a moment.

"Anyway." Joe snapped back to reality. "I was just telling the four of our viewers that tonight we're focusing in on Bond, James Bond." Joe showed the *Goldeneye* cartridge to Mike who grabbed another beer. "The Nintendo 64 multiplayer first person shooter—"

"They know what it is, Joe," Mike said, interrupting him.

"I was just giving the historical—"

"Anyone tuning in to this knows what the fuck Goldeneye is. I mean, it's not like we're talking about the movie here."

"—and background info on the game," Joe said, finishing his thought.

"I don't care about that stuff. And I don't think the viewers at home do either."

"They might."

"Guys, do you?"

A ping sound made him look towards the laptop. He didn't say anything.

"Well?"

"Just an emoji."

Joe looked over to see a comment from JoJo'sBizarreAdvertiser2 saying, "I like to hear that stuff."

"Aha!" Joe said proudly. "See?"

"Whatever," Mike said. "The rest of our capacity crowd of three don't need to know the complete history of a game twenty years old. We all lived it once."

"You don't know that they all did."

"And I don't care. Let's just play before I lose interest."

"I'm getting to that!"

"Wait, where the hell is Dan? We can't have Three Gamers with only two gamers."

"I told him we were starting at—"

Before Joe could say another word, the apartment door opened and in came the third gamer, Dan Stoddard, carrying a stack of red pizza boxes. Dan was six foot six, nearly three hundred pounds, with short black hair and thick glasses. He wore tan pants and a sweater.

"Sorry I'm late, guys, they didn't have the order ready when I went to pick it up. I had to wait twenty minutes."

"Speak of the devil!" Joe said.

"What do you mean, they didn't have it ready?" Mike asked. "We order the same thing every Friday."

Dan slid the pizza boxes onto the coffee table next to the beer case. "I guess they forgot this time. I don't think it was the usual guy, uh, what's his name?"

"Phil?"

"Yeah. It wasn't Phil. It was some hipster with a Force Awakens hoodie."

"Well." Mike turned to the camera. "That's strike sixteen, Chicago Phil's Pizza."

"Hire better staff, Phil," Joe said. "No hipsters please."

"I don't know that he was a hipster," Dan said.

"What was his moustache like?" Mike asked.

"Curled, like one of those pictures you see of old boxers," Dan said.

"I knew it, total hipster."

"As long as they got my pepperoni and mushroom right this time, I don't care." Joe opened the top box.

"And?"

Frowning at what he found, he looked at the second, third, and fourth boxes.

"Your silence is telling, Joe."

"Disappointed?"

"God dammit, make that strike seventeen, Chicago Phil's Pizza."

Dan ducked into his room and emerged wearing a white Legend of Zelda T-shirt and jeans. He went to the fridge and grabbed a Pepsi. He took his seat in the middle of the couch. His body sank into the remaining indented shape perfectly. "What are we playing tonight, guys?"

"As I was telling Mike a second ago, tonight is about—"

"Bond, James Bond," Mike interrupted.

"Classic. Sounds good," Dan said. "So, what'll it be then, the stack?"

Joe and Dan both looked at each other and said in unison, "Library."

"Let's get this going then," Joe said as he rose up. His knees cracked. He headed over to the television and bent down, shuffling around the consoles until he found the black Nintendo 64. He slid in the grey *Goldeneye* cartridge. Flicking the system on, he joined them back at the couch. "Okay, boys, everyone mic'd up?"

Dan and Mike each wore small clip-on microphones attached to their shirts. "Yup," they both said.

"Video stream going through alright, Dan?"

Dan checked a second laptop, this one beneath the coffee table. It showed what a viewer of the channel would see online: a huge dark rectangle, the television, with another screen inset in the lower right showing the three of them on the couch. Behind them, the wall covered in posters.

Joe waved his hand in front. There was a fraction of a second delay from movement to reaction on screen. The wall behind them was covered floor to ceiling in posters of sports figures: Teemu Selanne, Kirby Puckett, Lanny MacDonald; movies: *Gladiator, Blade Runner, Transformers*; and old video game inserts from Nintendo Power.

Dan pressed a button on the laptop to swap what was in the large view box. A viewer could do the same, alternating from making the television screen the primary feed or that of the shot of the three guys on the couch. Joe waved his hand again, the motion delay more interesting than watching Dan play with the laptop.

"Looks good," Dan said as he slid back to the couch.

"Okay, then, time to hit the books!"

CHAPTER TWO: NEW TECHNOLOGY

"—on the lookout for license plate number K-L-H 4-5-6, repeat, be on the lookout for a stolen car. Red BMW. License plate K-L-H 4-5-6."

The radio crackled as the voice of the dispatcher faded away. Frank took the last bite of his burger and crumpled up the wrapper. He tossed it in the empty bag and wiped his hands on his pants. He cracked his wrists and turned the car on, feeling the surge of adrenaline that always came with the promise of a high-speed car chase.

"Another bastard out taking what doesn't belong to him. Will they never learn that when they step on the innocent, Detective Inspector Sargent Frank Malone steps back? Hard."

He pumped the gas and smiled. He'd liked the sound of that monologue. Tough, compact, full of forceful vengeance, just like he was. He'd been talking to himself a lot lately. Maybe it was his age catching up to him or maybe it was just the ever-present solitude of flying solo. Either way, it beat the radio.

"No shame in talking to yourself, Frankie," he said. "At least you like the sound of your own voice."

The days of walking the beat and chatting up Sally the

Grocer or Jose the Street Sweeper were long gone. He was behind a wheel now, his days filled with driving up and down the streets of River City on the lookout for that one case that would rev his engine like he was revving that of old Betty.

"Thatta girl," he said, listening to the vintage purr of an engine made back when they knew how to do it right.

He rubbed the dark brown dashboard, marvelling at the analog displays and manual odometer. Old Betty was the last of the vintage cruisers on the force. He had a special letter that let him drive her until she finally croaked. They'd tried to replace her with something more modern, but he'd put up one legendary stink and they'd backed off, holding their noses in fear.

"Who needs all those stupid bells and whistles?" he'd grumbled to the brass.

"Malone, these vehicles are equipped with an on-board computer, GPS, can do zero to sixty in—"

"Let me stop you right there," he'd said to the suit. "There's no way I'm letting Sputnik tell me where to drive."

"But—"

"I've been on these streets longer than you've been alive," he'd said to the wide-eyed, civilian-class, degree-waving nuisance. "There isn't a shortcut on these streets that I didn't discover, a back alley I haven't stumbled down, or an uncontrolled railway crossing I haven't passed over. So just leave me with old Betty and take that ugly Jetson's car someplace else."

They'd known better than to force the issue. He'd kept his car and radio. Sure, they had to pay a special dispatcher just for him, but she made the coffee in the office anyway and Frank had proven his worth time and time again out on the streets.

Like he was going to do again tonight.

"Okay, carjacker," he said, as he rubbed the steering wheel. "You'd better watch your six because Frank Malone is coming in at twelve o'clock." He looked at the dashboard clock. "Okay, two forty-five."

That didn't seem right. He checked his watch.

"Okay, five forty-five."

He smacked the dashboard clock, but it appeared to have frozen in place.

"Don't worry, baby, I won't hold that against you. As long as you catch me one car thief."

He pulled out into the streets and merged with traffic. This had been his city for so long that each day was like going to the beach with a beautiful woman. You never knew what might happen, you dreamed of what could happen, and either way you ended up with sand in your socks.

"Give me a sign, City," he said softly.

Frank Malone had been around the block a few times, twice on Sundays. He'd seen more and done more in his lifetime than just about anyone, but he wasn't set on walking out into that great sunset just yet. There was still so much more to do, still so many episodes of Perry Mason he hadn't seen. He wouldn't retire, even though his body was begging him to; no, he would keep on going out there day in and day out until he finally fell apart and they had to scrape his pieces up in a dustpan.

"Traffic seems a little slight for this time of day." It was the tail end of rush hour, so most of the commuters were either delivery drivers on their way back to the depot, or people leaving late from the office.

"Somewhere amongst you all is a thief," he said, scanning the cars. "A snake in the grass who bit off more than he could chew when he took a car that didn't belong to him."

A red light was ahead. Frank pulled up slowly, driving alongside a truck transporting hogs to slaughter. The aroma of wet swine, feces, and the animal fear of death wafted in through his open window. Or maybe that was just the burger wrapper on the floor.

He leaned over and called out to the driver through two open windows, "Howdy, citizen, how goes it?"

"What? Huh?" The driver, a rotund man with tanned skin, looked around until he saw Frank leaning over in his seat. "Oh, hi, officer, I wasn't speeding, was I?"

"I hope not."

"So I wasn't?"

"Were you?"

"Not that I know of."

"Speeding is a citation, you know."

"No!"

"It is – I checked it myself."

"No, I mean, I'm sure I wasn't speeding."

"Good, that's what I like to hear," Frank said. "Now, tell me something, have you seen a stolen red car around here on your rounds?"

"You're kidding, right?"

"I never kid about crime."

The driver raised an eyebrow, then slightly shook his head and said, "Man, how would I know if a car I'd seen was stolen?"

"It was red, one of those fancy Eurotrash models that speeds through our free-market streets on smugness and import duties."

"What, like a Porsche or something?"

The light turned green, and the man seemed like he wanted to pull out, but Frank was still holding his attention. Someone honked behind them.

"You'd know it if you saw it, probably speeding the wrong way down the street, blasting something that sounds like it came from a computer, maybe leaving a trail of baguettes and bratwurst behind it."

A horn honked again, then another, then another, a crescendo of cars desperate to make the light.

"Shit, officer, I only see the usual, right, like people driving normal, okay? Now, can I go? I gotta get these pigs down to the plant, they're due for the chopping block in an hour."

Frank nodded. "The people need their bacon and ham, my good man, they need their tenderloin and ribs, their sausage and shanks, their—"

HONK!

"If you see something suspicious," Frank told him, "you call me, okay?"

"Okay, but how the hell do I do that?"

The horns behind them were almost deafening.

"Just call my name and I'll be there."

The light changed to red. The driver leaned back in his seat, muttering to himself. He rolled up the window.

Frank slid back into his seat. "Another set of eyes in the hidden network of the law." He pulled out and drove into the intersection, barely noticing the two swerving cars that collided behind him as they slid to avoid him, driving straight into oncoming traffic.

CHAPTER THREE: THREE BECOMES TWO

"You don't have to look at everyone else's screen," Joe said.

"It's not my fault everyone's on the same one," Mike said. "It's part of the game, so it's fair game. What say you, audience?" He turned to the camera. "Is screen watching a valid strategy?"

Pings from a dozen answers came in simultaneously.

Joe leaned over to look, keeping one eye on his quarter of the television.

"Well?" Mike asked.

"Fifty fifty."

"Dead again, Joe," Mike shouted. "Gotta keep those eyes on the game."

Joe grunted, waiting to respawn.

The three of them were lost in the low resolution, polygonal action on screen. The familiar greys, tans, and greens of the backgrounds blurred by in a flash of gunfire and digital screams. The Bond fanfare music punctuated fits of laughter and swearing, all while they drank beer during the fleeting moments they could go with one hand free.

"Almost had you."

"Look out!"

"Sniper kill!"

"Cheap bastard!"

The cameras broadcasted it all live: every kill, death, swearing fit, sip of beer, bite of cold pizza, wipe of the hands on greasy pant legs, punch to the shoulder of the one who took someone out from behind.

"What's our viewership at, Dan?" Mike asked.

"Almost a hundred."

"I can't believe there's a hundred people out there watching me take you two to school. Old—"

"Don't even say it," Joe said, interrupting him.

"It's my line, I have to."

A dozen pings of comments.

"Yes, I know Mike needs new material," Joe said to the audience.

"Old school!" Mike shouted.

They weren't superstars in the world of streaming. Others could pull in millions of people, while Three Gamers had a small, but dedicated following. It made a hobby into a side hustle. Their banter gave strangers a chance to feel a connection. The names in their channel chat were a familiar list of those who were here time and time again.

"He said it," Dan shouted. "How many is that?"

"Anyone at home dead from alcohol poisoning yet?" Joe asked. "It's got to be ten shots by now, at least."

PING.

"RichardtheLianHeart265 says he just vomited up his liver."

"Leave the jokes to the professionals, guys," Mike said.

Part of it was performance, a relaxed interpretation of hundreds of previously unseen moments that they'd shared since grade school. Who would have ever thought there would be an audience for what they used to call wasting time? Anonymous viewers, commenting, throwing out memes, making their own jokes, begging to be noticed, trying to feel like they were a fourth gamer on the couch; they were the unspoken validation each of the Three Gamers refused to acknowledge they craved, the proof that for every time their parents told them they were wasting their lives playing video games, there was a point in the future where the practiced camaraderie would attract an audience willing to pay, even a small amount, to watch it happen.

PING.

"Yes, PacoPoosDay, I did kick their asses back in the day all the time," Mike said.

"You wish," Dan said. "Only if you had the golden gun."

"Don't even need it anymore. BAM!" Mike shouted as he stood up and punched the air in excitement. "One shot, head shot, dead shot, Joe. Say goodbye to another round."

Joe dropped his controller, eliminated. "For a guy who's supposedly disinterested in video games, you're clearly enjoying yourself."

"How can you not when you're kicking so much ass?"

"Just don't say the line again," Dan said, frantically pressing on his thumbstick, desperately trying to dodge in game.

"BAM again!" Mike shouted. "Double sniper kill. That's fifty-six for me and, oh, look at your score, Dan," he said as he held up the whiteboard placed next to the couch. He pointed proudly to dozens of barely legible scrawls beneath each of their names. "Fifty-one, two, only fifty-three for you. And what's this? Joe?" he said mockingly. "You're only sitting at forty-three. Looks like you're barely hanging in with the big boys here."

"Turn off that god-damned golden gun. Instant kills are so cheap. They break the game."

"Yeah," Dan agreed. "How do you always end up getting that thing?"

"Muscle memory, I guess."

"We haven't played this in years," Joe said. "It's almost like your whole I-don't-care-about-video-games thing is just an act."

It was. Mike played the part of the curmudgeon who reluctantly joined in every night only to lose himself in hyper competitive showdowns with whoever was beating him. It had become schtick, the origins lost to an online persona that their audience both expected and demanded.

"I don't care about video games," he said. "I just like kicking your asses."

"With the cheapest freaking thing in the whole game," Dan said, taking a sip of Pepsi.

Mike ticked off another line beneath his name. "If it's in the game, it can't be cheap. Or are you suggesting the programmers of the *classic*," he said, rolling his eyes to the camera, "Nintendo 64 gem Goldeneye made some kind of error? That they forgot to ensure balance in an entire mode of play? For shame."

"You wouldn't be so far ahead if we were playing something else, like Mortal Kombat 2," Joe said, grumbling. He had a persona, too, the picked-on third man who always lost to the others and clearly didn't enjoy it. It had been going on so long that sometimes he wondered what had come first, actually not enjoying always losing to them, or playing the role of not enjoying losing to them.

Mike held the whiteboard one more time to the camera as if it was a giant cheque he'd won on a gameshow before putting it back beside the couch. He grabbed his beer. "No fucking way I'm playing Mortal Kombat 2. Old school is one thing, but all that will end up happening there is Dan using that purple bitch, uh…"

"Mileena?" Dan said in mock questioning.

"Right. The purple chick with that bullshit rolling move."

Dan smiled. "Hey, you said it yourself, if it's in the game, then it's not cheap, right?"

Joe placed the N64 controller down on the coffee table. They'd planned this out somewhat earlier, but the words were their own, based on a hundred similar arguments years ago.

"If you know how to block her, that move is nothing," Joe said.

Mike dismissed them both with a wave of his hand. "Dan just spams it over and over again. That's cheap, end of story."

"Guys?" Dan asked the screen.

PING.

"FrankieGoestoHollyOaks222 says just dodge it," Joe read.

PING.

"Cwood4Real thinks you just always sucked at Mortal Kombat 2," Dan read.

Mike pounded back the remainder of his beer. He seemed to take offence. Was it genuine anymore or an act? Or maybe it was from the buzz he was obviously sporting? "Fuck that," he coughed, his voice hoarse. "I'll kick both your asses."

"Then bring it on!" Joe said.

"Yeah, pop it in and let's see who can still handle it," Dan agreed.

"Alright, viewers at home," Mike announced as he rose from the couch to walk over to the huge DVD shelf. "Let's take a vote here." He pulled out the Super Nintendo cartridge of Mortal Kombat 2 and returned to the front of the television. "All those in favour of a change of pace, let your comments be heard. You want us to stop this Bond shit and go back even older school, a real grudge match, battle of the champions back before the analog control stick?"

PING.

Mike leaned down. "They're voting so fast I can't even read their names," he said.

"They just want to watch you get your ass kicked in sixteen bits."

"Big talk, big man," Mike said to Dan.

Mike popped the grey cartridge into the dusty Super Nintendo. "Last chance?"

PING.

"The viewers have spoken."

He switched the input on the television to the video channel connected to the Super Nintendo. Blurry pixelated footage of an archaic sixteen-bit game filled their stream window. "Time to bring it, boys."

"How many times do you think he's going to say the line?" Dan asked Joe.

PING.

"WhosJohnnyRock? says six," Joe said. "I hope you guys know what you're in for here."

"Mortal Kombat!" Mike shouted and tossed one of the Super Nintendo controllers to Joe.

Dan erased the whiteboard of the Goldeneye stats and wrote in M K II on top. It didn't take long before he'd scrawled in a line under Mike's name.

Joe snorted and passed the controller to Dan. "What the hell? How do you remember all the combos when you can't even remember your phone number?"

"Muscle—"

PING.

"Memory," Joe and Dan said in unison.

Dan joined in and Joe started scrawling lines. Soon Dan's Mortal Kombat 2 victories dwarfed them all.

"God damn it, you're so cheap!" Mike shouted as he fell victim to Dan playing as Mileena for the fifth time in a row.

PING.

"Or you just suck."

PING.

"He's right," Joe said. "And YourNiNight420 agrees, you're not very good at this game. Here's a secret for all you viewers, he never was."

"Turn that into a meme, people out there in internet land," Dan said. "Mike has always sucked at Mortal Kombat 2."

"This is bullshit," Mike said, grumbling. "I'm not going to subject myself to this anymore." He tossed the controller towards the screen, but the cord was caught in the great tangle on the coffee table and whiplashed back to land in one of the open pizza boxes.

"Just because you suck is no reason to wreck an antique," Joe said as he cleaned off the sauce covering the controller.

PING.

"GertrudeBeerStein says Mike's a little saucy."

"Weak, GertrudeBeerStein," Joe said. "You can do better."

"Move onto a real game. Like Super High Impact Football."

"I thought you were taking us to old school," Dan said. "Or

is this too old for even you?"

"The game is broken," Mike said.

PING.

"If you're keeping score at home, guys," Joe said, "that's about the twentieth time on this show that Mike has tossed his controller. Someone out there make a super cut, okay? We'll use it and send you a free shirt."

"Make sure you use footage of all my flawless victories," Dan said.

"First one who does gets a like from Dan."

PING.

Mike took a pull from his beer but said nothing.

"Can you imagine if they had footage of all the times he did it in high school?" Dan said.

"The super cut would be longer than Heaven's Gate!"

"Ha, ha," Mike said. "I didn't hear anyone taking me up on the Super High Impact challenge." He crossed his arms over his chest.

"Nobody wants to watch that, do you, guys?"

PING.

"Nope, they don't. See?"

"You're all philistines!" Mike said to the camera.

"Hey, Dan, how many controllers did Mike break on his SNES? Five? Ten? Twenty?"

"He personally kept Zellers in business through a few of those lean nineties years," Dan said, laughing. He ate another slice of pizza and wiped his hands on a paper towel.

Mike fumed.

PING.

"And it's not like you can even say unlucky in games, lucky in love. When was the last time you had a date? You've been single for, what, three years?"

This seemed to get a rise out of Mike. His drunken demeanour darkened. He furrowed his brow and snapped back, "Hey, I got a number just the other day on my route. Cute girl, works the desk at one of my stops."

PING.

"That's right, BladeRunner246, this does sound suspicious."

"Why don't you call her?" Dan said.

"Yeah, do it now on stream."

PING.

"Can't."

"Why not?"

"It hasn't been three days."

"What?"

PING.

"The *Swingers* rule?" Joe read off screen. "What the hell is that?"

Mike pointed to the camera with a huge grin. His mood brightened up instantly. "Yes! Who said that?"

"Uh, FavreauForLife420," Joe said. "But I still don't get it."

PING.

"You have to wait three days to call her after getting her number?"

Mike nodded enthusiastically. "See, I told you it's a thing. The Swingers rule!"

"You're taking dating advice from a twenty-year-old Jon Favreau movie?" Joe asked, incredulous.

"Who's Jon Favreau?" Dan asked.

"It's not advice, it's a way of life."

"From a nineties movie," Joe said.

"What movie?" Dan asked.

PING.

"Swingers?" he read off the screen.

"Yeah, dude, the Swingers rule is from the movie Swingers."

"Makes sense."

"Just call the girl. Maybe Three Gamers could have a special guest star tonight."

"Nope."

"Poll? You guys out there want Mike to call the girl from his delivery route? Comment yes or no."

The PINGs came in droves.

Joe leaned forward to read the quickly scrolling comments aloud. "Yes. Yes. No. Yes. Yes. Hell yes. Hell yeah. Of course. Do it! Yes. Oh, GOKUBOY316 thinks we should tell her it's a bikini-only party."

"Nice."

"I mean, we could use some more female guests, but I don't know if someone's going to come over to the apartment of three guys she's never met in a bikini. In River City."

PING.

"This channel is nothing but a sausage party," Dan read. "So?"

"No to all of you guys," Mike said matter-of-factly. "I'm not going against the *Swingers* rule, sorry."

"You can't be seriously basing your life around what a young Vince Vaughan says, can you?"

"First of all, I just rewatched it and it holds up. It's a great movie and it changed my life. I followed the rule with Julie and that ended up being a pretty good relationship."

"Except for the part where it ended," Joe said.

"Well, yeah, but apart from that."

"Three years ago."

Mike seemed momentarily melancholy as if he was lost in remembering his old girlfriend.

PING.

"I can't believe this, but the votes are turning your way," Joe said.

"See? We have a smart audience."

"Dude, your insistence in not calling this girl is stupid," Dan said as he reached for Mike's phone on the table and threw it to Joe.

"If you won't call her, then I will. I'll do the foreign guy voice again."

Mike leapt up faster than either of them expected and snatched the phone away. "No chance, Joe Evans. I didn't even put the number in my phone. Not yet, at least. It's bad luck."

"That can't be a Swingers rule, they didn't even have cellphones then."

"It's not. It's my own rule."

"So, what, did you write it down on a dollar bill?"

"It's all up here," Mike said, pointing to his temple in smug arrogance.

"You wrote it on your head?"

"I think he means he memorized it," Joe said.

"I've got a system."

"What kind of system?"

"A rhyme to remember the numbers. You know, a mnemonic device? It works like a charm. But I'm not telling you what it is."

PING.

"Oh, come on," Joe said. "I'll mute the feed if you're worried about one of our viewers beating you to the punch."

Mike leaned forward and pressed the mute button on the laptop. "Fine, as long as it's not going out online, I can tell you."

The PINGS had fallen silent, but the comments kept flooding through.

"All I have to do to remember her digits is to say the line. Eight three five, don't talk no jive, four two one three, to a girl like she."

Joe and Dan looked at each other in wide-eyed shock.

"That it?" Joe said. "That's the great mnemonic device? That's the stupidest thing I ever heard."

"Worked like a charm. I'll never forget her number now."

"Jive?" Dan said. "Where's that coming from?"

"From all those Blaxsploitation movies we watched last month."

"I'm unmuting the feed." Joe leaned forward to press the button. "We can't tell you what Mike said, guys, but you'll be happy to know it's heavily influenced by last month's Blaxsploitation marathon."

Dan ate another slice of pizza and leaned back on the couch, lost in thought.

PING.

"There's only so much Fred Williamson a man can take in a month," Mike said. "So stop asking us to do more."

PING.

"TheMack420 says we should move on to Rudy Ray Moore."

"This is all distracting us from the real story here. That you two won't play me at Super High Impact Football."

"Nobody cares about a shitty SNES football game, they want you to call this girl, but you won't for three days," Joe said.

"That's right."

"And you're remembering her number with a stupid rhyme. Does that mean you have other brilliant mnemonic devices that you're hiding up there? Like maybe for your bank card PIN or something?"

"Of course," Mike said, smirking. "I've got a whole train of 'em."

"Like what?" Dan asked.

"To remember our buzz code, all I have to say is four one four opens that door."

"Hey, that's not bad," Dan said, slightly impressed.

"Are you kidding?" Joe said in exasperation. "Why do you need to have a rhyme to remember our buzz code? It's the apartment number!"

"It helps," Mike said, shrugging.

"We live in the fourteenth apartment on the fourth floor – how hard is that? You can remember Street Fighter moves or complicated MK fatalities from twenty years ago but not your own buzz code?"

Mike grinned.

PING.

"Oh shit, do you secretly have rhymes for all of those, too?"

"Now that is a trade secret," Mike said.

"Viewers at home, if you think Mike is as insane as I do, please let us know. Do any of you think up stupid rhymes to remember simple common things in your everyday lives as well?"

PING.

"How about we just move on? We've been sitting here debating my memory for so long that the TV has gone into screensaver mode." Mike pointed to the black screen.

"And I think we lost about ten viewers," Dan said sadly.

"So, what next?"

"Super High Impact Football?"

"No!" Joe and Dan said in unison.

"How about we spend some time with a girl we all love?" Joe grabbed another Nintendo 64 cartridge from the stack, this one *Perfect Dark*. "I'd planned on doing a whole RARE theme tonight. Mistress Joanna Dark anyone?"

Dan sighed heavily and looked at his phone. "You know what, I'm actually kind of tired, guys. I think I'm going to pack it in early."

"Tired?" Mike looked at his phone. "It's only ten thirty?"

Dan rose from the couch with a sucking noise, leaving his indent behind. "I have an early morning tomorrow."

"On a Saturday? What did you take, OT?"

"Nope, going to my parents for breakfast."

"So?"

"We're having pancakes, and my nana will be there." He walked over to the front door and pulled it open to leave.

"Hey, where are you going?" Joe asked.

"I'm going to sleep over. It's a family thing. You know, that way we can all get up together and watch TV as my mom makes breakfast. You know how it is."

"No, we don't."

"See ya later, guys!" Dan said, waving to the screen before he stepped out and shut the door behind him.

"Do you believe that?" Joe asked Mike.

"I know, right? He's getting pancakes," Mike said.

"No, I mean he just ditched us and the stream to go sleep over at his parents. Probably in his childhood bed, too."

34

"I'll bet he was just fucking scared of playing Super High Impact Football."

Joe rolled his eyes and turned to the camera. "Sorry, guys, but I guess this marks the end of another episode of Three Gamers. Although I guess it's just Two Gamers right now… uh, anyway, signing off."

CHAPTER FOUR: NOURISHMENT

The silence of still night. A half moon filtered through the trees, casting thin tendrils of light onto the underbrush that crunched beneath feet moving through the woods in Assiniboine Park.

Why here?

A compulsion to move away from the paved ring road and delve deeper into the thick forest that weaved through the park.

Life all around.

An owl to the left, glowing eyes watching from a tree. Voices chattering on the branches, another echoing inside the skull.

Feed.

Hunger.

Eat.

Kill.

The darkness of the forest, the Assiniboine River to the north, following the path it had for millennia.

Closer. Move closer.

The banks of the river in sight; nothing but rocks and mud, broken branches, garbage.

Stirring nearby. Eyes. Small.

Feed.

Kill.

Impossibly fast, hands closing on the thing's soft fur. A cry of distress and thrashing panic.

Squeezing. The life ebbing. Frantic clawing at the dirt. Teeth ineffectually biting. A loud snap and the desperation was extinguished.

Feed.

Digging through the cooling body, pulling apart the flesh to get to the warm viscosity inside. The sick smell of raw meat.

Blood.

Hunger fading as teeth tore at flesh.

The forest watched. The river flowed by impassively. Something stirred curiously from the brush.

More.

Pouncing on four small forms. Confused scattering. One escapes. More blood to quiet the hunger.

The muddy water reflected a blurred image of a face and the moon above. The voices of the forest fade, then darkness.

Awake again. The woods are gone, replaced by four walls and a white roof. Moonlight danced on the ceiling through trees tapping against a window. Soft blankets crumpled at the base of the bed.

A dream?

Hands touched clothes covered in something sticky. Fingers to mouth, tentative flicks of the tongue, the taste of iron. Blood?

Something else: soft, downy, wisps of grey and black. Fur?

It was real?

The hunger faded.

37

For the moment.

CHAPTER FIVE: THE GUYS HAVE REGULAR JOBS

"Sign your name on the line here." Mike tapped his finger on the bottom of the LCD screen on his UPS hand scanner.

"What do I use? My finger?" the woman asked.

Mike rolled his eyes and reached to the side of the scanner, pulling out an attached stylus pen and passing it to the elderly woman.

"What's this for?" she asked.

"Signing your name," he said.

"I thought I was supposed to sign my name on the screen?"

"Yeah. You use this pen."

"But there's no paper?"

"It's not that kind of pen."

She examined the thin plastic like it was some kind of archeological artifact in the dusty backroom of a museum. "Where's the ink in this thing?"

Mike sighed deliberately. This woman was holding him up, like most old people tended to do when he made deliveries to their house.

"Ma'am, I'm on a tight schedule. I have a dozen more stops to make in the next hour and—"

"Do I have to put the ink in?"

There were only so many hours in the day he could waste with people who didn't understand technology. "It doesn't use ink, it's not that kind of pen."

"Doesn't use ink? Is this like one of those pens the astronauts use?" the woman said with renewed interest. She turned the stylus over and stared into the tip.

She stood four steps up in the doorway of small white bungalow on Valour Road while mosquitos buzzed around Mike's bare legs. The sun beat down on him from above. He was sweating. The armpits of his brown shirt were already soaked through. His deodorant had long since given up the fight. There wasn't much shade in the doorway, but there was a minefield of potted plants. While he hadn't kicked one on the way up, he just had this feeling that he was going to on the way down.

"I'm pretty sure astronauts use normal pens, maybe even pencils, I don't know. What I do know is that this pen is not for writing in an international space station, or shuttle craft, it's for writing on the little screen on the scanner. Your name specifically. On that line at the bottom." He tapped it again.

She looked from the pen to the screen and back again, piecing together the logic of what he was saying. "But if there's no ink, how will it write?"

"Just trust me on this one."

"Well, okay, but I've never…"

She trailed off as she carefully wrote her name in cursive on the line at the bottom of the grey LCD screen. Her eyes grew three sizes in surprise as she saw the flowing letters appear a fraction of a second later in the exact place she'd scrawled. "Goodness gracious, look at that! That is quite the pen!"

Mike had already written in her first and last names in the designated text fields; her signature was the last piece of the puzzle, the only thing keeping him from his next stop and, by proxy, the end of his working day in a few hours.

She waved the pen in the air, trying to see if it would write anywhere else.

"Perfect, thanks." He snatched the pen back, connecting it to the side of the scanner. He turned to leave. "Enjoy your box!" he said over his shoulder.

"It's a dildo," she offered helpfully.

His feet caught on one of the potted plants and he stumbled over, landing on the grass in front of her steps. His scanner flew three feet away. He scrambled back to his feet to look at her in shock as she stood on her step, smiling as she opened up the box. She had to be in her seventies and looked for all the world like one of the Golden Girls. Sophia resurrected. Had she said what he thought she'd said?

"Excuse me? It's a what?"

She tore the top open and reached in.

"No, no, no, that's okay, you don't have to show me!" Mike waved his hands to try to stop her before she took it out.

"It's really neat! A collector's item, from back when I was a kid."

"Oh god, it's used?"

"Well, of course, they don't make these things anymore, haven't for decades."

He cringed as she pulled out the contents of the box, a small statue wrapped in bubble wrap.

"Wait, what is that?"

"A Bilbo Baggins, Lord of the Rings porcelain statue. Surely you know who Bilbo Baggins is, don't you? I didn't think I was that out of touch."

"Jeez, I thought you said dildo," Mike said, chuckling. "Shit, you can tell it's been a long time since I've been laid," he mumbled to himself.

"I could help you with that," she said as he grabbed his scanner from out of the flower garden.

"No, that's alright, I've got it."

He looked up and saw her eying him like a piece of meat, licking her lips. "It's been a long time since I've been laid, too."

Mike froze like a deer in headlights. He hadn't meant to say it that loudly. He was sure she'd never hear it at her age. Now he was staring into the eyes of Mrs. Robinson's grandmother, trapped by his own big mouth.

"Why don't you come in and I'll get you some milk and cookies?" she said, smiling.

"I'm full from lunch."

"I could put on a Benny Goodman record and slip into something more comfortable."

"I'm deaf."

"Just because I'm old doesn't mean I've forgotten how to f—"

"Would you look at the time? I've got to get going, there's another call waiting for me. See ya around, okay, ma'am?"

Mike ran back to his idling truck, feeling her eyes on his ass the whole time.

"I'll order a Frodo next week," she called from behind him. "Wear something tight!"

He hopped up into his step van and slammed the door shut.

"Where do they find these people?" he said as he looked

out the side window to see the woman lifting her skirt and showing him her garters.

"Here's to you, Mrs. Robinson." He waved sheepishly.

* * * *

Miles Davis's *Someday My Prince Will Come* gently flowed through the tiny speakers of the computer tower on the floor beneath his desk. Joe leaned on an elbow as the tapping of seven other people on the office's keyboards provided a metronome percussion to the music.

He scrolled through the online news, mindlessly wasting time instead of facing the mounting workload that was piling up in his inbox.

Florida man dies when trying to perform dental work on sleeping alligator.

The office was bright, with huge open windows that looked out to the Red River that flowed through River City. An old train bridge spanned the river to the left. An ultra modern spire bridge to the French quarter crossed the other side of the river to the right. A small park wound its way alongside the banks. Some days Joe would take a walk on his break just to escape the claustrophobic office that confined him from nine to five.

River City Jets hope to break attendance records this year.

He should be doing anything but this, but his motivation had sunk into his shoes. Joe was a bureaucrat. He worked for the local film commission, the government agency that processed funding requests, administered tax credits, and tried to lure movies from Hollywood to the sleepy town of River City, Manitoba, Canada.

Marvel outlines the next phase of the cinematic universe.

The office was one of those fancy open-concept floor plans where the majority of them sat in corners or in the centre of the floor with no walls or divisions to speak of. The exposed beams and piping in the ceiling were freshly painted. The walls were decorated with posters of the many films that had been shot here in the city over the years. This was supposed to be a vibrant and interesting space, but he felt like the walls were closing in on him.

His email pinged. Another note from his boss, Marlena. She sent a minimum of a hundred emails a day, despite being only a few meters away behind a closed door in her four-walled partition. The rest of them had to suffer in the great open plains of grey carpeting and forest green walls.

"What does she want this time?" he grumbled, switching from the CBC page to his inbox.

At the top was a note marked "ASAP STAT TOP PRIOR-ITY!!!!!!"

"Six, it must be important."

He clicked. "Call all real-estate agents in the city and find out if we have any empty aircraft hangars that can be rented for three weeks in the fall."

He sighed deeply. "Again?"

This was supposed to be glamorous, a job in big-time Hollywood movies, but the film commission wasn't movies. Joe had come out of River City University with a degree in film studies and dreams of making it in show business. Like lots of people, he'd spent his teenage years goofing around with a video camera. He and Mike and Dan had shot skits, ill-fated prank videos, random monologues, scenes from a movie they'd planned to one day finish, but nothing clicked or went viral. He'd been forced to get a normal job, had stumbled across a listing for the commission and now he sat at a desk.

He wasn't an actor, didn't have Hollywood connections or family money; hell, he didn't even have a full head of hair. He was a guy with dreams living in the middle of nowhere in the middle of Canada doing work that seemed purposeless.

He pulled up his contact directory of real estate agents they'd worked with, dreading the phone calls he was about to have to make.

I could always go back to school. Or deliver pizza. Chicago Phil's was hiring...

Pushing thirty. Time seemed to be running out. He was a tiny fish in a tiny pond in a business that ate people like him for breakfast. Not rich enough to go to LA or Vancouver, crazy enough to try Toronto, or desperate enough to PA on the set of some big American TV production getting coffee or photocopying script pages. He wanted to make movies, but on his own terms: in River City, with the people he knew and had grown up with. But River City was a city desperate for outside attention. If he was honest with himself, he was, too.

He dialed the first number in the list and waited.

He was a minor online celebrity. The guy who shouted, "Sweet baby Jesus!" during their live streams. He'd been memed, but Three Gamers wasn't lucrative enough to ditch this job. He was stuck.

"Hello, Marshall Shultz, Premiere Reality," the voice on the other end of the line spoke.

"Yes, hello, Marshall, this is Joe Evans calling from the film commission... again."

"Oh, hello, Joe, what can I do for you this time?"

Joe could only imagine what Marshall was thinking right now, at his fancy desk in his fancy office with his fancy secretary and fancy shoe rack. He was probably twirling a fancy pen thinking *This idiot again?*

"We were wondering if there are any empty aircraft hangars available."

Marshal snorted. "Sorry, I don't think I heard that right – did you say aircraft hangars?"

"Yeah, you know of any?"

"River City isn't exactly a hotbed of aerospace engineering. All that we have are what the airport uses, and I wouldn't exactly call those empty."

"That's what I figured. Thanks, Marshall. Talk to you soon."

Joe typed a message to Marlena. "Marshall from Premiere Reality says no go on the hangar."

"T-minus two minutes," he said as he looked at his watch.

I could be a mailman. Maybe a cop. Maybe the guy that films court TV.

"T-minus one minute."

A grip, a best boy, a set dresser, transport coordinator. But the reality was that he was just Joe Evans, one of the Three Gamers with a few online fans who made supercuts of him saying his catchphrase over and over again.

"T-minus thirty seconds."

He had a fancy title and a desk, but was the bottom of a tiny ladder in a small office that operated on the kindness of a taxpayer grant. He should be thankful that he even had this.

"Five, four, three, two…"

His phone buzzed, the caller ID showing Marlena calling

him from ten meters away.

He picked up. "Hello?"

"What did the army say about that hangar?"

"You told me to call the real-estate people."

"I sent a second email."

Joe switched over to his inbox. There wasn't anything new. "Didn't get that one."

"Oh, I didn't press send. There it goes. You have it yet?"

A message appeared in bold. "RE: ASAP STAT CALL ARMY FOR AIRPLANE HANGAR ASAP TOP PRIORITY."

"Yeah, I see it."

"Okay, so what did they say?"

"I just got it now. I haven't called anyone yet."

"We need this yesterday, big time producer, big project. Get on it. Drop whatever else you're doing."

She hung up.

He could see her through the window of her office, scrolling Facebook. Marlena, the oversized personality that ran the commission; jovial, a massive ball of humanity that could glad-hand with the best of them, sweet talk a terrorist, and promise the moon only to forget the entire conversation a minute later. Scatter-brained, on medication for a myriad of problems, narcoleptic, impossible to predict. She could ask you for something one day, then yell at you for doing it the next, then want changes the third day. She lived through email, rarely left the office except to go on trade missions to LA, New York, Cannes, Toronto, a master at talking up the city, but hopelessly disorganized. It took a revolving door of people to pick up the slack for her.

He was just the newest one stuck in the door.

He sighed again as he opened their digital rolodex, looking

for someone from the department of defence. He found a site manager for the abandoned military base in the south end of the city and called her up.

"Geraldine Brewer."

"Hi, Miss Brewer, Joe from the film commission again."

"Look, Joe, I've told you, the old base is condemned, there's an infestation of dead pigeons inside, you can't rent it under any circumstances."

He laughed to try to diffuse the obvious tension. "No, not that this time. Marlena wants an aircraft hangar today."

"There are no air force bases here and even if there were, there'd probably be, you know, planes inside."

* * * *

The radio blared *The Doors* as Mike scanned the closest parcel on the shelves. "Okay, who's next?"

It was ten degrees hotter inside the step van. The air was heavy. There was no air conditioning apart from a small fan mounted to the visor that blew hot air in his face as he drove. The all-steel interior provided no circulation and on a hot summer's day, you could flash fry a chicken breast on the shelves in the cab. He'd tried.

There was a dozen more stops to go before he had to start his late afternoon pick ups. That meant a dozen more people waiting for their packages; the chance for a dozen more oddballs and weirdos to waste more of his time.

He sat back in the driver's seat and took a drink from his water bottle. The ice had long since melted. It was almost like drinking lukewarm bath water. The image of the old woman, rubbing her hands up and down the Bilbo Baggins statue suggestively, flashed back.

Jim Morrison seemed to be singing directly to him of the strangeness of people.

"No shit, Morrison," he said. "Especially the kinds of people who are home in the afternoon to accept a delivery."

Every day it was a soft parade: the retired, the unemployed, the work from home-ers, the disabled, the lazy, teenagers, housewives who just craved some adult conversation, people who begged for human contact during a day spent alone.

"I'm going to make sure that Frodo gets lost, lady," he said as he drove down the street towards his next stop.

"Why can't I have a babe proposition me, just once? Why is it always someone who needs a restraining order?"

The old lady hadn't been the first one to come on to him. A delivery driver fling seemed to be a fetish for some people.

"You lied to us all, porn industry!"

Harlequin gave people the wrong idea; even if he wanted to, there was just no time in his day to fill a desperate housewife's needs.

The boxes rattled on the shelves behind him as he drove over the potholed roads of River City's crumbling infrastructure. He was pushed to the limit every day, dashing from one end of his route to the other. Dropping off, picking up, picking up, dropping off, over and over again.

The first few notes of Aerosmith's *Love in an elevator* took over for The Doors.

"Nope," he said and pressed the CD button on the archaic stereo system in the truck. The radio died out and the techno beat of The Vengaboys blasted out of the tinny speakers.

"Much better."

The streets flew by. Time passed in waves. In and out of

the truck. Up and down stairs. He was just another guy living in River City, trying to get by and figure out what the hell he was going to do with his life. Single, going prematurely grey, working a side hustle as a mildly famous streaming celebrity, at least driving UPS gave him some freedom.

"It could be worse," he said. "I've got fresh air, the open road, the Vengaboys, a sunny day, a rolled-down window, no traffic, a cat running in front of my car—"

"Oh fuck!"

He slammed on the brakes. Too late. The van bounced over a small lump. He put it in park and got out, walking around to the other side. He bent down to see a dark red stain smeared along the pavement, fur mashed into the rubber of the tires, a silver collar sticking out of a pile of goo.

"Shit."

He walked over to a bush between two houses. There was nobody around. He broke off a branch and started poking at the chunks in his tire.

"Hey, mister, you seen my cat anywhere?"

He jerked around to see a pigtailed little girl holding a headless Barbie doll.

"Huh?"

"My cat. Fluffy. He got out and was running this way. Did you see him?"

A chunk of gore dripped from the stick in his hand. The collar dangled from the end. He swung it behind his back.

"Nope. Didn't see a thing."

He lobbed the stick away from the van. The collar caught on a bush and hung glittering in the sunlight, dripping blood on to the sidewalk.

"I'm really worried," she said. "He's not supposed to be out of the house."

"Oh, don't worry," Mike said. "I'm sure he's just dying to find you, too."

He ran back to the truck and peeled away, watching the girl in the rearview mirror.

"I hope you're happy, Fluffy," he said. "That kid's going to be scarred for life when she finds you smeared on the road."

* * * *

Another hang up, another call that led nowhere.

He opened Marlena's message and drafted a response. "Told that there are no aircraft hangars available in town. The only ones we have are at the airport and obviously those are taken."

This was one of the easier tasks he had. A few phone calls and that was that. Depending on the day, he might be preparing presentations of River City locations that could be used for script scenes, driving visitors around town as they talked on their cell phones and snapped pictures of old buildings, getting coffee, finding lost luggage, correcting letters, filling in a workflow database, itemizing expense reports, sketching driving routes for LA streets, scheduling meetings. He'd been promised a crash course in film production, a guidebook on how to get things done and a way to make more connections than a match three game. It was supposed to be his way in. But that was all just talk. The only thing he was learning was how far a person could be pushed before snapping and the only connections he was making were with the dozens of local officials and businesses that probably thought he was certifiable.

As soon as he hit send, he realized his mistake.

Oh shit.

The phone rang a second later. Her. "Call the airport and see if we could rent the hangar for three weeks in the fall."

"But they use it for the planes."

"Find out what it would cost to park them on the runway or something. I need that information for a huge project, super hush hush, big budget. Tom Hanks is in talks."

"Okay."

It was easier to just tell her what she wanted to hear than explain why it was impossible. Oftentimes she forgot about the request anyway.

Do I call the airport authority to ask if they would be willing to push out their planes for a project that might not even exist? How loud would they laugh at me?

If he didn't, this was liable to be the one time that Marlena remembered what she wanted.

"Tom Hanks is in talks… more bullshit?"

He'd been at this long enough not to take anything at face value. For every project that came across his desk, three quarters were ethereal and never got off the ground, another eighth went somewhere else. They were just trying to leverage whatever they could, find government grants, bounce phony promises off banks and investors. The vast majority of what Joe did went nowhere, and it was wearing on him.

"She loves Tom Hanks…"

He called the airport authority. As soon as the words were out of his mouth, Darlene burst out laughing.

"Why don't you ask the aviation museum if they would be willing to empty the facility?" she said, catching her breath.

"You have about as much chance."

He wouldn't even mention that idea to Marlena.

The phone rang again.

"Hello?"

"I found something," Marlena said. "Go to this website. H t t p colon—"

She read out every single individual letter of the search string which took nearly two minutes. When she finished, Joe was presented with a listing for a place outside the city called the Southport Aerospace Centre, promising high-tech jobs in a small-town setting.

"I'll bet they have a hangar. Call them," she said and hung up.

"This must be serious," he said. "She never does this much work on her own."

The website had a Geocities look and appeared at least a decade and a half old. The phone number twinkled in green.

"This looks like a high school project from 1996."

He called the number.

"Hello?" a voice answered.

"Yes, this is Joe Evans calling from the River City film commission. I was looking at your website and was wondering if you had any hangars on site, you know, for aircraft?"

"What?"

"It says here you're an aerospace centre. Do you have any hangar facilities? Maybe that aren't currently in use?"

"Shit, son, you're ten years too late."

"This isn't the Southport Aerospace Centre?"

"Hell, no. That place was torn down in 2002. Turned into a seniors' home."

He drafted a response to Marlena, sure that this was finally the end of the wild goose chase.

Moments later she responded. "Call the aviation museum and see how much it would cost to move all the exhibits outside for three weeks. ASAP STAT TOP PRIORITY +1 +1 +1."

"Fuck my life…"

* * * *

"At least I have you Vengaboys."

Overbearing heat, time constraints, frantic rushing, shitty River City drivers cutting him off, no parking on main roads; being a UPS driver wasn't glamorous, but it was the best job he'd ever had. In a weird way it was peaceful. He started with a full load of parcels, delivered them, then brought back more to be sent somewhere else. But more importantly, he was alone. No need to be in character, no people complaining that he'd messed up their Manhattan, that their steak was undercooked, that someone had taken a shit on the floor of the men's room, no shoplifters or drunk teenagers in the movie theatre, nobody expecting him to crack jokes all the time, no commenters meme-ing his off-the-cuff remarks, making fun of his waistline or hairline, creating polls to dictate what he did.

Alone. The only time to listen to his own thoughts. His phone rested on the tray next to the driver's seat, near the water bottle in the drink cup.

"I could call that girl…"

That's when he realized that he'd been single for three years. Since…

Julie, the girl who had broken his heart. He'd been so busy

that he'd missed the signals. She'd put up with a lot during the infancy of Three Gamers.

"How many days are you guys going to do this?" she'd said late one night after a marathon stream.

"We're trying to build our audience," he'd said to her. "You have to show consistency to prove you're serious about this."

"But five times a week?"

"This could be big. Donations, crowd funding, sponsorships. We're one viral stream away from getting noticed by the right people. We could quit our jobs and do this full time."

"Maybe you need to think about a more realistic dream."

"You sound like my mom," he'd said.

That had been the wrong thing to say. She'd walked away. It had turned ugly. He regretted how it had all ended.

"I wonder what she's doing now."

Talking to himself was therapeutic. He could practice jokes for the streams, work out bits, break up the monotony of the day.

"Facebook troll."

Stopping. Waiting in line at Starbucks, five minutes before he had to be back on the road, he found her.

"Engaged? In Calgary?" he said aloud.

"Did you say something to me?" a dark-haired woman in yoga pants next to him asked.

"Huh? Oh, sorry, I was just trolling my ex."

"Been there, done that," she said. "It's not healthy."

"I was just thinking that it was funny how time slips away. It feels like just yesterday I was walking on to the U of M campus expecting four years of Animal House."

"You were in veterinary studies?"

"Instead, it was just books, exams, teachers' office hours,

reading lists, student loans, and a useless three-year arts degree at the end."

"I heard vets were in demand," she said.

"Now I'm driving a truck. It was only supposed to be a temporary thing, to supplement income until things clicked with Three Gamers."

"Is that the name of your hospital?"

"Look at me. It's been years now. I'm stuck making the same rounds, single—"

"Single?"

"Waiting for that big break. What happened?"

"I'm Hannah," the woman said. "I—"

"Vanilla latte for Mike," the barista called out.

He moved up to the counter and grabbed his cup. He smiled to the woman. "That's me!"

"Mike, eh? That's a nice name."

"I guess. I didn't pick it, my parents did."

He took a sip from his cup and checked his watch. "Shit, Two minutes behind schedule. Well, see ya!" He pushed his way through the glass doors and left.

He jogged to his truck, took the steps in one quick bound. Twenty-nine years old. He'd be thirty soon. Was this the life he'd pictured he'd be living when he was thirty? Single, living with his two best friends, making a minorly popular online gaming show, driving around town with the same Vengaboys album on repeat in his truck? No, of course it wasn't what he'd pictured. It was better.

* * * *

The network was stable, emails answered, ethernet cables

stored securely, the laptop screens polished, and keyboards dusted. Everything was perfect and in its place.

Dan opened up his lunch box and carefully removed two sandwiches, a bottle of iced tea, banana, cookies, yogurt container, granola bar, and a small note. He unfolded it, saw well-formed letters in his mom's handwriting.

"Be all that you can be! We're proud of you! Love Mom and Dad."

He unwrapped the first sandwich and took a bite.

CHAPTER SIX: FRANK MALONE IS ON THE CASE

"How can one man in a car hide for so long?" Frank sipped on a cold coffee he'd been nursing for way too long.

He was parked in a prime spot, near the busiest intersection in town, Portage and Main, and yet, after two days of waiting, there was still no sign of the stolen car.

"How's the hunt going, Malone?" the boys asked him when he stopped into the office each morning to refill his thermos and grab a few donuts before all the good ones were gone.

"The guy's about to break, I can tell," he'd say to their unconvinced smirks.

"Face it, Frank, the car's been chopped into pieces and sent to China by now."

"That's your theory about everything, Jenkins," Frank had said.

"Because it's true. That's what they do with stolen vehicles now they—"

Frank had spun on the man, startling him with a wagging finger covered in powdered sugar.

"You'll change your tune when I come back here plus one stolen red Corvette."

"Wasn't it a BMW?"

"I'll come back with one of those, too."

But he'd been at this all day and still no luck. He couldn't go back empty-handed, it would kill his credibility. So he waited. Rush hour came and went. Frank looked everywhere for that red car.

"Where are you, Camaro?" he mumbled.

The roads were full of every other make and model: a sea of Civics, a mountain of Mustangs, a tide swell of Tiburons, and a never-ending parade of pick-ups. Yellows, greens, blues, blacks, silvers...

"Come on, boy, show yourself. I know you're out there and you know I'm out here, so why not just face the music? I promise I'll only throw the book at you."

Then, he saw it. In the distance, idling at the intersection of Main and King, the red car he was warned about. It had pulled out of a parkade next to City Hall and turned on to the streets without a care.

"You hide right in plain sight beneath the hallowed halls of municipal government. Clever."

Frank pulled out from his parking spot and merged into traffic. He let the guy get lured into a false sense of security as he drove obliviously down Waterfront Drive.

"Taking the scenic route, eh?"

Fancy new condos, reconditioned old buildings, a tree-lined park adjacent to the river – the guy sure was enjoying the neighbourhood.

Frank drew closer. He saw the license plate and read it aloud. He had to squint to make it out, since it seemed to be covered in some kind of blurry film. "Sure looks like K-L-H-4-5-6 to me."

He flicked on the siren. The shrill bleating turned heads and slowed traffic all around him. He pulled in behind the red car and waved it over to the side. The driver, to his credit, knew that the jig was up and complied.

"Don't think I'm going to go easy on you just because you surrendered, punk."

Frank put the car in park and stepped out, walking towards the stopped red car. He eyed the shine, the clear bumper, the sleek lines. What was the brand he was after again? Mercedes? Yeah, that sounded right.

He stepped up to the window and knocked once. It rolled down slowly. Frank looked in at a man in a pin-striped suit, a woman sitting next to him wearing a mini-skirt and a low-cut shirt. She looked half his age.

"Nice try, kid, but your little thrill ride is over," he said to the driver. "I caught you red-handed with the goods, now come along quietly so I don't have to get with the rough stuff."

"Excuse me, but what are you doing? Why did you pull me over?"

The man's voice was a nasally whine. He wore small glasses, sported a moustache and as fine a set of jowls this side of Tricky Dick.

"What am I doing?" Frank said. "My job. Enforcing the law. And why did I pull you over? It's the four thousand pounds of stolen steel you're driving around in. Seems like you couldn't keep your grubby little hands off someone else's property. And to do it in front of your own daughter… just makes me sick."

"Uh, I'm not his daughter," the woman said, leaning over and giving Frank a look down her shirt. "I'm his mistress, er, I mean, his secretary."

60

Frank grabbed the door handle and pulled it open, reaching in for the man's collar and clenching it tightly. "So I can add incest to the list of perversions you're into, eh? Nepotism, grand theft auto, and wearing stripes with plaid."

Frank jerked the man's tartan tie and started choking him. The man's eyes bugged out from the pressure.

"Wait, you don't understand!" The man coughed as his air was cut off.

"No, you don't understand, boss, I'm taking you downtown. And you, little girl, you should come, too. You can put in a complaint with the sex crimes division, make sure this guy is locked away for a long time."

"I can what?"

"Although, when the boys in lock-up hear what he was doing with his own kid, he probably won't last the night."

Frank yanked on the man's tie, trying to drag him from the car. His hands flailed. He tried to choke out words.

"You're hurting him!" the woman shouted.

"He's hurt a lot of people already. But with time and therapy, I'm sure you'll recover."

"No! He's still in the seatbelt!"

Frank looked down and sure enough, the man was strapped in tight. His trying to pull him from the car only served to press him against the hard fabric. "Don't think being safety conscious is going to save you this time, pervert. Let the man loose, little lady, so Uncle Frank here can take him to the big house."

She clicked open the seatbelt but held on to the man's arm. "There's been a mistake. This man isn't my dad and while I am fucking him, it's not what you think."

"So he's not putting his who-ha into your doo-dad?"

"Okay, so then it's exactly what you think, but we're not related! I just work for him, you know, like a boss and secretary thing."

"I don't need to hear what kind of roleplay games you're into, but if you're dropping the incest charges, then I guess he just goes away for GTA."

"But I don't think he stole this car. I mean, he's had it as long as I've known him."

"You're pretty brazen for a common street punk," Frank said as he yanked the man out to the ground and dragged him towards his cruiser. "But having balls doesn't keep you from going behind bars."

The man was frantic, dragging his shoes along the concrete and gravel. Frank had his car's back door open and went about lifting the man inside.

"You don't understand," the girl said, running over. She bounced in her tight shirt. Her skirt rode up her leg. She was thin, a redhead. If she was this guy's kid, Frank didn't see the resemblance. "He's the mayor."

"The mayor of what? Bullshit town? Look, kid, I know Mayor Jenkins and this tub of flavoured mayonnaise is not Mayor Jenkins."

Frank pushed him inside and slammed the door, wiping his hands as if he'd just thrown away a garbage bag.

"No! Didn't you hear? Mayor Jenkins retired, there was an election, lots of candidates, debates, voting – he won," she said, pointing to the man on the other side of the locked door.

"Sorry, doesn't ring a bell."

"It was on TV!"

"So's Canadian Idol and you don't see me giving a shit about that."

The woman looked confused, but she was insistent. "You still don't understand, that's the new mayor. Mayor Francis. He won in a landslide, was sworn in two weeks ago. Do you really not know any of this?"

"Hey, I'll have you know there's lots of things I don't know, okay, so if you're asking if I know what you're asking, then you're asking someone who doesn't know what you're asking."

"What?"

"Exactly," Frank said. He reached in to grab the police radio. "Car five three four here, I've just apprehended the perp on that stolen money-car deal. I've got him in the back seat ready to bring in. Might want to send a tow truck for the wheels. Parked on the corner of Waterfront and Alexander. Red ditty, license plate K L H 4 5 6."

"Sure thing, Frank, on its way," the scratchy voice responded.

The woman's eyes lit up when she heard him speak. "What did you say the plate was?"

"K L H 4 5 6," Frank said as he hooked the radio back on its cradle.

"That's it!" she said, beaming as she ran over to the back of the car, bending over and pointing at the letters. "You're reading it wrong. This is K L M 4 5 6."

Frank squinted, but he didn't see what she was saying. Somebody had rubbed Vaseline on the plate. It looked like an H to him. He walked around his open door and stepped closer, crouching down and following the woman's fingers. Now that he was within a few feet of the plate, the petroleum jelly had faded. The H had somehow turned into an M. He scratched his chin and looked back at the frantic little man in the back seat of his cruiser.

"So then, what you're saying is that this isn't the stolen car."

"No," she said.

"And that the little man I just dragged out and locked away is actually—"

"—Mayor Frank, the mayor!"

Frank sat in the hard-backed chair in front of the Chief's desk. The man was pacing back and forth, his hands gesturing wildly as he tried to maintain his composure.

"Only two weeks into his mandate. You rough him up, accuse him of incest and grand theft auto and all because—"

"If you'd seen the girl, Chief—"

"The fact that he's sleeping around on his wife is none of our business. You've already exposed that little secret to the press. Which has put you on his shit list, I might add. But what I don't understand was what prompted you to pull him over in the first place."

"The car matched the description sent over dispatch."

"He had a Mercedes, the stolen car was a BMW. They're not the same, Malone!"

"Do they both cost a lot?"

"Of course, that's what makes them luxury cars."

"And do they both come from those whiny European Union boys we bailed out in the big one?"

"I think they're both German actually."

"Even worse. Hitler's Sunday cruisers on our clean streets!"

The Chief ran his hands over his hair. He was new on the job, one of those HR types who moved up into the big desk. He wasn't a beat boy. He didn't have years out on the streets, but he did have a few fancy degrees and the right connections. He was trying to bring the force up to some kind of modern "sensitivity training" nonsense, make sure they were visible members of the community, touchy-feely stuff. People like him were why the police were losing their edge. Instead of busting heads, they were busting ballpoint pens filling out all the damn reports they were expected to file.

"Look, Frank, you're a valued member of the team and I get that you've been around a long time."

"Since you were still a gleam in your daddy's eye, Chief."

The Chief raised an eyebrow at that one. "Right, well, I know you're used to the way things were run around here in the old days, but this is the twenty tens – it's time to accept that change is here and move on."

"The bad guys still need catching, sir, that much will never change."

He nodded. "You're right and we all know that. But this is something else. Ignoring the fact that you got the make and model of the car wrong and misread the license plate number, you still roughed up a suspect. Mayor Francis has red lines on his neck that look like he'd been hung from a tree. People think he's into some of that David Carradine auto-erotic asphyxiation crap. You went too far, and we can't have that kind of behaviour on the force, okay?"

Frank shrugged. "As long as the bad guys don't resist arrest."

"Good to hear." The chief turned and put his hands on the back of his fancy chair. "Now I've managed to smooth things over with the mayor. I explained that you forgot your glasses that day and he's going to drop the issue, but I think that this whole thing exposes a larger problem, don't you think?"

"Sure do. Mayor Jenkins was the best thing to ever happen

to this city and now he's been given a silver watch, a one-way ticket to the beach, and the golden handshake of death. We'll never see his like again."

The Chief sat down in his chair and sighed. "That wasn't what I meant, Frank."

"So you don't think Jenkins was the best damn mayor we've ever had?"

"He seemed alright to me, Malone. But what I'm getting at is that maybe it's time for you to have a partner. Someone to watch your back, keep you from making these mistakes again."

"But Chief—"

The man held his hands up in surrender. "Look, I know all about your file and the special edict, okay?"

"No more partners. I've buried too many good cops in my day."

"I get that, I really do. But time marches on. You're the only cop I've ever heard of to have something like this on file. But let's face it, you got that edict from the previous mayor. And, sure, it says you fly solo and—"

"That I'm a lone wolf."

"Right. And while I can't force you to take someone on, I can certainly urge you to ask for someone to help you out. That's a request I wouldn't turn down, you understand?"

"That's why I'm not going to make it."

"I can also give you the warning that any more slip-ups like this and you'll be busted down to something in records to keep you out of the public's way."

"That edict was given to me for more than just my piece of mind, Chief. It's been with me for years now. An official letter that says I'm better off on my own. That the city is better off with me able to run where I have to, when I have to. That I don't have to be looking over my shoulder to make sure Baby Huey is keeping up."

"I know, I know. I looked into it. Lawyers did, too. It's been grandfathered into the collective agreement. I don't know what kind of shit you pulled back in the day to get that kind of deal, Malone, but I can't touch it."

"Grandfather? Shit, I didn't even know I was a dad."

"I'm just saying, think about taking someone on. Maybe a rookie you could show the ropes to. It might do you some good, make these last few years go by a little smoother if you catch my drift."

Frank rose out of his chair and shoved his hands in his pockets. "Sorry, Chief, but this big dog runs with his own pack. Now, if you'll excuse me, I've still got a stolen car to track down."

Frank turned and left the Chief's office.

CHAPTER SEVEN: BIG NEWS

"**H**oly shit, did you not go to bed at all last night?" Joe said as he exited the bathroom and saw Mike laying on the couch.

His head hung back, while the TV was stuck on the menu for the Die Hard 2 DVD. Fanfare music played its short minute loop before repeating again and again.

Joe walked into the kitchen and poured himself a bowl of Frosted Flakes.

"You know it's one o'clock Saturday morning?"

Mike didn't budge. Joe threw a wadded-up napkin at him. It lodged itself in the great tuft of hair in his armpits.

"I guess that *Rampage* reverse marathon wore you out, eh?"

"Why do you make me do these things, Evans?" Mike said through a cracking voice. He didn't move his head or stir at all.

"You mean you can't see the value in the complete destruction of the United States by giant monsters in progressively worse looking games for almost six hours?"

"I was seeing endless pixelated streetscapes in my dreams. I was punching buildings and eating screaming women. I was the lizard, the wolf, and the gorilla all at the same time. A horrible nightmare that never ended."

"You're thinking of the games. You're awake now."

"My brain, Evans. It's mush. Why did we do it?"

"Why did we do a Friday night marathon of Rampage Total destruction, Rampage Universal Tour, Rampage World Tour, the Rampage arcade ROM, and then the NES version?"

"Why didn't we just kill ourselves?"

"While that might have put our streaming numbers sky high, I have a feeling it would be a dead end creatively. Besides, we had our biggest audience ever."

"Tuning in to watch the two of us plow through the most monotonous gaming franchise in one night."

"Yeah. And we did it. We made it through the whole series."

"Why? Why did I think that wasn't going to be torture?"

"It was a viewer request."

"Do they hate us, Evans?"

"It seemed like a good idea at the time."

"I never want to see that lizard and monkey again for as long as I live."

Mike's head slowly tilted up. He rubbed his eyes and looked around the room. "So this isn't hell."

"Depends on what you wanted for breakfast."

"What time is it?"

"I told you. It's one o'clock."

"Fuck me."

Mike rolled his neck around, rubbed his shoulders, tried to restore the blood in his legs. Finally, he stood up. He shuffled into the kitchen and pulled open the fridge, taking out a milk carton and drinking from the spout. He pounded back the whole thing in one long gulp.

"Well, I guess you're not having any Frosted Flakes," Joe said.

"Did Dan ever come home?"

"The door to his room is shut, so maybe?"

They'd been about to move on to the second game in their reverse marathon last night when Dan had ducked out early. "Going to my parents for a sleepover," he'd said, and they'd continued on without him.

Mike slammed the empty milk carton on the counter. He grabbed a water bottle from the counter and moved down the hallway. He knocked on Dan's door.

"You in there?"

He waited a few seconds before opening the door to find the room empty. It was far too clean. There were no clothes in piles anywhere, the bed was made, the shades pulled down low, letting only a crack of sunlight in.

"Well?" Joe asked from the kitchen.

"As empty as our fucking heads for ever playing all those horrible games."

"We wouldn't be Three Gamers if we didn't play games."

"I was thinking about that. What if we just filmed us watching My Little Pony? We could get the DVDs, binge the whole fucking series. Maybe finally grab that lucrative ironic millennial crowd we can't seem to reach."

"Now I know your brain is mush."

Mike flopped down on the couch and held his head in his hands. He liked to act like he wasn't much of a video game guy, a casual player at best. Of course, this was as much a half-truth performance for the camera as it was for Joe. Mike had been gaming as long as any of them, but tended to play the same games for years and years, and rarely ventured beyond a few favourite genres. Part of his appeal to their fanbase was the airs he put on when he was forced to play something outside his comfort zone.

"Fuck that. I'm a closet Brony. We could change the name of the show to Two Gamers and a Brony."

"You sure it was only milk in that carton?"

"I dreamed I was watching Die Hard 2."

"After the Rampage dream?"

Mike rubbed his temple and dug for the TV remote in the couch. "Before, after, during. I don't know. It was a dream. Can't I be the lizard, the wolf, and the gorilla and be watching Die Hard 2?"

Joe joined him at the couch. "But why Die Hard 2? It's the worst fucking one!"

"What about five?"

"That's not real Die Hard and you know it."

"Two is underrated," Mike said as finally found the remote. He pressed play, skipping ahead a few chapters in the movie. "It has all the elements you need: John McClane, terrorists, Christmas, explosions, yippie kay ay mother fucker."

"It's the same exact thing as the first one – at least part three was trying something new."

"So did Die Hard 2," Mike said. "The first one was in a building, this one's in an airport. Totally different."

"Right! How could I ever get them confused?" Joe said.

"I'll give you that part three had some great moments."

"The whole thing was a great moment!"

"Hey, guys, how'd the stream go?" a voice said from the front door.

They both turned to see Dan walking into the apartment carrying a grocery bag. He was wearing different clothes than the ones he had left to go to his parents in last night.

"Hey, Dan, what do you think of this idea? Two Gamers

and a Brony. We do nothing but watch My Little Pony," Mike said.

"Catch that ironic millennial crowd that keeps eluding us, eh?"

"His brain is shit pudding," Joe said. "He's coming up with the stupidest takes. Die Hard 2 is the best one, watch cartoons for girls."

"And weirdos," Mike added.

"Yeah, and weirdos."

"Jeez. I leave you guys for one night and Three Gamers goes to hell." Dan sat down on the other side of the couch.

Mike flipped forward another chapter in the movie.

"Are we streaming right now?" Dan asked.

"What does it matter to you?" Mike asked.

"Nobody told me about this one."

"Relax," Joe said, looking at Mike's sulking face and wondering if this was all still a result of his supposed mind mush. "Mike just—"

"I'm just watching Die Hard 2 because I like it."

The movie blared on, the scenes of carnage and death like a comfortable old sock. They'd all seen it too many times to count. Joe felt like there was something going on with Mike. He wasn't saying anything, which was unlike him. Even before they streamed, he could never shut up while watching a movie.

Dan scrolled on his phone, nominally paying attention. He was so tall that the couch seemed to barely contain his body. He sat with his back straight and legs splayed out in front of him.

"Hey, Dan," Joe said. "What the heck do you do at your parents for so long every Saturday morning?"

"Oh, you know, sit around, talk about the week. Listen to Nana's stories – you know, family time."

"Even when my grandparents were alive, we didn't sit around and listen to them tell stories all morning. Although my grandpa had Alzheimer's so that might have turned out to be kind of interesting."

"With mine it's nothing but sports, reality TV, and how much they hate the Liberals," Mike said.

"I also signed up for online dating."

Mike spat out his drink all over the floor. He paused the movie and shifted in his seat. "Okay, what?"

"My parents, my sister, and Nana agreed. It's time to meet new people. I'm not getting any younger."

"You're twenty-nine," Mike said. "What's the rush?"

"Besides menopause?" Joe deadpanned.

"Guys, there's a time in a man's life when he needs to 'find that certain woman out there for you,' Dad said. 'There are some things that only a girlfriend can provide,'" Dan said in an impression of his dad's voice.

Mike looked like he was about to explode in laughter. "So, what, your mom made you an online dating profile?"

Dan shook his head. "No. But she did proofread it. She also swiped someone she thinks would be great for me. A gourmet who enjoys eating out, going to the movies, and cuddling. 'You like eating and movies, Dan,' she said. 'She'll be perfect for you!'"

"Your mom set you up on a date?" Mike said, chuckling.

"They made a lot of sense. I have been spending most of my free time in front of a television. Maybe it's time to branch out."

"I'm pretty sure I like food and movies, too, so maybe I

should call this girl," Joe said sarcastically.

"When are you meeting this perfect woman?" Mike asked.

"Tonight."

"Tonight," Joe said. "You're moving fast."

"Saturday night is apparently the most popular date night," Dan said. "Or so my sister told me."

"But what about the Three Gamers *Streets of Rage* marathon?" Mike asked.

"It's just a date."

"With someone his mom swiped on," Joe said.

"What if you get lucky? What are we supposed to tell the viewers? One of the Three Gamers is a no show. Again. But hey, this time he's on a date. People tune in to watch three gamers, not two gamers and an empty spot on the couch."

"You have been missing a lot of shows lately," Joe said. "We're starting to hear complaints."

"Really?" Dan asked, looking at Mike.

"How would I know?" Mike said. "I don't check the forums."

"Guys, I'll join in later. Streets of Rage games are two players anyway."

"That's not the point," Mike said. "It's about not letting things come into conflict with the show."

"It's live, scheduled programming," Joe added.

"Three nights a week is a lot," Dan said. "Maybe we should take a night off now and then. Live normal lives?"

"One night becomes two. Then it's a week. Then a month. We lose our consistency, we lose our fans. We lose our fans, we lose—"

"Money," Joe said, counting on his fingers. "Exposure. Possible sponsors. Future opportunities."

"Guys, you're getting way ahead of yourselves here. This date could be a disaster. Maybe I'll be back early, and I can tell the horrifying story while I play Streets of Rage 2. Who knows? Maybe it attracts a new audience."

"Lonely neckbeards?" Joe said.

"No, Dan's right. This could be our new direction. Turn the whole thing into a dating advice show." Mike laid it on as thick as he could with the sarcasm, ensuring that neither one would think he was serious.

"It's just a first date."

"Didn't her profile say she enjoyed food and movies?"

Dan nodded.

"Then it's a shoe in. Next step is marriage, babies, and you working as a clerk down at the DMV."

"I'm not going to back out," Dan said. "My parents would never let me live it down."

"Do what you have to," Mike said, crossing his arms over his chest. He was checking out again. He picked up the remote to the DVD player. "Can we at least finish Die Hard 2?"

He turned up the volume. Nobody said a thing, letting the explosions and gunshots do the talking.

Joe knew that Dan missing a couple of nights was the beginning of a slippery slope, but he was lonely, too, feeling the same things Dan must be.

This could be a good thing.

Girls tended to have friends that were other girls and they tended to want to set up single friends with other single people they knew. Maybe they could parlay this date into having women on the show, silence the commenters who claimed they were nothing but aging men complaining about movies and games.

Joe struggled to remember the last time he'd even been on a date.

"Hey, Dan, tell me about that website…"

CHAPTER EIGHT: LARGER PREY

The light of the moon shone on calm river waters gently flowing downstream. Driftwood bobbed on the surface. A hawk squawked off in the distance. Moving through the woods, returning to the familiar spot, hunger renewed, burning with a new intensity.

Forms in the darkness scattered. The foreign presence was to be feared.

A flickering firelight in the distance.

Moving closer.

Voices.

"Pass the grub, Kendra," a male voice said.

"Lemme finish first," a female voice responded.

Two people. Sitting around a campfire. Clothes hung from cords tied to the trees: stained sweatshirts, torn pants, wool socks, and jackets. A patched tent, held together with duct tape, faced the fire, semi-obscured by overhanging branches.

"Here," the woman said. "Done now."

She passed a can over to the bearded man with long braided hair and missing teeth.

He pressed a wooden spoon inside and pulled up a small serving of what looked like corn.

"Fucking hell, you ate the whole thing."

"Did not."

"One spoonful, that's it. What am I supposed to do with one spoonful?"

"Eat it, dumb shit."

"Then I'm not sharing the peaches."

"You don't even know they are peaches."

"I got a feeling."

"Yeah, some psychic. Your only power is knowing what's inside a can with no god damn label."

"More'n you can do."

A branch snapped. The two at the fire looked up.

"What was that?" the woman asked. "Someone out there?"

"Probably a fucking rabbit," the man said.

"Then catch it. At least we can eat something other than no-label cans."

The man threw the empty into the darkness and stood up.

"Here, bunny, bunny," he said. "Come to the fire, okay, Bugs?"

Too close.

Leaping, one hand over the mouth, another pressing into the jugular, piercing the skin at the base of the neck. Frantic clawing. Blood bubbling up over the gouging finger, air slowing. Heartbeat fading. Eyes dimming.

The man lay limp.

"You find that rabbit yet?" the woman called out.

She looked into the forest, trying to see through the veil of the night.

"Billy? You there?"

Silence. The man could never answer again. She stepped forward, curiously.

"Billy? Where you go?"

Closer. Closer. Out of the range of the harsh firelight.

"Billy? Quit it. You're—"

The eyes, pressing down, through the socket, finding the brain. A scream, but brief. Then she, too, was silent, laying next to Billy.

The fire crackled, smoke drifting upwards. A voice inside, barely audible, but there. Trying to communicate something.

Moving closer to the fire, looking deep inside the blaze. A face. Recognizable. The words made sense now. Directions.

"I understand."

First, though, the hunger burned. Dragging the bodies towards the fire. They alone wouldn't be enough to fill the void within. Something else was needed, something different, somewhere else.

These two would have to do for now.

CHAPTER NINE: FORUM COMMENTS ON THE DATING LIFE OF DAN STODDARD

JunkyCollector26: Looks like Dan and Lara broke up.
TheMack420: The foodie?
JunkyCollector26: The fat one, yeah.
Cwood4Real: <eyeroll>
TheMack420: *posted a video*

"I never thought eating cold fish could taste so good," the girl with the short, brushed back, dark brown hair said. Dressed in black pants and a multicoloured sweater, she was a full ruler shorter than Dan, but probably around the same weight. She speared a maki roll with a fork, sitting on a chair next to the couch filled up by the Three Gamers.

"What did you order?" Joe asked.

"The California roll."

"Vegetables, the fish of the ground," Mike said directly to the camera.

GOKUBOY316: LOL. That was hilarious. She was so dumb.
TheDoorsMan: Meme'd for life now.

BladeRunner246: He saved himself one hell of a headache.
GOKUBOY316: *posted a video*

"You know, guys, Lara was telling me that just by having a job in network tech, I'm systematically discriminating against women who feel marginalized in a male-dominated industry."

"Wait, what?" Joe asked.

"I'm also fifteen times more likely to rape someone I know than someone I don't."

"Why the hell would you rape someone in the first place?" Mike asked. "I didn't think you were that desperate."

"Or a sex offender," Joe added.

BladeRunner246: There's pussy whipped and then there's that...
GertrudeBeerStein: But he wasn't even getting any!
BladeRunner246: That's what made it worse!
GOKUBOY316: *posted a video*

"—as a member of the patriarchy I was born into a position of... uhhhh, fuck, I can't remember the rest," Dan said.

"Are you at least getting in her pants?" Mike asked.

"I don't think I'm supposed to."

"You shouldn't have skipped intro to women's studies," Mike said.

"Then he'd just hate himself."

"I think I already do?"

FavreauForLife420: If I was a woman, I'd totally go out with Dan. It'd be cool to hang out on stream with the guys.
LovinSpoonfulofCereal: I'm gay and I'd go out with him.

81

Cwood4Real: He's a little too desperate.
GOKUBOY316: *posted a video*

"You and your friends are entrenched in patriarchal privilege," Lara said.

"Then why are we all broke?" Mike asked.

TheDoorsMan: Lol. That was a good one.
   YourNiNight420: I think Mike hated her guts.
   BladeRunner246: Can you blame him? You see them leaving the apartment?
   TheDoorsMan: When?
   GOKUBOY316: *posted a video*

Dan stood at the apartment door, holding it open for Lara.

"Holding the door for a woman enforces archaic gender roles."

He started to go first, but she coughed and crossed her arms beneath her breasts. "Going before me shows that you consider me beneath you."

"I'm so confused. Do we walk in at the same time?"

"You should know this."

FavreauForLife420: She seemed a bit... of a handful.
   LovinSpoonfulofCereal: He's better off.
   TheDoorsMan: Plenty of fish in the sea!

Joe watched as comments flowed by, the screen filling up with the news that Dan had ended his relationship with Lara. Dan was back. Mike beamed. They were playing Halo 5.

"Who do you think would win in a fight, Mike, Master

Chief or Master Higgins?" Joe asked as he sat back against the couch, confident that things were getting back to normal.

"Who the fuck is that?" Mike asked with a furrowed brow.

"Master Chief is the guy you're playing as right now."

"With the gun?"

"Right."

"Who's the other asshole?"

"The shirtless guy in a grass skirt and baseball cap in Adventure Island."

"Does he have a gun?"

"No. But he does throw hammers and ride a skateboard."

Mike looked at Joe like he was insane. "What kind of question is that? A soldier in full body armour with a laser rifle against a half-naked skate punk? Who do you think would win? Why are you even asking me that?"

"Someone asked in the comments section. They wanted to know what you thought."

Mike turned to the camera. "Whoever asked that question is a fucking idiot."

Dan's phone beeped. He picked it up and scrolled through a message.

"Hey, guys," he said. "I'm on for tomorrow night."

"We're doing more Halo 5," Joe said. "People seem to like—"

"No, I mean, I've got another date."

"I thought it was officially over with Lara? This isn't just a break-up and make-up right away thing, is it?" Mike asked.

"Nope," Dan said. "She decided to move to Toronto to take a job working for a small non-profit feminist book publisher."

"You're better off," Mike said. "She was a nightmare."

"I don't know. I was learning a lot."

"Dan, they made a supercut of the first time you brought

her over," Joe said.

Mike paused the game. "Oh, shit, yeah, that was insane." He turned to the camera. "Sorry, guys, Halo 5 is on hold for a minute. We're going to watch that supercut of Lara's greatest hits."

"Dude…" Dan said.

"No, no." Mike waved him off as he moved to the laptop. "This is an educational experience for everyone. Ready, guys at home?"

"Credit to whoever took the time to do this, by the way," Joe said.

Mike pressed play on the video file, and it took over the screen and the stream.

"What is it exactly that you do here?" Lara asked.

"It's a form of two-way communication. People ask us questions live and we answer. Just a second ago some fuck asked me if the guy from God of War could beat the guy from Godhand. I have no idea what he was talking about, so I told him that. Audience interaction, it's what makes live streaming the entertainment destination of choice for today's youth audience."

Lara looked around the room as if encountering an alien civilization for the first time. The wall of DVDs, the movie posters, the tangle of game controllers, the open laptops, the cameras filming it all.

"This is some kind of nerd show?"

"Nerd show?" Mike said with a raised eyebrow. "There's nothing nerdy about what we do. We engage in intelligent conversations about video games and movies. Some call it art criticism. You can take a degree in that in college."

"Did you?"

"That's not the point," Mike said.

"Yeah," Joe added. "We also stream us gaming."

"It sounds to me like you guys just goof off on camera," Lara said.

"Not at all," Mike said, frowning. "We banter."

"So much banter," Joe agreed.

"Just you? There's no women or black people in your group? No visible minorities? No members of the LGBTQ community? Just three white people?"

Mike darkened with each word. Someone had edited his face to jump in to closeups with anger lines appearing over his head. "We've all been friends since high school."

"Was this a whites only high school?"

"I think there was a black guy? Joe, what was the name of the black kid we went to high school with?"

"Keyshawn, I think? Wasn't he on the basketball team?"

"That's an offensive stereotype," Lara said, pointing to Joe. "To not even remember the name of another student, assume that he was good at sports, as if that was the only thing to note about him."

"But that's all I knew about him! We ran in different circles!"

"Oh, so now he was a good runner, too!"

"Probably?" Joe said plaintively.

SMASH CUT TO:

Lara moving around the room, looking at the movies on the shelf. She pulled the DVDs of *Invasion USA* and *Missing in Action* starring Chuck Norris. "Typical jingoistic imperialist propaganda."

"In that one, Chuck Norris shoots a guy with a bazooka!" Dan said.

"Perpetuating the military industrial complex."

"The political ramifications of US foreign policy tend to fall by the wayside when Chuck Norris is faced with a bad guy holding a gun."

CUT TO:

Lara leaning right up to the lens of the camera and tapping it, not realizing it was on and that she was giving everyone a view up her nose. "This is what you use? How much do you make doing this? Not enough to quit your jobs. Dan said you were a UPS driver and you worked at some office."

"We've got a fanbase, receive donations and—"

"You work for tips?"

"Content creation is—" Mike began but Lara finally noticed the red light on the camera.

"Hey, is this being filmed?"

"Yeah, we're always on," Joe said.

"Oh god, why didn't you say something Dan? I—"

She turned and fixed her hair, taking a deep breath before spinning around and smiling. She was still way too close to the camera, her mouth taking up the whole screen. There was something green stuck in her teeth.

"I want to talk about misogyny. Particularly the misogyny I experienced working in the data entry department for a local metals company."

CUT TO:

Lara sitting on the couch, in Mike's spot.

"Why doesn't this game have gender neutral bathrooms?" she asked.

"Duke Nukem 3D?" Joe asked, confused.

"Is that what it is?"

"Yeah," Mike said, gritting his teeth.

"You're going into the men's room and there's a monster in the women's. That seems like all kinds of problematic."

"This game was made in 1996."

"Then it should have stayed there. You should really play more progressive games, Dan."

On screen Duke Nukem handed a wad of bills to a stripper who flashed him. *Shake it, baby!*

CUT TO:

Mike carrying a tray into frame. "Snacks, guys. I've got hot dogs!"

"Hot dogs?" Lara stuttered.

"Smokies, the best kind!"

"Blatant phallic imagery? In an apartment with three men? An apartment where I'm alone with three men?"

Mike rubbed his chin in mock thought. "I'm a man, and Dan's a man, that's two. But I'm not sure about Joe over there."

"Hey!"

Lara stared at the flaccid wieners on the tray, shaking in rage. "I feel so violated!"

"Oh, come on, it's just a hot dog. I'm sure you've had your share of wieners by now."

She shrieked in rage and batted the tray away.

"Hey!" Mike protested. "I just made those!"

"This is what women live with on a daily basis," she said as she stormed out.

"What? Food on the floor?" Joe asked.

The video ended.

"See what I mean, man?" Mike said proudly. "She just didn't fit in around here."

"I guess," Dan said.

"I don't know, Mike," Joe said. "Seeing it again like that isn't all that flattering to either of us. Also, you did kind of insinuate she was fat or that she'd sucked a lot of dicks."

"If you don't know, there's no way she did. Also, it was funny. Didn't you see the comments?"

Joe leaned in and read a few. "GOKUBOY316: That was SFF. TheMack420: LOL (crying emoji). Okay, but those are our fanboys and—"

"It's like TheDoorsMan said," Mike interrupted. "There's plenty of fish in the sea."

"Speaking of," Joe said. "The fans want to know what happened when you called that girl. It's been more than three—"

"Plenty of fish," Mike said curtly. "You'll meet someone better, Dan. In the meantime, Three Gamers are supposed to be rocking Halo 5."

Must have gone badly, Joe thought. He knew enough not to keep pressing.

Dan tapped on his controller, oblivious to Mike's glee at his failed relationship. Joe wondered what he really felt about it all.

"I can't believe you fucks seriously asked me if a trained, armoured space marine with a pulse rifle could beat an idiot with a hammer wearing a grass skirt," Mike said to the camera.

CHAPTER TEN: THE BOREDOM OF BOREDOM

Frank sipped a cup of the familiar sludge from the old Mr. Coffee machine. Another classic he refused to let them change out for a modern model. The boys knew better than to mess with what worked.

"Davis," Frank said to the man at the desk behind him, "it's been eating away at me."

"Huh? You talking to me, Malone?"

"Your name is Davis, right, Davis?"

"It's Travis Davis, but yeah."

Frank spun in his chair to face the man with less seniority than Frank's wallet. Recently promoted, Davis had the eager look of youth on his too-smooth face. He was thickly muscled, intense looking, like most of the newbies around here.

"Good," Frank said. "It's hard to keep up with all the changes around here sometimes."

"I've been at this desk for fifteen months."

"And I've been using this same coffee cup for twenty, what's your point?" Frank held up his ratty and stained Styrofoam cup in Davis's face as if that was all that needed to be said on this or any other subject.

"You can just get another one, you know."

"Why would I want another one when this one's been so good to me?"

"Because—"

Before Davis could answer, the bottom of the cup finally gave way, rotting through, dropping a half cup of lukewarm coffee onto the carpet.

"Don't even say it, Davis."

"I was—"

Frank held up a finger to stop him. "You were about to say it."

"No, I swear I wasn't."

"Good man."

They stared at each other in silence for a moment. The coffee slowly soaked into the thin layer of carpet between them.

"So?" Davis asked.

"So what?"

"You turned around to tell me something."

"Not so much to you, Davis, as to the space in which you occupy."

"What's the dif—"

"It's been nagging at me, what the Chief said. I haven't been able to get my mind off it; the idea that I might be slowing down. In need of someone to watch my back. It's been stuck there, in that little cubby hole part of my brain."

"And?" Davis said.

"The thought of having a partner again brings back a lot of bad memories."

"I've heard you don't—"

"I've had more than my share of partners killed in the line

of duty. Some were gunned down by bad guys, a few took a bullet to save my life. Hell, some went through simple twists of fate that could have been no more controlled than the weather."

Davis looked at the papers on his desk and pushed them aside, suddenly taking more interest in what Frank was saying.

"Then there was one who tried to bang my second wife at the disco from hell."

"He died, too?" Davis leaned forward.

"Yeah, but that's a whole other story. Remind me to tell you about it sometime."

"It sounds really interesting. Why—"

"The one common denominator of all these people I've seen take that last Cadillac ride to the sky was that they bit the big one and I'm the one left standing. Do you have any idea how many cop funerals I've been to in my life?"

"Seven?"

Frank scoffed. "I was at seven in the seventies, Davis."

Travis furrowed his brow, doing some internal math. "Wait, that was forty years ago, there's no way—"

"Let's just say I have no desire to sit through another one. Not only are they boring as shit, but it hurts too much to see one of my fellows cut down before their time. But especially if I'd been in the middle of teaching them the ropes. I hate wasting time like that."

"Remind me to turn down that assignment if it ever comes up," Davis said.

"That's the point. It's not going to come up. I'm not going to let it."

"Phew." Davis leaned back in his chair in relief.

"But that still doesn't change the fact that doubts are creeping into my brain. Doubts about my skills. You're younger than me, right?"

"Shit, I hope so."

"What do you newbies do to quiet that nagging voice that won't shut up in the back of your brain?"

"You mean my wife?"

"Is that who it is?"

Davis crossed his hands behind his head. "Sounds to me like what you need to do is to take some overtime, Malone. Stay too busy for any worries."

"Overtime? Huh…" Frank rubbed his chin in thought.

"Yeah, man, it's like a golden cash register. Double time. Triple time. You'll be rolling in bread."

"I prefer to eat my bread, not roll in it, but how you spend your extra pay isn't my business."

"No, I meant—"

"But it's a good idea, Davis. Crime seems to have taken an early summer holiday this year and I'm getting restless just driving around town all day looking for an invisible stolen car."

"Then overtime is just what you need."

"Now what exactly is getting posted these days? It's been a while. Are we talking like parade detail?" Frank asked.

"Nah, man, work events. Crowd control, look intimidating, that sort of thing. Evenings, weekends, whatever. Easiest money you can make. I heard Greenwood pulled in an extra hundred thousand clams in OT pay last year alone."

"I don't know if I could eat that much seafood," Frank said.

Davis snorted. "Malone, you're a real cracker, you know that?"

"Clams on crackers? Never tried that before either."

Davis just shook his head. "Just go see the duty officer, tell him you want to volunteer for OT and watch your bank account swell like my wife's ass." He laughed, but Frank didn't.

CHAPTER ELEVEN: MORE FORUM COMMENTS ON THE DATING LIFE OF DAN STODDARD

Queen's Another One Bites the Dust played as a dark-haired woman with huge, round glasses waved goodbye and walked out of the apartment door. With a sudden change of lighting, she walked back in, then left in reverse. The image shifted back and forth to her leaving with the wave, walking in and out, then leaving again.

WhosJohnnyRock: lol, nice cut job. It looks like she lasted more than one visit.

GOKUBOY316: You think the stink was really that bad?

Cwood4Real: Girls shit, too.

GOKUBOY316: Not like that.

Cwood4Real: You weren't there, you don't know if it was as bad as Mike said.

RichardtheLianHeart265: *posted an image*

Joe's face, frozen in a look of total disgust, with the words 'When you've smelt the smells of hell.'

RichardtheLianHeart25: does that look like the face of a man confronted with common human odours?

Cwood4Real: I swear sometimes this fanbase is full of chauvinist pigs.

GOKUBOY316: *posted a video*

Shannon's stomach groaned, the noise doctored slightly to sound like a dying bear.

"Are you okay?" Dan asked from beside her.

She frowned slightly. "Where's the bathroom?" she asked.

"Down the hall to the left."

Shannon ran off, leaving the three of them alone.

"So?" Dan asked. "What do you guys think?"

"She really has to go," Mike said.

Cwood4Real: Yeah, you keep posting that. People use the bathroom. It's normal!

GOKUBOY316: *posted a video*

"Sweet baby Jesus!" Joe shouted.

"What is it?" Mike said, grabbing the camera and rushing towards him. The view shook as he moved down the hallway. Joe stood, hand over his mouth at the edge of the bathroom.

The view turned to show Mike sniffing the air comically. He turned his lip up, shut his eyes, made a mock gagging face. "Oh god, what did she eat?"

"I don't know, open a window, open a door, knock out a wall, anything!" Joe pushed past him down the hall.

Mike pointed the camera inside.

"You can't tell this from home, people, but there's definitely an aroma in here."

He reached forward and grabbed their can of air freshener, shaking it ineffectually.

"Empty. She poured the whole thing out. It's given the room a certain je ne sais quoi. A melange of sulphur, shit, and pine trees."

"How can we ever use it again?" Joe said, coughing.

"Dude," Mike shouted. "Your girlfriend just tried to poison us. She took the evilest shit in our bathroom. She's... she's," he stuttered halfway between coughing and laughing, "she's SHIT-ler."

BladeRunner256: Lol. SHIT-ler. Classic Mike.

Cwood4Real: Okay, I'm done for tonight. Maybe I'll come back when you guys move on from poop jokes.

Cwood4Real left the chat.

GertrudeBeerStein: Did you just chase off the only confirmed girl in here?

BladeRunner246: Good riddance. She was getting annoying.

Joe leaned back from the laptop as the chat continued.

"The guys are having a field day with Shannon's epic departure last night," Joe said to Mike, who sat on the couch scrolling through Netflix.

"You think she'll ever be back?"

"Not if she sees the compilation video they've already made."

"That's fast. I'm impressed. What's it called?"

Joe returned to the laptop. "The annoying adventures of Media Boy."

Mike put the remote down. "That sounds better than the nothing I'm finding here. Put it on."

Joe opened the video and put it on full screen mode.

Shannon, wearing a hoodie and jeans examining the wall of DVD's. "You've sure got a lot of movies here. I mean, not as many as Media Boy but still quite a bit."

"Who the hell is Media Boy?" Mike asked.

Shannon pulled out a copy of *They Live* and flipped it over to look at the back. "Just this guy I know. He does a podcast about movies."

"He does have a lot of movies, guys," Dan added. "I saw his stuff last night. Lots of Italian horror."

CUT TO:

Shannon bent over, checking out their gaming console set up, then walking over to check out the games they had lined up on shelves. "You've got a lot of games, but I'm pretty sure Media Boy has more. He hosts a podcast about retro gaming."

"Does he have a turbo grafx 16?" Joe asked. "Because I've got—"

"A turbo duo," she interrupted him. "The ultra rare all in one CD ROM unit—"

"Yeah, I know what that is," Joe stopped her. "I've been telling the guys for years that we should get one but they're just too damn expensive."

"I think Media Boy has two. I could see if he'd sell you one."

CUT TO:

"This is Media Boy's favourite game," Shannon said, holding up a Chrono Trigger SNES cartridge. "His is complete in box though."

"Who cares about the box?" Mike said. "You can't play with the god damned box."

He turned to the camera and winked. Someone had added a twinkle effect.

"We've bought that exact same game on SNES, PS1, DS, and uh, others," Joe said.

"His is on Super Famicom," she said. "Media Boy only plays things on their original platforms."

"I don't speak Japanese," Joe said.

"Eh, who does?" Mike said as he shrugged comically.

"Media Boy does. And Korean. And Chinese, too."

"Also, you know, the Japanese?" Joe said.

"I'm still not convinced the Japanese aren't just an elaborate hoax," Mike said.

"Oh, Media Boy goes to Japan twice a year to find retro games for his podcast."

"Is he an elaborate hoax, too?" Mike mumbled.

CUT TO:

"Turtles in Time is the theme for tonight's stream with our special guest, Shannon," Joe said. "We were just about to—"

Shannon grabbed a controller. "Oh, man, I know this one. Media Boy is the best at it! He can beat the whole thing without dying. He hosts a podcast about the Ninja Turtles. He even did a speed run on YouTube, got like a million hits."

Mike clicked off the game. "Fuck the ninja turtles. I vote we do a reverse order watch of the entire *Deathstalker* series."

"I know those!" Shannon said. "Media Boy has a Blu-ray of the whole set. He did a podcast on them."

"Four player game," Joe interjected. "I vote Turok 2."

"Oh, man, Media Boy just did a podcast on that!" Shannon added. "He's like an expert."

"What about Turok 3?"

"The podcast was in reverse franchise order. He's doing the first Turok next week."

"Doom 2?" Joe asked.

"That was one of the first games I ever saw him beat."

"Contra 3?"

"He doesn't even need the Konami code."

"Resident Evil 4."

"Oh yeah, he rocks that game, too."

"Parodius." Joe was getting desperate.

"Which version?" she asked. "Famicom? Saturn?"

"Adventure Island!"

"And Wonder Boy," she added.

"Okay, so this Media Boy is a real Master Higgins," Mike said in frustration. "He's clearly beaten every game on earth, owns more movies and video games than us, too. We can all agree on that, right?"

"Totally," Shannon said.

"Is Media Boy his handle or something?" Joe asked.

"No, that's just what I call him."

"So what's his real name then?"

"Media Boy?"

"Right, fine," Mike said. "This Media Boy guy has more movies and more games than us, hosts podcasts, makes videos, too. But does he have one of these?" Mike walked over to the wall and pointed to his framed portrait of the famed baseball star Kirby Puckett.

Shannon's stomach groaned, but she ignored it. "His is autographed. It's got one of those big glass frames with the certificate of authenticity and everything."

The image zoomed in on Mike's frowning face next to his crookedly mounted, u-frame store, childhood poster. Text appeared below his face. 'That feeling when there's someone out there better than you at everything.'

"Fuck that!" Mike said as the video ended. "This Media Boy jerk is just some kind of elaborate joke, right? There's no way he exists."

"I wonder if he watches our show," Joe said.

"Sure," Mike added. "He even hosts a podcast about it." Mike rose and headed to the kitchen. "Whatever he's doing, he's not better than us."

"It's entirely possible he is," Joe said. "There's hundreds of people out there that have more viewers than we do. People who—"

Mike took out a cup from the cupboard and held it at waist level as he talked. "We're a growing niche. We keep it real. We don't sell out. Someone will understand our—"

"Hey, are you pissing in a glass?" Joe asked him from the couch.

"What's your point?"

Joe stood up and saw that, sure enough, Mike was peeing into one of their glasses, a clear liquid slowly filling it up as he faced away from him. "Our bathroom is currently nor will it ever be habitable for humans again after what she did in there last night. You saw the video!"

"I was there, too. But, dude, we drink out of those things!"

"I'm gonna put it in the dishwasher," Mike said, rolling his eyes.

Dan walked into the room, scrolling his phone. He went right past Mike and into the bathroom. "See, Mike?" Joe said. "He's going to actually pee in the toilet like it was designed for, not use a god damn drinking glass."

"Hold your breath," Mike called after him.

A few short moments and one flush later, Dan returned.

"Oh, hey, guys, get this, Shannon decided to move to LA with Media Boy to pursue his podcasting career."

"Then I guess you're single again?"

CHAPTER TWELVE: A DAY AT THE BIG GAME

"Say, anyone know if Ken Ploen still plays?" Frank asked the crowd of revellers in the blue and gold jerseys as they filed past him on their way to their seats. They carried beer in plastic cups, footlong hotdogs, bags of popcorn. It was just like he remembered. Mostly.

"His name's up on the wall," Frank said, pointing to a banner hanging from the stadium's edge. "Is that his parking spot or something? If it is, it's a primo one. Nothing but the best for that man and his magic arm."

His buttons were spit shined and he could see himself in his shoes. His slacks were so crisp you could build a house of cards on them and his shirt, despite the years, fit as tightly on him as it had when he'd been issued it so very long ago. He'd come dressed in his blues, as much for show as anything. If he was going to be earning so much money doing this overtime thing, he might as well give the people their money's worth and look the part.

He took a deep breath of the fresh air. Twenty-nine thousand people were crammed into the immense stadium that stretched all around him, curving to the sky with an exposed roof that allowed the sun to shine down on the boys as they played in the dirt. He'd taken a shift at the local football match. The hometown boys versus some foreign no-goodniks, just like when he was a boy. And a teenager. And an adult. The Blue Bombers had been playing the game longer than he'd been alive. The current place was a little fancier than the stadium where he'd sat on wooden bleachers and eaten cotton candy, but the sport was as pure as it had ever been.

"Some gig," he said to himself, remembering the times he'd been here with his brother Bacon and their dad. Was it really so long ago?

"What do you think, ma'am?" he said to a passing woman. "You think I could still put on the leather helmet and join in? Back in the old days, I used to rough house as much as anyone."

"Excuse me, officer?"

"Oh sure, I'd get skinned knees, but football is football. I think—"

"Sorry, did I do something wrong?" the woman in the green jersey asked. "It's not a crime to wear the visitors' jersey, is it?"

"I don't think so," Frank said. "I'd have to look at the book to be sure. The way they keep updating the thing... Tell you what, I'll let it slide today, but if it is, then how about you come by the precinct tomorrow and turn yourself in?"

"Uh, yeah, sure. I'll do that."

"Good on you, ma'am. Not everyone is that honest. Enjoy the game."

She shared a confused glance with her friend and kept climbing the stairs. Frank turned and soaked it all in. There were television cameras all over the place, men and women holding microphones and talking away to the viewers at home, telling them the stories of the match. Football was big business. When had all this happened? Clearly, he hadn't been paying enough attention.

"Cactus Jack's got to be out here somewhere," he said as he scanned the crowd of cheering spectators, rowdies, drunks, gluttons, parents and kids.

"Say," he said to himself. "There's a good chance my car thief is here, too. Now who looks like the kind of guy that would swipe a Ferrari that wasn't his?"

He scanned the faces for anyone suspicious. The supervisor had told him that they were only here to act as deterrent, but this was a chance he couldn't pass up. Besides, the stadium had its own internal security force – they'd call him should things get out of hand, or should someone need to be taken away to the drunk tank. For now, he was on watch for a sneak thief.

He crossed his arms over his chest and put on as grim a face as he could. "Alright, punk, show your face so old Frank can knock you down a peg."

"Who are you talking to?" a child in the front row asked him.

Frank looked down at the little picture of innocence, all dressed up in a team uniform, his face painted with a large blue B. That had to make it easy to remember how to spell his name.

"The bad guys, kid. The ones hiding in the shadows, just waiting for me to slip up so they can go out there and do whatever bad things are lurking around in their bad guy brains. Have you seen any of them, Billy?"

"My name is Braydyn."

"Of course it is, Billy. Now tell me, you've got the keen eyesight of a dwarf, have you noticed anyone lurking around, acting suspicious, like they're hiding the fact they stole a fancy car?"

Billy nodded.

Maybe his day was looking up. "Good to hear. Now tell me, Billy, where'd you see them?"

"Braydyn, leave the police man alone," a woman sitting next to the kid said. She wore a zip-up hoodie in the team colours and held a bag of popcorn by the tips of her fingers.

"Me and the kid here are having a little tete-a-tete, ma'am. That's French for head-to-head."

"Yeah, I know what it means, but if he's bothering you, just let me know. I've told him before not to talk to people trying to work."

"No bother, he's just offering his help. Citizen's duty and all."

"Oh, okay then," she said, turning back to the game.

Frank leaned in close, to talk to the kid without anyone eavesdropping. "Alright, kid, spill it. Where'd you see the bad guys?"

With wide eyes the kid gulped and mumbled out, "In my closet."

Frank slapped the side of his head as if it was the most obvious answer in the world. "Of course! That's why I haven't been able to find the guy. Talk about naive. A real criminal isn't going to come to a football game and try to commit another crime in front of all these people, he's going to do it somewhere where there's nobody around. And what place is more deserted than a kid's closet! Especially when that kid is at the very same football game!"

Frank pounded his hand into his fist. "Okay, Billy, take me to your place, show me this closet. It big enough to park a car in?"

Billy tugged on his mom's sleeve. At first, she didn't respond, but as he tugged with more and more urgency, she finally complied and looked over to him.

"What? What is it, Braydyn?"

"Mommy, the police man is going to shoot the boogeyman for me."

"Oh, that's nice, dear," she said.

"He's in my closet," the kid said.

"Yeah, yeah, I know." The mom leapt to her feet to cheer on the team along with the rest of the row.

"Can I go show him?"

"Huh? Oh, sure— OH, HEY, COME ON, REF!" She was barely paying attention, but parental permission was all he needed, so Frank leaned over and lifted the boy out of his seat. He deposited him beside him on the stairs and took his hand.

"Okay, kid, take me to your house."

* * * *

"It's nice to finally get out of the apartment for once," Joe said.

"You're filming this, right?" Mike asked.

Joe moved his phone over to frame Mike. "Not yet. I can only get about forty minutes of video on this thing, so warn me if you're going to do something meme-worthy."

"I have a feeling this whole date is going to be meme-worthy," Mike said.

"Just don't mess this one up for him, too. You haven't

exactly been treating the others all that well."

"I don't know what you're getting at, Evans," Mike said. "I've been the picture of politeness."

"We have ample video evidence to the contrary."

"We're not streaming this," he said. "You can edit the footage all you want. Hey, that's a good idea. Make a supercut of only my best stuff."

"You'd have to have some first."

"Just wait until we see what this Kim is like. I'm sure I'll bust out something classic."

A day at Investor's Team field, the home of the River City Blue Bombers, the city's Canadian Football league franchise – Kim's idea.

"You think she watches the show?" Mike asked Joe.

"It would explain why she doesn't want to be on it."

"But then Dan did say she was really into football." Mike dug out his phone and pulled up a screenshot, reading over the text below. "Kim, age twenty-three. Likes sports, ice cream, beer, partying. 'I'm a game day nut looking for someone to cheer on the boys with.' That's vague. It could mean the Bombers, or it could mean us."

"I don't think it means us. And did you screenshot her dating profile?"

"No, it's still up."

"You looked her up?"

"Of course. How else am I going to screen the people Dan's bringing to meet us?"

"Dude," Joe said, "I think it's hard enough for Dan to meet girls without you judging them before you even meet them."

"Someone has to," Mike said. "Have you seen his track record so far?"

"This one likes football, you like football. Take that as a chance for her to endear herself to you or vice versa."

"I don't have to endear myself to her, I'm not the one schtupping her."

"Please don't mention that when she comes," Joe said.

"What if it comes up in the course of normal conversation?"

"It won't, trust me. Look, here he comes. Be on your best behaviour, okay?" Joe waved to Dan as he climbed the stairs to their seats. A girl with pink hair and glasses, much shorter than he was, followed him. She wore a pink jersey and kept stopping to turn to watch the action on the field.

He waited for her. At a break in play, she followed him to their seats. The others in the row stood up to let them pass. Dan sat next to Mike and Kim took the seat next to him.

"Hey, guys, this is Kim," Dan said, leaning back so they could both see her.

She gave a little wave. "Sorry we're late," Kim said. "We had to get a quick schtupp in before we came."

Mike turned to look at Joe, his eyebrows arched, a huge smile on his face. He was about to say something when Joe just shook his head, stopping him.

"Well, he came at least," she said, snorting.

Dan turned beet red. "Yeah, so we've got a great view of the field here, eh?"

"Looks like Dan sprang for decent seats," Mike said, elbowing him playfully. "Didn't want to come across as a cheapskate so early in the relationship, eh?"

"Too bad that didn't carry over to the beer he brought over last night," Kim said. "Pabst Blue Ribbon? Seriously?"

"Geez, man," Mike said. "You couldn't get the good stuff?"

Kim just shrugged. "Whatever. It was still enough to get

into my pants, but don't think I'll schtupp for that shit more than once."

Mike looked again at Joe who just shook his head harder. Mike was about to say something anyway when Joe slapped his hand over his mouth.

"So, pink hair," Joe said. "That's cool. Was that for one of those charity race things?"

"No, I just like pink," she said.

"And the jersey? I thought the Blue Bombers, you know, wore blue?"

"I just like pink," she said.

"That's... logical," Joe said.

"Who won the coin toss?" Kim asked.

"Do you get points for that?" Joe asked.

Mike looked at him with a raised eyebrow. "No, it just determines who gets to pick what side they start on."

Joe did not care about football. His knowledge of the game came mostly from playing too much Tecmo Bowl in Junior High. Mike was the fan. The only time he refused to stream early was on game night.

"Is that good?"

Mike ignored him and turned to Kim. "We did. They chose to receive first."

"Fucking stupid," Kim said.

"What does it matter?" Joe asked.

"Are you kidding, with the wind picking up around eight o'clock?" she blurted out. "They're going to be kicking right into the cross stream. With this kicker they'll be lucky to make thirty yards. What a waste."

Mike looked impressed.

"Block 'em, you shits, block the run, block the run!" Kim

suddenly shouted out.

"Special teams, special teams," Mike yelled.

"Hey, Dan," Kim said. "You going to get me some beers or what?"

"Yeah, get us all some beers, Stoddard," Mike agreed.

"And none of the shit stuff," Kim said.

Mike patted Dan on the shoulder and waved him to go. "Don't cheap out again, man, trust me."

Dan stood up. Kim turned her legs to let him go past.

"Fake the run, these morons always fall for it," she shouted.

"So you're into football?" Joe said.

Mike nudged him to take out his phone. He did and pointed it at the two of them with the empty space in between.

The crowd erupted to their feet, and Joe had to quickly move the angle to keep them both in shot. He noticed just how much shorter than Dan she really was. She was barely five feet tall, and he was six foot six. Did he have a thing for short girls?

"See, what'd I tell you?" Kim said, holding up her hand for a high five. "Fake the run. The dumb fucks fall for it every damn time."

Mike high fived her and gave Joe, and the camera, a thumbs up.

Dan was back in a moment, gingerly holding four beers. He handed two to Sam and another two to Mike.

"They let you buy four?" Mike said.

"I convinced them that I was buying for the whole row. If I didn't have the DD bracelet, I don't think they would have let me."

"What a dumbshit rule," Kim spat. She had the plastic lid off her first one and pounded the whole thing back in one gulp.

"If you have to go up for beers two at a time you spend your whole fucking night in line instead of watching the game."

"This girl knows," Mike said, pointing at her with his thumb as he looked to the camera. "I've been saying that ever since they instituted that stupid rule."

"That's why you bring a dork to buy for you," Kim said, looking at Dan.

She and Mike high fived again.

"Get it, Dan," Mike said, looking from Dan to the camera. "You're the dork!"

Kim noticed him talking to Joe's phone. "You guys recording something?"

"Dan didn't tell you what he does?" Joe asked.

"No time. We've been too busy schtupping."

Mike was about to explode but Joe pulled him down and covered his mouth. "We have a streaming show. Three Gamers. Some of this might go into a video later."

"Whatever," Kim snorted. "More nerd stuff. Don't care. Dan, get more beer. I'm out."

Dan had reached into his pocket and took out a can of Pepsi. He looked at her as he popped the top.

"Did you smuggle that in?" Joe asked.

"I'm not paying six bucks for a Pepsi here," Dan said as if it was the most obvious answer in the world.

"He's always doing cheap stuff like that," Mike said, putting his arm around Dan. "This one time, he stuffed an entire bag of chips in each jacket sleeve to go to a movie theatre and—" Mike trailed off, spotting something a few rows down. "Oh shit, Dan, look!"

They all followed his finger to a police man talking to a boy in his seat.

"The cops are almost on to you!"

Dan lowered the Pepsi can under his seat as if he believed what Mike was suggesting.

The cop lifted the young boy out of his seat and together they started walking down the stairs.

"Maybe the kid saw you," Mike said, nudging Dan. "The little boy's going to make a statement."

"Come on, boys, let's see some fucking hustle," Kim shouted.

* * * *

"The problem with kids is that they've got no sense of direction. You ask 'em for their address and they give you a song and dance about how they can't spell."

The little boy sat patiently in the back seat, amazed to be in a real police car, even if it was one as old as his parents. The kid not knowing where he lived was a problem, but Frank had a workaround. He figured out where the kid went to school and what his last name was. Then he called in to dispatch and had them do a search on their magic computer. They had an address for him in no time and he pulled up in front of a completely normal suburban house, painted light blue. The kid brightened up.

"Is this your place, Billy?"

"Yes!" The kid bounced in his seat.

"Okay, so you show me where your room is, okay? Then you back off and let me take the bad guy out, alright?"

Frank helped him out of the car and together, they walked up to the front door. He was all set to ring the doorbell when he realized that it would only tip this Boogie Man off.

"This guy in your closet, he's part of some gang, is he?"

The boy just stared at him.

"With a name like that, he must be," Frank said. He'd seen it before with these types. They always had a code name they used to make themselves feel tough. "Boogie Man. Some kind of dancer? New slang for stealing cars?"

It didn't matter what the guy did, criminals like him were all just putty in the hands of Frank Malone. He'd sent so many of them to prison over the years that he was surprised they even bothered anymore. Shouldn't the word be out?

The house was quiet. There were no signs of anyone being inside. What was presented to him now was a dilemma. The place was locked up tight. The kid said there was a bad guy hiding in his closet.

"How to get inside without alerting the punk?" he said to himself.

He had to sneak in and catch the man unawares, so he didn't have time to load up some kind of Saturday Night Special. Just think of what they'd say back at the precinct if Frank bought it like that, cut down by a petty car thief stashed in a kid's closet.

Frank looked at the house. "You got a nice place here, kid. Your parents must do alright for themselves, eh?"

Billy picked his nose.

The house was a two story, with an attached garage and white picket fence. The kind of place they sold by the baker's dozen here in the suburbs.

"A life like this was never in the cards for me. Not twice divorced on a cop's salary."

"I hate celery," Billy said.

"Really? Not even with some Cheez Whiz spread over the

114

crack?"

The kid stuck out his tongue.

"There's no accounting for some tastes, I guess."

Frank looked at the fancy windows and shingles of the house and knew that he'd made the right choice to avoid this world. He had a higher calling and this opportunity to save a little boy was the gravy in his boat.

"I hope you learn something today, Billy. If you pick up on this when you're still in short pants, respecting the law, that is, then you have a good chance to live a straight and narrow life, contribute to society, pay your taxes, collect your pension, then fade away in an old folks' home with lots of little grandbabies to talk to. I can see it in your little brown eyes that you know exactly what I'm talking about."

He ruffled the hair on the kid's head. "You'll turn out alright. If we stop this Boogie Man. Now, Billy, you got a back way into this place?"

"There's a sandbox in my yard!"

"No wonder this Boogie Man is after you."

They walked around to the side of the house. Frank lifted the latch on the large wooden gate and crept into the backyard. It was eerily quiet. There was the aforementioned sandbox sitting in the middle of a freshly cut, green-grassed space of about sixty meters squared with a few abandoned kids' toys strewn about. The sandbox was a real top shelf piece of real estate. There was a bucket, a tractor, even a shovel.

"You've got it good here, Billy. When I was your age, we didn't have our own sandboxes. We had to crawl around in the old quarry down by the river. Didn't have buckets either, we had to use the chamber pots when they were empty. And trucks, shit, I had to push around an old tin can and go vroom vroom." He ruffled the kid's hair again, thinking back to those days in the North End, by the river, on the old farm.

Then, Frank spotted the patio doors. Glass, six feet across, seven high, clean as a whistle, reflecting a perfect image of him and the kid back out to a world that didn't know the evil inside the closet in little Billy's room.

"You got a key for those, kid?"

The boy just pointed to his truck.

"Yeah, I see it, you don't have to rub it in. It is one hell of a truck. Wait, that's it! You're a genius!"

Frank picked up the toy. Orange and blue plastic with green wheels and a little lever that allowed you to lift up sand. Quite an invention. Hell, if Frank had had things like this he might have gone into construction, put up skyscrapers and apartments instead of putting down villains and human waste.

He walked over to the patio door carrying the truck, looking from the shovel to the door and back to the shovel. The key was right there, the way to get inside and keep the bad guy from knowing he was coming.

"Watch and learn, Billy," Frank said, smiling.

"Truck!"

"Yeah, I know, it's a damn nice truck, would you stop showing off!"

Frank looked at the handle of the patio door, tugged it; sure enough, it was stuck tight, locked from the inside. That was where the truck was going to come in.

"Okay, kid, here goes."

Frank reared back and launched the truck point blank at the door. But instead of smashing through the glass in a great shower of twinkling stars, it bounced right back and hit him in the face, cracking his nose and sending a shooting pain through his teeth. He grabbed his prized nose and shouted in agony.

"Awww, fucking hell, that smarts."

"You're funny!" the kid said, laughing.

"You know something, Billy," Frank said as the dots in his vision faded away, "I'm beginning to see why this Boogie Man is after you."

His great plan thwarted, Frank took out his gun and fired once into the glass. The hole went straight through, but the pane stayed standing.

"Well, I'll be a gorilla's aunt. That's one hell of a door."

"Truck funny!" the kid laughed.

Frank saw the toy fly through the air again. He instinctively reached for his face to block the rebound, but instead, the toy flew right through the window, shattering it into a million pieces.

"Good work, Billy, there's hope for you yet!"

Frank reached in and unlocked the door, sliding it open, the track crinkling with the shards of glass that were everywhere.

"Now, take me to this closet. I want to meet this Boogie Man."

The kid pulled his hand and took him through a kitchen filled with stainless steel appliances decorated with sheets of white paper covered in the illegible scribbles of a madman.

Frank examined the red and blue swirls. They seemed to be drawn in crayon. "I'm looking into the mind of lunatic," he said in awe.

Billy tugged him again. They walked through a hallway and into what had to be the kid's room. The bed was decorated in dinosaur sheets with stuffed animals piled high on top. There was a shelf filled with books and another with toys, a dresser beneath the window with some framed photos on top and there, at the other end of the room, the closet door.

Shut. Locked tight. The hiding place of the Boogie Man.

"Is that where he lives?" Frank asked the boy in a whisper.

Billy just nodded and hid behind Frank's leg.

Frank led him to the doorway. "It's okay, kid, old Frank is here. Just stay back and let him deal with this."

Billy peered around the corner of the door, looking inside in wide-eyed curiosity.

Frank strode up to the door and took out his gun. He pointed it at the closet and said in his most imposing voice, "Alright, Boogie Man, if that is your real name. I know you're in there and you know I'm out here, so why don't you just make this easy for all of us and come out peacefully? No one has to die here on this shag carpeting, least of all you. Who it would assuredly be, by the way. I'm a crack shot. So, toss out your piece and come out with your hands up. If not, I start blasting on three."

He looked back to the kid and smiled, but the kid just stared at him.

No one was coming out.

He was going to have to do this the hard way.

"Alright, don't say I didn't give you fair warning. On the count of three then. One. Two. Three!"

Still no movement. Frank sighed. He hated having to do this, especially with the kid watching. But then we all had to see a dead body at some point. Billy might as well learn about what's inside people now.

Frank pulled the trigger, aiming dead centre at the door.

At each blast he moved the gun, putting holes in the door at every possible angle. There'd be no way to avoid being hit, unless the guy was some kind of contortionist. The kid covered his ears in fright.

When it was all over, there was only silence in the room.

"There, Billy, no more Boogie Man."

Frank walked over to the closet door and slid it open.

Empty!

"The bastard gave us the slip!"

He looked around the room frantically.

"Where could he have gone?"

Frank grabbed a stuffed bear and yanked its head off, looking inside but seeing only stuffing. He tore the tail off a stegosaurus, nothing again. He tossed the toys from off the shelf, pulled open the doors on a model car, flipped through every book; when the room was thoroughly searched and trashed, he'd still found no sign of him.

He shook his head. "I'm sorry, kid, looks like he's gone."

The kid started crying.

"Hey, don't worry. I'm sure if he comes back and sees this mess, he'll think twice about hiding out in that closet."

The kid still didn't shut up.

"Ah, come on, don't be like that."

"I want my mommy!"

"Would you listen to yourself? You're going to have to toughen up. Some day she'll be dead, and you'll be all alone. What are you going to do then?"

"Mommy!"

"Alright, alright, I'll take you back to the game."

* * * *

The empty beers piled up all around Mike and Kim. Joe ran out of storage space filming them making idiots of themselves. Dan sat uncomfortably, his Pepsi lost in the sea of beer cans. With the game almost over, the Bombers were down five points.

"A minute to go and ball on the fifty," Mike shouted. "You can do this!"

"You better last more than a minute when we get home," Kim said, elbowing Dan, slurring her words. "I don't need no minute man when I'm drunk and horny as fuck."

Dan went white as a sheet, but Mike just patted him on the shoulder. "Don't worry, a whole minute is still pretty solid."

"Better be solid," Kim said. "Don't want some pool noodle either!" She laughed like a pirate, deep and throaty, coughed up some phlegm and spat over the side of the railing.

"Excuse me, folks," a police officer said as he stopped at their aisle holding up a phone with a picture of a small child on it. "Have you seen this boy?"

"I'm not falling for that shit, Terminator 1000!" Mike said drunkenly.

"The robot masters won't rule this timeline," Kim added.

Joe and Dan shared an embarrassed look. "Sorry, officer, I haven't seen any kids," Joe said.

"Me either," Dan added.

The officer held his hand up to his earpiece. He listened to something they couldn't hear. "Motherfucker," he said under his breath and left them without another word.

"Run away, John Conner!" Kim called after him and Mike burst out laughing.

"More beers, Stoddard!" Mike called. "I'm not missing this last drive!"

By the end of the game, Kim had blacked out. Dan carried her out of the stadium. Her skirt rode high and the underwear she wore wasn't fit for a family audience. Mike stumbled around drunk, barely able to stay upright. They managed to get to Dan's car, passing a frantic woman talking to police saying, "—went with a cop, or a man in a cop's uniform. Oh please, you have to find him!"

"You going to be okay with her?" Joe asked Dan as he laid Kim into his car.

"I should be."

"You're lucky, dude." Mike punched him in the arm. "She's a keeper."

Dan just looked at the passed-out form of his date. "Not this one."

"Schtupping..." Mike said, laughing. "Lucky guy." He turned to Joe. "Come on, man, let's leave those two lovebirds alone. If we hurry back, we can catch the Sportscentre highlights."

CHAPTER THIRTEEN: CALL IT FORTH

The candles had been replaced and burned anew with the smell of brimstone. The dancing shadows played tricks with his mind. The crimson-robed figures formed a circle at the edges of the room, chanting slowly, almost humming. A newborn lamb bleated quietly on the plush velvet at the top of the altar. The protective pentagram had been repainted in blood graciously donated.

It had been weeks since the ritual and still no word from the dark one. They deserved more than whispers and shadows, therefore it was time for another summoning.

"It's too dangerous," some cautioned, but what choice did they have? Impatience rippled through their number.

"Evil one," he chanted. "We call to you. We, your loyal servants, beseech thee to make thy presence felt. Come to us. Come to us!"

"Come to us," the others repeated.

The candles slowly rose, as if someone were carefully turning the knob on a gasoline stove. Higher and higher, the flames nearly touched the ceiling. The lamb bleated in fear. He held it tightly by the neck.

"We offer this innocent life. As the blood spills—"

He drew the blade over the neck of the struggling lamb. The tender skin separated like overstuffed cellophane, pouring the dark red liquid down his hands, over the pillow, over the sides of the altar, to drip down onto the floor.

"—so we call to you."

Silence. The falling of the blood onto the floor echoed like the ticks of a clock. The flames burned impossibly hot. Sweating, he wiped his brow.

Waiting.

A collective breath held.

"Did it work?" a woman asked from his left.

"Shhh…"

Footsteps. Coming down the stairs.

All eyes turned to the doorway into the dark hall that led from the chamber. A line of candles stretched towards the wooden steps that seemed to hover in negative space. The footsteps approached. One by one the flames were extinguished.

"Something's coming," a man said from the wall.

"Of course something's coming, you idiot," he said back. "We called to it."

"I thought that meant, like, you know, on the phone or something," the man said sheepishly.

"Yeah, the direct hotline to hell that's just hanging right over there," he said back sarcastically, pointing to an empty spot on the wall.

The hallway was black. Everyone held their breath. Something was on the other side, waiting, watching them. Evil emanated back like a wave, heat, flowing into the room, mixing with the smells of sweat and burning candles.

"Is that—"

"Shut up."

"Who has called?" an inhuman voice growled from the inky blackness.

"Your servants, oh dark one. Those who awoke you and—"

"You claim mastery over that which you have sworn to serve."

"No, we—"

"Think to command?"

"To know your orders and—"

"Silence."

The tension in the room pressed thickly against them, pushing everyone against the wall. They backed away from the voice, compressed shoulder to shoulder as if by an invisible vice.

"You hold no sway over the power you have unleashed. You were merely the catalyst for events begun long ago."

"Well, yeah," a woman's voice said from his left. "We're the ones who b—"

"Do not presume so much," the entity said. The speaker's words died in her throat. She began gagging. Her hands went up to the hood and desperately pulled it back to show a face quickly turning blue from lack of oxygen.

"My mission is my own. My actions are my own. Father, mother; no lord do I serve."

"Then—"

His own air cut off; he struggled to breathe, facing the panic of imminent death.

"Clarity; the reawakened mind was fogged. Hunger burned, never satiated. The draining opened my eyes to something more… innocent."

"The blood of the lamb," he coughed out with extreme

effort, waving his hand proudly over the corpse that had let most of its life pour over the altar to the floor. It had spread outward, nearly touching the pentagram itself.

"Insufficient."

"What more can we give?" another voice said. "Say it and we will gladly offer it!"

The presence went silent. The sound of deep-throated breathing echoed in all their minds. He was quickly losing consciousness, but he had to know what the thing wanted.

"Only true innocence fulfils the hunger. Human, given freely. You do not contain this, any of you."

"Tell us what to do an—"

"Offer something else," the voice said.

"What?"

"Your lives."

The vice-like grip on his throat relaxed. He gasped air in panicked gulps. The woman did the same. He turned and saw her eyes growing in fear as one by one the flaming candles around the room were snuffed out, plunging them all into darkness.

"What's going on?" she said.

Before he could say anything back the last candle died. The room was as black as night. A scream from his right. Another from his left. Something hit his face. He wiped it with his hand to find blood, a chunk of something.

"An ear?"

The screams of the dying assaulted him. He couldn't see what was going on.

"Help!"

"Argh."

More cries, then a void. He gripped the altar tightly,

breathing deeply, wondering what he was going to do. Moments passed in total silence. Were they all dead?

"Hello?" he croaked.

Suddenly the candles all flashed to life at once, pounding his eyes with white light. What he saw would haunt him forever; corpses, everyone shredded, mutilated, torn, mangled, heads detached, limbs piled against the wall. Writing was on the walls in some hideous script, as if drawn by claws.

"Dear God..."

"You invoke his name? After renouncing him for so long?"

"No, I—"

That was when he realized why he was still alive. The circle. The magic had protected him. It was powerful indeed. He steeled himself, understanding that the horror in the room could not touch him.

"I am glad you have spared me, oh dark one," he continued. "I understand now that you—"

"You understand nothing."

The entity grinned as it stepped forward over the edge of the pentagram ring.

"What? How?"

The thing looked at his feet. He followed its gaze to see that the blood of the lamb had spilled over and disturbed the circle. He was undone.

"You offer so little," the thing said. "But it will suffice for now."

It leapt at him.

CHAPTER FOURTEEN: SHE'S THE ONE

"Well, it's over," Dan said, walking into the apartment carrying his laptop bag over his shoulder. He set it down on the kitchen table and went to the fridge to get a glass of milk.

"What is?" Mike asked.

"The Simpsons finally?"

"They put it out of its misery?"

"Not that," Dan said. "Me and Kim."

PING.

They were playing Total Carnage to an audience of nearly a hundred. Dan was late, but considering they hadn't expected him here at all, it was a step up.

"Seriously?" Mike said. "I thought things were going well."

"Really?" Dan said, surprised. "Why would you say that?"

"She drank like a fish, knew her football, and was putting out like a sailor on shore leave."

Dan turned beet red.

"Then there was that time she dropped her underwear live on stream and told you to meet her in your room in T-minus eight seconds before she started without you."

PING.

Dan spat out his milk all over the carpet.

"Guys!"

"What? Everyone watching saw it, too," Joe said. "Didn't you, guys?"

PING.

"What happened?" Mike asked. "I don't get why you'd split up when you had so much in common."

"We did?" Dan asked. "Like what, exactly?"

"Like the common desire to knock boots."

Dan put his glass down on the counter. "You need something more than that."

"Two girls at the same time?" Mike said.

"I think he means the fact that he's a software guy and she was a... what was she exactly?"

"She worked at the Baskin Robbins until she got fired for stealing sprinkles."

"Allegedly," Joe said to the camera. "Right?"

"Oh yeah, allegedly," Dan said. "For all legal intents and purposes."

"So?" Mike said. "Who gives a shit where she worked?"

"And there was also the whole thing with her hating video games," Joe said. "Remember when she called everyone watching us the only losers bigger than we were?"

"They are the only losers bigger than us!" Mike said. He turned to the camera. "But we love and appreciate each and every one of you from the bottom of our hearts." He held his hands over his chest and smiled condescendingly.

"And her drinking problem," Joe said.

"That *was* the problem," Dan said. "She's in rehab. Somewhere out of town. Some kind of isolated resort type place. She didn't tell me where. Said I was an enabler."

"You? But you hardly ever drink?" Mike scoffed.

"Yeah, but I paid for all of hers, so that means I was the one who was making it hard for her to control herself. Apparently, there were a few more reasons. I drained her life energy," he said, holding his fingers up to make air quotes. "Any of you guys know what the heck that's supposed to mean?"

"That sounds like something from Oprah or The View," Joe said.

"It sounds bullshit. But don't worry, brother," Mike said, patting the spot next to him on the couch. "We've got your back, and the stream is here for you."

Dan came to sit down next to him. "Thanks, guys."

PING.

Joe leaned forward to check the comment. "TheDoorsMan says there's plenty of other fish in the sea."

"You'll just have to go back to jerking off for a while," Mike said helpfully.

PING.

"FrankieGoestoHollyOaks222 wants to know if he can get her number. For when she gets out."

"Fuck off, Frankie," Mike said. "I called dibs."

* * * *

CwoodforReal: I almost feel bad for the guy.

PacoPoosDay: Don't. He's sunk to a new low.

MOTUClassic4Ever: What'd I miss?

CwoodforReal: Dan asking about K-Pop.

MOTUClassic4Ever: WTF?

GOKUBOY316: *posted a video*

Dan scrolled on his phone as the guys played a round of Street Fighter Alpha 2 on the PlayStation.

"What do you know about K-Pop?" he asked.

"K-Pop? Do you mean J-Pop? That's Japanese pop music."

"No, this says K-Pop."

"Huh?"

He showed Joe his phone. "Greta, age 20, likes K-Pop, Korean food."

"K-Pop?" Mike said, finally paying attention.

"If it's anything like J-Pop," Joe said, "which I assume it is. You know, only Korean. Then it's probably elaborate dance moves, catchy songs, weirdly pretty dudes."

PING.

Mike leaned over to check the screen. "WhosJohnnyRock says it's groups with short careers, guys that look like girls and girls that look twelve."

"So the same as J-Pop then, just... Korean."

Dan frowned. "I guess I could like that."

"Who the fuck are you kidding?"

TheMack420: How much do you want to bet he went into a deep dive?

WhosJohnnyRock: Who do you think he watched? BTS, H.O.T., Sechs Kies, Shinhwa, TVXQ!, BIGBANG, INFI-NITE...

FavreauForLife420: None of those are real band names.

CwoodforReal: They are, trust me on that one.

GOKUBOY316: There are some lines a man should not cross.

GertrudeBeerStein: Unless he's Korean.

GOKUBOY316: Sure, of course. Then it's okay.

* * * *

Dan sat in his darkened room. The light from a screensaver reflected off his glasses and a couple of old movie posters on the wall. His small bookshelf was filled with Star Wars novels and DVD shelf runoff. His blinds were drawn, very little sunlight seeping through. He walked over, lifted the shade, and was momentarily blinded by the natural light. Daylight. People were doing things on a Saturday. He closed them again.

He turned and looked at his dresser, covered in clothes, a dusty ovular mirror reflecting his crumpled shirt he'd worn all weekend.

"This shouldn't be so hard," he said.

He sat back down and scrolled through people on his dating app.

"Young, old, fat, thin, weird, scary."

He stopped on someone that looked promising. A photo of a smiling blonde with a slightly prominent nose and cutely crooked teeth. She looked like a bright, vibrant person; shots of her in a canoe, camping, hiking with other girls. There was something in her eyes that drew him; a pull deep inside that called out to a part of him he didn't really know. He couldn't explain it. He needed to talk to her. Maybe she could be the answer to the question he was struggling to pose.

"Kristin. Age 28. Likes: Camping, folk music, canoeing, the outdoors. Looking for a nature-loving person to get outside with. No funny business, friendship counts. Go slow and see how we match up. Nice guys only."

"What do you have to lose?" he said. "The outdoors aren't all that bad. You went to summer camp once."

She had a guileless face that interested him. In one shot, the red from the camera flash made her eyes look like the back headlights of a Kart in Mario Kart.

"God, Dan, you even think in video game metaphors. You have to get out more."

"Hey, dude," Mike shouted. "If you're through jerking it in there, we're about to start watching The Exorcist 3."

On the other side of the apartment, the guys were waiting for him. He looked up. Another night of these four walls, inside and alone. The compulsion kept growing within him. Get out. Do something with your life. You only live once. You don't have to stay cooped up here doing this forever. The others had been dead ends. This girl could be just what he needed.

He sent her a message. Simple, direct. To the point and honest. If he was lucky, she'd be as interested in him as he was in her.

He sat on the bed, letting his mind wander.

"Dude?" Mike called. "I put the DVD in. You're missing the boot up screen."

"Gimme a second," he called back.

He stared at her photos, scrolling the few she'd put up. It was weird, but her eyes seemed to have the red glow of the camera flash in almost all the shots. He scrolled back to the first few.

"Weird," he said as he saw them there, too.

He began to imagine all the things they could do together: pitch a tent in the woods, roast marshmallows, rent a cottage near a deserted lake, watch the stars, canoe down the Assiniboine. Maybe hike the Whiteshell.

He scrolled through more photos. The eyes were normal

now. Blue.

"I could have sworn…"

Then it hit him; it was the light coming from the screen-saver. He chuckled as the image shifted on screen from the rebel to imperial logos. It must have been tricking his eyes.

"You have been inside for too long," he said.

Kristin. It was a nice name. The kind of name you could hold hands with in the park. Go for ice cream. Watch the sky. Then, who knows? Marriage, sex, babies, retirement, grandkids, and death. Not necessarily in that order, of course.

"Dude? How the fuck long does it take you to whack that shit?" Mike called again.

The Exorcist 3 wasn't going to wait any longer. He shut his phone and left the room. He would just have to wait to see if she was as drawn to him as he was to her.

CHAPTER FIFTEEN: FRANK'S FALLOUT

The Chief had to read over the report a few times before he believed that it was real. He'd found a pre-printed form the force had stopped using in the nineties when they'd gone digital and typed on an actual honest to goodness typewriter. There were whiteout smudges where Frank had made a mistake and then written over the blotch in black ink.

"I didn't even know they still sold typewriters, Malone," he said as he read the nearly incomprehensible report.

Across from him, the grey-haired and leathery-skinned man in the dark blue button-up shirt was impassive. "I'm not replacing old Sheila for one of those grey boxes."

"You named your typewriter?'

"I name all my tools. Bertha is the piece that keeps me alive out there, Betty the cruiser, Shelby the car I drive."

"Let me guess, a Shelby GT?"

Frank reacted like someone had farted. "No, a Tempest. Why the hell would I drive one of those?"

"Just a hunch."

"Leave the hunches to those of us with a nose for 'em. No offence, sir, but you're the type more content to stuff his nose in a file folder than sniff out the faint traces of crime's stink on a corpse."

"What?" the Chief said. "That makes no… I'm just going to let that slide."

He didn't want to get into it with the old man right now. He was too busy trying to make sense of this report. No official codes, no chronological retelling of the events, just a large block of gibberish about how Frank had scared away a known gang member and repeat car thief calling himself the Boogie Man who'd been holding up in a little boy's closet. And that the little boy had come to him while he was working the most recent Blue Bombers game, requesting police protection.

"Problem, sir?" Frank asked him as he read.

"With your report? Plenty."

"Really?"

"Where to start?"

It didn't explain anything, in fact, it left more questions than answers. Like, for instance, why had Frank emptied an entire clip into a closet door? And why had he trashed four other rooms of the house before returning the boy to the football game?

"What stands out the most?"

"How about why you felt it necessary to point out the crowd cheering on a last-minute drive in the fourth quarter?"

"In case you wanted to know who won the game."

"Right. You know this whole thing was almost a public relations nightmare."

"The Bombers won, sir."

"I'm talking about the kid's mom. She'd been frantic."

"It did come down to the wire."

"They'd been about to issue an amber alert."

"I don't think those are for football games, Chief."

"Officers posted at every exit. They'd almost locked the stadium down. Then you show up with the kid and, we thought, saved the day."

"I did save the day. It's all in there."

"Then she calls back with a story. You were talking to the boy before he disappeared. She returns home to find the house a mess. The kid tells her you killed the Boogie Man. Surveillance footage confirms you were gone with the kid for nearly an hour and a half."

"He didn't know where he lived. I'm not sure how bright Billy is, really."

"A team of doctors and psychologists examine the boy. Mom thinks he's been abused or worse. People panic, thinking you've lost your mind and started a career as a child molester. They panic again. Maybe you'd always been one and were only just now caught."

"A what? Sir, I told you, it was the Boogie Man."

"The tests showed the boy hadn't been touched. That this was some bizarre misunderstanding."

"That's why I explained it all in the report," Frank said as if it should be obvious.

"I've managed to keep this whole mess out of the papers," the Chief said. "I've managed to convince the mother to forego any charges with the promise of a full police funded renovation of her home. I've even managed to keep the mayor from finding out. But I expected a detailed report from you, Frank, explaining your actions, and instead I get this short story straight from a retro men's magazine."

"You really think it was good enough to be in one of those?"

"This whole Boogie Man angle. You say the kid told you he

136

was a gang member and car thief, and that you interpreted that as imminent danger."

"Yup."

"The Boogie Man? Really? I mean, kids everywhere talk about boogeymen in their closets, it's a childish fear, nothing more. How could you—"

"Hold the phone here, Chief," Frank said, cutting him off with a raised hand. "Are you telling me there are more of these Boogie Men fuckers out there? That they're in closets all over town? And we're just sitting here doing nothing? My God, we're supposed to be protecting people!"

Frank rose to leave but the chief waved his hands to stop him.

"No! No, no, no. That's not what I meant. I meant that the boogeyman is a little kid's fantasy. There's no such thing. Sit back down!"

Frank had his gun out and looked at the Chief like he was speaking Greek. "With all due respect, sir, you just told me we've got an epidemic on our hands. I'm not about to sit here while—"

"I've got a team on it, Malone, just calm down and let me explain."

Frank slid his gun back into his holster. "I'm not sure we should hand this off to rank amateurs."

"Sit down, that's an order."

"But I'm willing to hear you out," Frank said and re-took his seat.

"Good. Now what I'd like to talk about is the same thing we talked about last time I called you in here over something insane you pulled. About getting a partner to—"

"Nothing doing, Chief. Loose cannon, lone wolf, need to

roll where the action takes me, remember?"

"That's just it. You are a loose cannon and I think you need some tightening up. A partner could help keep you from going off the deep end completely before you retire. Speaking of which, I've been having trouble finding your file to—"

"Don't worry about that, Chief, I'm sure it's in there somewhere."

"But records indicate—"

"Trust me when I tell you I'm not old enough to retire just yet."

"How do I—"

"That's all you need to know. But as to your other suggestion, I'm not a ball and chain guy, okay?"

The Chief sighed. "I was warned about you before I took this job. They told me you were a dinosaur."

"That's dumb. Those things have been extinct for, what, a million years?"

"Malone operates like someone from another decade, they said."

"One of the good ones, I hope."

"But they assured me that you had to be close to retirement age. You've been here longer than anyone. They also said despite your offbeat demeanour, you were still a good cop."

"False. True and true."

"Your file shows that you've solved some of the toughest and most bizarre cases this force has ever seen."

"Yeah, and?"

"And they told me that if I just let you do your thing, ignored what you said, you'd probably be harmless."

"Not to crime."

"But you're starting to prove them all wrong. You're causing more harm than good right now and something has to change."

The Chief reached into his desk and pulled out an old, yellowed paper.

"Now look, Frank, I dug out your special no-partner clause paperwork. I had the lawyers go over it and you're right, I can't touch it, not without renegotiating the collective agreement. But I did have them draft up a document that has you relinquish the order. That would allow us to give you someone to work with you, to keep you from making mistakes like this again."

"I told you before, I value my independence too much."

He'd been prepared for this and had the lawyers draft up something else.

"Then I'm afraid you leave me no choice. I have to suspend you. I'm putting you on administrative leave with pay. At least until this all blows over."

Frank's mouth dropped. "You can't! You wouldn't!"

"I can and I am. I'm sorry, Malone, but until you agree to work with me on this, I can't have you out there causing havoc. Someone's going to get seriously hurt."

"Yeah, the bad guys!"

"What if that little boy's sister had been in that closet playing hide and seek? You would have blasted her from here to Timbuktu. Did you stop to think about something like that?"

"You make it sound like just because she's young she's innocent. Maybe this Boogie Man is actually a Boogie-WO-man." Frank scratched his chin in thought. "You know, that would explain why I've been having so much trouble finding this car thief. I'd never thought to watch for little kids out joyriding."

The Chief looked up to the ceiling and wiped his chin. "Just hand over your badge and gun and go home. Unless you're willing to sign the form, that is. I could set you up with a rookie and have you back on the streets again in a half hour."

He slid the form forward, but Frank turned his gaze away from it.

"Then you leave me no choice – you're on suspension."

Frank undid the buckle on his holster and lay the gun on the Chief's desk. He took out his badge and placed it next to the pistol. He stared long and hard at the two items, lost in thought. Then, shaking his head slightly, he looked back to the Chief. Were there tears in his eyes? It was hard to tell.

"You win this round, Chief. But you'll come crawling back, I know you will. You've still got a GTA man out there."

"We've got people on that, Frank."

"Sure, but one of these days you're going to be up against something serious. Maybe a giant robot, or a giant insect, or a giant robot insect and then the only person who's going to be able to help you is old Frank Malone. Oh yeah, that's right. Then you'll come calling and I'll pick up that phone and say…" Frank mimed talking on the phone. "Hang on, Chief, I'm watching my stories. Oh, what's that? You're in desperate need? A giant robot insect? Well, then, you can just damn well wait until Patrick and Laurie finish kissing. Then, when those two crazy kids are done, I'll come back to save your ass from that metal cockroach. But it'll be too late, see, there'll already be a hundred and four dead bodies from here to Broadway and you'll cry, 'Oh, Frank, I was so stupid to have sent you home on administrative leave. Because of my error countless people have been trampled to death.' But I'll count them all for you, Chief. One hundred and four. Count them, tag 'em, and leave 'em on your doorstep. Then I'll go out and shoot that giant robot insect and save the city. So, what do have to say to that?"

The Chief blinked, trying to catch up. "I say just sign the form and you can stay."

Frank stood up straight. "You won't put a leash on this junkyard dog."

Frank turned and walked out of the office. The Chief watched him go, flinched as he slammed the door and then went back to reading over the report, confident he'd done the right thing.

CHAPTER SIXTEEN: LOVE BLOOMS?

J oe checked his watch, it was past their scheduled start time, again. "I guess it's another episode of Two Gamers tonight."

Mike took a pull from his beer. "How could anyone want to miss a Bonk marathon?" he said in his put-on sarcastic voice.

"He missed the NBA JAM tournament to go camping and the look at forgotten fighting games, that HE suggested. Who the hell would ever want to play Brutal PAWS of Fury and Rise of the Robots again?"

"God," Mike said, dropping the empty hard on the coffee table, "I wish I could have missed playing those two pieces of shit in the first place."

"He's missed SMASH TV, the Godzilla games, the Mad Dog MacCree trilogy, all just to hang out with this Kristin."

Mike opened another beer, flinging the cap halfway across the room. "I guess he really likes this one." His mood had darkened considerably the past few weeks. Joe didn't want him to just shut down and stew in his feelings; he was souring the streams, losing his quippy nature. Some of the commenters had started wondering if his heart was still in it.

"Why haven't we met her? If she's so special, he should want to have her meet his friends. He's brought others. You've brought exes here and if I had a girlfriend, I'd bring her by."

"Good thing there's no danger of that."

"You think he's worried you'll blow this one, too? She could just stay off camera."

"Maybe she's a hideous b—"

Just then the door opened and in walked Dan.

"Bonk," Mike stuttered. "Great graphics on the Turbo Whatsit sixteen, am I right?"

Joe quickly switched on the camera to start the stream. The red light blinked steadily.

Dan hung up his jacket and Joe noticed he'd lost a lot of weight. He was beginning to look gaunt and sickly. His skin was tightly drawn, sallow, like he was slowly shrivelling up like a grape left in the sun for too long.

"Hey, guys, what's up?" Dan asked.

"The Bonk marathon," Joe answered. "You're just in time."

"I can't. I'm just here to get my climbing shoes. I forgot to take them to work this morning."

He passed in front of the camera on his way to his room.

"Climbing shoes?" Mike asked. "You need special shoes to climb now?"

PING.

There were already a few dozen people waiting in the forum. Joe saw the first comment was from TMNTComics-sLuvR. "Yay, Dan!"

PING.

"Dan's looking svelte," TheMack420 wrote.

"He looks sick," YourNiNight420 added.

"Oh shit, does he have wasting disease? My sister's friend

143

got it. She looked like that thing from Lifeforce," Gertrude-BeerStein wrote.

Joe typed in a response, not wanting to say it aloud. "He says it's from all of the physical activities that he and Kristin have been doing."

But Joe wasn't so sure. This weight loss was too rapid to be accounted by simply a more active lifestyle. There was something odd going on.

PING.

"I for one like his new look," ECWMikeyFan wrote.

"Guys, diet and exercise can do a lot," Cwood4Real wrote. "You should try it some time."

Dan had always been self-conscious. Maybe he just wasn't eating as much now that most of his free time was taken up with Kristin. Or maybe he'd eaten so much with Lara that going back to his regular habits had been enough.

"Who knows?" he typed into the forum.

Dan came back into the room carrying a shoe box. "Found 'em! We're going rock climbing."

"Rock climbing?" Mike said. He took a swig of a newly opened beer. "In River City? Where the hell are you going, the gravel pits?"

"We're flying up to Banff tonight. Apparently, Alberta has some great mountains."

"Who would have known?" Joe said to the camera sarcastically.

"Leave the jokes to me, Evans," Mike said. He turned to see Dan cutting the tags off his never-worn shoes. "Taking a trip already? That seems fast."

Dan shrugged. "Sometimes people just click."

Joe saw deepening lines on Dan's face as he smiled. It was

almost as if he was losing weight in front of them. "Yeah, but a trip together – that's a big step for any relationship."

"You going to open her minibar?" Mike asked jokingly.

PING.

Dan stopped in mid cut. "Kristin's not like that, guys, she's... special. Says she wants to wait until marriage."

PING.

Mike darkened. "Who the fuck does that anymore?"

PING.

"She's big into rituals, you know, like traditions and all that."

"Not knocking boots is a ritual?" Mike said, confused.

"It's so we can get to know each other as people first without all that pressure. It was the way people did things for thousands of years, after all."

"Sounds like she's hiding something," Mike said.

PING.

"Like what?"

"I dunno, a sixth toe on one foot, a vestigial tail, some kind of weird growth on her ribs."

"She's not a mutant," Dan said.

"You don't know that for sure. What kind of girl won't put out before marriage? This isn't the fifties."

"Even the fifties wasn't like the fifties," Joe said. "You don't think Gidget was fucking and sucking at the drive in?"

"There, you see?" Mike said. "Even dateless Joe thinks there's something's wrong with this girl."

"Hey, I never—"

"Joe was also just saying that he thinks you're spending more time with this girl and not enough with your best friends," Mike interrupted him.

145

"Is that what you really think, Joe?" Dan asked as he finished cutting off the dangling price tag from the pristine shoes.

"Don't put words in my mouth. This is all him."

"Mike?"

Mike tossed his hands up in surrender. "I'm not keeping score like Joe is, but I've seen the tally and we're losing out."

Dan put the unblemished climbing shoes into a small carry-on suitcase. "She did ask to meet you guys, but she's not big on being on camera."

"They do turn off, you know," Joe said.

"She's not big on being around them at all actually. Something about how she always ends up with red eye. I think she used to get teased about that growing up."

"We said we could turn them off, dude," Mike said.

"What if we all went to dinner next weekend? You guys could meet her, she could meet you. No streaming, just a regular night out."

"Dinner? She's got you calling it dinner now? Jeez, man, she's changing everything about you!" Mike shouted in his put-on fake accent. "What's wrong with supper, or night food, or second lunch? Dinner. Ooh la la."

Joe dropped his face in his hands at Mike's embarrassing outburst. He was trying way too hard to make a joke. He was either desperate to find some reason to dislike this Kristin, or desperate to appear like he was.

"I'll be there," Joe said. "Dinner sounds fine."

"Of course, Evans is up for eating," Mike said. "Big shocker there."

"I'd actually like to meet this girl."

"What about you, Mike?" Dan asked. "Do we make it a foursome?"

"I thought you said it was just dinner?"

PING.

"Dude," Joe said in exasperation.

Mike waved them off. "I'll have to check my schedule, but if it's clear, I'm sure I can make the effort to think about showing up."

"Great. Next week then."

They stared at each other in awkward silence for a moment. The audience at home was getting a real treat right now.

PING.

"Well," Dan said, holding up his luggage, "I guess I'm off."

He shut the door, and they were alone again.

"There," Joe said, "you see. There's nothing wrong or weird about her. We're all going to meet for dinner next weekend. You'll see she's normal and you can get over this pathological hatred of his girlfriends."

"I didn't hate all his girlfriends," Mike said.

PING.

Joe leaned forward and read the comment. "GOKUBOY316 calls BS on that."

"What do you know, Goku Boy?"

"He said you didn't like the fat one, the smelly one, the one who liked Pauly Shore movies, the one who said video games were an illuminati mind control plot... They had names, Goku Boy," Joe said. "But he is right. Do you see the trend here, Mike?"

"Shut up, Joe. You, too, Goku Boy. I'm just looking out for him. I don't want to see him get hooked in by some scheming heartbreaking evil succubus demon woman."

Joe rolled his eyes. "I know you've been best friends forever, but you don't have to worry about him. He can take care of himself."

PING.

Joe read the comment. "LovinSpoonfulofCereal wants to know if you're in the closet? Oh shit, there's a thought. What do you say to LovinSpoonfulofCereal, Mike?"

"I'm done here." Mike rose from the couch and headed to his room.

"Hey? Where're you going? We still have the Bonk marathon!"

"You do it," he spat back. "I'm not up for bullshit 16-bit caveman games right now."

Joe turned to face the camera alone, holding up fingers and counting down. "Three gamers, two gamers, one gamer..."

* * * *

The CD in his CD player spun. The lights were dimmed. The rumbling of the spoken word intro to The Offspring's 1994 album SMASH spoke to him softly about relaxing in an easy chair.

I'm in my bed with a beer. It'll have to do.

The calming baritone promised him that 'music soothes even the savage beast,' but as Mike put his beer on his dresser and the first few notes of *Nitro (Youth Energy)* kicked in, he didn't feel soothed. He went into his small bookshelf, looking past all the Stephen King and Michael Crichton novels to find his school yearbooks, pulling out the whole stack, junior high through high school. He flipped through pages of class photos, individual student pictures, events and clubs, looking for the images of him and Dan.

"Photographic evidence," he said softly.

Since kindergarten they'd been inseparable. From Super Nintendo, Monopoly, Magic cards, poker nights, soccer, HeroQuest, sleepovers, movie nights, PlayStation, football, N64, RISK, beer, Axis and Allies, Xbox, graduations, dances, abortive clubbing attempts, sharing an apartment, to putting on a game streaming show – they'd done it all together.

"Best friends, for life."

Joe, too. The three of them had worked hard to build something special. They weren't famous celebrities, but they'd made a name for themselves.

Old pictures, days before complications, before responsibilities, just oblivious kids unaware of what was coming.

"I'd go back in a second."

Things were changing. Dan was changing. He was trying to move on to some new phase of life. Mike didn't know what to do. There was nothing wrong with wanting a girlfriend, but Dan was turning away from the show, from him, threatening to ruin everything.

"Three Gamers needs three gamers."

They were a well-oiled machine; three distinct personalities with three distinct sets of skills that together, formed an unbeatable triangle. Mike the quippy one, the leader, the Moe. Joe was the Larry, the dreamer, the punching bag, the nerd who made it work. Dan was the Curly; the innocent, also a punching bag, but surprisingly great at tech stuff and the best natural gamer of all of them, the one who could actually beat most of the games they played. Without him, it was just Mike and Joe, Larry and Moe.

"Two gamers doesn't work."

It's not that Mike didn't understand what a girl could offer, he'd dated. But a picture of the high school football team

149

brought it clear. Team. A girlfriend was no excuse to ditch
your buddies or forget the people who tuned in to see you
every week. Sure, getting laid was great, but—

"Shit, Dan isn't even getting any."

Kristin.

"Is that even her real name?"

There was something suspicious about her. Others were
fine coming over, why not her?

"Control issues."

Taking over Dan's life, changing him into something he
wasn't.

"Camping? Hiking? Climbing? He was never an outdoorsy
kind of guy, why now all of a sudden?"

Nitro (Youth Energy) gave way to *Bad Habit* to *Gotta Get
Away* to *Genocide* to *Something to Believe In.* Mike dug out a
package of old photos, four by sixes of their early behind-the-
scenes antics. Filming sketches, pranks, short films; so many
memories, the three of them against the world.

"Not quite."

Maybe their bond wasn't as strong as he'd thought. Joe he
didn't have to worry about, he was the Larry. But Dan. Curly
was the wildcard.

"Curly was the first to go, after all."

He had to figure out what power Kristin held over the man.

"It's clearly not sex."

Was she so hot he couldn't think straight? Did she exude
some pheromone? Maybe she'd cast a Voodoo spell on him.

"Or maybe you've seen too many movies."

But then maybe not. Whatever the sway was, he had to
counter it. Or barring that, win her over to the idea of letting
him have more time for streaming. Or hell, try the long shot

third option of convincing her to join in on their adventures. Did she have what it took to make their triangle a square? Could she be the Shemp?

"It's on Kristin," he said, sliding the photos back in the sleeve.

He didn't come to a fight to place second. He wasn't going to lose his best friend, not to a girl, not to anyone.

CHAPTER SEVENTEEN:
PREPARATIONS

S itting in darkness, senses closed off from the outside world, it waited. True communion would soon come, but now, patience. It didn't know how it knew that this one would provide the key, it only had a blurred understanding of events that had led to this point.

Wait.

Quiet, calm before the storm. Visualizing the transformation. New life emerging from a chrysalis into a world unprepared.

The fools that had awoken it had no conception of what it was that they were unleashing. That kind of innocence and naivete was merely an amuse bouche. It awaited true purity, not bumbling incompetence.

There was a sweetness, a unique taste and smell upon those that it craved. Crippling need burning inside, crying out for sustenance.

Wait.

Quiet the urges. Darkness and silence. The civilized world was stimulus overload. Solitude, communion with the stygian realms of the natural order. Allow events to take their course. Below the ground, cut off from the distractions of moving engines, steel, and concrete. Breathe. Think.

Wait.

"Lord, is there anything we can do for you?"

"We await only your—"

"Silence." It invoked fear in the thralls. They'd been destroyed once, but were allowed to serve. Whims change.

Cowering at the doorway, faint traces of light from above highlighted their shapes. The smell of pure terror.

"Why do you interrupt my solitude?"

"Forgive us lord, we only seek to—"

"Leave."

"What should we—"

"Nothing."

They turned to go but a mental signal forced them to stop. They couldn't have resisted even if they tried.

"Perhaps you can do something."

"Please, lord, tell us."

"Prepare. As you would have. Make ready the ritual. The pieces will be in place."

"Absolutely, master," they said as one and retreated.

Their steps faded away. The door above shut.

Wait.

Back in silence. Back in darkness.

Soon.

CHAPTER EIGHTEEN: DESPONDENCY

Every crack of the sidewalk pavement was as familiar as a line on the back of his hand. Every dark alley that most people wouldn't dare walk down at night was like a plucked grey hair from his ear. Every building, parking meter, hotdog stand; they were as much a part of who he was as his moustache. And yet, walking them as a civilian wasn't the same.

The sky was grey above him, but his heart was black.

"I just can't do it," Frank mumbled as he watched the thick sausage roasting on the grill. "I just can't be one of them."

"What's that, Frankie?" the man at the hotdog cart said. "A dog?"

"A dog, a cat, a hamster. Anything that isn't a cop."

"I've heard of police dogs, but hamsters?" the man in the apron said. "Do they really have those?"

"They could by now. I've been off the force for…" Frank checked his watch. "Eighteen hours."

"Finally retired, eh?" The man slid the cooked wiener into a bun and passed it over to Frank in a paper sleeve. "Must be nice to not have a nine to five anymore."

"Nice? Shit, no, it's hell."

154

"Ahh, you'll get used to it," the man said. He was stocky, with a day's worth of stubble and curly hair that poked out from under his white cap emblazoned with the name of the cart on it. "Donnie's Dogs."

"I don't know if I want to just yet," Frank said, piling onions on his hot dog.

"My old man, he worked at the furniture factory for thirty-five years. Never missed a day of work being sick. Finally leaves when his boss tells him he's too slow for the line. They gave him a watch and some cake. Even played some Sinatra for him at a party."

"That sounds alright. The Sinatra at least."

"Pops didn't know what to do with himself without working anymore."

"I can understand that feeling."

"Sure, sure. But see, after a few days of moping, he took up pickle balling."

Frank stopped in mid-scoop, his spoon inches deep in pickle slices. "Not with these in here, right? That's not sanitary, Donnie."

"No, down at the seniors' centre on Colony Street. Real popular, you know?"

"What people do with fermented vegetables isn't my concern. It doesn't sound like something that would take my mind off being on suspension."

"Suspension?" Donnie said, putting another line of dogs on the grill. "So you didn't finally retire, Frankie?"

Frank took a bite out of his dog piled six inches high with mustard, onions, pickles, and sauerkraut. A huge glob fell out on his shirt, leaving a yellow streak on the faded white fabric. "They'll have to drag me kicking and screaming out of that place, Donnie," he said with a full mouth, dropping more on his shirt. "This is just a temporary thing. Chief'll realize his mistake."

"Then you got nothing to worry about. Not like Pops did. He got cancer six months into his retirement. Died four months later."

Frank grabbed a napkin from the metal dispenser and tried wiping his shirt. The mustard just smeared in deeper. "Maybe he caught it from the pickles."

"Nah, smoking. Two packs a day for thirty years will do that to you."

"Not much point to the story then, is there, Donnie?" Frank said, tossing his trash into a bin nearby.

"Point is, enjoy the time while you have it. Could be gone tomorrow, you know?"

"The whole fucking city could be gone tomorrow without me."

Donnie laughed and waved Frank off. "Just go for a walk. Enjoy the sunshine. Watch some TV. Sleep in. Treat this as a vacation. You'll be back right as rain before you know it."

So Frank took a walk. Around the block, through the park, uptown, downtown. He stopped at every hotdog stand he found and heard the same thing from all of them. Enjoy your time off.

"Fuck that," he said to himself as he tried to wipe the fourth mustard stain off his shirt. "How can I enjoy myself when—"

His words died in his throat when a red car drove past him down Young Street towards a red light. The license plate was a blur, but that only meant the car was going even faster than he thought.

"Hold the phone, I know you."

Frank reached for his gun before remembering it was gone. "Stop," he shouted. "Po... police on suspension!"

He threw the napkin and ran after the stopped car, waving the last of his hot dog. The man inside had no idea what was coming. Twenty meters away, then ten. So close.

"Stop. Don't make me use this," he shouted, gesturing with his sausage.

The light changed green. His hand nearly closed on the bumper. The car peeled out. Frank fell forward. His hot dog went flying into the mud. He landed hard in a puddle, the wind knocked out of him. His shirt was soaked. He lay there in the dirty street, watching the pigeons attack what was left of his food, seeing the red car speeding away again to get lost in the city that used to be his.

"You okay, pops?" someone from the sidewalk asked.

Frank stood up, brushing himself off. The food was gone, he was covered in mud, grease, and mustard. He sighed as he fingered an inch-wide tear in his shirt.

"I'm fine, but this was my last shirt."

"So buy another one," the man said.

"What's the point?" Frank turned and headed for home.

CHAPTER NINETEEN: KRISTIN

Mike and Joe waited next to a huge fern in the lobby of The Elegant Knife, an upscale steak restaurant with classy decor and mood lighting in a reconditioned old warehouse in the waterfront district. The reservation was for seven o'clock, so Dan and Kristin were due to arrive at any moment. Mike had dressed up, while Joe wore jeans and a button-up shirt.

"Why the hell did you wear a suit for this? We're not at the Ritz."

"Sometimes a man likes to look his best," Mike said, straightening his tie.

"You want this girl to like you? That doesn't sound like—"

"Why do you care what I wear?"

"I didn't even know you owned a—"

"Every man should own a suit, Joe."

"You're trying to impress her. You're afraid he's serious about this one."

"Shut up, they're here."

Through the glass doors, they watched them walking holding hands. Dan held the door open for Kristin. She looked over the surroundings of the dark wood lobby like she was scoping out the joint for a possible purchase later, feeling the re-stained wood with a curt smile. She wore a navy sweater and ankle-length grey skirt. She carried a hemp purse with a colourful floral pattern etched on the side. She was blonde, with short pushed-back hair, a hooked nose, and a protruding Adam's apple. Her mouth was crooked, her eyes shining with intelligence.

She read over the note beneath an oil painting of a riverfront scene. Her posture made Joe think of Ichabod Crane in the old Disney *Sleepy Hollow* cartoon. She was long-limbed, gangly, straight-backed, slightly awkward in her movements, as if she was still getting the full hang of the whole walking upright thing. He wondered what her figure was like. It was impossible to tell in the baggy clothes she wore. He also wondered why he cared.

"Dan." Mike waved to catch his attention as if he couldn't spot them standing only a few feet away in the lobby.

He didn't call him Stoddard, dude, numb nuts, jerk store, man, or any of the other million things he used instead of a given name.

He's on his best behaviour.

"Hey, guys," Dan said as he retook Kristin's hand. "Waiting long?"

"Nope. Our table is just getting set up."

Kristin finally turned to take them in. She barely moved, but Joe saw her darting eyes judging them. He felt weirdly belittled, as if she didn't think they warranted the moving of any other muscle of her face. Again, he wondered why he cared.

"Hi, uh, Kristin, I presume," Joe said, holding his hand out to shake hers.

She nudged Dan in the side. He jerked to attention.

159

"Right, guys, this is Kristin, and Kristin, this is Joe and Mike."

She shook Joe's hand. Her touch was cold and clammy, like the skin of a garter snake. Could she be as nervous as they were?

"Nice to meet you," she said calmly.

"You, too," Mike said as he shook her hand.

"You guys are the roommates I've heard so much about?"

"Yup. And you're the Kristin we've heard so much about. Unless Dan's secretly dating two girls named Kristin. You're not, are you? Because that would make this pretty awkward." Mike's attempt at humour was met with a stony expression. She'd reacted as much as a gargoyle statue would have.

"No, this is her," Dan said. "The her."

"And you guys all host some kind of internet video game show?"

"That's right," Joe said, "it's called Three Ga—"

"It's not just video games," Mike interrupted. "We review movies, make films, discuss important news of the day."

"What he means is," Joe added as Mike went on, "is that it's a growing business. Yeah, we hang out and play games, but we have a following, returning viewers, paid subscribers, memes…" He found himself acting as defensive as Mike was about the whole thing. Why?

"Really?" she said flatly.

"It sounds more impressive than it is," Dan said.

"We're not some V-Logger prank people, let's players, unboxers or other a—" Mike stopped himself from swearing. Maybe for the first time in his life.

"I'm not sure I get it, but that's his thing, not mine," she said.

"You should come by the apartment sometime for a recording. See what old Dan here does for fun. At least when he's not out with you," Mike said.

Kristin seemed unenthused. "I don't know, I'm not into the idea of broadcasting my life to strangers."

"You could always just watch," Joe offered.

"Fridays and Saturdays are our biggest nights," Mike said. "That's when—"

"Oh, Dante and I are usually out Friday and Saturday nights."

"He could come, too," Mike said.

"She means Dan." Joe nudged him.

"But she said Dante?"

"Kristin likes Dante," Dan said.

She linked her arm through his. "It sounds more sophisticated. Less like someone living in his parents' basement." She ruffled his hair like he was six.

Joe caught Mike's glance of WTF but before he could say anything stupid, the maître d' appeared. "Mike, party of four, your table is ready."

They were led to a quaint table in the corner below another oil painting. This one was of a biblical scene that Joe didn't recognize. People were dragged in chains past a huge iron gate as soldiers in strange armour prodded them with spears. Lit candles cast a wavering red glow on the odd scene. As he took his seat he read the caption. *Through the Gates of Hell.*

Fancy folded napkins made small towers on crisp white plates, but he couldn't take his eyes off the painted image, seeing so much detail everywhere. The thing looked like it belonged in a museum. Or a church. He realized that he and Mike were the only ones sitting down. Kristin had frozen in place, lingering on the painting.

161

"Not this one," she said. "A table near a window."

"Of course, madame, I'll move you right away," the man said.

They were given a spot next to a window looking out onto the waterfront. People were paddling canoes, a water taxi motored by, tourists took snapshots with their phones, trees blew gently in the breeze. Joe had to admit the view was much nicer than in the back of the room.

"Much better," Kristin said, waiting for Dan to pull her chair out for her. Like an obedient lapdog, he sprang into action.

Mike was about to say something, but Joe elbowed him in the ribs, and he bit his tongue. He picked up the crimson leather-bound menu and pretended to be more interested in it than in what Dan was doing for his date.

Joe grabbed his. Calligraphy, high prices; the place served a bit of everything despite being known for steak. Fine cuts of beef, fish, chicken, and pork.

"Looks nice," Mike said, reading over the menu. "Hope there's no vegetarians here. Wait." He looked up at Kristin. "You're not, are you?"

"Good evening, I'm Rodrick, and I'll be your waiter. Can I start anyone off with drinks?" A trim and bearded man with manicured eyebrows in a black vest appeared out of nowhere, flashing too-white teeth and too-tanned skin.

"Red wine for me and he'll have water," Kristin said.

The waiter stood with his hands behind his back. His dark vest was immaculately clean. He turned to Joe and Mike.

"Beer," Mike said. "Domestic."

"Uh, yeah. Two," Joe said.

"I think we can order right now, too," Kristin said.

"Absolutely."

"I'm going to have steak, blood rare, and he'll have the brisket."

Mike raised an eyebrow as he frantically looked over his menu.

"Oh, can I have a Coke, too?" Dan said. "I don't think I want just water."

"Certainly," the waiter said.

Kristin shook her head. "Dante, you shouldn't."

He looked in her eyes and something in that brief glance must have changed his mind. He turned back to the waiter. "You know what, cancel that. I'm fine with water."

"Not a problem. And you, sirs?"

"Steak. Also blood rare," Mike said.

"Uh, I guess the chicken?" Joe said. "But not blood rare, please."

* * * *

"She had me call all the location managers in the city, then the wildlife commission, then someone from natural resources, only to find out that, and this is interesting, untouched prairie grass as found in the 1800s is almost extinct. The guy from natural resources told me that we've pretty much fu— err, ruined what was here through years of farming and development."

A thin line of blood dripped down the side of Kristin's mouth as she chewed. She ran her finger alongside her chin and wiped it off, licking it clean in one quick motion. "I did my degree in environmental sciences. I wrote a paper on that very topic. It's a shame what happened to the land here."

"Yeah," Mike agreed, "like that whole acid rain and hole in the ozone layer stuff. Oh, and nuclear power."

"Kristin set us up doing volunteer work for the Save the Elms committee," Dan said.

"So, you're going to go and chain yourself to the redwoods or something?" Mike asked.

"They don't have those here," Kristin said curtly.

"Crap, then you're too late..." Mike said.

Kristin spooned up the remaining blood on her plate and quietly slurped it back. When it was all gone, she slid Dan's plate over and did the same with his.

Joe caught Mike watching in stone-faced silence.

The smiling waiter returned, seeing four empty plates. "And how was everything?"

"Excellent!"

"Great!"

"I thought the steak was a tad undercooked and the seasoning on the potatoes a little heavy, but other than that I'd say a deserved three-star review," Kristin said.

The waiter was unfazed. "Dessert?"

"Too much sugar," Kristin said. "Unless you two wanted something?"

"Oh no, we hate sugar," Mike said. "It's much too..."

"Sweet?" Joe offered.

"Is this four separate bills?" the waiter asked.

"He'll be paying for the two of us," Kristin said, motioning to her and Dan, "but they're... you're not together, are you?"

"Me and him?" Mike said in horror. He noticed Kristin's eyebrow raise. "Not that there's anything wrong with that, but no. Three Gamers are not, you know, three gamers in the biblical sense of the word."

The waiter dropped the bills down. Dan gathered up his and Kristin's and paid in cash. Mike and Joe carded theirs. They all rose and walked through the restaurant back toward the lobby. Joe watched Kristin's gaze turn back to the painting again. The booth was empty. The candles had nearly burnt out. She stopped. Her eyes seemed to catch the red light, glowing with an odd internal fire. Dan took her hand.

"Just a second," she said and stood motionless in place, locked on the odd biblical scene. Dan and Mike chatted quietly, not paying attention.

"She likes red meat," Mike said. "That's a good sign, I guess."

Their words fell out of focus as Joe watched her. She was rigid. What was it about that picture that was so fascinating? Joe tried to understand the draw. The oil images stylistically looked as if they'd been painted hundreds of years ago but the detail was incredible, almost as if the people were moving.

Then he realized they were.

The soldiers stabbed out with their spears, piercing the skin of a ragged prisoner. Blood poured from a wound in his abdomen. His mouth cried out in a silent scream beneath a flame-filled sky. The line slowly dragged their heavy chains along the rocky ground. He could almost hear the screams, the sounds of torture. Something flew by above the men. A bat? He'd barely seen it in his peripheral vision.

The lights in the restaurant dimmed. The candles flared upward, the fires burning impossibly huge for such small bits of wax. Kristin swayed in place. The landscape of the picture expanded outwards. The table seemed to shrink inside, then the floor, gradually the image creeping towards her. She was going to be absorbed. Joe wanted to scream but his throat seized up.

Shadows. Stretching out from her. Inhuman shapes on the floor and walls. She turned her head. Her eyes glowed red. Mouth twisted into a grin. Fangs. The room evaporated. The fires of hell surrounded them, yet Mike and Dan continued talking obliviously.

Rocks, boiling lakes, crucified bodies, spears dripping blood, whips across skin, the cries of tormented victims, the overpowering smell of—

"We should all go and play pool," Kristin said.

In a flash it was all gone. Joe stood gazing at a completely normal painting in a mundane, if overpriced restaurant.

"Joe?" Dan said. The others stared at him strangely.

"Zoned out there for a minute, I guess." He shook his head.

"There's a great place in the next building over," Kristin said, taking Dan's hand. "Split a table three ways?"

CHAPTER TWENTY: COMPETITION BRINGS OUT THE WORST IN PEOPLE

"I knew this was coming," Joe said. "I've seen it all before."

"Would you stop?" Mike said. He looked up from his shot to see Joe leaning on the pool cue upside down. Dan and Kristin sat on chairs watching, holding hands.

Sharkey's Pool House was a happening place; dozens of pool tables spread out across the massive third floor of a former textile factory. On one end was a bar constructed of refinished old wood covered in the labels of beers from around the world. A team of serving girls in short plaid skirts roamed the room with trays piled high with beer and Sharkey's famous kettle chips.

They'd taken a table at the edge of the space, gathered around the dimly lit green rectangular surface.

"How long do you plan on lining up that shot for?" Dan asked.

"As long as it takes," Mike said. "It's how the pros play."

"Just because you grew up with a pool table in your parents' basement doesn't make you a pool shark," Joe said.

"At least I'm not terrible at it like you, Evans," Mike spat.

"You're a regular River City Fats."

"Would you just let me break already?"

"I'm just saying we haven't even started and you're already taking ten-minute contemplations of your shots. They charge by the hour, you know."

"There's a science to a good break, okay?"

"We could always make this more interesting," Kristin said.

Mike leaned up to see her smirking with a cockiness he found off-putting.

"Oh yeah? What are you talking about, quarters?"

"Let's start with loonies and see how it goes."

Dan just sat there passively. Joe ground his cue into the floor like an idiot. This would obviously be between the two of them. But why was she challenging him? Was this some kind of competition for Dan? Would beating her push her away? If she won, would she be more willing to hang out with them? Let Dan out every now and again? What was the hidden meaning here?

"Too rich for your blood?" she said mockingly.

Was she just super competitive? The obvious course of action was to kick her butt and assert his dominance.

"You're on," he said.

"I'll break," Kristin said. "Otherwise, we'll be here all night."

She leapt up, chalked her cue and bent down, eyes laser locked on the board. With a smooth, practiced motion she struck, knocking more than one ball into the hole.

Joe whispered into Mike's ear, "She looks good."

Mike grimaced.

Loonies became twoonies, then fives. She was some kind of shark, and he was stuck with a complete guppie for a partner.

Joe walked up, leaned over, took a half second glance, then

just blasted away as hard as he could at the first ball he saw. His shot careened wildly around the table, accomplishing nothing.

"What are you doing?" Mike shouted. "You're setting her up and leaving me with nothing!"

"Isn't that the strategy?" Joe said.

"You're supposed to be trying!"

The pile of money on the table was enough for one hell of a night out and it was all going to her if he didn't pull out a miracle soon.

Dan flubbed his shot.

"That's okay, Dante, I got this," Kristin said.

Mike ground his teeth as he looked over the table. Then he saw the path to salvage this whole night.

"Six ball, corner pocket." He leaned over and with a quick smack, his ball was sunk. "Seven ball, side pocket." Another crack, another score.

He was on fire, but Kristin was ahead on points, and he was playing catch up. It might be teams, but Dan and Joe were hopeless. The real competition was him and Kristin. Man versus woman for the championship of this one little table at Sharkey's.

Mike sank his next two shots, cleaning the table and winning the game. That put him neck and neck.

"Okay, tied," he said. "Now how about we make this one really interesting?"

Joe fingered through the cash on the table. "There's, like, seventy-five dollars here."

"What are your stakes?" Kristin asked.

"Loser pays the tab."

"This would pay it," Joe said, pointing to the pile of

accumulated cash.

"You're on," Kristin said.

He grinned. He'd finally clicked on. This was going to cost her.

"My break," he said.

One, two, three balls sunk. It looked like he had it wrapped up, but then, something went wrong, the crack didn't angle right, and he left her an opening.

"Oh hey, they have a Daytona USA cabinet here," Joe said. "Is it too late to pull out?"

"We've been playing pool for fifteen years and you suck just as bad now as you did in my parents' basement. Even a monkey could learn this game."

"Yeah, but I choose not to."

Kristin turned to Dan. "You could use more practice, too."

"I'm good just watching," Dan said and replaced his cue on the rack.

"Awesome," Joe said. "Day-tona!"

He wandered away to the sit-down cabinet at the far end of the hall. He'd be a while. It was down to the two of them.

"Okay," Mike said. "The dead weight is gone. May the best player win."

She smirked.

Dan sat in silence, as if in a trance.

Kristin leaned down to line up her shot. She looked up at him. "You can't win, you know."

"We'll see," he said. "I've got a few tricks up my sleeve."

"So do I."

The noises in the room drifted away as she looked at him. The people slowed to a crawl, moving as if in molasses. The ceiling fans froze in mid air. His breath began to fog in front of his face. A chill ran over his arms. But at the same time, he was sweating. A wave of warmth radiated outwards from where Kristin leaned over. Behind her, Dan had frozen in place.

The eyes.

There was something wrong with the colour of her eyes. Shifting from blue to green to brown, then to a deep shade of... red? No, it must be a trick of the light. The world was on pause. The two of them were the only ones moving in real time. He saw a waitress bent over flirting with a table of drunks, the hem of her skirt in mid sway. A shot at the table next to them was locked in the air, faces captured mid laugh, words silently muted, a room of statues in still life.

What was going on?

Kristin sank a shot and looked up at him.

"You shouldn't be afraid."

"What?"

Was he frozen, too? Had he spoken? The words seemed to evaporate on his tongue.

She sank another shot.

"People grow up, their priorities change, you just have to face that."

She moved around the table, lining up another shot, brushing past him.

"You've got a routine, and it scares you that it's changing. It should."

She looked up at him. Her skin was bathed in the yellow light of the overhang. But the eyes, he was positive now, glowing, flaring red like pulsing headlights. It wasn't just a trick of the light.

"I have big plans for him."

She sank another shot, then walked over to the stool where Dan sat in blissful ignorance, unmoving, not even blinking. She slung her arm over his shoulder and looked towards Mike. She leaned down and planted a kiss on Dan's cheek.

"We're going to be very happy."

Mike gasped. The light from the lamp above the table cast strange shadows from the forms of Dan and Kristin. Impossibly bright, a dark form stretched behind them, out across the floor. The shape... two points on the head, a long dangling pointed... tail?

Is anyone else seeing this?

Nobody moved. He could see Joe in the distance, hands locked in mid turn on the steering wheel of Daytona USA. A glass fell from the hands of a drunk, beer in mid air, tiny golden pockets hovering.

The shadow. It moved, danced behind them. The tail curled like a snake. Growing, shrinking, breathing with life. It wasn't a human shadow; it was as alive as anything in the room, but not locked in time.

"He's a great guy, you know. If you only paid more attention."

She kissed Dan again and the colour seemed to drain from his face. Pale skin, as if he was sick. He didn't react to the touch. Was he hypnotized? Was the whole place?

Sharkey's Pool Hall had been put on pause. Mike could see every tendril of smoke in the room, every ball frozen in mid shot, each football player on the television trapped as statues.

What's happening?

Kristin walked back to the table and lined up another shot. Her crooked teeth gleamed.

"Maybe you'll realize what you've lost."

She wasn't human. How could she do this? None of Dan's other dates had the power to freeze time. But she wasn't just dating Dan; she was changing his name, converting him into some kind of neo-hippie wannabe hipster, pulling him away from the show and his friends. What was she after?

Trapped outside of time, unable to breathe, sweating, mute, watching a shadow form with horns and a tail mimic her? Was he losing his mind? Was he having a seizure?

She lined up her next shot, never taking her eyes off him.

"One." She sank a ball.

"Two." Sank another.

"Three." And pocketed the final one. "That's the game. You just didn't stand a chance."

She put a hand on Dan's shoulder and stared at Mike with red eyes flashing like strobes. His brain throbbed with a pounding migraine. He shut his eyes to stop the horrible assault. He wanted to scream but nothing came out. His lungs had stopped working. A rising panic bombarded him.

"So, who won?" came Joe's voice and he was jerked back to reality with a sudden, desperate intake of breath.

Time flowed at normal speed; the crowd in the bar moved, shots were sunk, ceiling fans spun, football players ran, the waitress giggled and handed out beers, a crash as a glass fell and splashed its contents all over the floor. Everything was as if it had never happened.

Dan was chatting to Kristin with no sign that he'd ever been in a trance at all. Her eyes were no longer red. Had he just imagined everything?

"Dude," Joe asked again. "Who won?"

"She did," Mike said.

"How much did you lose?"

"Besides the pot, the tab and my dignity, I'm not sure..."

Mike watched Kristin as she rubbed her hand over Dan's shoulder protectively. He eyed her for any sign of what he'd just seen. The eyes, the shadow on the wall, anything, but all he saw was a gangly blonde girl who was winning the heart of his best friend.

CHAPTER TWENTY-ONE:
DEMONOLOGY

"I'm telling you time froze."

"You can't be serious," Joe said.

"Everyone was a statue and I know it sounds crazy, but it's true. You were in mid turn on Daytona, a waitress was bent over, someone dropped a glass and it just hung there, in the air."

"It doesn't just sound crazy, Mike, it sounds insane."

"Her eyes were glowing fucking red, man. Like traffic lights. Her shadow had horns and a tail. It moved like it was alive."

"None of that is possible," Joe said. "It's all completely... insane!"

"Just stop and consider what I'm saying." Mike paced the room, hands gesturing wildly. Joe could only watch, worried that his friend was finally losing his mind.

"I did consider it. Time stopping? Glowing eyes? Living shadows? Just what the hell are you insinuating here?"

"Shouldn't that be obvious? She's a demon!"

"Those don't exist, Mike. This is River City, Manitoba, not... uh, hell."

"Look at the evidence logically."

"Evidence? Logically? You said time froze. I don't

remember—"

"Because you weren't in the free bubble."

"The bubble that only you and her were in."

"Exactly."

"I don't even know what to say to that."

"Let's move on from the time freeze bubble then."

"Please, let's."

"Consider her influence over his life. Trips, taking up new hobbies, changing his wardrobe. She ordered for him. She even changed his name!"

"Dan's just one of those guys that goes all out. We've seen that before. Many times. Shit, remember when he was researching Korean boy bands?"

Mike scratched his chin. "Shit, maybe her influence stretched back before he even met her. What sinister purpose would she have for—"

"Okay, you've lost it."

Mike spun in place. "Fine, let's presume she didn't do that, it doesn't seem to fit the MO."

With the way Mike was carrying on, Joe didn't want to mention what he'd seen with Kristin and the odd painting at the restaurant. It would only encourage him. He still wasn't even sure it had happened in the first place. It could have been an undigested bit of beef...

"What I do know is this," Mike said, pacing again. "She's got her hooks in deep. Deeper than any of the others."

"You ever stopped to consider that he just likes her more than the others?"

"No."

"Then—"

"Dante? What the fuck is that? And what is he getting out

of it all? She's not putting out, she's not rich, she doesn't have Hollywood connections that I know of. What the hell can she offer that you or I couldn't?"

Joe shook his head "I can't conceive…"

"Me either!"

Mike was getting agitated. He needed to calm him down.

"Maybe he really likes spending time with her," Joe offered. "Getting away from the cameras and—"

"Or maybe it's mind control." Mike spun, wagging his finger at him. "Hypnosis, subliminal suggestion. If she can stop time, it's not a far leap to think she can manipulate minds."

"Yes, it is!"

"The way he just sat there like a zombie while she was kicking our asses at pool. It was like some kind of trance."

"He could have fallen asleep. We'd just had a big meal of red meat. It was getting late."

"Holy shit, that's it."

"Finally, you're listening to reason."

"No. The bloody meat. She was sucking that juice back like it was chocolate milk."

"I think the French call it au jus."

"Do demons like raw meat? That's something we need to look into."

"Dude, plenty of people like their steaks rare. You ordered—"

"How many of them have glowing red eyes? You saw her pictures on the dating profile."

"Camera flashes."

"There were no cameras at Sharkey's."

Finally, Joe realized he had to face the reality that Mike

wasn't going to let this go. He knew that admitting what he'd seen was only going to encourage him, but what were the odds of each of them hallucinating from bad beef? Especially since he had the chicken.

"Look," he said haltingly. "I know you're going to take this the wrong way, but I might have seen something, too."

"How? You were frozen stiff."

"Before. In the restaurant. She was looking at a painting on the wall. It sort of grew. Nobody else noticed. I thought it had to be a trick of the light, but I could have sworn her eyes were glowing red. The thing came alive and... then it was gone. I wasn't going to tell you, but then you started going on about—"

"So you believe me."

"I'm not saying that. I'm just saying maybe there's something here we're overlooking."

Mike stomped to the refrigerator and took out a beer. He popped the cap on the edge of the counter and took a sip. "Now you need to hear about how I saw her drain the life energy out of him with a kiss."

"I knew I should have kept my mouth shut. That's even more insane than the time stopping thing." He rose to leave.

"No, it's true. One kiss and he went pale, like a member of the Edgar Winter Group. Haven't you noticed that he's lost a lot of weight lately?"

Joe was partway towards his room when he stopped. It was true. He had noticed that Dan was looking thinner, paler, but—

"People lose weight all the time. He's in IT. He spends most of his day indoors. None of that's proof of her being an energy vampire."

"Oh shit, like in Lifeforce. You think that's what she is?"

"No!"

"Right, off track here. Those things couldn't talk, and she ordered for him," he said, counting on his fingers. "Told him what to eat, what to drink, what to think. All verbally. Mind control."

"Dan's always been malleable, you're reading too much into this. He could just be in love. Eager to please."

Mike took another sip. "In love? No way. I mean, she's... I don't know, nothing special. Big nose, gangly, no real figure... he could do better. We get offers from weirdo chicks all the time in our forums. Some even send pics. Some much hotter than Kristin."

"Let me get this straight, Mike," Joe said. "You're saying that because you don't think Dan's girlfriend is good looking, then she must be a demon? Did you ever hear the expression beauty is in the eye of the beholder?"

"What's that shitty old video game got to do with this? Wait, are you implying that Kristin looks like the beholder from Eye of the Beholder? That's what she really is? Those eight-eyed monsters that take over your brain? That I hadn't thought of. Not a demon, a beholder. Using an illusion spell. Fuck, if you're right, he's really in for it. We never could beat that fucking game."

"Are you even listening to yourself anymore? I sure as hell don't know why I am," Joe said. "Now you're suggesting that Dan's girlfriend could actually be a beholder from a Dungeons and Dragons video game. I don't know if that's worse than you trying to prove she's a demon."

"Maybe she's both," Mike said, awestruck. "That's an angle neither one of us thought of."

Before Joe could say another word, the door opened, and Dan walked in.

"Hey, guys," he said.

"Oh hey, we were just talking about you," Joe said.

"Nothing bad, I hope."

Joe saw what Mike meant now. Dan was looking thinner than ever. He wore a workout shirt like he'd just come from the gym that hung off him like a tent. His skin was so pale it was almost translucent. His elbows and knees protruded awkwardly. His veins were visible in dark blue lines. Was he sick and not telling them? But apart from that, his hair was combed to the opposite side, and he wore coloured contacts that made his eyes a rich, bright blue.

Mike opened his mouth as if he was going to say something, but Joe shook his head. He stayed quiet.

"Of course not," Joe said. "We were just thinking about playing—"

"Eye of the Beholder on Super NES. Maybe we can finally finish the damn thing."

"That's a fun game. And an excuse to use the Mario Paint mouse. But if it's this weekend, I can't. I'm going to Folkfest."

"Since when are you into folk music?" Mike asked.

"Kristin says I should broaden my musical understanding away from just Weird Al and heavy metal to more international music."

"Weird Al is international music. He's from America. And what the fuck is wrong with Weird Al?" Mike spat.

"Kristin says he's childish and immature."

"What the fuck is childish and immature about the guy who wrote Fat? Got more chins than Chinatown? That's high concept stuff!"

"She told me about the workshops at Folkfest, how they bring in bands from Africa and South America. There's this great group from Paraguay that she says is really brilliant."

He slipped past Joe into his room and in a flash was back, dressed like a hippie: cargo pants, multi-coloured shirt, bean hat, hemp necklaces. A brand-new tent still in its package slung under one arm and a huge backpack with pots and pans dangling from the outside slung over the other. He pulled on his hiking shoes. "Oh yeah, I almost forgot to tell you guys, but I bought a condo!"

"What?" Joe asked as Mike simply froze in shock.

"Yeah, I'm moving out at the end of the month. One bedroom, parking space, en-suite laundry, the works." He tied the laces of his shoes. "Kristin thought it would be good for me." He rose and opened the door. "See ya Monday!"

And with that he was gone. Mike turned to Joe with a look of horror on his face.

"It's even worse than I imagined."

"You may be—"

Suddenly the door opened, and Dan ran back in. He went straight to his room and came back out carrying a bright yellow bag. "I almost forgot my scrapbooking supplies."

Then he was gone once more. Mike took a long sip of beer, working over something in his head. After a long while he sighed deeply. "You see? She's won. Scrapbooking, Folkfest, camping… he hasn't touched a controller in weeks. This isn't the Dan we knew. Not anymore."

"You know what, I'm starting to believe you," Joe said, hardly able to comprehend the words coming out of his own mouth. "Only a fucking monster wouldn't like Weird Al."

"She's got him moving out. Not only is our rent going to go

up," Mike said, pointing to the television shelving unit, "but that's his N64! Two of those PlayStation controllers, a few dozen of those DVDs, Blu-rays, the working Super NES, all his."

"Oh fuck, I didn't think of that. What are we going to do? Buy another N64?"

"Hell no. I'm not giving up that easily. Besides, I'm not paying eBay prices."

"Then what? Trawl the pawn shops?"

"No, we're going to save him. But first we have to figure out exactly what we're dealing with. Demon, energy vampire, beholder…"

Mike sat on the couch and pulled out the laptop from under the table. He opened the feed to their channel. "We start with a poll of our viewers, see if anyone's dealt with this before."

He typed out a question: "ANYONE HERE EVER DEALT WITH A GIRL STEALING THEIR FRIEND BEFORE? PERHAPS THROUGH MIND CONTROL?"

"Why'd you type it in all caps?" Joe asked.

"It's more pressing if you do that."

"So, what? We just wait to see what our fans say?"

"That could take minutes," Mike said, shaking his head. "No, now we go to Google and do a search. I'm thinking roommate controlled by new girlfriend, to start."

He clicked over to the browser and typed it in. They were met with a listing of pages, mostly dealing with relationship advice, college questions, reddit threads, but one stood out. Mike pointed to "DEMONS: SUCCUBUS."

"That one."

"A succubus, really?" Joe said. "Wasn't that a fucking South Park episode?"

"Exactly. Don't you see?"

"No, I don't."

"You've heard the expression write what you know. The South Park guys must have seen this before."

Mike clicked the link. The page opened up to an all-black site with blinking red and yellow letters with pentagrams everywhere, like something out of a bad Geocities fan page.

"God, this hurts my brain," Joe said.

"Look here. It says: a female demon is called a succubus. The succubus draw energy from men to sustain themselves, often until the victim becomes exhausted or dies. So the succubus IS an energy vampire!"

"Remember the succubus in Darkstalkers the arcade game?" Joe asked.

"If Kristin looked like that, I'd probably let all this slide. But there's more here. It says the succubus will devour the soul of a man completely after the act of intercourse."

"Dan said they hadn't slept together, so how does that mean anything?"

"Don't you see, that's the proof. She's getting him to buy a condo, step one. Step two, they'll announce an engagement. The whole time he'll be getting weaker and weaker. Step three, she'll get him to write a will, take out life insurance, then POW, step four, marriage. Step five is sex city. Step six, she kills him, and step seven, walks away with the insurance settlement, the condo, the N64, the working Super NES, two PlayStation controllers, and some sweet DVDs and Blu-rays."

"Shit..."

"Everyone will feel so sorry for her, too. A widow so young. Think of the Facebook posts. Then she'll be free and clear to do it all over again. In fact, how do we know she hasn't already done this before?"

"Look," Joe said, "I think you're placing entirely too much stock in this one insane website we found. Let's at least see what some other people say before we go jumping to any conclusions."

Mike scrolled back to the Google search page. He clicked on another site, this one purporting to be about witches, demons, and demonology. He scrolled through the text until he stopped at the listing for succubus.

"This place says the succubus will use her powers of suggestion to control the man and will him to do her bidding. Folkfest? Scrapbooking? That sell it enough for you?"

Joe read over the text again. "I'm not ready to accept it just yet. Look again."

Mike scrolled back and went to a third website, this one called "DEMON POWERS OF WOMEN: SUCCUBUS."

"The succubus desires to be impregnated with the seed of a man," he read.

Joe scratched at his neck. "Okay, but she's not sleeping with him."

"Remember her dating profile." He clicked away on the laptop to a folder marked "Not Porn."

"Not porn? Is this where you keep all your porn?" Joe asked.

"No, but that's what I wanted you to think. Reverse psychology. That way you wouldn't look inside. I keep lots of private stuff in here."

"Yeah, but now I know where it all is."

"Shit…"

Mike clicked on a screenshot, from a month ago, a dating profile for the username "outdoorsygirl23." Sure enough, there was Kristin's picture, complete with creepy red eyes.

"Why did you screenshot her dating profile?"

"I was looking for clues. And I figured she'd take it down now that she was dating someone. That someone being Dan."

Mike pointed to one line of text in the information box. "Look, right there. Says she wants to have a family some day. Game, set, and match."

"Someone wanting a family isn't proof they're a demon."

Mike closed the laptop. "Dude, we've found corroboration from three different sites. Succubi use mind control, Kristin has totally mind-fucked Dan. Succubi drain energy from men, he's looking haggard and thin and he goes to bed early. Succubi want to get knocked up. She wants kids and is totally going to push him for marriage."

Joe rubbed his chin in thought. Mike was taking a wild leap here but, strangely enough, he could see where it was coming from. Dan had changed so much in the past few weeks. He was barely the same person. Hell, she was calling him Dante now. But to accept that this was all a demon plot was a little much.

"Do you believe me yet?" Mike asked to break the silence.

"While I will admit that this is getting a little eerie, I still think that we're jumping the gun. It's quite possible that there are, in fact, three crazy websites out there on the net."

"Come on," Mike said. "One I could picture, there's nuts everywhere. Two, okay, but three? Three to me says trend, like this is something real out there and people are talking about it."

"Three also says conspiracy theories, tin foil hats, alien abductions."

"Shit, I never thought of that – she could be an alien!"

Joe rubbed his eyes. "Please don't go there."

PING.

Someone had responded to their question on the forum.

"Let's see what our fans think," Mike said.

"There's Canucklehead420," Mike said. "From Vancouver."

Joe read the comment aloud: "This totally happened to my bro. Met this girl who took over his life, made him change everything about himself, turned him onto folk music, the environment, all kinds of shit. They were supposed to get married, and he died mysteriously. Police said it was an accident. I'm not convinced. She moved away, I think to River City, but it could have been Regina. She blocked me on Facebook."

Mike tapped the screen as if that was all that needed to be said, but he spoke anyway. "What do you say about that, Mr. Skeptic?"

"I say that it's a coincidence. People die in accidents all the time. Vancouver is a big place – I'll bet there's a fatality every day, maybe more."

"Canucklehead420 says she moved here!"

"Or Regina."

"Come on, who moves TO Regina?"

Mike started typing in a response to Canucklehead420's reply, asking him to add him on Facebook and tell him who his friend was in a DM.

"Why do you want to know that?" Joe asked, reading along.

"A hunch."

Mike opened his Facebook and they sat looking at the home page screen for a solid ten minutes, waiting. Neither one spoke.

"You think he'll do it?"

"He watches the show, doesn't he?"

"Yeah, but adding a viewer as a friend? That just seems like crossing some kind of line."

"It's the only way."

Then, a change on the page. A new friend request. Mike opened it up and saw that Canucklehead420 was actually a guy named Jesse Long who did, in fact, live in Vancouver. Mike agreed to add him and immediately sent him a message.

"Does your late friend still have a profile up here?"

They stared at the screen until a response came in.

"Yup. His name is Derek Voth."

"Do you remember the girl's name he was dating when he died mysteriously?"

They waited again for the response. The three dots stayed on screen for what felt like an eternity before the words appeared.

"Kristin something."

Joe's mouth dropped as a pit opened in his stomach. Could it be possible?

Mike perked up. "There, you see?"

"It could still be a coincidence."

Mike quickly found the Derek Voth profile. It was public. They scanned it for information.

"Posts are fairly standard, links to news stories, photos of cats doing stupid things, photos of a guy with short brown hair and thick glasses on a boat, the same guy in contacts going camping," Joe said. "I'm not seeing anything here."

"There's lots of shit to go through yet," Mike said.

"How long are you—"

"There. Look at that, Mr. Skeptic."

A photo of this Derek Voth with a girl who bore a spitting

image to Kristin.

"Holy fuck, it's her!" Joe said.

Joe didn't know what else to say, he was at a loss. Photographic evidence that maybe Mike's whole theory wasn't completely batshit.

"Check his relationship status."

Mike acquiesced. They were both shocked to see it showed Derek Voth *in a relationship* with Kristin Smith.

"I'd say that about wraps this up."

"I'm not ready to concede that just yet. It could be someone with the exact same name as her, who looks just like her, but isn't her. Like a doppelganger who just happened to live in a different province and just happened to move to River City or Regina."

"You think doppelganger is more plausible than energy vampire, beholder, or demon succubus?" Mike asked.

"I'm not sure what I think anymore," Joe admitted.

"There's only one way to find out for sure," Mike said. "I need to add her as a friend."

"Do you think she'll add you back? You were kind of a dick to her."

"I'm her boyfriend's best friend. If she wants to stay in his good books, she'll want me on her side."

Mike clicked on add friend by her name. Her profile was locked down. The screen only showed her picture and current city as River City. Everything else was behind privacy walls.

"And now we play the waiting game."

They sat in silence and stared at the screen. A minute passed, then five, then ten, then thirty, then an hour. Finally, Joe came to a realization. "Wait, didn't Dan say they were going to Folkfest? She probably doesn't check her Facebook out there. Hell, she might not even have service in the middle of Bird's Hill Park."

"Shit," Mike said. "Then I guess we have to wait until Monday to know for sure."

"What do you want to do until then?"

"Let's try to kill that fucking Beholder."

CHAPTER TWENTY-TWO: IN THRALL TO THE DARK LORD

"Lord, you must feed. You're looking—"

"Looking what, thrall?"

They cowered in fear as a wave of anger emanated over them.

"You've drained all that you could from the others, we—"

"You defiled the sanctity of the unholy sanctuary?"

"The smell was—"

Piled in the corner of the room were the husks of those who had dared to presume they could summon. There was little left of them.

"I can remove your noses if you wish."

They grovelled, desperate to keep the last shreds of their humanity. Decaying, their state of undeath wasn't permanent and could be ended with a whim.

"You exist only to serve."

"We feared that—"

"Your concern is… admirable. What have you brought?"

The woman held a small bundle wrapped in red cloth in her arms. It had upon it the faint smell of tiny life.

"A morsel," she said, presenting the bundle forward.

The cloth fell away, revealing an infant with pink skin,

waving hands, and brown eyes.

"Stolen in the night, I assure you," she said. "No one—"

"Leave it and be gone."

She laid the bundle down on the concrete and backed away in a half bow. Her fellow thrall followed suit. The two of them stood at the entryway to the sanctuary, waiting.

"You remain?"

"We were hoping we could..."

"Could what?"

"Watch."

With only a thought, the door slammed shut, encasing the room in darkness. The infant let out a soft confused coo.

Closer. The smell of new life was intoxicating. A snack. Nourishment until the ritual could be completed.

Reaching out, touching the soft, plump skin. Fingers wrapped around the larger hand.

It was all over in a flash.

Tiny drops of blood fell from wet lips to the cold concrete.

CHAPTER TWENTY-THREE:
FRANK BUYS A NEW SHIRT

The mall was the last place Frank wanted to be. Surrounded by shoppers on all sides, listening to the faint hum of muzak in the background, passing the elderly dressed in workout gear marching up and down the halls; it was like a different planet. "Should be out on the streets," he grumbled. "Doing my job instead of... this."

He would have been, too, if not for the suits.

"Break my ass," he said.

"Excuse me?" an elderly woman asked, walking beside him.

"They said I need to work as part of a team, can you believe that?"

"Who said?" She had hair as white as new underwear and glasses as thick as a bottle of scotch.

"That I can't keep on being a lone wolf, as if that was a bad thing."

"There was a wolf out near the perimeter a few years back. It ate a few stray cats and—"

"I'm the one who's been busting the real bad guys all these years. If you knew half of what I did you'd soil yourself."

"You soiled yourself?" she said, aghast.

"No, you would have."

"I'm not that far gone," she said. "I might even be younger than you by the—"

"Let's just agree to disagree on that one, okay?"

He made a sudden right and left her to her laps around the mall. He wasn't here to chat.

"It's got to be around here somewhere." He moved past rows of stores with bright illuminated signs, banners advertising sales, and crowds of people coming and going.

"It's all that new Chief's fault," he said quietly. "Thinks he can kill me with kindness. I'll wait him out until he comes crawling back on his hands and knees begging."

There was only one problem with his plan so far. The waiting game was taking longer than he expected. He'd figured that after a day without him the city would crumble into anarchy and that the Chief would have him on the horn faster than a Viking at a mead party. But here he was, weeks into his forced vacation and still the phone stayed silent. Every so often he'd pick it up to make sure it was still working only to be met with the dial tone of disappointment.

He finally couldn't take any more hot dog walks or *Littlest Hobo* re-runs; he had to get out of his apartment. He figured it was finally time to buy a few new pairs of socks and he still had to replace his lucky shirt ruined by that car thief still on the lam.

"That guy's racking up one hell of a IOU," Frank said as he looked for old Vincenzo's menswear store. It was somewhere in this mall, but he'd walked around the place twice and hadn't seen any sign of it. The whole monstrosity looked nothing like it had years ago.

"Bad enough before," he said, stopping in place, looking around at the glass elevator, the fountain, the kiosks selling perfume, trying to orient himself.

When he was growing up, this was nothing but a huge field. They used to run horse races on a track before someone had the bright idea to turn the whole thing into a three-level shopping mall. He could still smell the shit.

"Hey, buddy, you got something on your shoes," a man said, passing him.

Frank looked down to see a mashed in turd dangling off the edges of his shoes.

"Thanks, pal."

He rubbed his foot along the edges of a planter and spotted the illuminated mall directory sign. With newly clean soles, he walked over to read the list of stores.

"Vincenzo's, starts with a V."

He ran his finger over the names but nothing matched.

"Shoes, clothing, toys, electronics, make-up, underwear, whatever the hell this place I can't even pronounce sells… No sign of the old man."

He looked around again. "He was on the north side near the parkade. There used to be an arcade across the hall. It was always good for a few truant busts after getting a quick hem."

He recreated the faded image of the mall's past and found a path that looked familiar. He cut through the centre, cutting off the old lady on her return lap and found the spot that Vincenzo's should have been but wasn't.

He walked in anyway.

"Hello, can I help you?" a lanky man in a vest and striped pants said. His thin moustache was gelled into points and his hair had more pomade than sense.

"Where's Vincenzo?"

The man raised an eyebrow in confusion. "I'm not sure I know who you mean."

"You know, fat little Italian guy makes the best shirts in town."

"Not here – I've been in this location for ten years."

Frank looked around the store, a wall of mirrors, sinks, and chairs. Near the counter was a display wall for razors, creams, and sprays with names in languages he didn't understand.

"Vincenzo change careers?" He read the signage aloud. "Upright Male Fine Barber shop?"

The man nodded proudly. "The best cuts and shaves to make you look and feel like a modern man."

Frank took a contraption with a half dozen small blades set into a padded head off the shelf. "This some kind of fruit slicer?"

"That is the newest in shaving technology, the ultra shave 3000. Swedish design, optimal blade angle to provide maximum comfort and the closest of shaves. We're the only dealer in River City authorized to sell them."

Frank put the tool back. "What the hell is wrong with a good old-fashioned straight razor?

"This cuts down on skin irritation and accidental cuts, completely sensitive skin friendly."

Frank reached into his sock and took out his wooden-handled straight razor. He flicked it open to gleam in the lights above. "I can strip the skin off a watermelon with this in a minute flat."

The man jerked away from the blade, holding his hands up in fright. "Please, take whatever it is you want, just don't hurt me."

"What?"

The man ran over to the cash register and opened it up, grabbing a wad of bills and rushing back to Frank. "Here, the store isn't worth my life."

"I don't want your money."

The man ran back to the counter and came back with a check book in a large leather billfold. He scribbled away and tore off a yellow lined cheque. "It's made out to cash for everything in the account. Six thousand eight hundred dollars. There's a place around the corner that'll cash it without ID. Please, I don't want to die!"

Frank folded the razor back up into the handle and shoved it in his sock. "I'm not here to jack you, I'm looking for old Vincenzo's place. He used to make the best shirts on this side of the river, but if he's moved, just tell me where to and I'll let you get back to whatever the hell you think you're doing here."

"You're not here to rob me?"

"I'm a cop. Well, on suspension right now, but still a cop."

"So you're not going to slit my throat?"

"Of course not, I just need some new shirts."

The man snatched the cheque back and tore it into strips. He took the pile of cash and replaced it in the register.

"Fashionable Male. Next aisle over. You can't miss it."

"Try me."

The man put up a 'back in five minutes' sign and personally led Frank to the place. "Here you go, you're their problem now."

Before he could thank him, the man had darted out of sight.

"Time to get a shirt."

The mannequins in the store window didn't seem to be wearing men's clothes, but the sign did sale Fashionable Male.

He saw a guy filling a rack with more spikes in his hair than a cactus. He wore something tight, shiny, and decorated in belt buckles.

"Can I help you, sir?" the man asked as Frank walked in.

"Shirts. Starched. Collars, buttons and pockets. And sleeves that roll up when you have to get arm deep in shit."

The man raised an eyebrow and motioned with his finger for Frank to follow him to the corner. "These just came in from Paris. All natural fibres." He held up a dark green shirt with arms that didn't match and odd drawings down the side. "Machine—"

"Did someone have this out painting?"

"I assure you, this is quite new."

"Where the hell am I supposed to wear this? One of those love-ins I keep hearing about? I need one colour. Either white, blue, or dark blue. I'll settle for grey if that's all you have."

"This isn't your style, how about this?" The man showed Frank a hooded shirt with fur at the edges and huge buttons the size of a doorknob.

"What am I, a fur trapper? I need shirts, not a taxidermist's nightmare."

"Hmm… when I look at you, I picture a man who likes to make an entrance, who needs to feel important."

"Keep talking," Frank said, liking the cut of this man's jib.

"I think I have something just for you." He began to walk away and that was when Frank saw the crime. He grabbed the man by the arm and stopped him in place. "Don't move."

"Sir?"

"Shh." Frank held his finger up to silence him. He wished it worked on the horrible music playing.

"What's the matter?"

Frank pointed to a curtained area. A thin man carrying multiple shirts on hangers in his arm slipped inside. "Shoplifter. Five'll get you ten that he's going to go in there and put those things on and try to slip out without paying."

The man furrowed his brow. "But that's exactly what—"

"I'm a cop. I know how to handle these people. Just get to your phone and dial 9 then 1. When I give the signal, dial the second 1."

"You don't understand—"

"I know, I know. This day and age your markups are so small that you can't afford to let one of these guys get away, I get it. Just be thankful that I'm here."

Frank walked over to the curtain, looked to the bottom, saw a man's socked feet poking out. Heard the man humming.

"Singing as you steal, eh?"

Frank swung the curtain open. The guy was standing in his underwear with a cellphone in his hand, in the middle of taking a selfie. He screamed in girlish terror as Frank shouted, "A-HA!"

"That's all the evidence I need to send you away." Frank grabbed the phone.

"Hey!" The man reached for it, and they struggled over the device.

"Trying to delete the proof, eh? Sorry, but I'm going to need to put a date stamp on that." Frank stepped down on the man's feet as hard as he could. The guy cried out and let go of the phone.

Frank waved it over his head proudly to the shopkeep. "Press that one now, Johnny, I've got the evidence."

"My phone, my phone! He's got my phone!" the man in his

underwear shouted.

"Put your pants on, shoplifter, the boys in blue will be here any second."

Frank noticed the screen. In the struggle, the selfie was gone. In its place was what looked like some kind of worm in a bush. He squinted, trying to figure out what in the hell it was.

The clerk came over. "I've called mall security."

"Good, maybe they can tell me what the hell this thing is," Frank said as he showed the man the phone.

The clerk's eyes grew three sizes. "Your dick?"

The man with his pants down shrugged sheepishly.

CHAPTER TWENTY-FOUR: DIVIDE AND CONQUER

"Okay, she's pulling out now."

"Are you sure you want to cross this line?"

"You said so yourself," Mike said, "there's something wrong with her. Strange powers, the dead ex, the fact that she hasn't added me back on Facebook. I'm just following her around to see what the hell it is she does all day – it's not a big deal."

"It's stalking."

"It's intelligence gathering. Spies do this shit all the time."

"You're not a spy!"

"But I am trying to expose her and her intentions."

There was a pause on the other end of the line. Finally, Joe continued, "Just don't get caught."

Mike looked at his reflection in the rearview mirror: aviator sunglasses and fake moustache. "Don't worry, I'm in disguise."

He checked her locked Facebook page on his phone again. What the hell was locked away behind that friends only designation? It had to be incriminating evidence. She was pretty smart to not add him back, he'd see it for sure then. But she didn't expect the lengths that he was willing to go to learn the truth.

"You're at her place now?" Joe asked.

"I can see her walking to her car."

Kristin lived in a modest, three-story brick apartment building tucked away on a tree-lined street in the east end of town. It looked like a thousand other places all over River City.

"Tan Corolla. She's got a prime parking spot."

"Only a demon would drive something so practical."

He watched her get in and check her mirrors, then buckle her seatbelt.

"Well?" Joe asked.

"She's safety conscious."

"The bitch."

She backed out slowly, while he ducked down out of sight in his truck. Mike had arranged to get a flex route today and he'd made trades with some of the guys to take a portion of his load off.

"You sure you can do this while working?" Joe asked.

"I've got it all covered. I should have a solid hour or two of time to shadow her before I have to go do pick ups."

"In your work truck."

"A UPS truck is the perfect cover. She'll never suspect that this simple common delivery truck is, in fact, a covert observation van."

"That's certainly some kind of logic," Joe said. "But what if you lose her?"

"Hey," he said into the phone, "I'm not some rank amateur here. I might not be a cop, but I've seen a lot of cop movies. I think I know how to tail someone."

He laid the phone down on the dash and pulled out after

her. He stayed as far back as he dared. They drove for a few minutes until she pulled into the nearby Safeway. He took a spot in the lot a few rows away. "She's at the Safeway," he said.

He took the phone and got out, following her inside the store. It was surprisingly busy for the mid afternoon. He spotted her moving towards the perishables.

"She's in the produce section," he said.

"Demons eat vegetables?"

"About to find out."

Kristin, unaware of Mike's presence, went about gathering onions, tomatoes, and peppers. She picked up a cucumber, a solid twelve inch long one, balanced it in her hand, held it at eye level, checked the size against that of her mouth, then broke it in half and dropped the two pieces in her bag.

Mike flinched instinctively.

She stopped at the cantaloupes and began testing their firmness.

"Now she's squeezing melons," he whispered into the phone.

"Sounds hot," Joe replied sarcastically.

* * * *

Back at his desk in the office, Joe held his phone to his ear, listening to Mike tell him everything Kristin was buying as if it was of great import. *Wow, she's shopping. Obviously only demons do that. This is so stupid. Why did I let him convince me this was a good idea?* Suddenly, Marlena came running out of her office. "Joe, stop what you're doing. Wait, what are you doing?"

He covered the phone with his hand. "Um, just conversing with a producer about something."

"What's the budget?"

"I'd say about one fifty."

She frowned. "Sounds like small potatoes."

"Melons actually."

"Is that what people say now? I'll have to remember that the next time I'm in LA. Small melons." She started to turn back around. "Thanks."

Then she stopped, seemingly trying to remember why she'd just come running out of her office. In a moment, it hit her and she spun back around. "Wait, Joe! I need you to take this sweater." She held up a black fleece hoodie with the company logo emblazoned on the side. "To Prairie soundstages. Meat Loaf is complaining that he's cold, so I told the people at Bison Gal Films that we'd help out."

Of all the times to be sent on a pointless errand.

"We were going to give him one of these sweaters anyway," Marlena said proudly. "But instead of waiting for the wrap party, we'll do it now and look like heroes." She handed him the sweater. "Keeping Meat Loaf warm in River City. I like the sound of that. Oh yeah, you can't use your car for this, it's some insurance thing. Call the car rental place to get one, then get over to the set ASAP stat!"

She ducked back into her office and shut the door.

"What's going on, Evans?" Mike asked.

"Hang on, dude," Joe said.

He put his cell phone down and picked up the office land line. Couldn't Meat Loaf get his own sweater? Or barring that, couldn't someone from the studio who'd hired him pick it up? They had PAs for this kind of thing. Who was he kidding? If there was one thing he'd learned about the film industry, it was that shit rolled downhill.

He dialed the car rental agency and they picked up on the second ring.

"Excelsior Car Rentals."

"It's River City Film Commission here. I need a car. Anything ready right now?"

He heard them tapping on the keys through the phone line. "I can get you a 1991 Nissan Stanza in powder blue."

"As long as it works, I'll take anything."

"Well, let's hope it does then!"

In minutes he was out the door and walking across Portage Avenue towards the car lot, carrying the sweater in one hand, his cell in the other.

"Evans, what's going on?" Mike asked. "You sound like you're outside."

"I'm off to see Meat Loaf," he said.

* * * *

"Meat Loaf? How the hell do you know what she's shopping for?"

Crouched behind a display of cereal, Mike watched Kristin comparing the nutritional information on two packages of tea. She dropped one in her basket and put the other back on the shelf. She started to walk away, and he darted over to see what it was that she'd rejected. It might be a clue.

"Excuse me," someone called to him.

He jerked around to see a balding man in a red vest looking at him inquisitively. Kristin left the aisle.

"Huh, I was just… er…" Mike stammered.

"I know what you were doing."

"You do?"

"I keep telling your dispatcher that you're supposed to come to the loading dock. That's where the pick-ups are. This way." The man waved for Mike to follow him.

Shit!

"Possible issue here," he said to Joe. He could hear the noises of a busy street through the phone.

"Ditto," Joe said.

Mike saw Kristin walking towards the other end of the store as he followed the manager to the back. He was beginning to doubt the wisdom of his disguise.

"Right here." The manager pushed open a set of swinging doors and led Mike into the warehouse. It was dark, filled with pallets of food in crates and boxes with labels from all around the continent. On one side was the freezer and refrigeration room. "You guys are so fast. I just placed the order and BAM, you're here!"

"Well, uh, you know us. We try to be prompt."

"Prompt? This was incredible. Maybe forty seconds!"

"Fibre optics," Mike said. "You know, that whole 5G thing they keep going on about."

"Interesting," the man said, handing Mike a box covered in shipping labels. "I saw a video the other day that said 5G was a conspiracy to give us all brain cancer. Big Pharma has a vaccine in the works. They won't get me, though, I only use payphones."

"Isn't that incredibly inconvenient?"

"So is brain cancer. You should really throw away your cell. Trust me."

Mike looked at the phone in his hand, broadcasting faint

street noises. "But I—"

"You probably already have a tumour, like the size of a golf ball." He tapped the box in Mike's hand. "Look into it. You'll thank me."

"I'll do that," Mike said, looking into the manager's blank stare. "Thanks for this then." He darted back into the store. He couldn't see Kristin anywhere. *Shit. She must have already paid.* He dashed outside, just in time to see her driving past.

He tore to his truck.

"In hot pursuit," he said to Joe as he hopped in, threw the parcel in the back, and gunned it after her.

* * * *

Joe pulled up to Prairie Soundstages, River City's soundstage complex. It was, from the outside, nothing more than a large square cube, with loading doors and a gravel parking lot. But inside there would be a hundred people working on the latest film to come to town: cast, crew, office staff, the producing team. He'd been here countless times giving visitors guided tours. He pushed inside the double entrance doors with the sweater under his arm. A young brunette girl was manning the front desk. She rose and ran to block his way into the stage. "Uh, excuse me," she said. "Where are you going?"

"I'm Joe from the film commission. I was asked to bring this to Meat Loaf," he said, brandishing the sweater. "Apparently he's cold."

"No one told me about that."

Joe shrugged. "I was sent by the film commissioner to do this."

"I'm going to have to call that in," she said and went to the desk. "Wait here."

Joe tapped his feet, listening to Mike detail every street Kristin drove down while the girl called upstairs. The soundstage complex lobby wrapped around past a commissary and led to stairs that allowed access to the upper-level offices. Closed doors at the end of the aisle opened up into the stages themselves, the construction and loading areas. Meat Loaf would be in there somewhere.

The girl hung up the phone and came back. "I'm sorry, but no one here knows what you're talking about. You can't just walk in claiming to have a delivery for legendary singer and actor, Meat Loaf – you could be a stalker or something."

"My friend is the stalker, I just work for the film commission and was asked to bring this sweater to the legend that is Meat Loaf, okay? I didn't ask to do this errand, but here I am anyway."

"That's the other thing – Meat Loaf's not even shooting here today. Your story doesn't add up. I want you to know that I called security."

This stupid errand was threatening to turn into a big schmoz. "Look, if you just call the—"

"Security!"

"I'm going," he said and walked out. He grabbed his work phone and called in to the office. Surprisingly Marlena answered on the second ring.

"Is that you, Shaemus?"

"No, Marlena, it's me, Joe."

"Joe? I can't talk right now, I'm waiting on an important call from Ireland."

"I'm here at the soundstage and they're telling me that they don't know anything about Meat Loaf needing a sweater.

He's not even here shooting today."

He heard her pop some chips in her mouth and loudly chew them close to the phone. "I'm just about to go meet him for lunch, so why don't you bring the sweater back and I'll take it?"

Joe covered the receiver. "Fucking hell, bitch, mother fuck. Why the fuck didn't you just take it in the first place!"

He composed himself and uncovered the phone.

"Sure thing, Marlena," he said. "Be right back."

* * * *

"What could she possibly be doing at a dry cleaners?" Mike said as he stepped out of his truck to follow Kristin inside the small shop in a strip mall. The place was barely bigger than the counter. Mike slid into a chair and grabbed a newspaper, holding it in front of his face to pretend like he was waiting, eavesdropping on her conversation. She held up a light blue dress.

"—bloodstains out? I've tried everything."

"Sure, we'll do the job for you."

Mike couldn't tell where the little man that ran the place was from, because his accent was so thick.

Kristin seemed relieved. "I'm so glad. It's my favourite dress."

"It's nice," the man said, turning it over in his hand. There was blood on both sides.

"If this works out, I've got some more you can have."

"Bring them when you pick this up," the man said. "Trust me."

More bloodstains?

"Blood on her dress," he whispered to Joe. "Covering something up for sure."

* * * *

"What on her dress?" Joe asked as he ran up four flights of stairs to the office, carrying the sweater in his free hand. He went straight to Marlena's door, but the room was empty. "Where'd she go?" he asked the room.

"Out for lunch with Meat Loaf and the producers of that alien movie," one of his co-workers called back.

"Any idea where?"

He was met with a shrug.

"Fucking hell." He called Marlena and she answered right away.

"Shaemus?"

"No, it's Joe. I have the sweater, where did you go?"

"Muffin shop," Mike's distant voice said from the phone in his other hand.

"Lunch," Marlena answered. "Chez Ami. Bring the sweater there. Also, I'm driving, so I can't really talk." She ended the call.

"Chez Ami... fucking hell."

"No, the muffin shop," Mike's voice said from the other phone.

* * * *

"She's at the muffin shop," Mike said. "I repeat, the muffin shop. She appears to be ordering a muffin." He rubbed his chin as he watched Kristin take a brown paper bag from the server.

"It looked healthy, maybe bran. Do demons need fibre?" he whispered.

* * * *

"I don't fucking know," Joe answered as he pulled into the parking lot of Chez Ami. "Correction. It could have been chocolate," Mike said back. "Maybe blueberry. Hard to tell."

"Who cares?" Joe said as he walked up to the door of Chez Ami. He pulled but it was locked tight. That was when he realized the place was deserted. There was a closed sign on the door.

"It's closed," he said.

"No," Mike answered, "it's not. I'm inside now."

"Chez Ami."

"She's at the muffin shop," Mike said. "Weren't you listening?"

Joe grabbed his other phone to call Marlena, but there was a text from her: "Going to Cafe 526 instead."

"For fuck's sake," he said and ran back to the car. "She's moved again."

* * * *

"Yeah, I know," Mike whispered back. "We're in some kind of oddball bookstore now. Weird place."

Dark purple curtains, African masks on the wall, beads dangling from the ceiling, and shelf after shelf of curios and jars with handwritten labels surrounded him. A faint aroma of incense wafted from the counter.

"Madam Ovidie's House of the Occult," Mike whispered as he stood behind a shelf, pretending to read a book on witchcraft, watching as Kristin perused another shelf. She pulled out a book about spells and rituals, asking the shopkeeper a question Mike couldn't hear clearly.

"Demons read," he whispered to Joe.

* * * *

"What kind of books?" Joe asked as he drove around the busy parking lot of Cafe 526.

"Got to be evil," Mike said back. A crashing sound.

"Mike? You okay?"

"Yeah, I just knocked over a jar that says it's eye of newt."

"I don't think that's real."

"Tell that to the woman saying I have to pay for it. Ten fifty? Really?"

"There!" Joe said as he spotted the last parking spot in the entire Cafe 526 lot.

"Where?" Mike asked back.

"I'm trying to do three things at once here, man." He pulled in and shut off the car.

"And I'm not?"

Joe closed the door and walked into the restaurant. The place was jam-packed with people.

"She's buying a—"

The cacophony of the mingled conversations drowned out Mike's voice through the phone. Cafe 526 was an upscale French restaurant, one of Marlena's favourites to schmooze with clients. Another refurbished old building with a ceiling of exposed beams and black painted piping. A chalkboard next to the counter with the cash register detailed the day's specials. He couldn't see Marlena anywhere in the crowd.

Mike said something else, but he couldn't hear it.

He flagged down the maître d'. "Have you seen a group of people with Meat Loaf here?"

"I'm sorry, sir, we don't serve meat loaf."

"Not the food, the guy. You know Paradise by the Dashboard Light?"

He was met with a blank look.

"I would do anything for love, but I won't do that?"

"Do what?"

"You know... that!"

"But what's that?"

"Where?" Joe looked behind him.

"No, in the song?"

"Oh, that. It's, you know, screwing around."

"Really? I figured it'd be something else."

"I didn't write the thing. But is he here?"

The maître d' shook his head. "His party was, but they didn't have reservations. I did hear a woman say they were going to try Ray and Jerry's instead."

"Fucking hell," Joe said in frustration as he went back to the car.

* * * *

"She's stopping for lunch. Steak. Of course it would be meat."

Mike followed Kristin into the Ray and Jerry's parking lot. She disappeared inside the 1950's style steak restaurant. He checked his watch – he was past due. He looked at the growing list of parcels he had to pick up on his scanner, then looked behind him at the ones he still had to deliver.

"This is more important than work," he mumbled.

He was running out of time. Tailing her hadn't yielded a trump card. He needed more than circumstantial clues. He had to go inside.

"Come on, you devil, show me something really evil."

He parked and followed her.

* * * *

Joe's work phone pinged with a text from Marlena: "Where are you? Need sweater."

"I'm five minutes ahead of you," he grunted.

"I'm going inside," Mike's voice came from his other phone. "Where?"

Joe parked and walked inside Ray and Jerry's. It was a vintage restaurant, a River City institution. With a dimly lit interior right out of a Rat Pack movie, the furnishings were red leather. The booths were deep and plush, the walls wood panelled, and the clientele was probably the same as it had been in the fifties. The waitresses, too. They were grey haired and wore pink skirts. It was an expensive place, at which he'd never eaten.

He spotted Marlena at a table on the other side of the room. She motioned him over. He lugged the sweater around tables and waitresses carrying trays loaded with red meat. A team of producers, Marlena, and Meat Loaf were all midway through a steak lunch.

"Joe's here," Marlena said, smiling.

All eyes at the table looked up but no one knew who he was or why they should care. Five guys in designer shirts with cellphones laid out next to their plates and Meat Loaf. The man was smaller than he imagined, more wrinkled, with short grey hair, a far cry from the screeching behemoth in the puffy shirts.

"Uh, hi, Mister Loaf." He waved.

"Joe brought you a sweater, Meat," Marlena said, smiling. "We'd heard you were cold in the soundstage."

Joe handed Meat Loaf the sweater. He seemed to like it. "What size is this?" he said as he checked the collar. "Extra large? I haven't been an extra large since the nineties."

"Try it on and see if it fits," Marlena said.

Meat Loaf pulled on the sweater and, sure enough, it was a tent on him.

Marlena shot Joe a dirty look, silently saying, "Why didn't you bring more than one?"

He didn't feel like telling her that it was the one she had given him.

Meat Loaf handed the sweater back. "Does it come in large?"

"I'll go back and get one for you."

"Don't rush, stay a while, have lunch. I'm sure we can make some room for you. The steak here is great."

"Sorry," Joe said. "If I'm gonna beat rush hour, I've gotta make like a bat out of hell and—"

The table fell silent as he trailed off. *Oh shit. Did I make a faux pas?*

One of the producers blanched. "Are you making fun of him?"

Joe shook his head. "Oh no, no, no. I'd do anything for a laugh, but I wouldn't do that."

More silence before Meat Loaf burst out laughing. The

table quickly followed suit. "For crying out loud," he said, "that was good."

"You took the words right out of my mouth," Joe said, grinning.

Meat Loaf stopped laughing and scrunched his face up. "Two out of three ain't bad." He burst out laughing again.

"Well, I'm going nowhere fast, and since I'm all revved up and have some place to go, I guess I'll see ya later, Mister Loaf."

"I couldn't have said it better," Meat Loaf said.

Joe took the opportunity to duck out before he did one line too far. As he passed the bar a hand grabbed him by the arm and pulled him.

"Shut up and get down."

It was Mike, hiding behind a menu.

"What the hell are you doing here?" Joe asked.

He pointed to a table in the corner. "Look at what she's eating."

He followed the finger to spot Kristin, alone at a table, blood dripping from her mouth as she ate a nearly raw steak with her hands, biting off huge chunks. She licked her lips, then leaned down and licked the plate. She reacted as if she'd had an orgasm, falling backwards in her seat.

"Holy shit."

"I know, right? Is the steak really that good here?"

"I don't know, but what the heck—"

"Hey, guys!"

They turned in shock to see Dan behind them, carrying a bouquet. He'd dressed up in a suit neither knew he owned.

"Dude, what are you doing here?" Mike dropped the menu, scrambling to act naturally.

"Meeting Kristin for lunch. Oh, hey, there she is!" He waved at her. They all turned to see her waving back.

"You guys here on a lunch break?" Dan asked them.

"I was here for Meat Loaf," Joe said.

"Oh yeah? It good here? I've heard the steak is. Why don't you guys come over and say hi?"

"The jig is up," Joe said quietly as the three of them walked over to the table. Kristin's plate had been licked clean. She rose and kissed Dan on the cheek, leaving a bloody red impression of her mouth.

"What are you all doing here?" she asked.

"Uh, business lunch, you know how it is."

Joe pointed behind him. "I was just meeting Meat Loaf."

"Whatever the reason, I'm glad you're here. Today's a special day," Dan said.

Kristin grinned. Joe couldn't help but notice a thin line of blood dripping from her mouth. She looked flushed, renewed. Had she gained weight? She seemed thicker. Dan, on the other hand, looked like an extra in a zombie movie; tired, with sunken cheeks and sallow skin.

"What's going on?" Mike asked. "Why is this a special day?"

"Kristin's agreed to move in with me."

She licked the blood off her lips with a quick flick of what seemed like a too-long tongue. "My lease was coming due anyway, it just made sense."

Mike's mouth dropped.

The two of them hugged. Joe elbowed Mike to notice the shadow cast from the dim lamp on the wall behind her. The image of the two of them was all wrong. Wings, a tail. The form moved, like it was alive, watching him.

Mike saw it, too. His eyes were three sizes too big. Joe

scanned the room; nobody else seemed to notice. But then why would they, their faces were locked in mid conversation. Steak dangled on forks in mid air, glasses in mid tilt, words dead on the tongue. Time had stopped. Again. The walls of Ray and Jerry's melted away, flames roared up in their place, burning everything into ash. A shape hovered above the melted ceiling below a red sky. It passed the corner of his eye but when he turned his head, it was never there. High above, rocks, sheer cliffs. Below them, the fires of hell. To the right, bodies writhing in torment crucified to jagged crosses. Charred things lumbered in slow lines towards the edge of the peak in the distance. Their flesh pierced with spears held by twisted shadow things, rivers of blood poured from open wounds, mixing with the dirt.

He and Mike stood on a tiny island of rock. That was when he realized that Mike was seeing it all, too. Neither had been affected by the pause. But where the hell were they?

Mike pointed to the left. A pair of eyes, glowing red. Where Kristin and Dan should have been. Pulsing, beating, like flares, expanding outward, wrapping them in oppressive heat. He shut his eyes as he felt his skin begin to melt. He tried to scream but his tongue liquified and he gagged. Fat crackled, flesh poured down his body, the pain was—

"I can't wait to spend even more time with my guy here," Kristin said.

Joe blinked and it was all gone with a popping sound. Everything he'd seen, vanished in a flash. People were moving, eating, talking as if they'd never stopped. He saw Meat Loaf laughing with Marlena, waitresses dropping more drinks down in front of hungry people. Normal again.

He looked to Mike who'd gone completely white. He was

217

staring at Kristin and Dan. She hugged him and looked right at them from his shoulder. Joe swore he saw her eyes glowing blood red.

"Congratulations," he stammered, "that's a big step."

Mike just stood in abject terror. Kristin's mouth turned into a twisted grin full of fangs. Right in front of them, out in the open. He needed evidence. He held his phone up. "How about a photo of the happy couple?"

CHAPTER TWENTY-FIVE: WE NEED PROFESSIONAL HELP

"I can't believe I'm saying this," Joe said, "but you might actually be on to something." Even saying the words out loud made him question his sanity, but after the evidence Mike had compiled and what he'd seen with his own eyes, Joe was starting to come around to the theory that Dan was dating something not quite human.

"I told you."

"Energy vampire, demon, succubus, I don't know what the fuck she is, but the change in his personality, the complete rearranging of his life, the rapid weight loss, he... doesn't look well."

"Distancing from his friends, her glowing red eyes, the living shadow, and whatever in the hell it was that happened in the restaurant."

Joe didn't even have words for that just yet.

"She was taunting us," Mike said as he scrolled through the pictures he'd taken of her during her day out. "She knew what she was doing all along."

He turned his phone to Joe, going over it all again. "The cucumber, the bloodstains, the muffin, the bloody steak, the fact that she drove a Corolla."

"That part I'm not so sure of actually," Joe said.

"Then there's this picture." Mike stopped on the last one, Dan and Kristin, smiling, hugging together with the shadowed form of wings and a tail behind them.

"I see it, the shadow, the red eyes," Joe said. Then he noticed something different about the picture. "Wait, they both have red eyes."

"What?" Mike snatched the phone away. He zoomed in on the faces, scrutinizing them magnified four hundred percent.

"Maybe it was the flash all along," Joe said.

"You were there, man. The time vortex. The room became—"

"Hell. Or at least what I assume hell looks like."

"You always laughed at me for my interest in the para-normal. Everyone meme-ing old Mike watching Ghost Investigators. But the proof is right here in your face. Digital film. Completely un-doctorable."

"Well…" Joe trailed off, staring silently at the photo. He knew he'd seen her eyes lit up when they'd first looked at it. But now, Dan's were red, too.

"Wings, a tail, probably even horns if we look hard enough."

Red eyes. Glowing. Two sets. The longer Joe looked, the bigger the flare around them seemed to grow. Slowly expanding outwards. Impossible. But it was. Four became two became one huge halo of red, leaking outwards to the edge of the image. Taking over. Ray and Jerry's was gone, in its place a mass of red light. Something moved in the apex. Fire? Dancing, writhing. A body slinking in the motion of a burning flame. Long, gangly limbs, slender torso, imperceptible details. Locked on the movement, his gaze kept zooming towards the shape in stutters. He wanted to look away, but he was drawn to that rhythmic motion. Fluid, seductive, hypnotizing. Blurred details of a face, obscured by pixels and digital artifacts. Who was it? The mouth moved. Talking to him? He tilted his ear closer. The screen was warm. He could feel the flames radiating outward. Faint whispers. Male, female? Human? *What?* Something sharp touched his earlobe, dragging along the flesh like claws. Trapped in place, helpless as they traced along the helix, into the antihelix, towards the canal. Inside the ear. Heat, moving deeper, towards the centre of his skull. *Help. Mike, help.* A stabbing in his brain and—

"Dude? You paying attention?"

The phone in his hands had gone dark, the screen covered in fingerprints. He touched his ear, came back with a faint line of blood on his finger. "Sorry," Joe said. "What were you saying?"

"I said demons wouldn't walk around looking all demon-like, they'd be sneaky about it. They'd use a disguise. That's why she looks human. Demon magic must be attuned to human vision, not a camera. She can't fool a megapixel."

"What makes you the expert on demon magic?"

"Google."

Joe swiped back on his phone to see the image of Dan and Kristin.

"See?" Mike said proudly. "The shadow knows."

Joe stared again at the photo, desperate for some alternate explanation. A trick of the light? A false shadow cast by potted plants, a waitress walking behind them? The more he looked, the less he could explain it. And then there were the eyes. Four. Glowing. No, it was two again. Now one? Growing outward and—

221

He clicked off the phone and laid it face down on the edge of the couch. Sweat dripped down his neck. His heart pounded. *Do not look again.*

"And Facebook is the nail in the coffin."

Mike took out the laptop and opened Facebook, typing in Kristin Smith's name and getting a full page view of her open profile.

"I can't believe she was so arrogant to finally add me back. There's enough breadcrumbs here for us to make a salad."

Joe watched Mike scrolling through old posts at lightning speed.

"This post from over a year ago about 'New Beginnings,' this one about moving on from pain, this one about starting over." He tapped the screen as he moved past. "Comments from friends, all in Vancouver, mind you, wishing her good luck coming to River City."

He kept scrolling, to a photo of Kristin standing with her late ex Derek Voth. "And this 'My heart is broken, R.I.P. My love.' The balls on her, acting upset when she knew she was the one who killed him."

Mike kept going further and further back through Kristin's online life. Photos of parties, campfires, graduations, nights out, fancy dinners, canoe trips, her with smiling babies of relatives, then, the clincher. "Game, set, match." He pointed to another post from four years ago, "Devastated, R.I.P. my amazing boyfriend. Can't function right now. Impossible to think you're gone @Lyle Unger. We had so much to look forward to."

"She's done this at least twice before!" Mike said, jabbing the screen with his index finger. "It says he died of a sudden illness. Endocarditis. What the fuck is that? It sounds so made up. And no one saw through it until us! Two dead boyfriends… that's some baggage I sure wouldn't want to check."

"It could still be a coincidence…" Even saying it, Joe didn't really believe it.

"One, maybe, but two? That's a trend. So she moves here and goes after Stoddard."

He slammed the laptop shut and started pacing the room excitedly.

"Eat your heart out, Bagans, you hack fraud. How many seasons and you've found shit. We've got a real goddamned black widow, the kind you see on Cold Case Files. I wonder how long she's been doing this for. Her Facebook only went back six years. She could have killed dozens of men before this came out."

"Or used a different account," Joe said.

"You're right, but we can't worry about that right now. We have to stop her before she gets whatever it is she's after. Is there, like, some kind of soul quota? And if she hits it, then what? Fucking hell, there's so much we still don't know."

"So, what do we do? Go to Dan with this and expect him to believe us?"

"He's in too deep," Mike said. "We're going to have to go to the experts. And I'm not talking about Zak fucking Bagans."

* * * *

"Excuse me, what did you say?" the sergeant at the desk asked in wide-eyed shock.

Mike tapped the Formica desktop and repeated himself. "I think you heard me. We, meaning the two of us" – he pointed to him and Joe – "have substantial evidence and reason to believe that our soon-to-be ex-roommate is dating a demon, or more specifically, a succubus. Before you suggest an energy vampire, you should know that we have proof she's drained the souls of at least two men in Vancouver and is currently in the process of doing it to one now. We'd like you to arrest her, or put a warrant out, maybe a restraining order, whatever it is you do in these situations."

The sergeant just laughed, his great belly jiggling like Santa. Behind him were the inner workings of a police precinct: cops chatting, paperwork typed, coffee sipped.

"Okay, okay, I get it," he said, composing himself. "This is a Halloween prank. A little early, right, guys?"

"It's not a prank," Joe said. "I'll admit it sounds insane – hell, I thought so, too – but there's a lot of circumstantial evidence here."

"I'm going to circumstantial evidence your ass if you two jokers don't take a hike. We have real crimes to go after here, not this late-night horror movie bullshit you're spewing."

He pointed to the exit behind them.

"Isn't there anyone who'll hear us out?" Mike pleaded. "A man's life is at stake!"

"Out!" the officer shouted and pointed more forcefully to the exit.

They turned and started to trudge their way outside, when the man suddenly called after them. "You know what, come back here, guys." He seemed to be holding back laughter, or gas. It was hard to tell. "I think there actually is someone who can help you. He's one of our best, handles this sort of stuff all the time."

"Really?"

"Oh yeah," the man said, grinning, "he's a regular Ghost-buster."

"Demon," Mike said.

"Whatever." The big man waved dismissively. "Just give him a call. He's... uh, into this kind of crazy shit, so I'm sure he'll take the case."

"He's not here?" Joe asked.

"No, he's, uh... on vacation. Only gets called up for the really good stuff, you know? I'll put his private address on the back, just for you guys."

Mike perked up as the man scribbled on, then handed him a business card from a stack in the desk. He read it over. "Now we're getting somewhere. Thanks, officer."

"Sergeant."

"Whatever."

"It's not the same thing."

"If you don't give a shit, it is," Mike said and turned to walk to the exit.

Joe chased after him, surprised as hell that they'd gotten any help at all. "What's it say? Is it some kind of paranormal investigator? Like Fox Mulder?"

Mike read the card looking more than pleased. He dramatically turned the card around and held it up for Joe. "It sure is."

Joe read the name aloud. "Detective Inspector Sergeant Frank Malone."

CHAPTER TWENTY-SIX: LIKE MINDS THINK ALIKE

"And that's all we know," Mike said to the old man sitting on his decaying couch in frayed slacks and a stained yellow undershirt.

"I'm glad you guys came – I was beginning to think the city had forgotten me."

The man stood up and walked over to the window of his small apartment. The place was a mess, with food wrappers all over the floor, old TV guides stacked beside the couch and a plate of what looked like last night's TV dinner on the small coffee table. He wasn't much better. It looked like he'd slept in his clothes for the past week. He pulled back the yellowed curtains and looked out on to the streets as he spoke.

"I'd almost been doubting myself," he said, "wondering if maybe my time was up."

Mike looked to Joe who just shrugged.

"I know what you're thinking, I can see it on your faces." The man never turned around to look at them, just kept on talking. "How could the famous Frank Malone think that? The man who's saved the city more times than Superman, faced the worst this world has to offer – how could someone so strong have a moment of weakness?"

226

He shook his head as he stared out the window.

"To tell you the truth, I'm not sure either. Maybe it's this strange new world of cellphones, computers, and cars that drive for you. Bean counters running things, sensitivity trainers, or maybe it was just a bad bottle of Jack. All I know is, I was sitting here in my room watching re-runs, ready for my own personal sunset. Then you two came."

He spun around and looked them both over. "Two people I've never met before telling me they've got proof their best buddy is dating a demon. A man drained to death by a creature from beyond the night. Two citizens who need the help of the best there is, the best there was, and the best there ever will be."

"Bret Hart?"

"Who?"

Frank pushed aside a stack of newspapers laying on the big recliner that was the focal point of the room. One headline read "Missing Newborns Baffle Police." Underneath was a brand-new shirt, still in cellophane. He tore the plastic off and shook it out. It was half buttoned up, so he slid it on over his undershirt. "I'm glad the boys had the sense to send you my way and I'm glad you had the sense to come. You see, a story like this – demons, time vortexes, fire eyes, soul sucking – you take that to a normal cop, and you get laughed at, maybe even tossed into the drunk tank. But you take a story like that to me, and I listen. While the rest of those pimple-nosed twerps are worrying about what report to file, I'm taking care of business. And let me tell you something, fellas, I've taken care of a lot of business in my day."

"Then that's it? You believe us?" Joe asked incredulously, still not sure even he did.

Frank scowled. "Of course I believe you. I've seen this before. Demon women bleeding a man dry – hell, sounds like one of my ex-wives."

"Yeah, but we mean that literally."

"You think I don't?" Frank lifted the back of his shirt to show them a horrible circular scar on his lower abdominal area. The skin was all wrong, like it had been chewed up or badly burned; off colour, textured like sandpaper. The wound was old, long since healed over, only leaving the awful scar as sign of whatever it was that had happened.

"Jesus Murphy, what the hell did that?" Mike asked.

"I'll tell you about it sometime, but right now what we need to do is work out a plan to expose this succubus for the monster she is, save your friend, and save my job."

"So, what do we do?" Joe asked.

"I've got a plan that can't fail," Frank said, rubbing his hands together proudly.

They stared at him, waiting for him to say more, but he just grinned, as if that was all that needed to be said.

"Uh, and? What is it?"

"What's what?"

"The plan?"

"I'll go and arrest her," Frank said. "The second she realizes who she's up against, she'll confess the whole thing and we can be in the corner booth at Joe's Diner before the bar rush."

Mike looked to Joe, who was starting to doubt the idea to come here in the first place.

"But what if she's, uh, more careful and won't talk?" Joe said.

Frank cracked his knuckles. "Elbow grease should loosen her tongue."

228

"Look, a confession is all well and good," Mike said, "but I've seen cop shows. Lawyer shows, too. Shit, I've seen entire movies set in courtrooms. We're going to need more than that."

"He's right," Joe said. "With the right lawyer, even a confession isn't enough to convict."

"Blast," Frank said, pounding his fist into his palm. "You guys are right. God, I've been out of the game too long to forget about shyster lawyers getting demon women off with only a warning. We're going to need something more concrete, I guess."

"Okay, so what then?"

"Look," Frank said. "There are three of us now and one of us has a cop's mind, which is really worth two and a half, two and three-quarter non-cop minds. So even if you only used half your brains, we'd still have three and a half, three and three-quarter regular minds. But if you both think really hard, maybe get up to seventy-five percent, hell, two-thirds would do, then we'd have like four and a quarter, three and seven-eighth minds, and that's pretty much a cabinet meeting right there. So we take those four and three-sixteenth minds and we put 'em to work on this problem and between the three of us, we're bound to come up with something."

Mike looked at Joe who could only shake his head in confusion.

CHAPTER TWENTY-SEVEN: THE DOUBLE DRAGON MOVING COMPANY

The mud-stained, dark grey moving truck pulled up to the modest brick apartment building. Three men in brown coveralls stepped out onto the quiet tree-lined street. Joe adjusted his zipper and looked at Kristin's soon-to-be ex-home. "I still can't believe that this is the best plan we could come up with."

Mike attached a fake moustache to his face and adjusted the brown hat on his head. "What do you mean? This is outstanding."

Frank folded his hands over his chest proudly. "Going undercover is a proud tradition of the police force. I've been some places that would turn you whiter than a sheet. This one time I had to wear a—"

"She's going to recognize us!" Joe said, interrupting the man's story before it could start.

Mike handed him another fake moustache from the three-pack they'd bought at the local costume store. "That's why we're wearing disguises!"

Joe looked at the tiny patch of black fur and gave up,

sticking it below his nose in defeat.

"I tell you, posing as the movers is iron-clad, foolproof stuff."

"Worked for the Three Stooges," Frank said.

"She'll never suspect us," Mike added. "She's totally the kind of person who wouldn't look twice at the so-called hired help."

"What are you basing that on?" Joe asked.

"She seems like a bitch."

"Can't argue with that logic, kid," Frank said.

"But what's our cover? Mario and fucking Luigi?" Joe pointed to Frank adjusting his fake black moustache over his real one. It looked completely ridiculous contrasted with his stark white hair and leathery nose. "And let me guess, he's Wario? Waluigi?"

"No. That would be stupid," Mike said.

"Then what?" Joe asked.

"Just leave it up to me." Mike waved his hand to stop the argument and led them to the buzzer panel of the apartment. He pressed the number for Kristin's suite.

She answered, "Hello?"

"Uh, yes, hi. It's the movers."

"Today? I wasn't expecting you guys until tomorrow."

Mike covered the buzzer with his hand. "Shit, the jig is up."

Frank pushed him out the way and leaned in. "Look, lady, some asshole obviously fudged the paperwork on this one but we got a lot of jobs to do, lots of people to move from point A to point B. A few even to point C. So just let us come in and do the job, okay?"

"But I'm not all packed yet."

Frank blanked, covering the intercom with his hand.

231

"Boys?"

Joe leaned in and waved Frank's hand away, speaking into the intercom. "It's all a part of the service. You let us handle it all while you relax or go for coffee or fried chicken or something."

The intercom went silent, but a moment later, it crackled to life again. "Well, okay. I'm almost ready anyway. This'll give me more time to unpack in the new place."

The buzzer for the door latch sounded. They headed up to the third floor, spotting Kristin standing in the doorway waving them forwards.

"Hello, ma'am," Frank said.

"Hi." Kristin looked them over. Joe did his best to keep his hat pulled down low and avoid eye contact.

"I'm Billy Lee and this is my brother Jimmy Lee," Mike said in a terrible attempt at a false accent.

"And you are?" she asked Frank.

"Uncle Bruce."

"Ok-ay. Billy Lee, Jimmy Lee, and Bruce—"

"Lee, that's right," Frank said.

"You're—"

"Brothers," Mike said.

"The, uh, Double Dragon moving company," Joe added.

"Double? But there's three of you."

"These two idiots need supervision, ma'am," Frank said. "Don't worry. I've got plenty of experience."

"Moving or supervising?" she asked.

"Both. Even at the same time."

"Alright," she said. "Then I guess you probably want to come in and get started."

"It would make the job a lot easier," Mike said.

She led them inside the apartment, a disaster room full of boxes, some shut, some open. Most had Sharpie markings showing what was either inside or to go inside. Pots and pans, clothes, books, couch, television, empty shelves; the job wasn't too big.

"This is the stuff," she said. "I'd like you to be especially careful with the ones marked 'china', they're fragile."

Frank nodded. "I know what you mean – those bastards never could make anything to last."

"It's my great-grandmother's fine china and incredibly valuable. Please treat it like it was your own great-grandmother's fine china."

"Got it, toss it down the coal chute the day she dies and get blasted drunk." Frank looked around the room. "Where is the coal chute?"

Kristin frowned. "Maybe I should just take those ones." She reached for a box marked 'VERY FRAGILE.'

"Nonsense, we're the professionals." Frank snatched the box from her. It tinkled like there was broken glass inside.

"Okay, so you know the address to take it all?"

"Sure do," Mike said. "Dan's new condo. No problem."

Kristin tried to look under Mike's hat. "How did you know his name? Say, do I know you?"

"It's on the requisition form, ma'am, from Kristin Smith's place to Dan Stoddard's place," Joe said, trying to salvage the whole operation.

That seemed to appease her. "I guess that makes sense. Well, okay then. I'll head over and wait for you guys there. I'll try to figure out where to put all this stuff before you show up."

Frank rubbed his hands in readiness. "You going to have

room with all his stuff in just a tiny condo?"

"He doesn't have any stuff. I've helped him purge the unnecessary junk he's been holding on to."

"What about the video games?" Mike asked.

Joe stomped on his foot hard to shut him up.

"He's not going to need those anymore. But why do you care?"

"We, uh, just see a lot of video games being moved around, you know," Joe stammered. "From, uh, point A to point B."

"Sometimes even point C," Frank added.

"Well, his are going to point V, Value Village."

"But they're valuable," Joe started. This time, Mike stomped on his foot to shut him up.

"He's not a teenager anymore. But you won't have to move those, just this stuff."

"And we'll do a bang-up job, ma'am," Frank said.

"Great to hear. Then I'll let you get to it. Bye!" She left the apartment.

Frank shut the door slowly behind her. "I see what you mean, boys. Nothing human could be that normal."

"Did you hear what she said about getting rid of all of Dan's stuff?" Mike asked. "He's too old for video games. Value Village—"

"You think she meant the N64?" Joe interrupted.

"She couldn't be that evil," Mike said. "Or could she?"

"If she's a woman," Frank said, "she sure could be."

Joe looked around at the mess of boxes and clutter, wondering where to start their search. "Okay, she's gone. Now what do we do?"

"We find the proof." Mike walked over to one of the boxes, looking inside.

"Are we actually going to move all this stuff over to Dan's place?" Joe asked, looking at the sea of boxes and trying to internally calculate how much time it would take to do the job.

Frank tossed a couch cushion aside, looking underneath for any clues. "If we don't, we'd be pretty piss poor movers, now, wouldn't we?"

"Aren't we just pretending to be movers?"

"Undercover goes both ways."

"Well, shit."

* * * *

Mike ripped open a box that had already been taped shut, tearing the top flap. Inside, he found a stack of books placed carefully in even rows. He slid one out. "*Jane Eyre*, sounds suspicious." The next one down was *Anne of Green Gables.* "Does hell have green gables?"

"They'd probably be red or black or something," Joe said.

"Blast."

He kept digging, pulling out more books and tossing them on the floor. "Nothing but classic literature. Come on, there has to be something harder than this."

Then he found it, at the bottom of the pile. A black book with blood red lettering and strange symbols drawn on the cover. He took it out slowly. The lettering seemed to cast an ethereal glow on the sides of the cardboard. He could swear the book was burning at the touch, almost like a small heating pad.

"The Encyclopedia of Demons and Spells," he read the title aloud. "Put this in the proof column."

235

"But why would a demon need a book *about* demons?" Joe asked, looking over Mike's shoulder.

"To scope out the competition obviously," Frank said as he pulled out an old lollipop from inside the couch. He sniffed it once, rubbed it off on the couch arm, then stuck it in his mouth.

* * * *

What surprised Joe the most about Kristin's place was that she had obviously spent a lot of time decorating it. Instead of the usual stark white walls that were the norm in a rental unit, she had painted them a deep indigo, with crimson and forest green accents. She'd hung ornamental decorations everywhere; Celtic imagery, crosses, other symbols he didn't recognize. Empty hooks left in the wall showed where she had taken down pictures that rested on the ground covered in blankets. He pulled the wrappings off and started to look through them; landscapes, a bowl of fruit, what looked like a Dali reproduction, a motivational poster with a cat, a charcoal drawing of a tree. The frames were old, possibly thrift store finds.

So far, the place looked just like the apartment of any girl who was into pagan imagery and liked Wiccan themed decorations.

"You think she's going to repaint the room after?" he asked, pausing in his flipping.

"Who cares?" Mike answered.

"That's her damage deposit gone if not."

"Could you just stick to finding proof that she's a demon?" Mike said.

Joe flipped the next picture in the stack, a rock in the mist. He froze on the next one in the stack.

"Oh my God." It was *The Gates of Hell*, from the restaurant. She'd brought it home.

"What is it?" Mike asked.

"The painting from The Elegant Knife."

"How the hell did she get that?"

"An art thief, eh?" Frank said with interest.

Joe spotted a price tag still stuck to the frame. "No, it looks like she paid three hundred dollars for it."

"Sounds like the seller was the real thief," Frank said, going back to his search.

Mike regarded the picture quizzically. "It looks like a heavy metal album cover."

"It's hell," Joe said.

"It's not that bad."

"No, I mean literal hell. Torture, stabbings, devils, lakes of fire, and—"

"Like I said, a heavy metal album cover." Mike went back to the boxes.

Joe pulled out the picture and held it up in front of his face, scanning over the detail, trying to understand what it was she would have seen in it.

"It's detailed, but it's fucking weird," he said softly. "Guys stabbing people, smoke billowing to the blood red sky, the waves of…"

He trailed off. The slow flowing lava in patterns edging downward. A cry of pain. His eyes darted to the right. A man doubled over in agony with a spear in his gut. Naked, blood poured over his fingers as he looked up at Joe, silently pleading *help me*. The picture was heavy, his hands were getting sweaty. Heat radiated outward. He caught his reflection, hovering in the centre of the glass, fading, then gone. He looked behind him, but instead of seeing the bare walls of Kristin's apartment, he saw a blackened sky and distant mountains bathed in blood.

"Back in line," a voice cried out.

Feeling a prodding in his back, he turned, saw a hideously twisted horned thing jamming a spear into his bare skin. Bare? He wore tattered rags. His ankles were bound with chains. Pulled forward, he fell hard onto the rock floor. Dust filled his nostrils, the smell of sulphur. The spear pierced him deeply in the kidney. He screamed, grabbed at the weapon, felt it three inches inside his body.

"Up, dog. Move," the thing yelled at him in a guttural, dismissive bark.

"How? Where?"

"No questions for the damned," it said again and rammed the spear in deeper.

Joe screamed, feeling the blade slicing up into his lung, cutting off his air. He couldn't breathe. Bulging chest, crackling bones; the spear burst through, erupting in a shower of blood and flesh from his sternum.

He sucked in air, but could only bring in fluid. Panic, gargling blood, clawing at the thing that only laughed at him. *I'm not here. I'm not... help!*

Pulling at the face, his fingers gouging eyes and ripping skin. The monstrous visage torn away, leaving only a bloody skeleton, laughing inhumanly.

"No!" he shouted.

"Relax," Mike said. "It's her money. If she wants to waste it on some shitty picture, she can."

He was back in the room. Nothing had changed. He held the frame in his hands, stared at his own reflection where the skull had been laughing. His skin was intact. He put the painting down and felt along his ribs. They were fine. He took a deep breath. Normal.

"I'm fine," Joe said. "I'm okay."

"And an art critic, too, from the sounds of it," Frank said.

* * * *

With the sweet sugary lollipop melting away in his parched mouth, Frank dug around inside the dark green couch. His fingers brushed over all kinds of things that had fallen between the cushions. You never knew what could slip out of a pocket and get lost down there; in addition to incriminating evidence, you could often pick up a few bucks in the process. So far, he was up a buck twenty-five and a matchbook, but he knew if he kept on digging, he'd find something sinister. He wasn't about to let another demon woman have her way with an unsuspecting man. Once bitten, twice shy; words to live by.

He slid his hand in deeper, through a hole in the back of the couch, right through tattered fabric, down, past his elbow to his shoulder. That was odd, he should be touching floor by now. He touched something sticky. Had this woman let a bunch of food fall in here?

He shoved his head close, reached out, trying to feel what it was. Jelly? Pudding? It felt almost like a membrane. He pressed into it, his finger poking through the thicker shell, finding something softer inside.

Juice?

He retracted his hand, but halfway out something caught. The warm liquid on his hand began spreading upwards from his fingers, to his palm, then up his wrist, slinking along his forearm, higher, higher.

What the fuck?

He tried to jerk his arm back. Stuck. The thing moved past his elbow, slithered up his shirt. Helpless, he felt the liquid inching up his shoulder.

"Little help here, boys."

Pulling, one fast yank before the crawling thing hit his neck. He launched himself backwards, landed hard against an end table, knocked a lamp off. That's when he saw that his arm was gone, eaten away to the bone. He moved his fingers. Brittle white bones moved back.

The lamp behind him shattered to the ground. The sound jerked him around, to see the thing in a million pieces.

"Hey, watch it!" Joe said.

"It's not my fault," Frank said, "it's my…" His arm was back to normal.

The leathery skin, the lines and scars, the swelling of joints from years of overuse. Nothing crawling upwards, no gelatinous ooze. He was holding a partially chewed dog bone. Dried blood caked the rawhide that had fallen inside the couch however long ago.

"I might have found something important, boys," he said.

"What?" Joe asked, looking paler than he had a few moments ago.

"Chew toy. Demons always have one."

"So do dogs," Joe said.

"Did she have a dog?" Mike asked.

"Dan never mentioned anything about one."

"Then I guess we can put this one in the clue category," Frank said.

* * * *

The more books Mike sifted through, the more he found Kristin's reading material skewing towards the arcane. "Why would she need three copies of Dante's Inferno?" Mike asked as he tried to figure out what was different between each one.

"Probably reminds her of home," Frank said.

"Maybe she had a class?" Joe answered.

"A class of evil." Mike flipped through the pages of one. A few were marked with flowing cursive writing.

"I think I took that – the homework was hell," Frank said as he dropped the old dog bone into a plastic bag and went back to digging around inside the couch.

Page after page of notes told him nothing, so Mike moved on. The boxes of books were emptied, their contents spread across the floor.

"Put these into the evidence pile," he said. "I'm going to check her room."

He walked into the bedroom and hit the light switch. Nothing happened.

"Didn't pay your electric bill, eh?"

Something screeched in the darkness.

"*Did* she have a dog?"

He squinted, trying to make out what had made the noise. He took a tentative step forward. The door slammed shut behind him. He spun and grabbed the doorknob. Burning heat seared his palm.

"Fuck!"

241

He wagged his hand in desperation to cool it off. Something hit his head, knocking him off balance.

Wings flapping. A dive bomb, talons across his neck. Feathers brushed his scalp. He covered his head as he was raked on the arms. He dropped to his knees, tried to roll out of the way, but more things attacked him, ripping out huge chunks of flesh, pecking and burrowing their beaks into his body. Searing pain from a thousand bleeding wounds assaulted him.

"No, stop. Don't."

Crawling, he found the door. The handle was cool. An impact against his back, flattening him to the wood. His hand moved in a wide loop, hit the light switch, flicked on the light. He jumped back in shock when he found that he was standing in the open doorway. The room was illuminated in red, and he saw what it was that had attacked him.

"Guys, come quick."

He was joined at the door by Frank and Joe, who looked over his shoulder at the bizarre lighting choice.

"Talk about a red light special."

"What the fuck is that?" Joe pointed.

In a flash Frank had his gun out and aimed at the corner of the room where a large white owl perched on a wooden log that jutted out from the wall. The yellow eyes glowed with savage intelligence.

"Don't anyone move," Mike said, frozen in place, trying to figure out what was going on. "I don't think he saw us." He watched the eyes of the beast for any movement before realizing that it was stuffed. It couldn't have attacked him. Then what did? Did anything?

"Relax," he said. "I think it's dead."

"Let me make sure." Frank started to squeeze the trigger.

"No, no, no!" Mike pushed the pistol away.

"You can never be too careful."

"Gunshots would only bring up too many questions."

"Better that than to have your head scalped by a trained murder owl."

"Do they have those things?" Joe asked.

"You'd be surprised," Frank said grimly, refusing to take his sights off the taxidermized thing.

"It's alright," Mike said, waving them off. "I've got this, I was just, uh, caught a little off guard is all."

He snapped a photo of the owl with his cell phone, trying to forget what he wasn't even sure had just happened. "Would you call this decorating style Satan chic?"

* * * *

Frank stuffed his backup gun away and left the guys in the bedroom. He went back to the mess of boxes. The couch had turned up little, the books another dead end, but there were still so many things inside taped up cardboard cubes that they hadn't examined. He went to work opening.

One was nothing but unmentionables, another assorted pots and pans, another dish towels. He was getting antsy. Where were the severed heads, the shrunken limbs, the vials of blood, the books bound in human flesh?

"Come on, girlie, show old Frank where you've got the bodies..."

He looked at the box marked with the fine china and rubbed his chin in thought. "If I were incriminating evidence, I'd probably hide somewhere no one suspected." He grabbed the tape.

* * * *

Joe opened a box labeled 'scrapbooks.' Inside, he found bright covers decorated with glitter, ribbons, cut out shapes and odd symbols. "The whole box is full," he said. "It looks like she's been into this for a long time."

The others weren't paying attention.

Digging deeper, he found one book dating all the way back to the mid nineties with the writing inside that of a small child. She'd drawn pictures of herself, her family, pasted toy ads from magazines and affixed photos inside. He found a list of her favourite foods, favourite songs, names for future children.

"Seems like she was pretty normal." He flipped more pages.

He found a tiny piece of newspaper glued to one page: a black and white photograph of a child with a block of text. He read it aloud, "Tragically Ewen Rochester was taken from his family... Holy shit. It's an obituary."

He read the story, a small child that had drowned in a pool at a birthday party. The kid looked so innocent, even processed through decades old newsprint. A crooked grin, bright eyes, messy mop of hair swaying as if—

"Underwater?"

The image wavered, blurred, as if it was moving. No, as if he was looking up, from underwater, seeing the boy looking down at him from the edge of a pool. The kid pointed, mouthed something muffled.

"What?"

Pointing excitedly, he ran away.

244

"Hey, where are you going?"

Fluid in his lungs. Gagging. *Air. Need air. Get to the surface.* He tried to move his legs, kick off from the bottom of the pool, but he was dead weight. The sun glared overhead. He tried to shout, could only gargle. The world began to go black. He reached up, begging the boy to come back.

The sharp intake of a desperately needed breath jogged him back to the present where he was still looking at the newsprint obituary glued on the page.

"Daydreaming?" He rubbed his hand over the back of his neck. A trickle of water dripped down from his hair. He caught the whiff of—

"Chlorine?"

He slammed the book shut and threw it to the side.

"Fucking hell."

There were still more scrapbooks to look through. He hesitated. He put the first one back into the box and shut the lid. He took a deep breath and grabbed the next one on the pile. More confident writing on the cover, more elaborate decorations; she would have been older when she made this one.

He slowed his breathing and looked inside. School assignments, animal drawings, small books made for a child, photos of a freckle-faced girl he assumed must be Kristin.

"So far, so normal."

He turned the page to see a polaroid picture of a small blond boy wearing a Power Rangers shirt.

"Who's this?"

He turned the page again. His mouth dropped. Another obituary pasted in the centre.

"Child dies in house fire..."

245

He stared at the face in the photo wondering how it had happened when a thin line of smoke drifted up from the picture, towards him, reaching out like a—

He slammed the book shut and threw it in the box with the other one.

"Fuck no. I'm not going through that shit again."

* * * *

Keeping one eye on the owl, Mike pulled open the drawers of Kristin's nightstand. Then he looked under the bed. Finding only a lone sock, he stood back up and looked around the room."Where would I—"

Movement. Someone was in the bed, under the sheets, writhing around. Not one, two. Touching each other, the outlines of their hands sliding down and around the clinging sheets that obscured them.

"Who?" His words faded out as the two forms stopped and turned to look at him. Smooth profiles of what appeared to be living mannequins under Kristin's sheets. They sat up. He backed away a step. They watched.

He tentatively clasped the edge of the sheet. The two things under the covers didn't budge. His heart pounded in his chest. Why didn't he just run the fuck away? Because he had to know what was underneath.

He jerked the sheets as hard as he could with a scream, tossing the fabric over to the corner of the room. Nothing but a clean mattress.

"Dude?" Joe called from the other room. "You—"

"I was just, uh, thinking about how little use this bed must get."

The mattress was spotless. No blood or other stains. He lifted it up and examined the box spring. More nothing. "I need a black light to be sure..."

He dropped the mattress down and looked around the turned over bedroom. "Where is she hiding the evidence?"

The closet. It was the only place he hadn't checked. The shut doors beckoned him.

"It's got to be in there."

He pulled on the handles.

* * * *

Frank dug through the box of china, but all he could find were dishes and plates wrapped in bubble wrap. "There has to be something in here." He tossed a plate over his shoulder. Then another went flying. Cups, saucers, a sugar bowl.

He froze on a creamer, noticing the design on the trim of the china. Fancy, intricate lines of brightly coloured shapes. No, not shapes, people, bent in all kinds of weird positions, moving. Moving? How could they be... no. They weren't moving, they were fornicating.

He stared in awe as the tiny people on the edges of the plates thrust and rode each other like bulls.

"Great Gatsby..."

They stopped. Tiny sketches of penises quivered in the white space of the plate. As one the figures stepped out, off the edge, down to the centre of the creamer, moving in a legion of naked paintings of mini-people.

He threw the thing into the wall, and it exploded.

"Whoa," Joe said, looking up. "What are you doing?"

"I, uh... saw a cockroach," Frank said.

"On the wall or on the china?"

More of the tiny things marched forward on the next plate down, nearing the edge of the box. He threw that one like a frisbee. Joe ducked as it whizzed past his head.

"Oh shit!"

Frank looked in the box at the rest of the china. Hundreds of those tiny nude figures, expanding. He could see their glowing red eyes.

"Fuck this," he yelled and started lobbing them over his shoulder in waves.

* * * *

"Hey! Watch the—" Joe shouted as the plates flew in the air.

He dropped the scrapbook in his hand and lunged to catch a flying plate Frank had flung before it hit the ground and shattered. He latched on just in time. It was as light as a feather, off white with an intricate floral pattern painted on.

Frank threw the next one in the air, and he leapt for it, too.

* * * *

"You need to come see what I found," Mike said, walking out of the bedroom. A plate flew at his face. He ducked in the nick of time as it whizzed by and landed on the bed in the other room. "What the hell?"

"Nothing's stopping the little naked people." Frank threw plates and cups over his head. "They just keep coming."

Joe scrambled, trying desperately to catch all the china Frank was throwing around the room.

"Little help here," he said, his arms filling.

Mike ran to join in, grabbing a teapot just before it smacked the floor.

"God damn you, naked people, leave me alone!"

They moved like lightning and somehow, between the two of them, they were able to catch everything Frank threw.

"I'll bet there are more in this one," he said and moved to the next box.

"No! Stop!" they cried out in unison.

* * * *

Frank looked up to see both of the kids holding stacks of plates and bowls like French waiters. "Whatsamatter with you two? Going to a tea party?"

"What the hell are you doing?"

"Isn't it obvious? I'm trying to stop the tiny naked people from escaping the plates."

"The what?" Joe asked.

"There's still three more boxes of that china stuff to check through, I've—"

"You were seeing something," Joe said as he placed his stack carefully on the ground. "See?" He held up a plate. "No tiny naked people anywhere."

"Look again, smart guy," Frank said.

Joe examined the plate. He seemed taken aback when he realized what the pattern on it actually was. "Okay, so there are tiny naked people. That's an... odd china pattern but—"

"Guys, the plates aren't important. What I found in the bedroom closet is," Mike said.

"Live naked people?" Frank asked.

"Something much worse." Mike waved them towards the

bedroom.

"Just give me a minute." Frank grabbed the tape on another box. "I want to check through this other box."

"Just get in here," Mike said. "That stuff can wait."

Frank followed. The two guys stood facing the closet. He looked over their shoulders to see that the narrow space had been converted into a makeshift shrine with a small altar. A photo of a bespectacled man rested on top.

"That the guy?" he asked.

"That's Dan," Joe said.

He looked normal. Dark hair, all his teeth, brown eyes. His photo was in the place of honour on the strange platform. Surrounded by burning candles, symbols drawn on the walls, and a small bowl filled with red liquid in front of the photograph.

Frank dipped his fingers in the viscous fluid and tasted it. "Pig's blood."

"How the hell do you know what pig's blood tastes like?" Joe asked.

"It's part of the job," Frank said.

A gently pulsing wave of frost seemed to radiate outwards despite the burning candles and cramped interior of the closet. Their breaths fogged in front of them.

"This is just fucking strange," Joe said.

"It's like nothing I've seen before," Mike said. "Except maybe in one of your fucked-up Italian horror movies."

"Why would she have this?" Joe asked.

"He packing heavy sausage?" Frank asked. "Guy I knew in, let's just say top secret circumstances, had what the ladies might call heavy—"

"Yeah, we get it, but what's that got to do with anything?"

Joe asked.

"Well, after a night with him he left this one girl so obsessed that she tried this voodoo thing to make him come back for round two."

"What did she do?" Joe asked.

"Besides give him VD? That's why he wasn't interested, by the way. That girl had more crabs than Red Lobster."

"No," Mike said. "Did she try to kill him? Mind fuck him with voodoo?"

Frank laughed. "If anything, he mind fucked her. But he also fucked her. Which is why he got VD in the first place."

"What the hell is the point of this story?" Joe asked.

"The point is, a woman scorned often turns to voodoo if she's predisposed to that sort of thing. And this looks just like that sort of thing."

"You see, Joe?" Mike said. "Even Frank thinks she's doing some kind of dark magic, demon stuff, or whatever the fuck it is."

Joe looked like he was trying to figure out just what rational explanation there could even be for this whole scene. There didn't seem to be one. The kid had to learn that not everything had one either.

"It's also one hell of a fire hazard to leave candles burning like that." Frank picked one up to blow it out.

"Was I right or was I right?"

"Certainly looking that way," Joe said.

"Does this not sell my theory that she's up to no good? Demon no good."

"Bad taste in china, too." Frank blew out the candle.

"You both need to see what I found," Joe said. "It's just as bad as whatever the hell this is."

Joe handed a scrapbook each to Frank and Mike. "Take a look inside."

Frank flipped through the pages. "Great Gatsby, the woman is a hell fiend." He turned the book to show them a picture of teenage Kristin in a red cape and fake horns with her eyes glowing red.

"That's Halloween, keep going," Joe said.

"There's more?"

Mike blanched as he read through his book. "You're right, this *is* way worse. She was dating a guy named Chet in Junior High." Mike showed them both an obituary pasted onto a page. "Says he died of alcohol poisoning at a hockey team rookie party."

"And that's not all," Joe said, pointing back to the other room with his thumb. "She's got a whole stack of scrapbooks with a whole stack of dead men inside."

"How the fuck did she fit a corpse in one of these things?" Frank asked, flipping through the pages, looking for the body the others had found.

"Not actual bodies, Frank," Joe said. "Obituaries. From guys she knew in the past. I counted. Combined with the ones we knew about on Facebook, there's seven dead exes."

"Seven?" Mike said in shock. "She's some kind of serial killer."

"And Dan is next."

Frank skimmed the rest of the book, but all he found were photos and glitter embellishments.

"So," Mike asked. "Do you think we have enough proof to go to him with yet?"

Frank tapped the picture of Kristin in the devil's costume. "Uh, hello?"

Joe frowned. "I'm not sure. Would it do any good? If he's really under her spell, it might not matter what we come to him with, he could dismiss us as crazy, or tell us to fuck off and never speak to him again."

"We can't just let her win," Mike said. "Not when we have so much goddamned evidence."

"If your friend is under the spell of a demon woman, he won't hear anything you say. He'll just think you've got sour grapes," Frank said. "He'll say shit like, 'Frank, you just can't handle that I'm settling down. I'm not able to get blasted drunk every night with the guys, I can't go down to the Five Hundred Club and dance with that cigarette girl anymore. You'll have to find another chum to order fifty Alicia's pierogies at two in the morning with before you wander home pissed out of your head singing Johnny Dagon songs,' well, not those anymore... something more like Sinatra or Burton, but you get the idea. He'll be all, why can't you be happy for me, Malone? Why do you have to be such a—"

"Is there something you need to get off your chest, Frank?" Joe asked.

"Me? Of course not. I'm just trying to tell you, your friend is probably so deep in her spell that he won't even know what he's saying anymore. You have to break it first."

"How do we break the spell?" Mike asked.

Frank took one last look at the devil girl's photo and slammed the scrapbook shut. "The only way to break crazy is with crazy. And I know just the guy. But if we're done here, let's get all this stuff moved to the condo before she starts to get suspicious."

CHAPTER TWENTY-EIGHT: CLOSING THE WEB

"The dark one seems ravenous lately." They moved down the dimly lit hall towards the closed door where it waited.

"Demands increase with each passing day," the other thrall replied. "Sustenance is becoming more difficult to acquire."

His rotting face betrayed no signs of any emotion. They were both beyond annoyance or impatience. His cloak was pulled back, showing greying flesh, a gaping wound near the jawline, and solid white eyes that were not as blind as they appeared. An insect scurried from a hiding spot at the back of his head.

"The transformation approaches."

"I can feel the dark energies gathering."

A bit of skin fell from his temple to land on the cold concrete. "I can, too."

"Are there suspicions?"

"Some."

"Do we have orders to—"

The door to the sanctuary opened and they were both cowed by the presence of the dark form, invisible within the inky negative space. They knew they were being judged by one who could destroy them with but a thought.

"There are none that can stop what is in motion," it said.

"Of course, oh dark one, we merely—"

"Chatter incessantly."

She bowed low. Even the presence of the dark one was too much. It only served to remind her of all that she'd lost. She should not have such thoughts. At least not where they might be sensed.

"Forgive us, lord." The other thrall dropped his head even lower. "We merely wish to serve."

"Have your brought what was asked?"

"Indeed." The other thrall motioned to her. She opened the folds of her robe to reveal, clasped in her greying hand, dangling from the legs, a still form. Red with birth blood, life never given the chance at what she'd lost.

"A husk," the dark one said flatly.

"We had to take what—"

Impossibly fast the tiny corpse was pulled from her hands and sucked into the stygian space. Neither one had seen a thing. They shared a panicked glance.

"It won't provide much. But it will do. For now."

Her companion thrall bowed again. "We will get another."

"It must live."

"Of course," she said.

"Was there anything else you wished?" he asked.

Silence.

The thought of what went on in that chamber would have sent a chill through her body were she still alive. A tiny voice at the back of her mind cried out, but the words were like a whisper at the edges of her thoughts.

"Perhaps there is," the dark one said.

CHAPTER TWENY-NINE: DIVINE INTERVENTION

"Listen to this," Joe said. "St. Lucia's is not only the oldest building in River City, it pre-dates the city itself."

"How does that make sense?" Mike asked.

"It came from France."

"Of course it did," Frank said dismissively as he drove.

"Taken apart brick by brick and shipped first to Quebec, the components were brought over before the railway had been finished."

"How'd they do it then?" Mike asked.

"According to Wikipedia, in boats portaged down the river."

"I'll bet that was an arduous and time-consuming process."

"Kind of like this conversation," Frank said.

Joe kept reading from his phone. "The entire church had been painstakingly rebuilt to be the cornerstone of the city as it grew from wild frontier town into bustling metropolis."

"And now it's probably only used for weddings, film shoots, and maybe the occasional historical tour."

"If you two are done with this needless exposition dump, you might want to look out the front window," Frank said.

"Why?"

"Because we're here."

He'd parked the car in front of the moss-covered grey brick cathedral. Just like the article said, it was a masterpiece of old-world gothic architecture. The three of them stepped out into the night. Two floodlights illuminated the great arched front. The exact image seen on postcards sold in River City souvenir shops. Frank took a deep breath of the crisp downtown air. "Smell that, boys?" he asked.

"Urine?" Joe said.

"Cigarette smoke?" Mike added.

"The smell of a living city. The smoke is the breath of industry moving the gears of progress and the urine is the leaking fluid of society that drips out from the dangling dick of the country. You can't have one without the other. For every action there is a reaction, and for every law-abiding citizen there's a gutter dwelling criminal out there waiting to prey on them."

"Really?" Joe asked. "Those numbers don't add up at all. I'd always thought that crime was going down as a percen—"

"You can't believe the news rags, kid, and the TV is full of crackpots. The only thing you can trust is a man who's seen it all from the ground floor." He waved his hands around at the city that surrounded them. "I could tell you the names of all the Pollacks who built these buildings, the Ukrainians who laid the brick, the Irish that did the electrical, the Scots that put up the drywall, the Brits that laid the carpet, the—"

"Who built the church then?" Joe asked, interrupting Frank's train of thought.

"How the fuck would I know? What am I, two hundred?"

"We're here for a reason, right?" Mike asked, looking at the old building skeptically. "You said you knew a guy who could help us?"

"He's not just a guy, he's—"

* * * *

"Father O'Hoolahan at your service," the impossibly old, prune-faced man in the priest's garb said. He held out his weathered hand to Joe and Mike. "Malone here tells me you've got a problem with one of Satan's henchmen, or rather, hench-women."

"You believe us?" Mike shook the man's clammy hand.

"Without a doubt," the man said with a faint Irish brogue.

Mike caught the overwhelming aroma of alcohol. The man's eyes were glassed over, his teeth yellowed, his fingers jittery. Either the guy was falling apart from age, or he was drunk. His clothes were old and worn, more grey and yellow than black and white. He swayed slightly in place, as if he might fall over at any moment.

"How much did Frank tell you?" Joe asked.

"Enough to know what it is you're dealing with."

"Great, so?"

Father O'Hoolahan motioned for them to follow him over to the pews of the church. The arched ceiling above them stretched up to a great stained-glass skylight of Jesus on the Cross. The wooden beams converged to a point on either side. The faded plaster walls and dark wood trim, intricately carved in relief, were marked with the grain of a thousand years of history. The delicate pews were worn from countless use. The entire room seemed to hum serenely of its own accord. A peaceful silence overtook them as they sat.

Joe tapped Mike on the shoulder. "I'm pretty sure that guy's hammered," he whispered.

"Communion wine?"

Frank sat down last. "How've you been handling things, Father?"

"Oh, you know, we're not all that busy these days, but I keep myself going with the little things. Why, just the other morning I was down in the cellar making sure the communion wine was fit to serve and I got to thinking that it'd be a good time to have someone fix that rickety back door. I called up old Julio, the man I usually call for these things, but you see, he wasn't home. So I spoke to his wife and she said, oh no, Father O'Hoolahan, Julio has gone to the lord. Which I took to mean he had died and left me unawares, but as it turned out I simply misunderstood her, on account of her thick accent and she, in fact, said that he had gone to the store. Then I asked when he'd be back and she said, why sorry, Father O'Hoolahan, but I just don't know. You see he had to pick up quite a few things and then stop at the Home Depot for a new saw or some such tool. Then I asked her if I could leave a message but..."

Frank seemed to hang on every word, but Joe and Mike just stared at each other in shock as the man rambled on for a solid five minutes. When he was all done, Frank tapped him on the shoulder. "Good to hear you're keeping busy doing the Lord's work. Now we've come here on urgent business."

"So you said," Father O'Hoolahan said solemnly.

"Our best friend is being lured by a demon. She's got him under some kind of mind control, taken over his life, changed his name, his hair, his hobbies. Now they're moving in together. And he looks awful – we're pretty sure she's draining his life force."

"Like the movie Lifeforce? Is she... naked?"

"No," Mike said. "That's the worst part."

"No," Joe interrupted. "The worst part is that we think she's planning on killing him. We have reason to believe she's done this at least seven times before."

"Lilith herself," the old man gasped.

"Her name is Kristin," Mike said.

Joe sighed heavily, as if he was debating a controversial topic internally. "We've also seen things."

"Shit, I've seen some things, too," Frank said. "Have you ever seen a fish that walks like a man but—"

"Not like that," Joe said. "I was talking about the red eyes, the shadows, wings and a tail—"

"The painting, the scrapbooks, the altar..." Mike continued.

"Go on," the priest said.

"I've tried to explain them in a million ways, fever dreams, drunken hallucinations, contact highs, nothing does it. They were real, I'm sure—"

"The fish men were, too," Frank said, pouting.

"Visions of hell, a painting come to life, the deaths of people in the scrapbooks as if I was there myself—"

"Living owls, time vortexes, torture," Mike added.

"Demons can weave spells on those around them," Father O'Hoolahan said.

"She wasn't even there half the time," Joe said.

"The things touched by a demon can themselves become possessed with evil."

"So is there nothing safe from her... evil?" Mike asked.

"Not anymore." Father O'Hoolahan patted them paternally on the shoulders. "You've come to the right place, my friends."

"You've seen this before?" Joe asked.

"Absolutely. I've been in this world for many years, more than Malone even, and in that time I've seen many a thing. Why, one time I saw this little person dressed up in a child's costume dancing on the pier for nickels and this man in a woman's costume pushing a pram came along and—"

Frank whispered to them behind his hand, "The man's a legend."

"—and the policeman said, 'Who here's seen the woman with the beard?' So I raised my hand, but you see I was just a little boy then and no one could notice me through the crowd, but I raised it regardless and, well, fortune shone down on me that day because he saw me and called out, 'You there, boy. What did you see?' So I stepped to the front of the crowd and pulled myself up to my full haunches and said proudly—"

Mike whispered back as Father O'Hoolahan continued to ramble, "Where's this story going?"

Frank whispered, "Damned if I know."

"—so the man said, 'Thank you, boy, you just might have saved Christmas for a hundred orphans throughout the River Valley.' And, you know, that made me really proud to hear, so much so that I didn't notice the carriage barreling down on me from the south side trolly tracks—"

Joe whispered now, Father O'Hoolahan unaware of their conversation as he spoke, "Do we interrupt him?"

"I wouldn't," Frank said, shaking his head. "He has a tendency to start over."

"We just let him go on?"

"Yup."

Ten minutes later, Father O'Hoolahan was done and looked to the three of them as if he'd just realized they were there. "So, what was it you needed?"

261

"A way to save our friend from a demon succubus!"

Father O'Hoolahan clasped his hands together. "Grave tidings. Most grave tidings. I haven't dealt with a case like this in... oh, fifty-three years. That one was a real pickle, back in the fifties, it was, and the girl was an American, I believe, up here for the exhibition. A group of men came to me much like you yourselves are and said, 'Father O'Hoolahan, we need your help saving our friend from a demon who's out to suck more than just his soul away—'"

This time, Mike had no patience to let the man talk and interrupted him, "Okay, okay, we get it. Just tell us what to do?"

Father O'Hoolahan blinked, came back to reality like he'd been asleep and swayed in place. "Yes, the demon woman. The lure of the succubus is strong and not easily defeated. Getting the man away from her charms isn't enough. Her spell can transcend geography, time and space. You have to sever her power to truly free him."

"We have to kill her?" Joe said in shock.

Father O'Hoolahan shook his head gravely. "My boy, you wouldn't have the first idea how. Only the power of the lord can defeat a demon like her."

"So, then you have to kill her?" Mike asked.

"I'm afraid my demon killing days are done."

"So, then I have to kill her." Frank stood up.

Father O'Hoolahan grabbed Frank's sleeve. "Even you, Malone, are not righteous enough to slay the demon. I'm afraid that only a true warrior of God can do that."

"Where do we find one?"

Father O'Hoolahan pointed to himself and beamed proudly.

"But I thought you said you were too old to kill her?" Mike

said.

"Fuck you, I'm not old."

"But you—"

"I said my demon killing days are done because it's fucking ten o'clock already. It's past my bedtime. Tomorrow we can do it."

"Great, so then just come with us tomorrow and we'll take her out," Mike said.

Father O'Hoolahan chuckled. "I'm afraid killing her won't stop the curse. For, you see, her power transcends even death."

"Then what the hell do we do?"

"You have to break her spell first, free him from her control, then, when he sees her for what she truly is, then and only then can she be sent back to hell forever."

"How do we do that?" Mike shouted impatiently.

Father O'Hoolahan rubbed his chin. "You should show him all the things that she has taken away from him, the ruin she has done to his life, good things turned bad. When he realizes the sway she's held over him, if the lord wills it, he should be able to break the hold."

Frank pounded his fist into his open palm. "Great, so we take him out for strippers and beer and he's home free."

"It might not be that simple," Father O'Hoolahan said. "What was it that he most loved to do and can no longer do because of her?"

Joe and Mike each looked at the other, each knowing exactly what it was. Almost in unison they said, "Goldeneye."

"We get him to stream his favourite game and it frees him from her influence?" Joe asked.

"That seems a little too easy."

"You'll only free him, boys," the old priest said. "You'll still have to kill her."

"That's where I come in," Frank said proudly.

CHAPTER THIRTY: REMEMBER YOUR LIFE

"Alright, he's on his way, is everything ready?"

Joe checked over the camera and microphones. They were all in working order. "The stream is set. I've put out the word to the viewers, I've ordered the pizza, and beer is in the fridge."

"The stripper?"

"I left that up to Frank."

"You invited *him*?" Mike asked incredulously.

"He seemed really disappointed that he wasn't going to get to shoot anything, so I told him he could help."

"I'm not sure that guy's playing with a full deck."

"Considering what we're about to try to do, I sometimes wonder if we are."

Mike checked his hair in the mirror. "You heard the priest, we have to break her spell."

"I know, I know, it's just that if you asked me a few months ago if I ever thought something like this would happen, or even *could* happen, I would have laughed in your face. Succubus. Shit, it all seemed so simple then, the three of us, the show, none of this horror movie science fiction bullshit."

Mike put a hand on Joe's shoulder solemnly. "We totally had

the perfect lives. Work, streaming, minor internet celebrity."

"I wouldn't say that my job was perfect. Marlena is a handful."

"UPS is no picnic either. That's not the point."

"So, what is the point? I'm lost already."

"The point is we had jobs that paid the bills and allowed us to do what we were put on earth to do."

"Stream video games for a faceless audience?"

"You *could* call it that. I call it engaging in the scholarly pursuits of pop culture. Becoming the masters of all things designed to entertain us and sharing that expertise with other likeminded souls. But that woman messed it all up. Worse than the others."

"Yeah, none of them were eating his soul. At least, I don't think so."

"She's turned him against his own past, made him forget our mission to keep doing exactly what we've been doing as long as we can. And she wants to drain his life force with demon power."

"Allegedly."

"Would you stop with that? You've seen shit. I've seen shit. That drunk priest's seen shit. Even Frank has seen shit. This isn't fiction anymore. You can't put your head in the sand. If we don't do something to stop her, then it really is all over for him, us, the show, maybe even the world."

"Let's not get ahead of ourselves here."

Mike patted away a wrinkle in his collared shirt. "We don't know what her endgame is. We have to assume that since she's a demon, it's nothing good."

"I guess that does kind of make sense. In a I-can't-believe-any-of-this-is-happening way. But is *Goldeneye* enough?"

Mike smiled. "Come on, what guy would walk away from a night of pizza and beer with his buds, playing his favourite game, and getting a private show from a—"

"You call this a burlesque house?" a voice interrupted him.

They turned to see Frank standing in the open doorway with a woman in a high collared, vintage beaver fur coat. She looked impossibly old, her face resembling a painted raisin.

"Finally! I was worried you weren't going to make it," Mike said.

"I had to circle the block three times to find a parking spot," Frank said.

"Is that your date?"

The fur coat was so large that it completely obscured the woman's figure. Mike could just see the points of heels jutting below where the coat nearly reached the floor.

"Date? Hell no, this is Southside Annie, the best go-go girl this side of the Mississippi," Frank said.

"Her? But she's so…"

"Experienced," the woman interrupted in a deep-throated smoker's wheeze. "Now if this is a five and tenner then I get paid fifty upfront, but if you're looking for the full merry-go-round then I want a hundred. That'll get you a ride on the carousel, but any more and it's another twenty." She walked into the room with complete confidence, looking at the books and movies and games. "Where's the cage? The catwalk? The donkey plank?"

"This is an apartment," Joe said. "We don't have any of those things."

She shrugged and opened up her coat. "I've worked with worse."

"Southside Annie here is the best of the best," Frank said,

joining Mike on the couch. "She's swung more tassels than a shriners' convention in a tornado. I saw her dance for Deef the Chief in Cold Lake the night that Kennedy was shot and let me tell you something, that was a night to remember and not because of the news."

The woman shucked off the fur coat and threw it down the hall towards the bedrooms. Mike blanched to see that she was wearing thigh-high boots with garters, black underwear, and nipple tassels. She was bone white, wrinkled, partially deflated but clearly a woman who'd once been a stacked, statuesque show-off. Parts of her sagged in conflicting directions, but she looked like an old pro and moved with a fluidity that belied her age. She spun her breasts a few times to get the handle of the tassels and Mike's eyes circled around and around, hypnotized.

"Hey, hey, hey, Annie, hold the show, the guest of honour isn't here yet." Frank picked up the coat and slung it back over her shoulders. He turned to them. "Where should I stash her, boys?"

"Uh, you can use my bedroom," Joe said as Mike seemed frozen in place, head still circling around and around, unable to answer. "Down the hall on the left."

Frank led the woman away.

* * * *

"Where does he find these people?" Joe asked. He flipped open the laptop to see a chat room quickly filling up with regulars. With the two geriatrics gone, the party room was almost set. The entertainment was here, all they needed now was the guest of honour.

"Has Dan texted yet?"

Mike just stared open mouthed at nothing. Joe could swear he could see after images of the spinning tassels burned in his retinas.

"Earth to Mike." He snapped his fingers in front of the man's face.

"What? Huh, oh, sorry. I, uh, wait, what's going on?" Mike blinked and looked around the room like he was confused as to how he got there.

"Dan, any word?"

Mike dug out his cellphone. "There's a text. Says he's on his way and he's bringing a—"

The door opening interrupted Mike's words.

"Hey guys, I'm here."

The two of them watched Dan walk in with a tall, lanky man with large, rounded glasses who wore a sweater over a bright blue collared shirt. He stopped in the doorway as Dan hung his coat up. The man coughed once, and Dan shook his head as if he'd forgotten he was there. "Oh yeah, this is Harry, Kristin's brother."

"Hello, gentlemen, a fine abode you have here."

"Apartment," Mike said, frowning. "It's an apartment."

Harry laughed. "Well, there's no place like home, is there?"

Mike turned to Joe with the fury of a thousand suns written on his face. He could understand how he felt. Harry instantly gave an impression of hubris. He spoke with an accent that had to be put on. Kristin didn't have one. A hipster, exactly the kind of person they'd both avoided like the plague.

"I figured with Harry we have four people to play Golden-eye," Dan said.

"It sounds like a fascinating enterprise," Harry said.

269

"And it is a night to celebrate, after all," Dan said, grinning.

"That's right." Harry threw his arm over Dan's shoulder. "It's not every night I get to fete the arrival of a new brother-in-law!"

"Wait, wait, wait," Mike said as he picked up a beer. "I thought you said Kristin moved here from Vancouver? Alone. So, then, why in the heck is her brother here, too?"

"Visiting my good man. Like any brother, I do occasionally feel lonesome for family. One quick plane ride over the majestic Rockies and the vast plains of Saskatchewan. Nothing could stand in my way on my quest to be at her side to receive the amazing news of her impending nuptials to this fine gentleman here!"

He hugged Dan in close.

"Okay, what the fuck did you just say?" Mike asked, confused.

"Uh, he says Dan and Kristin are getting married," Joe said.

In a great stream of brown liquid, Mike spat out a mouthful of beer all over the carpet in shock. "Holy shit! Married?"

"Would you stop doing that! You don't have to do a spit take every time someone gives you shocking news."

"Maybe you don't," Mike said before turning back to Dan and Harry.

Harry slung his coat on a hanger and Dan placed it in the closet.

"What in the actual hell? When did this happen? And when is the whole wedding thing going to take place? And what the fucking shit, man? We find out from her brother?"

Dan took a place on the recliner next to the couch, letting Harry have the seat between Mike and Joe. They both recoiled as the man plopped down in the groove that had been worn in by Dan's larger frame. He didn't fill it.

"Kristin thought we shouldn't wait any longer. When two people know they're right for each other everything just kind of fits, you know? I can't see myself with anyone but her and she feels the same way, so why put it off? She's moved in, we both want to have kids at some point. There's no point beating around the bush, right?"

"Not anymore, clearly," Joe said.

"That's it? You move out, get engaged, and start wedding planning? All in a matter of a few months?"

Dan nodded enthusiastically, as if it was all the most normal thing in the world. "It all seems like a crazy dream, but it's true!"

"When's the ceremony?" Joe asked.

"Four weeks."

"Four weeks! Holy shit again!"

Harry put his arms around Joe and Mike, hugging them in tight. "I'm as happy as you are!"

"Why so fast?" Mike recoiled from Harry's arm as if it were made of snot.

"We found a last-minute cancellation for an absolutely amazing venue. We're not religious so we don't need a church. It might be tight trying to get all the preparations in order, but she's really organized and I'm sure she can get it all together. Flowers, decorations, you know, all the stuff that goes into a wedding."

"Do I ever!" Harry said, beaming.

Mike looked over Harry's shoulder to Joe and mouthed, "No church?"

"Demon," Joe mouthed silently back.

"What's more amazing is that Harry has agreed to be my

best man," Dan said proudly. "I can't imagine anyone I'd rather have beside me on that special day."

"Hey," Mike said. "I've known you since we were five years old."

"And me since we were six," Joe added.

"Don't worry," Dan said, "you guys'll both be there, plus one of course."

"Then tonight…" Mike trailed off, deflated.

"Is now officially a bachelor party!" Harry clapped his hands in excitement. "Now I understand that you fellows like to play the odd video game?"

CHAPTER THIRTY-ONE: DO NOT GIVE UP

FavreauForLife420: That was an epic blowout.

WhosJohnnyRock: You think that's it for Three Gamers?

Cwood4Real: Could you blame Dan if it was?

TheMack420: They should just get that Harry guy to replace him.

GertrudeBeerStein: He kicked all their asses.

YourNiNight420: Embarrassing really, but it started so innocently.

GOKUBoy316: *posted a video*

Focus locked on the television, flashes of gunfire on their faces, the four of them frantically tapping on their N64 controllers. "You must have missed this a little bit, right, Dan?" Mike said.

"It has been a while," Dan said.

"How many times did we do this back in the day?" Joe asked.

PING.

"WhosJohnnyRock guesses a thousand," Joe read. "Sorry, WhosJohnnyRock, you're underestimating how little we went out in junior high."

Cwood4Real: The calm before the storm

ECWMikeyFan: All downhill from there.

FrankieGoestoHollyOaks222: You should put that in B & W with sappy music.

TheDoorsMan: Tell me you made one of Harry smoking their asses.

GOKUBOY316: Of course! :) *posted a video*

"Bang, headshot, Evans!" Mike cackled with glee.

"Oh, ho, ho, a fine aim you have there, but watch out for he who comes from behind!" Harry said.

Three shots later and Mike's quarter screen filled with blood. He looked over at the whiteboard. Harry was kicking all their asses.

"Joe?" he said.

"It ain't over yet," Joe said nervously.

"Revenge is a dish best served cold," Harry said.

PING.

"GOKUBOY316 says he's already making a compilation of how many times you've died tonight," Dan said.

"Hold off on that one, GokuBoy," Mike said. "I've got some tricks left."

"I thought you were experts at this particular cartridge?" Harry said as he killed Joe again.

"You guys are getting your butts kicked," Dan said.

"Dude, time to step it up," Mike said. "Get serious. Use teamwork."

"You do know he can see our screens," Joe said, dying again.

"We know this level. Form up!"

A montage of gameplay clips showed Mike and Joe working

together. When Mike's avatar turned a corner, Joe would cover his rear. When Joe sniped, Mike would guard him. They blasted anything in sight and the kill numbers rose. It wasn't enough. Harry was some kind of Goldeneye savant, and he picked up their strategies in an instant, racking up kills.

"Goddamn this fucking stupid old game needing one TV for four fucking people!" Mike shouted over more images of him dying.

One kill, two, three. The time in the round counted down: three, two, one. Game over. They'd lost.

"Ho, ho! A rousing game!" Harry said.

GREATBonkers378: "That NOOB had skillz!

GertrudeBeerStein: "Nah, Mike blows at this game."

BladeRunner246: Three Gamers should be called Three LAMErs LOL ROTFL"

FavreauForLife420: "Dudes did step up!"

TMNTComicsLuVR: "I thought for a second there was a comeback for the ages on the way."

Canucklehead420: Nope, they just got p0wned.

GOKUBOY316: *posted a video*

Mike stood at the fridge. "Anyone want a brew?"

"I'd love some refreshment. I'm quite parched after that vigorous electronic contest."

Mike tossed a can to Harry who caught it one-handed. Mike stared at him, popped the top off his own can and pounded half of it back before belching loudly. In split screen, Harry popped his own beer can top and drank the whole thing in one gulp. He then belched even louder, squished the can

275

into a flat pancake against the side of his head, and deposited it on the coffee table like it was a coaster.

'Flawless victory' text effect appeared under a freeze frame of Harry's face.

RichardtheLianHeart265: Nice one!

YourNiNight420: Who would have thought that skinny dude could pound it back like that?

Cwood4Real: Chugging a beer isn't as attractive as you guys think it is.

GertrudeBeerStein: But chugging a beer then kicking their asses in Mario Party is!

GOKUBOY316: posted a video

"How about we go full Mario Party on this bachelor party?" Mike said, holding up a handful of Wiimotes, dangling from their wrist straps like dead weasels. "Full waggle?"

"My grandmother has one of those in her retirement home," Harry said.

A fast cut of the guys in hyper speed, moving their Wiimotes, gesticulating in blurred motions, the footage from the game shown in five hundred times speed. Mike's screams sounded like lost Chipmunk albums while Harry dominated them in almost every waggling minigame. Mike's frustration grew, animated steam shot out of his head, finally it exploded in a primitive plug-in special effect, freeze-framing on his photoshopped headless corpse.

PaçoPoosDay: Lol Good one!

MOTUCLASSIC4EVER: You could see him about to explode!

276

TheMack420: Yeah, that's the joke.

GertrudeBeerStein: How long that take you?

GOKUBOY316: Check this one. *posted a video*

"See if you can handle old school, sixty-four bits of Mega power." Mike held up the original Mario Party N64 cartridge.

"SAUcyGAL245 thinks I'm going to win here, too," Harry said, reading the screen. "Thanks for the vote of confidence SAUcyGAL245." He waved to the camera.

"He's picking this up pretty fast, eh, guys?" Dan offered.

The screen cascaded into a divided shot, in each small square a different image of Mike losing it: fuming, his face turning red, screaming, close-ups of his hands spinning the joysticks on the three-pronged controllers, his fingers mashing the buttons, an extreme pixelated zoom in of sweat on his brow, his eyes darting, his score plummeting. Faster and faster, a multiplicity of faces, a kaleidoscopic view of a man going insane, shouting in violent rage, frantically twirling the tiny grey stick at the centre of the N64 controller, faster and faster, around and around, harder and harder until, in a great fury of circuits and plastic the entire green three-pronged controller exploded in his hand. The images merged back into one shot of Mike falling back to the couch, covered in shards of plastic and sweat, defeated.

"Looks like I am the champion!" Harry said, laughing as his character, WaLuigi, danced a victory dance on screen.

GertrudeBeerStein: That was impressive as fuck.

FavreauForLife420: They should hire you as a full-time editor!

GOKUBOY316: Watch this one! p*osted a video*

"Mario Kart. Circuit. A shot for every place out of first you end up. 150cc."

"150cc?" Joe asked.

"150cc," Mike repeated.

"Dude, I don't know," Dan said. "150 cc is pretty intense."

"This is your goddamn bachelor party and you're going to get shit faced."

"It is the prescribed turn of events," Harry said, agreeing with Mike.

"Alright, but you suck at this game," Dan said warningly.

"Not tonight. Tonight, I'm red shelling all your asses."

An impossibly kinetic montage of game footage intercut with Mike taking shots. A barrage of shells; blue, red, green, banana peels causing skid outs, giddy Mario characters speed boosting past him, Mike falling off the edges of rainbow roads. Then, after the bombardment, four full races of the circuit, he ends up in last place. Joe in fifth, Dan in fourth, and Harry, somehow miraculously in second.

"I believe the rules were a drink for every place out of first?" Harry said.

A quick cut of Mike in the kitchen, lining up shot glasses, filling them with a red booze, then the same footage of him pounding them all back as Harry toasted. "To the groom! Long may his marriage last and many a child it produce!"

More frantic edits of the rest of them downing their shots, with Mike doing a seemingly endless row. Anyone counting would know that this montage showed him taking way more than seven drinks, but the screen fragmented with endless little loops of him shooting on repeat, circling around an image of him in the centre of the screen looking like he was going to throw up. A caption in comic sans flashed beneath him. "The Worst Gamer in all of River City."

GertrudeBeerStein: Man, you're on fire GOKUBOY316
  GOKUBOY316: :)
  Cwood4Real: Should we really celebrate alcoholism like this?
  FavreauForLife420: That's why we're all here.
  TheMack420: And the laughs.
  TheDoorsMan: What was the deal with the stream cutting off when Mike called for the stripper?
  TMNTComicsLuVR: I guess they didn't want to get booted for adult content.
  YourNiNight420: Must have been wild as F
  Cwood4Real: Why do guys always want strippers at bachelor parties?
  JunkyCollector26: It's tradition!
  GertrudeBeerStein: What I wouldn't give for GOKUBOY316 to have had a chance to GIF the fuck out of that wild show!
  GOKUBOY316: Totally. I guess we'll just have to imagine how insane that was!

* * * *

As Mike pounded back the last shot, he slammed the tiny cup on the table and grunted. "Okay, the kids stuff is over. Dan, you're about to turn into a one-woman guy and we all know the way you usually plow through chicks." Mike elbowed Dan while winking at Harry. He held a hand up to block his mouth and whispered, far too loudly to actually prevent anyone from hearing, "The guy gets around. Kristin better watch out."

Joe nearly choked on a pretzel.

"Before you settle into the same chick night after night we thought we'd give you one last shot at what the rest of us bachelors get to experience anytime we want. Enjoy this, buddy, because it's the last fun you're going to have for a long time. At least if Kristin has any say. Joe, get the camera ready."

"I don't know if we can stream this…"

"Just do it, it'll get our views to the goddamn moon!"

Mike was falling over himself, slurring his words, blasted drunk. Harry turned to the hallway and waited intently. Dan raised an eyebrow. Joe hesitated. Mike grabbed the camera for him and pushed it too hard into his chest.

"Come on, man, this is for Dan!"

PING.

Joe could see the comments piling up. People wanting to know if they were really going to livestream a stripper. How was he going to get them out of it? Even if he cut off this camera, there were two more recording.

"Frank, hit the lights and the music," Mike said.

PING.

Mike turned to the empty recliner in confusion, finally realizing that Frank was nowhere to be found, nor had he been all night so far. "Frank? Hey, Joe, you seen Frank?"

"Shit, I forgot all about him. The last time I saw him he was taking the str—" He trailed off, realizing that Frank and Southside Annie had gone into his room hours ago and never come out. He stared down the hall wondering just what in the heck had gone on in there.

"What's wrong?" Mike asked.

"My room…"

"Well, go get them. This is Dan's party. And get it all on

camera. The viewers are waiting."

Joe carried the camera cautiously down the hall towards his room. The closer he got, the slower he moved. He dreaded what he might find. The door was shut. He could hear noises. He put his ear to the wood and listened.

"Oh, mama!"

"Ride 'em, big boy!"

He recoiled in horror, trying desperately to stop his mind from picturing what they might be doing in his room, on his bed. He knocked haltingly. "Uh... Frank?"

He didn't know why he reached for the doorknob. Maybe it was the shots he'd taken overriding his common sense. He also couldn't explain what had possessed him to open the door itself. The sight was forever burned into his brain, worse than a hundred childhood nightmares.

In the darkness of his room, Frank and Southside Annie, their legs and arms in places they didn't belong. Full frontal nudity, geriatric sweat, inhuman noises; panting, grunting, thrusting, shouts of passion, grey hair and wrinkles—

Joe unleashed a primal scream. He dropped the camera. It shattered, cutting the stream just in time to keep anyone at home from seeing more than a brief flash of the nightmare fuel he'd have to face during the darkest hours of his remaining years. He ran, curled into a fetal position behind the couch, rocking back and forth, jabbering madly as his brain struggled to comprehend what he'd witnessed.

"They coming?" Mike asked him.

"Oh God, yes..." Joe said. "Too many times..."

"Good, then Dan, prepare for what I hear is the best show this side of the Mississippi."

"You don't understand..."

"You said he was coming—"

"They both are... I think."

Mike pounded the table in anger. "What the fuck? This is about Dan's good time, goddamn it. Frank?" He awkwardly rose from the couch. "What's going on in there?" Mike walked down the hall towards the bedroom.

PING.

Joe killed the stream. He didn't want anyone else seeing what Mike was about to.

Dan checked his watch. "You know, it's getting late, and I promised Kristin I'd be up early to help her at the farmer's market. You ready to go, Harry?"

"I was looking forward to this vaudeville act, but I am your ride. Joseph, I have had a wonderful time. Electronic entertainment is a refreshing change of pace. Kudos to the hosts!"

Dan and Harry rose and walked towards the door. Joe saw their scheme fading away. Nothing they'd planned had worked or was enough to break through Kristin's spell. All that was left was to just come out and tell him and hope he didn't flip out.

"Dan, there's something we've been meaning to talk to you about," he said.

"Oh yeah?" Dan stopped at the door, slinging on his jacket.

"You see, Mike and I—"

A blood-curdling scream from the direction of the bedroom cut him off.

"What was that?"

"Mike must have found Frank and Southside Annie fucking."

"Now that is a show!" Harry ran off to see.

The perfect opportunity: he had Dan alone. He had to say something now or they'd miss their chance.

"Mike and I were concerned about Kristin. We found out some things about her."

Dan frowned. "Oh yeah? Like what?"

"Before I get into that, let me assure you that whatever we did, we did out of concern and love, but mostly love. For you. Okay?"

Dan sighed. "If you're going to tell me that some of Kristin's old boyfriends died, I already know that. That was one of the first things she told me when we started dating."

"She did?"

"I mean, that's some pretty big baggage, right? She was worried how I'd react if she told me later, so she got it out of the way early."

"About all of them?"

"Uh huh. Sometimes life just deals someone a rotten hand and that's what happened to her. A car crash, an overdose, a sudden aneurysm, an undiagnosed heart condition, it might sound a little crazy, but those things can and do happen. I totally understand her decision to start over."

"You do?"

"Who wouldn't want to move away from all that pain? Can you blame her? Having so many dead exes is bound to mess with your head a little. That's more than her share of bad luck and heartache. Harry told me the whole family supported her decision to leave Vancouver and come here to River City."

"What about the weird pagan stuff she's into? That Gates of Hell painting?"

Dan laughed. "I don't get that one either, but she thought it was cool. Why judge her taste? So much death in your life is

283

bound to skew you. She turned to Wiccan rituals to keep her head together. Did you know she even made a shrine to try to keep me from dying? Some book taught her some kind of nature spell that was supposed to protect me. She was so embarrassed, but eventually showed it to me. I told her that I don't mind. If she wants to pray to tree gods or whatever, I'm cool with that."

"Moving in, rushing into marriage?"

Dan just shrugged. "Well, what can I say? She is pregnant."

"Wait, what? I thought—"

"I don't tell you guys everything, you know."

"She's having a baby?"

"Hey, I want to start a family. How long do you think I can just sit around and play video games? Eventually you need to grow up and move on with your life. She's just as excited as I am. After seeing so much death she's got a pretty strong appreciation for the fragility of life."

"I never looked at it that way." Joe was reconsidering everything he'd thought these past few weeks. "Are you going to tell Mike?"

"Not yet. He seems to be taking this whole thing pretty badly."

"Yeah…"

"Don't worry, man," Dan said, patting him on the shoulder. "I know what I'm getting into."

Any more words froze in Joe's throat as he threatened to tear up. How could he have been so blind? How could he have let himself get so carried away by Mike's crazy demon theory? Dan had known about those things they'd found all along, and he didn't suspect that his girlfriend was a demon, he just accepted them as a part of who she was. A different religion, a painful backstory, it made sense. Their imaginations had gotten carried away with them. They'd seen things they'd wanted to. None of it was real. It seemed insane now when confronted with the truth.

"Thanks for the bachelor party. It was nice to have one last night like the old days."

"Yes, indeed, I had a wonderful time," Harry said, coming back with a huge grin. "Those two back there sure gave me a new appreciation for the human form." He slung on his coat, not a broken man at all. "You'll give Mike our thanks, won't you? When he snaps out of his... stupor?"

Joe just nodded. He couldn't say a thing for fear his voice would crack.

"Alright, see ya at the ceremony and reception," Dan said.

Dan and Harry left, leaving Joe feeling more alone than ever before.

* * * *

"This might be the last stream we do," Joe said to the blinking camera light. "Maybe for a few weeks, maybe forever, I don't know. What I do know is we fucked up. Dan's gone. He's getting married and nothing makes sense anymore. Thank you, guys, for supporting us. I just really need to rethink a few things that have happened recently. Anyone out there ever, like, thought they'd seen something? Were so convinced of it? Then wondered if it had really happened at all?"

PING.

"No, TheMack420, I wasn't high. Not that I know of. Mike might have been drunk, but I was sober. It was all so real. But it couldn't have been."

285

PING.

"Hypnotic suggestion. Interesting theory, RichardtheLian Heart256. But who would have been doing it? Myself?"

PING.

"Yeah, I guess it is possible, GertrudeBeerStein, that I have telepathic powers and don't realize it. Anyway. What I thought I saw, I couldn't have seen, so I must not have seen what I thought I saw. Which means I was either going crazy or wanted to see that thing so bad that I let myself believe that I'd seen it because deep down, I just didn't want to face the truth that I'd never seen it in the first place, because it was never real in the first place. But I'm facing it now."

PING.

"Things are changing. Consider this a hiatus. I'll try to keep you guys updated, but... I don't know. There's just... so many things I don't know right now. Three... I mean, two... I guess, one gamer, signing off."

PING.

PING.

CHAPTER THIRTY-TWO: WEDDINGS BRING OUT THE BEST IN PEOPLE

"And so, if there's anyone here who has any objections to this union, let them speak now or forever hold their peace."

Mike reached into his suit jacket and took out a small, folded piece of paper. He cleared his throat and moved to stand up. Joe grabbed his arm and yanked him back down. "No," he mouthed silently. Mike relented, a look of defeat washing over him.

The priest continued when it was clear no one was going to say anything. "So, with the power vested in me, I now pronounce you man and wife. You may kiss the bride."

Dan bent forward and took Kristin in his arms. He kissed her deeply and with surprising passion as the crowd erupted in applause. A harpist took up the cue and played the wedding march as the happy couple walked down an aisle covered in rose petals.

Outside, beneath a canopy of old elms near the river, Dan and Kristin beamed. They'd rented the old fur trading outpost, now turned popular wedding venue. White folding chairs lined up in neat rows on the lush green grass, stretched from the steps of the historical site. The massive trees muted the noise from the city, giving the whole place a peaceful and secluded air. The reception was scheduled later in the preserved outpost itself, while for now the wedding party were off to take photos in the park-like setting.

"I had my doubts they could pull this off so fast," Joe said as he admired all the decorations Kristin and her team had put up, "but I'd say it looks pretty good."

Mike pouted. "Why didn't you let me stop it?"

"You'd make a complete ass of yourself. And there's no point. The dude is in love. He's married now and we just need to accept that."

"I won't. Not to her. Not to that thing…"

"She's not a demon, man, get over it."

"How can you just forget all that we saw? Red eyes, living shadows, the scrapbooks, the painting, the deaths, the shrine, the—"

"We've gone over this," Joe said, rubbing his eyes in frustration. "There's perfectly rational reasons for everything we thought we saw. Red eyes, shadows, I looked around online and there are all kind of reports of people seeing things in photos that aren't there. Shit, the dude who wrote Sherlock Holmes went around telling everyone he had photographic proof of fairies, for fuck's sake."

"I know what I saw."

"You know what you wanted to see. And he already knew all the so-called dirt we uncovered. Face it, this whole thing is on us."

"So, what do we do now?" Mike asked.

"We still have two hours till the reception."

"I don't exactly want to hang around here and watch the happy couple posing under the trees."

"Then let's go pick up our dates."

* * * *

Southside Annie stood in the open door of Frank's apartment. She wore an impossibly tight black dress. It propped up and pushed away twenty years of gravity. Her make-up was immaculate. She was a real experienced pro. She leaned on the frame and eyed the two of them with a cat's hunger. "Don't you boys look cute in your monkey suits." She licked her lips.

"You don't look too bad yourself," Mike admitted, temporarily forgetting the images he'd seen of her and Frank back in Joe's room.

"Keep it in your pants, stud, I charge by the hour."

"If I can't score with one of the bridesmaids, I might just take you up on that."

"Is Frank ready?" Joe asked.

"Hold your goddamn horses, I'm coming," the old man shouted from another room.

Southside Annie moved out of the way to let Joe and Mike come inside the as-always messy apartment.

"Just finishing up," Frank said.

They turned towards the sound of his voice and saw the man leaving his room. Joe's mouth dropped, while Mike froze in shock. Frank wore a wig and a dress, with full make-up, expertly applied, presumably by Southside Annie.

"How do I look, kids?" Frank posed and twirled in place, obviously proud of his disguise.

"What the fuck are you doing in drag?" Mike asked.

"We're supposed to be your dates," he said as if it was the most obvious thing in the world. "It would look pretty funny if you didn't come with a couple of hot young bobbysoxers."

"You can't come looking like that, people will think we're insane!"

Frank snorted. "I've gone deeper undercover than this before, kid. Hell, one time I had to dress as a gorilla and infiltrate a secret ape society. You think a wig is tough, wait till you wear a full body merkin for two weeks straight. That's a smell I'll never forget."

"Just wear a suit. There's no way in hell I'm walking in there with the oldest cross-dresser in the country as my date," Mike said.

Southside Annie coughed her smoker's cough. "He ain't the oldest, kids. Fella I know back in Regina, Uptown Bruno, he's the oldest. Guy was crossing before Newfoundland joined confederation. He makes Frankie here look like a hog painted with lipstick."

"Thanks, Annie," Frank said, obviously finding a compliment in that statement somewhere.

"Just get changed!" Mike shouted. "The reception starts in an hour!"

* * * *

The old fur trading outpost's hall was more log cabin than ballroom. Crammed with circular tables and high-backed chairs decorated in white linen, at one end of the room the bride, groom, and wedding party all sat in a neat row at the long head table. It was a small wedding party: Harry on the groom's side and Kristin's best friend on the other. Joe, Mike, Frank, and Southside Annie were seated in the corner of the room at a table next to the one with Dan and Kristin's parents. In the centre of the table was a place setting of tree saplings in little bags and a fishbowl lined with photos of the happy couple. Two goldfish swam happily inside. Frank brushed dust from his suit. He hadn't completely wiped the lipstick off. Southside Annie pounded back the bottle of red wine on the table like it was free. Which it was.

"Real nice turnout," Joe said, nibbling at the bread service.

Mike played with the napkins, staring at nothing.

"Reminds me of my first wedding," Frank said. "Although we didn't have any fancy fishbowls at the table, just knives and forks and a hunk of red meat to share."

Southside Annie wiped some wine from her mouth. A few drops fell into her cleavage. "My first time was at the end of a shotgun."

Frank nodded. "A proud tradition."

"This is the first wedding I've been to since I was a kid," Joe said.

"You were married as a kid? What kind of royal family were you born into?" Frank asked.

"No, it was my cousin."

"Yeah, I figured as much. Keep the bloodline pure and all that. So where was it? Luxemburg? The Ottoman Empire? Sweden?" Frank asked.

"No, no, no. My cousin married someone else. I was only six years old," Joe tried to explain.

"She broke your heart," Frank said. "I can understand that. I've had my ticker cracked a few times before myself."

"No—" Joe started, but Southside Annie waved her hand to

stop him. "Best to leave it be, boy, he's not going to catch up any time soon."

* * * *

The food came in waves: bread, salad, soup. He barely noticed the bison roast until Joe elbowed him in the ribs. "You should try this."

"Why bother?"

"Dan's parents sure seem to love it."

He pointed to the next table over where Dan's mother and father devoured their roast sloppily.

"How many bottles of wine do you think they've had already?" Joe asked, barely containing laughter as the two parents ate like mad dogs.

"Not enough." Mike grabbed one of the bottles from the centre of the table.

Speeches. The best man and maid of honour telling tearful stories of how wonderful the new couple were, anecdotes from their childhoods that purported to show the beautiful souls they truly were, how bright their futures looked.

Bullshit.

Mike drank wine and stared a hole through the woman that had fooled everyone, even his best friends. He didn't believe for one second what Joe had told him about Dan understanding Kristin's past, how there were perfectly legitimate reasons behind all the deaths. None of it could explain away what he knew he'd experienced at Sharkey's. She'd manipulated them all.

"Not me," he mumbled and took another swig from the bottle.

"Dude, maybe you should slow down," Joe said.

"Yeah, even Southside Annie's taking it easy after the second bottle," Frank added.

"It's all a giant con," he said.

"Annie, you secretly hiding bottles up your—"

"Not that," Mike said. "The show. The whole kit and caboodle, this wedding between my former best friend and a killer, a soul-sucking demon—"

"Don't worry about him," Joe said. "He's just bitter it wasn't him up there telling the funny stories about Dan."

"I was there from day one."

"You were at the hospital when his mom popped him out?" Annie asked.

"Kindergarten, soccer, football, Magic, Fireball Island, movie nights, SNES, Xbox, fuck, I'm the guy that told him to go into the tech industry."

"Do you even know what Dan actually does?" Joe asked.

"Something to do with setting up people's internet, that's not important. Dan owes me. He should trust me. Who told him to get contact lenses instead of wearing those big round coke bottle glasses he wore in junior high? Who told him to take up weightlifting so he'd be able to hit harder on the football team? Who told him what Super Nintendo Games to get so we could swap when we were done with 'em? Who told him what movies to see, what music to like, when to move out and where? Who did more for him than me?"

"Sounds like you were the one in love with him," Southside Annie said.

"What? No, I'm the one who…"

He stared at Kristin as he spoke, laughing with Dan as they rose together to start their speeches.

Look at her, the crooked, toothed grin, new bride's glow, the pale white skin, the glowing red eyes... the shadow of wings and a tail behind her...

"Holy shit!" he blurted out. "Look at that!"

"Speech time," Frank said. "Better pass the sauce, Annie, this could take a while."

* * * *

"And that was when I knew that this was the right guy for me. He had the missing piece to the puzzle I needed, that—"

Joe felt Mike poking him in the ribs to get his attention as he listened.

"What?" he whispered.

Mike pointed frantically.

But at what? Beside them, Dan's parents gnawed on more roast, across from them Southside Annie's hand kept inching up Frank's leg, all around them people listened intently. A few even wiped tears away. But Mike just pointed, pale-faced. Was he going to spew from all the wine he'd downed?

"What is it?" he whispered with venom.

He pointed to the stage.

Dan and Kristin spoke, but their words slowed to a crawl. The lights in the room flickered. Dan moved in slow motion, Kristin stopped completely. The candles on the tables flared upwards, singeing the saplings. He looked around the room, saw everyone trapped in some kind of stasis.

What the hell is going on?

Glowing red eyes. He saw them, so bright he couldn't tell who they were even coming from. The shadow on the wall stretched and pulsed outwards, danced in the glare.

Wings. A tail. Horns. Moving, alive, cascading over the room around them. The lights in Harry's eyes dimmed, became solid black orbs. Kristin's sister's face was sucked inwards, the moisture pulled away until all that was left was a greyish husk. Everyone in the room's skin turned to dust, their flesh rotting away in an instant. The roof cracked and crumbled around them. The night sky glared red with fire.

The city stretched in the distance, but the buildings had decayed into a post-apocalyptic wasteland. Things in dark robes crawled through the ruins of the park. Everything was gone.

Joe turned to Mike who brought his hand up to his mouth as if he was trying to stifle a scream. He said something that Joe couldn't make out.

What?

No words came from his mouth.

What? What is it?

He swallowed hard, felt the burning of ashes in his throat, then tried again.

"What?"

Everyone was looking at him. Had he shouted that?

"Joe, you okay?" Dan asked from the stage.

It was all back to normal. Kristin looked at him with a crooked grin.

"I, uh…"

Mike stared at him, shaking his head in panic, hand over his mouth, completely scared shitless. He'd seen it all, too. Then, Mike stumbled to his feet, pushing his chair away. He bolted for the door. He only made it a few feet when he started to blow.

* * * *

Someone screamed in horror. Frank turned from the eyes of Southside Annie to see one of the kids running around like a sprinkler, launching chunks of green and tan in all directions. He held his hand in front of his mouth, but only served to send streams of vomit out either side. It went everywhere: in hair, in drinks, down shirts. It was total chaos as the room erupted in mad panic. "Reminds me of my second wedding," he said and turned back to his date's endless legs.

CHAPTER THIRTY-THREE: THE LONELINESS OF SOLITUDE

"I'm glad you boys called me." Frank walked into the room carrying a brown bag and wearing a long black raincoat, dress shirt and slacks. His collar was loosened, a black tie dangled undone at his neck. "When you said you had all-new information about a certain unresolved issue, you just about made my day."

"Thanks for coming," Joe said. "You're the only one we can really turn to about all of this."

Frank pulled out a bottle of Jack Daniels from the bag and placed it on the table in front of the television. "Now tell me where you saw the red convertible so I can make the arrest. Then we can celebrate with my good pal Jack here."

"Convertible?" Mike said, confused, pausing the Xbox. He put the controller down on the coffee table. "We wanted to talk to you about our friend and his now wife."

"Isn't he demon food by now?"

"That's why we phoned," Mike said. "See, when they were talking, we saw—"

"So you didn't see the car I've been after for months now?"

"No, we saw a vision of hell on earth!"

"You weren't the ones getting married," Frank said. He

unscrewed the top of the bottle and took a swig, before holding it out to the two of them. "Let him realize the mistake."

"I'm not going to just give up on him," Mike said.

"It's the normal course of events when a buddy gets married. I've seen it all before. I know just what you need to take your mind off it."

"A plan to get our friend back?" Mike said.

"A good old-fashioned blackout bender. We start with Jack here and then, when we're all warmed up, we go meet some of my crew. They'll help you see that there's more to this world than a guy who'd ditch his buddies for a dame."

"Look, Frank," Joe said. "We're not the blackout drunk types. Well, I'm not. We were kind of hoping that you'd help us figure out our next move. Maybe call Father O'Hoolahan again. She might think she's won, hell, she had me convinced for a minute there that I was crazy, but then I saw—"

"Your pal shooting his guts all over her parents?"

"Before that."

Frank took another sip of the bottle and held it to them. "Okay, the guys can wait for a few minutes. Give me the details and we'll work this out."

"It's hard to explain," Joe said. "It started with the eyes. Then the whole room sort of melted and—"

"Everything was gone. The whole city. Wiped out. I think her marrying Dan is just a first step to something much worse."

"Yeah, alimony. Been there, done that."

"No, you're not getting it," Mike said. He looked around the room for something to use as a visual aid. "See, it's like the levels in Call of Duty." He grabbed the Xbox controller and unpaused the game. "You start small, you see a few bad guys, you shoot them."

Frank watched the screen wide-eyed. "What in the world is this?"

"Yeah, it's pretty great, eh? The graphics here make Goldeneye look like a bowl of puke."

As soldiers on screen jumped out of a helicopter and were immediately fired upon, Frank's mouth dropped.

"You start small, but then the real story kicks in and it all goes to hell in a handbasket. Global politics, thermonuclear war, the destruction of cities—"

In a flash of movement, Frank pulled his gun, fired four times into the television, exploding it in a shower of sparks.

Joe and Mike jerked back in fright, knocking over the bottle. "What the fuck!"

"Did I get 'em?" Frank said in a daze.

Something was wrong – he looked like he was reliving old memories, locked in a loop. He sat with his gun pointed at the now ruined television, breathing slowly, sweat beading down his forehead.

"Are you okay?" Joe asked.

Frank blinked and came back to the real world. "Yeah, yeah, I just had a flashback to something that happened to me when I was over in the Middle East working under cover for old man Trudeau. Iran. I had half of… oh shit, that's classified. Now I'm going to have to kill you."

"You never told us anything!" Mike pushed away from him on the couch.

"Relax, kid." Frank put his gun back in its holster. "I wouldn't kill you. But it is classified, so keep your mouth shut."

The tone in his voice told them both that he meant it.

Joe stared at the wreckage of the television in dismay. "You just blew up our set."

Frank bent over and picked up the bottle of Jack from where it had fallen to the floor. He held it upside down and nothing came out. There was a huge puddle on the carpet next to the coffee table. "And you just spilled the booze. I think that makes us even."

"What? How?"

"You can still make it up to me. Let's go." Frank rose to his feet and motioned for them to follow.

"Where?" Joe asked.

"I'll introduce you to the old gang. Between the five of us, I'm sure we can figure out what in the hell you were getting at with that fancy canasta machine metaphor. Hell, they might even cheer you two Roy Orbisons up."

* * * *

"Boys, I'd like you to meet the gang." Frank waved his hand towards a table where four old men sat nursing drinks. They were all as old as Frank, maybe older. Stooped, wrinkled, grey-haired and frail, they looked like escapees from an old folks' home. "Gang, these here are the boys," Frank said. "Seems their buddy went and got himself married to a she-devil and they're depressed."

The four old men at the table grunted and shook their heads in understanding.

"Introductions are in order. First is my oldest pal, Derek." Frank tapped a tall, heavyset man with Coke bottle-sized glasses and a thin grey-blond crew cut. "We grew up in parts of this city that weren't even parts of this city yet, eh, Derek?"

"Sure did, Frankie. There were more pigs than people back then."

"Still are," Frank said, grinning.

Next, he pointed to a stooped, leathery little man with thin wisps of hair sipping away at a glass of tomato juice. "This is Fuller. He used to be called the Brick Layer for what I think are obvious reasons."

"He slept with a lot of fat women?" Mike asked.

"Shit, no, he worked in construction. Show a little class, kid."

"Next up we've got old Russ." Frank pointed to a rotund man in stretched sweatpants pulled up impossibly high with his shirt tucked in the front. He struggled to fit in his chair but waved his stubby hand in greeting.

"And what did they call him?" Joe asked.

"White Lightning," Frank said.

"I don't get it."

"And you don't want to," Frank said threateningly.

"Does it have anything to do with the Burt Reynolds movie?" Joe asked.

"Don't bring Burt up around these guys," Frank said. "He's a bit of a sore spot."

"Burt Reynolds?" Fuller asked. "The fucker who walked away from Evening Shade just when it was getting good?"

"Oh God," Frank said. "Now you've got him going."

"What kind of asshole splits from big tits Loni Anderson? And what kind of asshole walks away from fucking Evening Shade! That was fine television and—"

"Okay, Fuller," Frank said. "We've all heard this rant before. Let's move on. I still have to introduce Marvin." Frank gestured to the fourth man at the table with massive hearing aids in his ears. "Marvin doesn't hear so well anymore, so you'll have to speak up."

"Talk louder," Marvin said. "I can't hear you."

"I said you're going deaf, old man," Frank shouted.

"Only from listening to you for so long."

"Okay," Mike said. "So, this is the geriatric crew. And you think these guys can help us, why?"

"Because what we have here are four of the best friends a man could ask for," Frank said. "No matter how many times the world has tried to kick me under the door mat, they've been here. Through thick and thin, the five of us together, a bottle in hand and a shoulder to puke on."

"Sometimes a bottle to puke in, too," Derek said. "Pull up a seat, boys."

Joe and Mike took empty seats at the table. The place was a dive bar; tables rotting away, peeling walls, yellowed photos hanging in cracked frames. The room had the permanent odour of smoke infused into it. A thin haze in the air showed that the years of cigars and cigarettes had fundamentally altered its makeup. The bartender looked like he might still be in prison. He was covered in so many tattoos that it was hard to tell what was ink and what was his shirt. A handful of bikers and street people sat drinking at the other tables. Frank's friends had claimed their own corner and seemed to have been given a wide berth by everyone else.

"Tell us your story, kids," Russ said. "Life is breaking you down?"

"First thing's first, we need some whistle wetting." Frank waved to the waitress and shouted, "Two rounds of the usual, Shelley, and don't stop till one of us blacks out."

302

When she came to the table, she put a shot and beer chaser in front of each member of the group.

"Our best friend married a demon," Mike said.

The old men all nodded like they knew exactly what he was talking about.

"Not the first and not the last," Derek said.

"Happened to every one of us at one point," Fuller said.

"That's right," Russ added. "If there's one thing that never changes in this world it's that women will always strive to take a man away from his friends."

"But this one is a literal demon, not just a bitch," Mike said.

"Pussy'll do that to you," Marvin said.

"He could be dead by now. She could be sucking his soul this very minute."

"She could be sucking lots of things this very minute. But they don't do souls all in one go," Fuller said. "It can take years of nagging."

Joe looked around the table, seeing five men who could be his grandpa, sitting around in this hellhole of a place, drinking. It was depressing as fuck.

"It's a part of life," Derek chimed in. "You grow up with a bunch of fellas that you'd go to war with – shit, some of us did." He laughed and the other geezers at the table joined in. "But then, that little dowsing rod in your pants starts looking for water."

"The never-ending story," Fuller said. "Man gets suckered in by a woman and bled dry. Next thing you know he's fifty pounds heavier, bald, and pissing every five minutes. Which reminds me." Fuller rose from his seat and waddled away towards the bathroom.

"Even happened to me a few times," Frank said. "But I was

one of the lucky ones. I had the gang here to fall back on."

"What about the rest of you?" Joe asked.

Nods and grunts. Marvin spat on the floor in disgust. "Not me. I never gave in. I had too much to do with my life."

"What was it you did?"

"Unemployed mostly. But I used to host a television show about card counting."

Frank laughed. "Yeah, old Marvin there was a real Rock Hudson. Beat the women off with a stick. And now look at him."

Joe took a long look at the grinning Marvin, nearly deaf, bragging in a dive bar about a life of solitude. He blanched, thinking of what was in store for him and Mike. Maybe being sucked dry by a demon wasn't that bad, after all?

"I won't let Dan go through it," Mike said. "I won't let that demon mind fuck his soul straight to hell."

"Good on you, boy," Fuller said. "The only thing a man really has is his friends and his dignity. A woman'll try to take both away if you're not careful."

"We're just going to have to take drastic action," Mike said.

"Like what?" Joe asked.

"Kidnapping, reprogramming, maybe get O'Hoolahan to do one of those exorcisms I've heard so much about."

Joe suddenly had an image flash through his mind; the three of them here, in this same bar, fifty years from now, stooped, grey-haired, senile, crooked fingers ruined from gaming, reminiscing about the old days. Incontinent, never having done a thing with their lives. He panicked and shouted out, "Pregnant."

"Who is? Russ? Nah, he's just a little soft around the edges, is all," Frank said.

"No, Dan!"

"A man pregnant?" Frank said in shock. "Shit, the things they can do now with science."

"No, Kristin is pregnant. Dan told me before the wedding, but I was sworn to secrecy."

"He what?" Mike said. "I thought they weren't even fucking?"

"He sure the thing is his, then?" Derek asked.

"He was," Joe said. "I guess they were. I don't know. It's just… can demons get pregnant?"

"This must be her plan," Mike said. "We have to go get him. Tonight. Now. Before it's—"

"It already is too late, fella," Fuller said as he returned to his seat. "That man's life is over."

"To the memory of a good kid." Russ raised his glass. "Even if I have no idea who he was."

"To a life once lived," Derek added.

"To another screaming shit factory," Frank said.

They all looked to Joe and Mike for their toasts, but Mike just pulled out his phone. "I'm texting him right now, telling him we're coming over. Joe, check out Kristin's Facebook page, see if she's going to be around. We might need that gun of yours, Frank."

"Got it right here." Frank pulled a revolver from his sock, laying it on the table.

Mike frantically started typing a text to Dan while Joe opened Facebook. He found Kristin's page and saw a recent status update, a photo of the two of them with a massive block of text underneath. He started reading it as the old man downed their shots.

"He says he can't do anything right now," Mike said. "What

305

the fuck?"

Joe finished reading the text and almost dropped the phone. A pit opened in his stomach. What he'd read floored him.

"What? What is it?" Mike asked. "She post an ultrasound picture with one of those cute little—"

"She's dying," Joe said.

"Who is?"

"Kristin." None of this made sense, but he re-read her status update and it was real. "They found something during a routine test. They did some follow ups, got a second opinion. I don't know how to put this, but she's been given six weeks to live."

"There," Derek said. "Problem solved."

"The universe has a way of working itself out, eh, boys," Fuller added.

"That makes no sense," Mike said haltingly.

"What doesn't?" Marvin asked.

"Looks like this is a cause for celebration." Frank waved the waitress over for more drinks.

"I don't understand it either," Joe said.

"What's to understand," Russ said. "You two were thinking of committing the kind of crimes old Frankie here would have to arrest you over. Not too smart to plan it all in his face either."

"Suspended, Russ," Frank said. "I'm not here in an official capacity."

"Good, cause I think I ran over a kid on the way in," Fuller said.

"So my best friend…" Mike trailed off.

"Is about to become a widower," Fuller said.

"Here's to demon women biting the big one before they

can bleed a man dry." Russ raised his glass.

"To a man saved before it was too late," Frank added.

Their glasses high, they looked to Mike and Joe who were both shell-shocked.

"Guys," Frank said. "Isn't this exactly what you wanted?"

"I guess," Joe said.

Mike tentatively grabbed his glass, lifting it up to join in the toast. "Right, uh, to getting exactly what we wanted?"

"Cheers!" the geriatric crew all said as they clinked their glasses.

CHAPTER THIRTY-FOUR: TRUST THE PROCESS

"It is nearly time." The dark presence meditating in the black room spoke through vibrations in their minds rather than sound. "For transformation."

"But the child," the male thrall said. "This wasn't part of the—"

"It is of no consequence."

"There are things that can be done," the female thrall said.

"Unnecessary."

"The book of rituals," the male thrall said. "I found something worrisome, about—"

"You presume I was unaware?"

"Of course not, but—"

A searing pain wracked the mind of the thrall. He fell to his knees, hands over his rotting ears, screaming in pain. Black blood poured through clenched fingers, dripping down the side of the greying skin. His brain expanded within his skull, threatening to explode outwards.

"Please…"

"Dark one, he merely wished—"

She, too, was wracked with an attack on the inside of her mind. She fell to her knees as a surge of energy passed through her decaying brain in waves, swelling it like a balloon about to burst.

"Neither of you are necessary for what I must do. I allow you to exist. Question me again and I will paint the walls with what remains of your brains before I feast on your corpses."

The waves of mental attack ceased. The two thralls collapsed to the concrete floor in supplication.

"We hear and obey."

"Leave me. There are many things to consider. As the ultimate goal nears, some refuse to heed the warnings given. They must learn what it means to meddle in affairs they shouldn't."

The two thralls rose to their feet.

"What can we do, oh dark lord?"

Silence.

The darkness of the room, an extension of the one that was inside became still. Finally, the path forward appeared in their minds.

"Thy will be done."

CHAPTER THIRTY-FIVE: THE ROAD TO THE TRUTH

The funeral was on a Tuesday. A hundred people, dressed in black, tears flowing, stood shell-shocked in the rain in the very same place they'd come for the wedding. The old fort was a gloomy and depressing place under grey skies. Harry had given a simple service for his sister. Wicker idols surrounded the urn and a small photo of Kristin. Her ordeal had been mercifully brief. Facebook updates detailed the rapid decline, the few days in the hospital, the transfer back home for the end. To the world it was heartbreaking. Mike didn't know how to feel.

He watched Dan standing at the edge of the room, where he'd stood to give his speech at the wedding, talking with mourners, shaking hands, accepting hugs and well-meaning pats on the back.

"He looks okay, all things considered," Joe said. "He's gained some weight back. There's more colour in his face."

"It's probably from all the food people were donating," Mike said, thinking of the friends and family who'd banded together to try to help by cooking meals for the couple. He wondered if anyone would have done that for him.

"You think we should have maybe given something better

than Popeye's?" Joe asked.

"If either one of us had tried to cook, she might have died even faster," Mike said.

They watched the people all pay respects to Harry, Dan, and the parents.

"You ever think how fucking fragile life is?" Joe asked. "Just a few weeks ago, Kristin was alive, vital, happy to be married, and then, bam, she's wasting away and gone before anyone can do anything about it."

"No."

"What do you mean, no?"

"Joe, we both know what she was."

"Oh, for fuck's sake, we were obviously wrong – she's dead."

"It has to be a part of the plan."

"She's going to burst out of the urn and yell surprise before eating him at her own funeral?"

"Shit, now that would be one hell of a way to go out," Frank said, approaching them, holding a plate of tiny sandwiches.

Joe ignored him. "Seriously, Mike, it's time to move on from this whole demon thing. The woman is dead."

"I can't," Mike said. "I don't know why, but this is all—"

"It's not a part of anything. And you need to lay off. Whatever we were on to was bullshit. It's time to be there for Dan."

"You want me to grab you guys a plate, too?" Frank asked as food fell from his mouth.

"Anything good on the spread?" Mike asked.

"Sandwiches, cookies, those little date squares."

"Sounds like my kind of buffet." Mike started to leave for the food area.

Joe grabbed his shoulder. "Don't you think we should go

and say something to the man?"

"What is there to say?"

Joe just shook his head in disappointment.

"See if he wants to come over for a beer," Mike said. "We could stream something he likes, I dunno, EVO on SNES. He was always going on about one."

"You think that with his pregnant wife dead he's going to want to get drunk and play video games for an audience?"

"He might want to take his mind off it."

"I've got a bottle of Jack in the glove compartment," Frank offered.

"Just go stuff your face," Joe said. "I'll talk to him."

"You heard the man," Frank said. "Let's eat."

* * * *

Joe waited in the receiving line, amidst other mourners patiently queueing to pay their respects. He watched Mike and Frank shovelling food in their mouths as if this was some kind of party. He figured Mike had to feel as bad as he did about all of this, even if he wasn't admitting it. How could he not? They'd harboured a grudge against Kristin, stalked her, even thought she was a supernatural creature, and now she was dead, lost to whatever it was that the doctors had found inside her. "I'm sorry," he muttered to the silver-framed picture of Kristin on the small table. In the photograph, she was practically glowing; dressed all in white, smiling on her wedding night, when the world still seemed so full of possibilities.

"I'm really sorry," he muttered again.

"Why?" the woman in front of him in line asked. "Did you

spill something on my shoes?"

"Huh? No, I was just talking to the picture."

She looked at him like he was insane. "Why? She's in the urn, not the picture."

He didn't know this woman. She appeared to be in her early thirties, wore a modest black dress and light makeup. She held the funeral pamphlet in her hands. He wasn't sure if he should laugh or not.

"Are you with the widower or the deceased?" she asked.

"Dan's. Er, widower."

"Me, too. Co-worker. You?"

"Roommate."

"I thought he lived with Kristin? Oh shit, did you guys have some kind of poly thing going on?"

"No, he left us to be with her."

"No wonder you're depressed," she said. "It's okay, those kind of relationships never last anyway."

"Wait, that's not—" he started, but she'd moved up to shake the hands of Kristin's parents.

He was fighting back tears, but didn't feel like it would be fair if he cried. Especially after all they'd done.

The line moved and he shook the hands of Kristin's parents. "So sorry for your loss," he said.

Next was Harry who moved past the outstretched hand to come in for a hug instead.

"Thanks for being here, friend," Harry said.

Then it was Dan's parents. They looked as out of it as he felt. Pale, sallow, sedated. His mom seemed to have really caked on the makeup.

"Mr. And Mrs. Stoddard," he said. "So sorry for… everything."

"Thanks for coming, Joe," Mr. Stoddard said with a frog in his throat.

"It means a lot to see you here," Mrs. Stoddard added.

"It was a lovely service," Joe said awkwardly. "Unconventional but nice."

"Kristin never was one for organized religion. Neither were we really."

"I had no idea she had so many friends," Joe said.

"Most of these people are probably just here for the free food," Mr. Stoddard said, eyeing Mike and Frank.

"Mike's still processing all of this."

Mrs. Stoddard nodded. A flake of white fell from her face.

Joe didn't know what else he was supposed to say; he'd never had to do this before. "It's tough when someone who had so much, uh, spark goes young."

"She had lots of life," Mr. Stoddard said. "Dan loved that about her."

"Not anymore though," Mrs. Stoddard said. "She's just a pile of ashes now."

"Uh, yeah. I guess so," Joe said.

The woman ahead of him was still talking to Dan.

"So, uh, what happens now?" he asked. "Is she being buried somewhere? You guys spreading the ashes?"

"Dan will give them a good home," Mr. Stoddard said.

"Which reminds me, Joseph," Mrs. Stoddard said. "We're having a more intimate reception at our house later. For the closest friends. We'd love for you to be there. It would mean so much to... Dan."

Joe saw Mike and Frank waving to him with sandwiches in hand.

"Yeah, we'll be there," he said. "It's the least we could do for our oldest friend."

"Excellent," Mr. Stoddard said.

"We'll make the arrangements and see you around seven, okay?"

Then it was time to shake Dan's hand.

Red around his eyes, clothes ruffled from too many hugs, traces of lipstick on his cheeks from consolatory kisses, but he looked almost relieved in a way. His eyes shone with fierce colour, and he stood to his full height.

"I'm so sorry, Dan."

"Thanks," he said, his voice strong.

"I don't even know what to say but we're here for you." Joe moved in to hug him.

"That means a lot."

Dan was thick, compactly muscled. Joe had never actually hugged him before. Was he always like that? It just went to show how little they'd actually connected, despite knowing each other for almost twenty years. He resolved to correct that.

"Whenever, whatever you need. Just call," Joe said.

"You're coming to my parents later?" Dan asked calmly.

"Absolutely, I promise."

"Glad to hear."

He moved on to the next person in line.

Joe joined Mike and Frank at the buffet table.

"I'm telling you," Frank said. "I met the guy, and he was an asshole."

"You met Johnny Dagon?" Mike said incredulously. "But he's been dead forever."

"You ever think I could have been alive forever, smart ass?"

"You are pretty old," Mike said. "But Johnny Dagon was big

in, like, the fifties and sixties."

"He was retired when I—"

"Guys," Joe interrupted. "I have some news."

"If it's about Johnny Dagon, I know he's dead," Mike said. "That's what we were arguing—"

"It's not about old crooners, dude, it's about a private family-only reception Dan's parents are having later tonight. We're invited."

"Can I bring a date?" Frank asked.

"I, uh… guess so? Not really sure it's that kind of party, but you do you."

"I hope she will later," Frank said. "That's why I'm inviting her."

"Why would we want to go to another funeral after we already went to one?" Mike asked.

"If you want to repair the relationship with Dan, this might be a good chance. Also, they'll probably have more food there."

Mike sighed heavily, crumbs falling from his mouth. "You really think it's a good idea?"

"You could pitch him on your streaming EVO idea."

Mike looked at Kristin's photo and urn, lost in thought for a moment before finally nodding.

"Great," Frank said. "Two parties in one day. Things are starting to look up!"

CHAPTER THIRTY-SIX: DEEPER DOWN BELOW

Mike pulled up to the unassuming two-story suburban house on a cul-de-sac in Western River City. Two cars were parked in the driveway, both with Budget rental stickers on the back window. The interior lights were off, a faint red entryway light shone on the front door instead. "I guess we're not the last one's here," he said.

"I don't see Frank's piece of shit car anywhere – you think he got lost?" Joe asked.

"I sort of hope so."

He parked and they both climbed out. The blackened skies of the afternoon funeral service had become heavier with the fall of night. A static charge in the air said a storm could break out at any moment. Wind blew dust and debris in his face as he looked at the Stoddard's house, where he'd been a thousand times over the years.

"Why no lights?" Joe asked.

"Maybe it's part of the service?"

"I dunno," Joe said. "His parents didn't give me any details."

"Let's get this over with." Mike walked up the driveway.

"You might want to, you know, show some sympathy for Dan. Maybe seem like you're upset about this whole thing."

"Why would I do that?"

"He's our friend and his wife just died."

"Allegedly. We don't even know if demons can die."

"Just promise me you won't bring that up in there," Joe said. "It's already going to be awkward as fuck without you accusing the corpse of being about to kill everyone."

"Oh shit, you think she was going to kill everyone? Not just him?"

Joe pressed the doorbell. "I'm not talking about this anymore."

They waited on the front step for a few minutes. Nobody came to the door. Mike quickly grew impatient. He hadn't wanted to come in the first place. He wasn't good with this kind of stuff, even if he could let himself believe that any of it was real.

"There," he said. "You see? Nobody's here. This was all some kind of—"

The door opened. Dan's parents stood in the darkened foyer. They wore strange black housecoats, while their faces were pale and sallow. Heavy bags surrounded eyes that didn't seem to be focused on either Mike or Joe.

"So glad you two could make it," Mr. Stoddard said with a hoarse voice.

"We were wondering when you were going to show up," Mrs. Stoddard added.

"Sorry," Joe said. "We were just in the middle of watching *The Dead Zone* for, like, the two hundredth time."

"What? I like that movie," Mike said.

"I did, too, the first hundred and sixty times I saw it."

The parents moved aside to let them in, peering out into the night behind them before shutting the door and locking

318

it.

The house was completely dark. Mike looked around, re-membering the sleepovers, the birthday parties, the summer afternoons playing Magic: The Gathering. The place hadn't changed a bit. Come to think of it, it looked like it hadn't been cleaned since the last time he was here. A layer of dust covered everything. The mirror on the wall to his left was dull with grime and there were stains on the carpet visible even with no light.

"Looks like you guys have been busy," he said, not sure why they would have let everything slide so much. They'd always been neat before.

"Busy doing work for the master," Mrs. Stoddard said.

Mike caught a reflection of the back of Mr. Stoddard's head in the mirror. Something darted out of a bald patch around his ear.

"Yeah, I can see why you guys would be distracted with all that has been going on," Joe said. "You should see how messy Mike's room is."

"Yes, the room is very important," Mrs. Stoddard said.

They sure are acting weird, Mike thought. *They on something? Maybe quaaludes. People their age still do those, right?*

"Come," Mr. Stoddard said. "Further into the abode."

"We have prepared much nourishment," Mrs. Stoddard added.

They waved to follow them down the hallway towards the dining room. Candlelight flickered dimly inside. This must be some weird pagan thing that Kristin had wanted.

The dining room table was covered with serving trays sealed under warming lids. Twin candelabras with five tall candles each lit the room in a dim amber. The electric lights in the room were all off. Mike noticed that even the bulbs had been pulled out.

"You guys have a power outage or something?" he asked.

Joe elbowed him in the side, shaking his head.

"There is much power in here," Mr. Stoddard said.

"Yes, much," his wife added.

Three people sat in the adjacent family room on the couch in the darkness. It must be Kristin's parents and Harry. None of them rose to greet them. He saw the urn and the photograph from the funeral on an end table near the couch. The television was dark. What the heck were they looking at?

"Did you guys already do the service or what?" Mike asked.

"And is Dan here?" Joe asked.

"Dan had to step out for a moment," Mrs. Stoddard said. "He's out meeting someone."

"Like a lawyer?"

"She could be," Mr. Stoddard said. "I'm not sure what her occupation is."

"Her?" Joe asked.

"Indeed. With Kristin gone, he should really continue his search for a suitable mate," Mrs. Stoddard said.

"Whoa," Joe said, taken aback. "That's a little fast, don't you think? She's not even in the ground yet."

"Oh, she's not going in the ground," Mr. Stoddard said. "She's a part of the ceremony tonight as much as you are."

"I fucking knew it," Mike said. "She's not dead!" He moved over to the end table in the family room where the urn rested next to the photo.

"Dude, shut up."

Mike picked up the urn and looked to the three forms on

the couch. "Are you all in on this, too? Is this like a whole demon family situation?"

The black shrouded trio sat immobile on the couch.

"I'll bet this urn isn't even full of ashes," Mike said. He unscrewed the top and tipped it over. "See?" A stream of grey ash fell to the floor.

"Oh God," Joe said, hiding his face in his hand. "You just couldn't help yourself, could you? I am so sorry about this, Mr. And Mrs. Stoddard. He'll clean it up. Harry and Mr. And Mrs. Davis. I don't even know what to say to apologize for this idiot."

The three people on the couch didn't even seem to notice what was going on. Mike stood confused as ashes poured all over the carpet and his socks. Joe walked over to the couch and bent low to wave his hand in front of Harry's face.

"Harry? You guys okay?"

"I don't understand," Mike said.

Joe pulled his phone out and swiped on the flashlight. He pointed it at the family on the couch and screamed.

"She is dead?"

"So are they," Joe said.

Mike turned to see the glare of the flashlight illuminating three corpses, sitting perfectly rigid on the couch, throats slashed, bodies gutted and greyed. Their mouths hung open, their eyes were vacant.

"What the fuck is going on?" Joe asked.

"We invited you to the reception," Mrs. Stoddard said.

"We prepared so much for you to eat." Mr. Stoddard pulled away one of the warming lids. On the silver serving tray a mound of entrails steamed. Mrs. Stoddard pulled another away to reveal what looked like a pair of lungs.

"How about some red?" Mr. Stoddard said, pouring thick crimson liquid into a crystal glass. "It's so much better when it's fresh."

He handed the glass to his wife who drank it. The liquid that had to be blood poured over her mouth and began leaking from a gash in her throat that opened up anew.

Joe screamed and turned to run, hitting face first into the patio door and knocking himself back on his ass in a daze.

"I don't understand any of this," Mike said.

"And you don't have to." Mr. Stoddard grabbed a huge knife from the table and slowly walked towards them.

CHAPTER THIRTY-SEVEN:
CATCH AND RELEASE

Joe awoke from a dreamless sleep to a yellowed ceiling bathed in the morning sunlight. He sat up, neck aching, head swimming. Familiar posters on the wall, UHF, Silent Rage, The Thing. Dust on his spill-over DVD shelf. Clothes on the floor of his closet, boxes of comics piled haphazardly below hooks full of t-shirts and hoodies. He plopped his feet to the floor and stepped in something cold and damp. "Ewww, what the fuck?"

His pale-skinned feet had landed in a puddle of strong-smelling dark liquid. He bent over to take a sniff. "Whiskey? Why the fuck is there whiskey in here?"

"Because you love the stuff, kid," Frank said from the bed.

Joe spun to see Frank laying on his side with the blankets pulled low. He was shirtless and sweaty, staring at him intently.

"What the fuck are you doing here?"

"You didn't ask that last night."

"What the hell are you talking about?"

Frank yawned and ran his hand over his messy black hair. But hadn't it been grey before? No, almost white. Had he discovered Just for Men?

"Leisure Suit Larry, that little pervert, turned you on and… here we are."

The bedroom door opened. Someone came into the room. *Oh shit.* He spun around to see a gelatinous mound of flesh waddling in, completely naked, huge girthy breasts and stomach swaying as wide hips moved the great mass.

"Marlena?"

"Joe, glad you're awake." She held a cellphone to her ear and covered it with her other hand. "Put all of what you're doing on hold. I need you to find out if we can use the old Sugar Beet factory for a project next month. ASAP stat on this one."

She climbed into bed next to Frank and lay on her back. He slid on top of her.

"Old Sugar Beet factory? I've never heard of that. What is it now?"

"Top priority," she said calmly.

"I thought I was the top priority," Frank said.

"Just get to work," she said.

"Yes, ma'am!"

Joe turned away, not wanting to see even the first signs of coupling. He slid on a pair of boxers and bolted to the door. He skidded to a stop when he realized Kristin stood in the way.

"Jesus Christ, is this some kind of orgy?"

"You are such an idiot," Kristin said. "You only see what you want to see." She snapped her neck to the side with a crack. Her skin pulled apart at the collar. She reached up and dug her hands into the folds and began jerking downward. Her flesh tore away in strips, leaving her a meaty mess, dripping blood on the carpet. Joe could see her exposed organs pumping, intricately woven muscles, her entire internal structure.

He backed away, caught between her and the bed.

"Just look a little closer next time." She took a step towards him.

He screamed, woke up again, this time in complete darkness. He couldn't see a thing. "Blind, I'm fucking blind."

"No, you're not," Mike's voice said in the pitch black, "we're just locked up somewhere without any nightlights."

"Mike?" Joe asked. "Is that you?"

"Who the hell else would it be?"

"I don't know. I was having a fucked-up dream."

"Did it involve being offered organ meats made of the Davis's?" he asked. "Because that shit wasn't a dream."

"Oh God, now I remember. They must have knocked me out with something," Joe said.

"No, you knocked yourself out when you ran head-first into the patio doors. They just carried you down here."

"Then how did they get you?"

"They had a big fucking knife. I'm not Jackie Chan, I can't kung fu my way out of anything."

"What's going to happen to us?"

"I don't know," Mike said. "Something about how we're going to feed the master, whoever that is. I'm guessing it's Kristin. She's through whatever transformation she had to fake her own death to do and now she's going to eat us and Dan. Maybe even this new girlfriend he was out to meet."

"That's... an explanation, I guess."

"You have a better one?"

"Of course not. But in my dream, Kristin was trying to tell me something. I don't remember what it was, but she was pulling off her skin and then trying to—"

"Kill you. See? She's even haunting you in your sleep."

"So, what do we do?" Joe asked. He wasn't bound and rubbed the feeling back into his arms and legs. "Is there a way out of here?"

"Not that I can see." Mike paused, then burst out laughing. "Get it? See? Because it's so dark in here, neither one of us can see a goddamn thing."

"Is this really the time to crack jokes?"

"I don't know what else to do, man. We're trapped in a dungeon, nobody knows we're here, and two nutcases want to turn us into organ stew. Oh, did I mention there's a demon out there?"

"Wait, somebody does know we're here," Joe said.

"Frank!" they both said in unison.

* * * *

"You ready yet, Annie, or you still trying to learn how not to walk bow-legged?" Frank wiped shaving cream off his face and looked at himself in the mirror. He saw a man flush with post-coital glee, and felt better than he had in a while.

"You got a real high opinion of yourself, Wildcat," Southside Annie said from the bedroom.

"Oh, come on." Frank left the bathroom to catch her doing up her girdle with one of her sweet gams perched on the bed. "You know a ride on the Frank express isn't like any other ride in town."

"Express is right," she said. "You were missing all the stops on the way like you were behind schedule."

Frank grabbed his new and mostly still clean shirt from the floor and pulled it over his head. His spent Johnson dangled below as he buttoned up. "I just wanted to get you to your destination before closing time, baby."

She eyed his nakedness with a raised eyebrow. "Next time I'll take the subway."

Frank pulled on his yellowed underwear and socks. "Anybody can drive one of those things, you're stuck on a track. Driving a bus takes real skill with the wheel and stick."

She pulled on her silver miniskirt and black sweater, fixed her hair and chuckled. "Alright, Wildcat, I get it. You're not the only guy I've been with who has a high opinion of his own skills. Not even the only guy this week."

"Wait, so who's the subway in this metaphor?" Frank asked.

"Worry about that later – weren't we supposed to be at your two buddies' party hours ago?"

Frank pulled on his raincoat and ran his hand through his grey hair. "Who the hell goes to a party on time?"

* * * *

"You have any idea how long we've been down here?" Joe asked.

"A few hours, I think," Mike said. "But they took our phones."

"Smart."

"But they don't know the passwords."

"Sure, but now we can't phone for help."

"I doubt there'd be a signal down here anyway," Mike said.

"Any idea where we actually are?"

"The basement of Stoddard's parents' house. But it doesn't look at all like I remember. They redecorated to dungeon chic."

"Wait, so this is Dan's old house?"

Mike didn't answer.

"Mike? You there?"

"Yeah."

"You didn't answer. Is this Dan's old house?"

"I nodded. That usually means yes, you know."

"Fucking hell, Frank better get here soon."

* * * *

The radio played Burton Cummings as Frank drove South-side Annie through the gloriously lit, neon-soaked streets of River City. He took her past all the old joints, taking his time to breathe in the pre-rainstorm air of a city that was soon going to be washed clean.

"Smells like rain," he said.

"Smells like piss, too."

"One'll solve the other then."

The address the boys had given him was in the west end of town, on the other side of the Assiniboine River. He could have taken the perimeter highway and saved twenty minutes of driving time, but he liked the buildings and grime.

They pulled to a stop at a red light. Frank looked over to his date, his favourite lady of the evening. He watched her fixing her make-up. Sure, she'd been around the block, but when the block was so good, who cared?

That was when he saw the car pull up next to them. A red convertible, idling at the stop. The man inside was shifty-eyed, dressed in black.

"Holy shit," Frank said.

"What?" Southside Annie asked. "You think red is too much

for a funeral?"

The man in the other car saw Frank looking. He motioned with his head to the light. Frank nodded back; cop and criminal sharing an understanding that went beyond words.

"I think red is too much for a criminal!"

"Hey, you knew I was a pros—"

The light changed. The convertible sped away. Frank slammed on the accelerator and peeled after it. Annie was launched hard into the seat, smearing lipstick all over her face.

"He's not getting away from me this time."

* * * *

A tiny door opened, at about eye height, but it was hard to tell when there were no reference points. A blue rectangle shone inwards, lighting a point on the floor. It gave enough illumination to allow Mike to see Joe laying against the wall nearby. Then, the light was cut off by a face.

"Good news for you two," Mr. Stoddard said in his gravelly voice.

"You're letting us go?" Joe said.

"Of course not. You have a larger part to play. The good news is the master is looking forward to feeding on your organs and flesh."

"Yeah, that is good news," Mike said sarcastically.

"Unfortunately, the master is indisposed at the moment. You'll just have to marinate for a while longer, I'm afraid."

"When Dan finds out you two are planning to kill his best buds, he's going to be pretty pissed," Mike said.

The door slid shut, cutting them off again from the light.

"Maybe we should start working on getting ourselves out of here," Joe said.

* * * *

The red car faded away down Portage Avenue, leaving Frank and his poor old reliable domestic in the dust. He was doing a hundred, but that thing was doubling him. He'd blown it. Again. "Blast," he said, pounding on the wheel. He let the car slow down to the speed limit.

"Don't worry, Wildcat," Southside Annie said. "Thirty years ago, you would have had 'em for sure."

"Thirty years ago, that punk would have been nothing more than his dad's bad intentions."

"Maybe I knew the guy?"

"It's alright, Annie," Frank said. "I'll get that bastard one of these days. Guess we'd better get to that party before they run out of the good stuff."

He turned off Portage onto the Clement Bridge, crossing the river towards the address he had been given.

* * * *

"Find anything?" Joe asked.

Mike rubbed his hands along the cold brick walls, looking for any kind of loose brick, latch, or way out.

"No. You?"

"Nothing yet, but there's got to be something, right?"

* * * *

Frank parked the car behind another one on the cul-de-sac with a name like all the others in this cookie cutter neighbourhood. The house mentioned on the note was dark, as if they'd packed in for the night. The driveway was full, however, so someone had to be home. "You sure this is it?" Southside Annie asked.

"Of course," he said. "But I left my reading glasses in the glove compartment, so you want to double check the paper the kids gave me?"

He handed it to her. Southside Annie pulled out some glasses from her cleavage and looked down her nose at the note before checking the house number. "Yup, this is it," she said.

"Maybe the action is around the back." Frank started walking around the side of the house.

* * * *

"Someone's coming," Mr. Stoddard said, staring off into space.

"Not the dark lord."

"No."

"What do we do?"

"Hide. Surprise them. The master could always use more sustenance."

"Where?"

"The closet, hurry."

"Let me just take something for the road." Mrs. Stoddard grabbed a pile of entrails as the two of them ran to hide in the hall closet.

* * * *

Frank peered through the patio door into the house. He could see candles lighting up a nearly untouched buffet. A few people sat like statues on the couch. He waved at them, but they didn't seem to notice him at all.

"Well? What do you see, Wildcat?"

"There're people in there. Must be watching the TV. One hell of a spread of grub, too. Don't see the boys, but I guess we can just go on in."

He pulled on the door handle, but the thing was locked tight. "Goddamn it. Hey, guys, let us in?" He tapped on the door a few times, but nobody budged. He turned and looked around the yard. "No sandbox," he said. "Guess I'll have to use Old Faithful." He took out his gun and aimed, but the sound of a click stopped him.

Southside Annie stood holding the door open.

"How'd you—?"

"Call it a trick of the trade," she said, shoving a hairpin back into her hair.

Frank replaced his gun and walked into the room.

"Hey, everybody, sorry we're late. We were a little busy getting busy if you catch my drift." He walked over to the buffet table and reached for a warming lid.

"Uhhh, Wildcat, I don't think these people care that we're late," Southside Annie said.

"That's good. I don't care if they care anyway."

"No, Frank, they're not going to care much about anything anymore. They're dead."

"I thought this party was a little too quiet."

He lifted the lid and took a whiff of the delicacy on the

plate. It smelled rank. "No wonder, this grub's gone sour."

He replaced the lid and walked back over to where Southside Annie stood checking out the bodies. She tested pulses, held a compact under noses, listened to chests, then gravely shook her head.

"Don't see the boys here anywhere," Frank said.

Southside Annie spotted a trail of blood on the floor, leading to the hallway closet. She quietly pointed to it.

Frank pulled out his gun. "Someone did a piss poor job of mopping," he whispered.

Southside Annie put a hand on his shoulder as he moved cautiously towards the closet door. They held their breath, listening. He motioned for her to stop. Frank held one hand out, slowly reaching for the closet door.

Something was definitely moving around on the other side. He heard shuffling noises, muffled conversation. Was it the boys hiding? Was it whoever had killed those poor people on the couch? Only one way to find out.

"When I give you the signal, hit the lights, Annie," he whispered.

She moved towards the staircase leading up and held onto the banister, reaching her hand over to the light switch that would illuminate the chandelier high in the ceiling. Frank looked up, saw bulbs, which was one up on the other sockets in the house so far. He only hoped they weren't burnt out.

He nodded slowly and counted to three with his finger on the trigger. When he hit three, he pulled open the closet door just as Southside Annie hit the switch.

He screamed. The two people he saw inside screamed. Southside Annie screamed. Then Frank fired his whole clip.

* * * *

Joe heard the gunshots from the floor above. "Holy shit, you hear that?"

"Gunshots?"

"Frank!"

Mike moved to the door and started pounding. "Help! We're in here. Uh, in the basement!"

"Help!" Joe shouted.

* * * *

"What the hell were those things?" Southside Annie asked, looking at the couple in dark robes with rotted skin. Blood had smeared all over their faces from the length of entrails they'd been chewing on. Contact lenses had fallen from the eyes of one, revealing nothing but white eyes.

"Actual honest to goodness goddamned Boogie Men," Frank said in shock.

"One's a woman."

"No such thing, eh, Chief?" Frank said proudly. "Then what the fuck are those?"

Faint muffled shouts drifted up from the floor beneath them. Southside Annie put her hand on Frank's shoulder to quiet him. "Listen."

"Help!"

"The boys!"

"There's got to be a basement," Southside Annie said.

* * * *

Mike pounded hard, frantically crying out.

"He has to have heard us," Joe said, his voice already hoarse.

"God, I hope so," Mike said. "Help!" he shouted again.

Just then the tiny slot in the door opened, sending a searing line of light into Mike's eyes. He blinked away temporary blindness to find Frank's smiling face looking back at him.

"So, this is where the party is, eh?"

He unlocked the door. A lightbulb dangling from the ceiling illuminated the hallway. There was another door across from them, shut tight.

"Frank," Joe said, coming out into the hall, "are we glad to see you."

"Usually, she's the one the guys are glad to see." Frank gestured to Southside Annie standing beside him.

She waved at them. "Hey, boys."

"Southside Annie, I could kiss you," Mike said.

"Sure, but that puts you on the clock."

* * * *

"Great Gatsby, you're right. That's people in there," Frank said, replacing the lid on the food plates. "What the hell kind of party was this?"

"Dan's parents were some kind of... zombie cannibals," Mike said, grabbing the huge, curved knife from the table and swinging it around a few times. "They wanted to chop us up with this and add us to the spread."

"For their master," Joe added.

"Who's that?" Frank asked.

"It's got to be Kristin," Mike said.

"You mean the dead girl?" Southside Annie asked.

"He means the dead girl he poured all over the carpet." Joe gestured to the pile of ashes still laying near the three dead Davis's on the couch.

"Ahh, someone'll vacuum that up, don't worry."

"Just what in the hell is going on here?" Southside Annie asked.

"The beginning of your doom," a gravelly voice shouted at them from the hallway.

They all turned to see Dan's parents, standing upright, blood-soaked, blank-faced, moving awkwardly towards them.

"Now I *know* I shot the shit out of those two Boogie People," Frank said.

"Fool," Mrs. Stoddard said. "You can't kill what's already dead."

They backed away. Frank frantically dug in his pocket for bullets to reload his revolver. Southside Annie pulled out some mace from her purse and took aim. Joe slid a chair in their way. Mike stepped to the side. The ghouls passed through the doorway.

"The master will make meals out of all of you. You cannot stop his—"

Mr. Stoddard's hoarse voice was cut off when Mike swung the huge knife and severed his head completely from his body. It flew through the kitchen, but the body kept moving.

"What the…"

"Do it again," Joe shouted.

Mike swung the blade, taking Mrs. Stoddard's head clean off as well.

The two bodies began stumbling around, tripped over the chair and fell on top of each other. Joe quickly pinned them down with another chair and sat on it.

"The master cannot be denied," the dead couple cried out.

Frank finished loading his gun and aimed at the heads. "You've had enough red meat, how about some lead salad?"

"No, wait," Joe said, struggling to hold down the squirming corpses. "We need to know what we're up against here."

"Yeah." Mike leaned the huge blade on his shoulder. "Who are you working for, Stoddards?"

"That one knows," the head of Mrs. Stoddard said, looking at Joe.

Mike turned to him. "What? You been holding out on me, dude?"

Joe pushed down on the chair, trying to understand what they were talking about. He remembered the dream, Kristin in white looking at him before pulling off her skin. "Kristin…" he said haltingly.

"There." Mike turned proudly to the heads. "We know your evil demon bitch boss lady, so tell us where to find her and we'll take her down, too."

The heads laughed, horrible rattles from beyond the grave. Southside Annie covered her ears and Frank raised the gun again.

"You are such a fool," Mr. Stoddard said. "The dark one is—"

"Dan," Joe interrupted.

CHAPTER THIRTY-EIGHT:
ILLUMINATIONS

"What the fuck are you saying, Joe?" Mike said.

"He knows," Mr. Stoddard's head said.

"He doesn't know shit, so shut the fuck up." Mike punted the head as hard as he could. It flew against the wall above the fireplace, splattered hard and slid to the ground, leaving a streak of red in its wake.

"Stop to think about it for a minute. I know it seems farfetched, maybe even preposterous, but it's true. When we saw the shadows, the glowing eyes, the weird visions. Every time you thought you saw a tail or wings, or felt the time bubbles. What's the common denominator?"

"Six," Frank said.

Mike tried to picture all of those moments. What was Joe hinting at? Kristin's glowing eyes: they'd shone when she and Dan had stood beside each other at the pool hall, again when they were giving speeches at the wedding. The shadow behind them had... Suddenly the realization Joe pushed him towards was right in front of him. "Each time they were together."

"You weren't seeing just her shadow, you were seeing his. Or more precisely, both of their shadows."

"But I've been his friend since kindergarten," Mike said. "I would have seen signs before, wouldn't I?"

"I don't know. Why don't you ask his mom?"

Mike bent down to look into the white glazed eyes of the severed head of Mrs. Stoddard, the woman who'd baked them cookies for afternoon snacks, made pancakes the mornings of sleepovers, driven them to soccer and football games, trailed behind them as they rode their bikes to the mall, who'd done a million things over the years that had never once come close to trying to feed him to her son. Blinking, with rotting skin and goo leaking from the stump of her neck, she wasn't the same person. She wasn't even a *person* at all.

"Mrs. Stoddard?" he asked tentatively.

She tried to bite him, and he jerked back.

"I don't know if you're in there, but I need to know just what in the fuck is going on. Is Dan a demon? Where is he? What's he after? Can we stop him?"

The head seemed to calm, blinked awkwardly, and looked at him as if it had only now realized he was there.

"Mike?" it said. "Is that you?"

"It is, Mrs. Stoddard."

"I can't feel my legs," she said.

He looked over at Joe who sat on the chair that held down her flailing body.

"Don't worry, they're still moving around."

"Where's Gordon?"

"He's checking out the fireplace." Mike looked over his shoulder to see the head of Mr. Stoddard rocking back and forth on the hearth.

"Dan..." she said.

"Yeah?"

"We…"

"You what?"

She mumbled something. Mike leaned in closer. She bit down on his ear, and he whiplashed his head back. She clung tight.

"Get it off, get it off!"

Southside Annie grabbed the hair and started pulling, stretching Mike's ear.

"Ow, ow ow, ow!"

"The bitch won't let go," Annie said.

Frank calmly walked over to the table, grabbed one of the tray-warming lids, flipped it around and swung hard, knocking the head clean off, launching it against the far wall, where it splattered and slid down to lay next to the head of Mr. Stoddard.

Frank grabbed two of the serving trays from the table and slid the organs off. He took them over to the heads and, using the lids, propped up the heads in the centre. He pulled out his gun and pressed it against the temple of Mr. Stoddard.

"Okay, buddy, we tried it the kids' way, now we do it mine. Spill the beans or I spill your brains. Assuming you still have any."

"Naive fools. The ritual cannot be stopped. The dark one has awoken. He will fulfill his destiny to bring on the end times."

"How does he plan to do that?"

"Amassing energy to unleash his true power."

"How does he amass energy?" Joe asked.

"He devours," Mr. Stoddard said. "And soon he will devour you all."

"Doomed," Mrs. Stoddard said. "You are all doomed!"

They started laughing. Southside Annie covered her ears. "God, again, it's horrible."

Frank put the lids on the two trays, muffling the heads.

"That answer your question, kids?" he asked.

"Fuck, no. I still don't buy it," Mike said.

Joe scrolled through his phone as he pinned the bodies down. The blue light cast a cold glow on his grim visage as he read.

"Look at this." He waved them over.

They crowded around the screen to see a photo of Dan with a dark-haired girl in glasses. They were sitting in his condo on the couch, below the painting of Gates of Hell. She wore a floral print dress and smiled brightly. Their eyes glowed red from the flash.

"Who the heck is that?" Mike asked.

"Says her name is Jennifer," Southside Annie read.

"Is he dating, already?"

"It sure looks that way."

Mr. Stoddard's serving tray vibrated. Frank walked over and lifted the lid.

"More souls for the dark one! His power grows stronger! You are all going to hell. You are all doo—"

Frank slammed the lid back down.

"So, your buddy is getting back out there," Frank said. "Sounds like that's a bad thing."

"Maybe he's just not processing his emotions," Mike said. "His wife just died and—"

"Who dates someone new the day of his wife's funeral?"

"I knew a guy who took me *to* his wife's funeral," Southside Annie said.

Mike stared at the phone trying to figure out an answer for

what was going on. "He never did like to be alone. Maybe he…"

The trays vibrated again. Frank lifted the lid of Mrs. Stoddard's tray.

"He feeds! He gains more power to destroy you all. The ritual is nearly complete!"

"What fucking ritual?" Joe said.

The other tray vibrated, and Frank lifted that lid.

"From the book of evil. On the altar of despair. We called and were answered."

"Where is this book and altar?" Joe asked.

"We would never reveal the secret place hidden away from the light," Mr. Stoddard said. The two heads laughed.

"Is it in the basement?" Joe asked.

The two heads stopped laughing and tried to look at each other.

Frank slammed the lids back down.

"Sounds like it is to me."

"Maybe there's something down there we can use to stop this," Joe said.

* * * *

"Nothing in the cell we were kept in," Joe said.

"Nothing in the storage area," Southside Annie added.

"Nothing behind the furnace," Frank said.

"That just leaves the locked door." Mike stared at the heavy wooden portal covered in scratches and dust.

Joe reached for the handle. "Locked."

The two trays on the ground vibrated. Frank lifted the lid of Mr. Stoddard's.

"Do not disturb the sanctuary of the dark one."

The other tray rattled. Frank lifted that lid.

"You idiot, you weren't supposed to tell them that!"

Frank pulled out his gun. "I've got a surefire lockpick right here, boys."

Southside Annie stopped him. "Let me, Wildcat."

She took out her hairpin and went to work.

"Stay away, whore!" Mrs. Stoddard said.

"Hey," Frank said. "That's working girl to you."

"Slut, whore, cunt!"

Frank dropped the lid on her head to silence her screams.

"I've heard worse," Southside Annie said. With a click, she had the door open. She pushed it in to reveal a room bathed in darkness.

Joe and Mike shone their cellphones inside. An altar lay toppled in the centre of the room. The remnants of old candles rested in sconces on the wall, but what was even more shocking was the pile of desiccated corpses pushed into a corner. The meat had been sucked clean, leaving skeletal remains in tattered robes. There had to be at least a dozen bodies.

"Jesus, how many skeletons in the closet does this family have?" Frank said.

"What is this place?" Joe asked, shining his light on the deep gouges in the brick walls, and faded symbols drawn on the floor.

"Looks like a few bachelor parties I've run," Southside Annie said.

Mike crouched low, finding a book on the floor. Bound in heavy leather, with thick pages written in red ink, he shone his light over the words.

"Whatever it is, it's not English."

"Of course it's not English, you fools," Mr. Stoddard's voice called from the hall. "The words of evil are written in the ancient tongue of… evil."

The other tray rattled as Southside Annie walked over and took the book. "Looks like Latin to me."

"What'd I tell you, boys? She's an old pro. Can you read it?" Frank asked her.

"Nope," she said. "But I recognize it from my time in Catholic school."

"Then what good is this book to us?" Mike asked.

"Nothing," the head of Mr. Stoddard said. "So leave it exactly where you found it and return home. The dark one will soon complete his transformation and you will all be dead. There's absolutely no reason to keep the book at all."

The other tray rattled. Frank lifted the lid.

"Would you shut the hell up!" Mrs. Stoddard said. "You practically told them that the book contains the way to stop the master's plan. Fuck, what an idiot you are."

They all looked at each other. "Are you thinking what I'm thinking?" Joe asked.

"That it's pretty convenient to find exactly what we need at the exact time we needed it?" Mike said.

"It doesn't matter what you've found," Mrs. Stoddard said. "The master will devour you all."

"The dark one has developed a taste for pure things," Mr. Stoddard said as he eyed Joe. "You will be perfect."

"What's that supposed to mean?" Joe asked.

"Dude? Is he implying what I think he's implying?"

"We imply nothing," Mrs. Stoddard said.

"Okay." Joe grabbed the two trays and flung them into the

dark room with the skeletal remains. "We're done with you two."

"Can any of *you* guys read Latin?" Southside Annie asked as she flipped through the book.

"No!" Mr. Stoddard said from inside the room. "No one can. Not anymore. That's the dead language of bibles and private schools. So just fuck off and—" Joe slammed the door shut.

"Bibles!" Frank said.

"Father O'Hoolahan."

CHAPTER THIRTY-NINE: OUR FATHER

"I can't believe St. Lucia's doesn't have a phone," Joe said, scrolling through online listings.

"The place was built pre-electricity," Mike said.

"And contractors ain't cheap," Frank said as he drove.

Southside Annie flipped through the book in the front seat. The night sky was filled with swirling, inky black clouds that seemed poised to break into a storm at any moment.

"Are you sure we need this guy's help?" Joe asked. "He can't be the only person who can read Latin in River City."

"It's one in the morning. What are you gonna do, post on Facebook and hope somebody DMs you?"

"I know what a few of those words mean," Frank said from the driver's seat.

"Don't worry, Wildcat." Southside Annie patted his leg. "It's Latin to me, too."

Mike scrolled his phone, looking for something that might help. He absent-mindedly clicked over to CBC, checking to see if there'd been any important news while they'd been locked up.

"Body pulled from the Red River," he read to himself. "Identified as Shannon Emily, age twenty-five. Shannon

346

Emily? Where have I heard that name before? Emily hadn't been reported missing and authorities are considering whether the case is a suicide or accidental drowning."

He typed her name into Google and found her Facebook profile. "Holy shit, Shit-ler!" There looking back at him was the girl Dan had briefly dated, the one who had fouled their bathroom so badly even six thousand flushes hadn't been enough to get rid of the aroma.

"What about her?" Joe said. "She moved to Vancouver."

"They just pulled her from the river."

Mike clicked on her Facebook profile, which was a ghost town of inactivity. It showed her current city as Vancouver. There were a few scattered posts, things like "go Canucks," or "miss the sunshine." There were no photos, no mentions, not even any links. A few friends had left notes saying "miss you," or "when are you coming home," but she hadn't responded.

"She's dead?" Joe asked.

"Looks like it."

"Are you thinking what I'm thinking?" Joe looked over at him.

"That we shouldn't have left our car at Dan's parents?"

"No. That Dan having one dead ex and one dead wife is a pretty big coincidence."

"Is it?" Frank asked from the front seat. "How big? Asking for a friend."

"Quick," Joe said. "What was the name of that girl who came to the Bomber game? Kim... something. Comeau, that was it."

Joe typed in her name on his phone and found her profile. Mike leaned over to look. It was also devoid of activity since an initial announcement that she was going to rehab.

347

"What are you thinking?" he asked Joe.

Joe found and typed in the number for the rehab centre. He dialed, holding up his finger for Mike to stay quiet.

"Hi, yes, I was wondering if it would be possible to speak to a patient there. Yes, I am aware of the time and I'm sorry, but it's a family emergency. The name is Kim Comeau."

Joe waited, listening.

"I see… Has she already been discharged? No? There was never any one by that name there? Huh, I must have the wrong information. I'm sorry to have bothered you."

He hung up.

"So she went somewhere else," Mike said. "Big deal."

"I'm not sure you're seeing what I'm seeing here."

"What I'm seeing is—"

"Guys," Frank said. "We're here."

* * * *

Leaving the car parked across two spots and half on the grass in the otherwise empty lot, the four of them stood at the parish door while Frank pounded and called to the father. After what felt like ten minutes, the door opened slowly, and the bent form of the wrinkled old priest appeared. He held a candle and smelled like wine. "Frankie, a little late for confession, isn't it?"

"Not this time, padre," Frank said. "I've got those two kids with me. Seems like there's a new wrinkle in their demon story and it might be in this old book."

Frank grabbed the book from Southside Annie and handed it to the old man who licked his finger and flipped through a few pages.

"Latin?"

"We need your help translating it, Father," Joe said, stepping forward. "We were wrong before. Our friend's woman wasn't the demon, he is!"

"Allegedly," Mike added.

Father O'Hoolahan's eyes bugged out as he read. He shut the book and waved them inside. "Not here," he said. "The night has eyes and more than a few aren't friendly."

The old man led them inside the church. Southside Annie examined the historic building with interest while Joe and Frank told the man everything that had happened. As he listened to the crazy story, he rubbed his chin in thought.

"—so that's the deal, Father," Joe said, finishing the recap. "The book should have the way to stop our demon ex-roommate, but none of us can read it."

"Alleged demon ex-roommate," Mike said curtly.

"It's a good thing you came to me," Father O'Hoolahan said. "A very good thing. Why, just the other day I was thinking to myself that this whole demon business was going to come to a head. I was preparing for the worst."

"How?"

"Ensuring the sanctity of the communion wine, for one, also—"

"But can you translate?" Joe interrupted.

"Of course."

They sat looking at each other in silence. Nobody moved. The father smiled paternally, holding the book. Frank slung his arms over the pews.

"So will you?" Joe asked.

"Oh!" Father O'Hoolahan said. "You wanted me to do it now?"

"The severed heads of Dan's parents said he was almost through whatever transformation he was undergoing, so I'd say that puts us in a time crunch," Joe said.

"You know," Father O'Hoolahan said. "This just goes to show that you have to trust in God's will. I've been fighting the spawn of Satan for ages, sent more than my share back to hell, too, but it'd been so long since any popped up that I was beginning to wonder if I'd been forcibly retired. If maybe the Lord had forgotten about me. Then, lo and behold, you four show up here and tell me that your supposed she-devil is actually a he-devil."

"Do those actually exist?" Mike asked.

"Oh, sure. They call them an incubus."

"And what do they do exactly?"

"Oh, the usual: drain the life of lovers, try to impregnate women, mind control…"

"You've seen an incubus before?" Mike asked.

"Probably delivered my share of 'em back in the old days, too. Sometimes you can just smell that a baby is evil when they come out of that little flesh tunnel. They kind of look at you cock-eyed, like they're confused as to why they're not still in hell."

"One of mine was like that," Southside Annie said from the far stained-glass window she was examining. "He went into law."

"Figures," Frank said. "Breaks a mother's heart to see."

"There's no wings, tail, glowing eyes, fangs?" Joe asked.

"Depends what the mother was laying with."

"You're getting carried away here," Mike interrupted. "This makes no sense. I've known Dan for twenty years. Are you telling me his parents were demons, too?"

"They certainly weren't human anymore," Joe said.

"Well," Father O'Hoolahan said, "it all depends who his real father was. See, the incubus impregnates a woman in order to create new demon life. The child born of demon/woman relations begins life as an indistinguishable human only to become a demon as it matures. A female baby will become a succubus, the male an incubus."

"Dan's mom fucked a demon?"

"Or his dad was one," Joe said.

"No, your friend was right. You see, upon birth, the new demon life absorbs the power of its creator, killing the original succubus or incubus and beginning the process all over again. It's a part of their curse."

"So, if Dan has a baby he'll die? Is that why he killed Kristin?"

"Allegedly," Mike said.

"You're assuming your friend is a low-level incubus. Satan has many servants. The friend you knew was just a kind of chrysalis phase of something much worse, a higher-level fiend. You see," Father O'Hoolahan said, brandishing the book, "he's been awoken by a dark ritual from the mists of pre-history. Now that he's matured, so to speak, he's spreading his wings. If what the book says of this creature is true, he is going about feeding on the souls of some, impregnating others. Satan's minions can only survive so long here on earth under God's life-giving sun. It drains them. All natural light does. It must feed to sustain itself for its dark mission."

"There you have it, boys," Frank said proudly. "Straight from the Lord's mouth. Your pal is a real no-goodnick."

"What I'm hearing is you saying Dan's mom boned some incubus and never told his dad."

351

"She wouldn't be the first wife to do that," Southside Annie said.

"Just goes to show you, shit runs downhill." Frank said.

Father O'Hoolahan waved his hand. "No, no, no. There's more here than any of you realize. Something much worse."

"What could be worse than you telling us our friend is a demon?" Mike asked.

"Your demon friend killed his pregnant wife recently, correct?"

"Allegedly," Mike said.

"We're pretty sure he did," Joe said. "Why is that important?"

The father pounded a fist into his open palm. "He isn't a regular run of the mill lower-level incubus. The ritual in the book was to awaken one much more powerful. This one knows its fate. It doesn't impregnate a woman to simply create a new demon life, it does so that it can kill and absorb not only the woman's soul, but that of the unborn as well."

"Is that bad?" Mike asked.

"Is that bad? Is that bad?" Father O'Hoolahan said, flabbergasted as he looked to Frank. "Can you believe this guy asking me if that's bad?"

"I can believe anything, Father," Frank said.

"Well, is it bad?" Mike asked again.

"Oh, it's bad," Frank answered.

"It's worse than bad, it's terrible. An incubus who absorbs enough of the power of life, strongest in the pure and innocent – and what could be more pure and innocent than the unborn – that demon gains tremendous power, the power to rip asunder the veil that separates hell and earth."

"So, he could open a portal to hell?" Joe said, incredulous.

"A way to call forth the armies of Lucifer to make war on an unsuspecting humanity. Millions would die, society would crumble, it would be the end times."

"Jesus Christ," Joe said.

"Can he be stopped?" Southside Annie asked. "I kind of like this place."

The old man stood up, stoically. "I think so. I've got exorcism gear in my closet, but it's been a while – I might be a little rusty."

"Can the book help?"

"It gives me the monster's true name and realm. I can work with that."

"How much of this pure life energy does he need to open the portal?" Joe asked. "Dan may have already killed multiple women and at least one unborn baby."

"We should hurry. There's no telling what could happen should he be allowed to absorb any more souls."

Joe checked his phone, scrolling to Facebook. He blanched, holding up the phone for all to see. "We might be too late."

Mike leaned in and read the updated Facebook status aloud, "Dan and Jennifer in a relationship. Holy shit, he moves fast."

"And did you see how many likes it got?" Joe said in disgust. "Did people forget about Kristen already?"

"We should go immediately," Father O'Hoolahan said. "If the relationship is far enough along to announce on the internet, then who knows how many times they may have knocked boots? A demon seed is the most cunning seed there is. She could already be pregnant. We may not have much time left to stop him."

"Alright," Frank said. "We know who the enemy is, we know what he's after, and there's no way in hell... er, heaven that I'm going to let him open a portal to Satanville into my city.

There's enough assholes out there as it is without a bunch of demon-spawned shitheads running around. It's time I called in a little backup. Give me that phone, kid."

Joe handed Frank his cellphone. Frank stared at it, confused. "Say, how do I dial this thing?"

"What's the number?" Joe grabbed it back.

* * * *

The phone rang and a hand in the darkness reached over to answer. "Hello, who is this?" the Chief said, still half asleep and mostly under the covers. He held the receiver of the emergency line against his ear, his head resting on his pillow. The phone was only to be used in the utmost of crises. It had only rung once before and that had been for a suspected terrorist attack, a false alarm. What could it be this time?

"What is it, honey?" his stirring wife asked.

"Shhh, it's the hotline."

She fell back asleep almost instantly. It had been a nice quiet evening. They'd watched a few episodes of Hill Street Blues on DVD, then gone to bed. The emergency line had jerked him out of a particularly nice dream about Veronica Hamel.

"Hello? Who's there?" he said again into the phone.

"Chief, I hope you're wearing a diaper for this one because you are about to shit your pants."

That voice. He knew that voice. Was it—

"Malone? How the hell did you get this number?"

"There's no time for small talk, Chief, you've got to listen to me. Something real bad's on its way straight down the Highway to Hell. Seems one of Satan's helpers is trying to

354

crack open a gate to the hot place and we're going to need all the back up we can handle if we can't stop him. Get a pen so I can tell you where to send the boys in blue."

"Malone, I'm not in the mood for this. It's late and I've got a lot of work to do."

"But sir—"

"But nothing. I don't want to hear from you." He clicked the phone back onto its cradle and rolled over, grabbing his wife around the waist.

"Who was that, honey?" she mumbled.

"Just that nutcase I was telling you about. He sounded drunk."

* * * *

Frank stared at the phone, confused. "He hung up on me?"

"Well?" Joe asked.

"Looks like we're on our own on this one," Frank said.

"Guys, it's Dan," Mike said. "My best friend. Even if he is this powerful demon thing, he wouldn't do anything to hurt us. We're bros."

"He's no longer the man you knew," Father O'Hoolahan said. "He's a part of Satan's army now."

"Every army needs to be fed, Father," Frank said, taking out his gun. "And I'm going to give this one a lead lunch."

"Do we have to kill him? Can't we cure him or try to reason with him first?" Joe asked.

"Maybe there's something in that book to reverse the curse and stop him from doing all this gate to hell stuff," Mike said.

"I'm afraid we don't have time to read the whole thing," the priest answered. "We can't let him grow more powerful. We have to destroy him."

"I don't know if I can kill my best friend," Mike said.

"Leave it to me." Frank put his hand on Mike's shoulder. "I've killed lots of people's best friends."

"Neither of you understands," Father O'Hoolahan said. "A demon such as he cannot be killed by earthly means. Only a blessed warrior of the faith stands a chance. It's on my shoulders this burden falls." He broke out in a coughing fit and fell back to a seated position on the nearest pew.

"But you're so old – how can you do anything?" Joe asked incredulously.

The father braced himself back upright. "I will perform the exorcism and banish the demon from this dimension."

"What about this Jennifer girl?" Mike asked. "If she really is preggo then won't that baby turn out to be an incubus or succubus, too?"

"It must die as well to end the curse once and for all."

"This is getting heavy. Kill our best friend and an unborn baby," Joe said, shaking his head. "I don't know if I can handle all this."

"I've got some plan B in my purse," Southside Annie offered.

"Neither of you has to worry," Father O'Hoolahan said. "All you need to do is stay back and let a man of the Lord do his work. Now take me to this Dan so I can vanquish the spawn of Satan."

"You heard the padre, let's lock and load and hit the road," Frank said.

"Any chance of you guys dropping me off at home first?" Southside Annie said.

CHAPTER FORTY: (UN) HOLY SHIT!

T he night was as quiet as the grave. Even the crickets had preferred to sleep rather than sing at this hour. The streets were nearly deserted as the group drove through a city at rest. Frank pulled up to Dan's condo and put the car in park. The five of them looked out the window at the unassuming, multi-storied, depressingly modern building with a patio that overlooked the city. "This is where the hell-spawn lives?" Father O'Hoolahan said, looking up from the book of evil. "I'd expected something more sinister."

"There's nothing worse than a condo, padre. Paying a mortgage and condo fees? Without even owning any land? Cubic space..." Frank said. "It's a deal straight from the devil himself."

"Especially in this market," Joe said.

"So, what do we do?" Mike asked. "Ring the doorbell and ask him if he's a high-level servant of Satan out to destroy the world?"

"I doubt he'd just admit to that," Southside Annie said.

"And even if he did, we don't know what to do. You find anything in that book yet, Father?" Joe asked.

Father O'Hoolahan flipped another page intently, tracing

the lines of text with his finger. "Not yet, but I'm working on it."

"You keep reading. Mike and I will scope the place out first."

"I think I've got more experience scoping out places," Frank said. "Let me."

"Can we trust you not to shoot anyone?"

"*Any*one?"

"Let us do this, okay?" Joe said. "You need to stay here and... uh, guard the father and Annie."

"I can guard myself, thank you very much." Southside Annie pulled out a straight razor from her stocking.

"Okay, then, you guard Frank and the father. Either way, just stay in the car."

"That doesn't sound very heroic," Frank said.

Southside Annie leaned over and whispered something in his ear. He perked up. "Really? Just like that? Alright. Kids," he said to Mike and Joe, "you've got ten minutes to learn the layout and find out what you need to find out. Then we go in blasting."

"I guess that's as good as we're going to get."

Joe and Mike exited the car and walked down the sidewalk towards Dan's unit. The sky above was black, making the place feel more sinister than it should. The building was three stories tall. The main floor was one suite, while Dan's occupied the top two. A flickering light danced on the window that was his television room.

"You know, I still don't buy this whole Dan-is-a-demon idea," Mike said. "How could my best friend actually be some kind of monster?"

"I'm not going to pretend I understand it either," Joe said.

"But we've seen some crazy shit the past few weeks."

"You think he would tell me if I just asked him?"

"That all depends on if that awakening ritual was legit or not. He might not even be Dan anymore."

"Then we need to find out."

"How?"

"Spy on him through the window. It's the only way to know for sure."

"Okay," Joe said. "But he's on the top level."

"The balcony."

They went around to the back of the building. The third-floor bedrooms had a walk out balcony, with just enough space for a couple of chairs. It gave the owner a tiny sanctuary to gaze out at the stars, at the back of the Superstore parking lot adjacent to the condo compound, or far beyond that, the distant downtown lights.

"Up there," Mike said. "We can look in without him knowing. Is this new girl still there?"

"I don't know," Joe said. "He hasn't updated Facebook in a while."

"The light's on. They're either watching a movie or boning."

"I sure hope it's the former," Joe said. "But how do you propose getting up there? It's too high for a boost."

Mike looked up at the third-storey balcony twenty feet above them; concrete, with a railing made of wrought iron. "You wouldn't happen to have a grappling hook, would you?"

"Sorry, left it in my other pants."

Mike looked around the grounds for something they could use. There were no hoses, sprinklers, or ropes laying around.

"Huh…"

"What about an extension cord for a block heater?" Joe

said. "Frank might have one in that old beater of his."

"Stay here and watch. I'll go check."

Joe stared up at the blinking light in Dan's window, thinking back to everything that had led to this point; wondering if it was really happening or if he'd lost his marbles at some point. Before he could answer the question, Mike was back with an extension cord looped around at the top into a kind of lasso, fashioned into a crude grappling hook. He started twirling it, then let loose. His first three throws were wide, short, and in the trees. Then, growing frustrated, he tried again, and the loop hooked over one of the protrusions on the railing. He tested the hold, pulling down a few times and it stayed.

"Seems tight."

"You go first then."

Mike leapt up and dangled on the cord about a meter off the ground. The loop gave way, and he came crashing down on the grass.

"Okay, fine, not so tight then," he said, trying to not show any pain.

He retied the loop, tighter this time, and threw it again. Again, it connected with a railing protrusion. After a few tugs to show that it was secure, he hauled himself up and waved Joe to follow.

Joe had a spotty history with rope climbing dating back to elementary school. He never could manage to get anywhere and was the butt of jokes whenever he tried.

"You can do this," he said softly.

He leapt up and pulled, struggled, used all his strength, managed to make the ledge after Mike had pulled himself up and over. Crammed together in the tiny space of the balcony, they peered into the bedroom through a gap on the closed curtains.

The television mounted on the wall flashed through scenes from *The Notebook.*

Shapes moved on the large king-sized bed; two bodies under the sheets. A woman lay on her back, sheets clenched in her hands, head shaking back and forth as a larger form on top moved rhythmically.

"I feel kind of dirty watching this," Joe whispered.

"Shhhh."

Dan looked up, eyes glowing red. The shadow behind him cast by the flickering television moved strangely. Living shapes that weren't human, wings and a tail.

Joe gasped. Mike stared in horror.

Dan thrust again and Jennifer stopped moving; frozen in a moment of ecstasy. Dan quivered briefly then something started happening to her. She seemed to sink into the bed as if it was made of sand. Dan opened his mouth. A thin tendril of smoke began to leak from Jennifer's nose and mouth, drifting right up into his.

"He's absorbing something from her," Joe said.

Dan inhaled the strange smoke and after a few moments it was all gone. Jennifer lay prone beneath him. He pulled out and off her and slid off the bed, standing up to his full height. His nude body glistened with sweat. His dangling member glowed with a greenish otherworldly light. He walked towards the balcony where they were watching.

"Oh shit, hide!"

They climbed over the side and hung from the iron bars. Joe looked down. It was a fourteen-foot drop. Not so high that the fall would kill him, but it would probably fuck him up. He didn't know how long he could keep his grip.

Through the space in the bars, they saw the naked Dan walk outside on to the ledge. He put his hands on the banister, dangerously close to theirs and stared at the night sky lost in thought. He shuddered, stretched out some kind of kink in his back. Two great wings unfurled from his shoulders. Leathery, criss-crossed with dark veins, claws at the end, like a bat's. They looked large enough to carry him up and into the air.

Something writhed near their eyes. Joe choked on a gasp when he realized he was looking right at Dan's penis. It was alive, moving around like a moray eel, swimming against some invisible current, snapping at bugs as they flew by. He saw a pointed tail that dropped from just above Dan's bare ass.

Dan said nothing, didn't look down or notice their dangling forms. He'd completely transformed into a demon, like something out of a bad horror novel. How could this be the man they had known for so long?

Joe wondered just what it was he'd sucked out of that Jennifer girl. Had it killed her?

Dan took one more look at the sky and then turned and walked back inside his bedroom. He closed the wings tight around his body. His tail dragged behind him.

Joe looked over at Mike who'd gone white as a sheet.

"You believe it now?" he asked softly.

"How... how is that him...?" Mike stammered.

"It is. Or was. Or is and was. I dunno. Either way, we need to get the others."

Mike looked back towards where they'd left Frank and the car, then at the drop beneath them. "Right... how exactly?"

CHAPTER FORTY-ONE: THE FINAL COUNTDOWN

Frank checked his revolver, Southside Annie swung her straight razor a few times in the air, and Father O'Hoolahan slung a rusted sword into a scabbard on his back. "I'm still not clear on what the plan is," Mike said. "Barge in, perform some kind of exorcism on Dan, then do what amounts to an abortion on the possibly already dead girl?"

"Simple and effective, I like it." Frank stuffed the revolver into his belt.

"God's given us a chance to save the world. We must act now before the monster knows we're here."

Father O'Hoolahan looked like a Don Quixote cosplayer. He'd brought his whole kit, and it was right out of the middle ages: a plate of dented armour over his priest's robes, a conquistador style helmet of gold on his head. He carried a huge crucifix in one hand and vials of holy water strapped to a bandolier around his waist. The sword should have been within easy reach, but judging by how much trouble he had getting it on there in the first place, it seemed unlikely he'd be able to use it effectively. Despite the get up, Mike doubted he'd be much help at all.

"What happens if your exorcism doesn't work?" Mike asked.

"Pray that it does, my son." Father O'Hoolahan gently tapped him on the arm.

"Joe, help me out here."

"Dude, I don't know what the fuck is real anymore. You saw Dan. This is out of our wheelhouse. Trust the experts."

Mike looked at the so-called experts. A senior citizen cop, a washed-up prostitute, and a drunken Irish priest in four-hundred-year-old armour.

"We're fucked," he said.

"No," Frank said. "Your friend is."

They crept up to the street level entrance of the condo. There were no lights on above the door that led to the second floor. Had Dan gone back to bed? Was he… sucking more life out of this Jennifer girl?

Mike reached out and tried the handle. "Locked. I guess we can't go in and kill my best friend."

"Annie?" Frank said.

Southside Annie removed a hairpin from her head. "You guys would be lost without me."

She leaned over and began to go to work on the lock. Frank grabbed her ass, and she jumped in surprise.

"Frank!" she said.

"Put it on the tab, babe."

She had the door open in moments. She stepped aside and proudly motioned for them to enter.

"Say, Father," Joe asked. "How many of these demon things have you killed in your time?"

The old man started counting on his fingers, eyes looking off into the distance, mouthing equations. "What year is this?"

"Why does that matter?"

"Never mind, carry the one, plus two, let me think, there was that time in Prague… well, I guess you could say none," the man said.

"None?" Joe nearly shouted in shock.

"Shhhhh!" Frank turned to them halfway into the apartment.

"If this is really the high-level incubus demon I think it is, then it's the first time anyone's faced something like this. I've only dealt with minor level demons, imps, that sort of thing."

"But you *have* done that before, right? You've killed those imp things?"

"Oh, oh, of course. Imps, Cacodemons, Lost Souls, Spectres, Barons of Hell, Spider Masterminds, Cyberdemons, Zombiemen, shotgun guys…"

Joe frowned, realizing something about what the man was saying.

"Those are just Doom enemies."

"Yeah, and I've killed a shit ton," the father said.

"Guys," Frank said. "Radio silence from here on out."

They crept up the stairs of the condo, the four of them inching up to the second level holding their breath as if that would somehow prevent them from making any noise. The stairs creaked under their weight. Mike felt a palpable sense of dread, like the air was heavier, weighing down on them as they climbed. The faint aroma of sulphur wafted up his nose. A pulsating warmth emanated from a source above them.

They came to another shut door at the top of the stairs.

"Annie," Frank whispered in the lead. "Hand me that hairpin."

At the back of the line, Southside Annie passed along the

hairpin from hand to hand. Frank took it and began to work on the door.

"You sure you know what you're doing?" Joe asked.

"You think I've never... God damn it." Frank held up the broken hairpin.

"Great, now what do we do?"

"Anyone have a credit card?" he asked.

"Sure. Visa, Mastercard, Amex?"

"What, no Discovery?"

"Just take one!" Mike said, holding out his cards.

Frank chose the Amex, bent back down and fidgeted with the door. Seconds later he spat in disgust. "Fucking hell." He rose up with a broken card. "Hand me the Mastercharge."

Frank snatched the next one and moments later, came up with another bent and mangled card. "Okay, now let me try the Visa."

"Hey, I need those things." Mike pulled the cards away.

"You want in or not?"

Frank reached for the last card and the two of them struggled. Joe reached between them and turned the knob, surprised to find it unlocked.

"Uh, guys," he said, pointing to the slowly opening door.

Frank straightened his tie. "See, I knew I could do it."

He rubbed his hands together in anticipation and waved them onward. Mike grabbed his shirt and held him back.

"We're really doing this?" he asked.

"I'm not about to let some demon bring about the apocalypse on my watch," Frank said. "I've still got some dry cleaning to pick up."

* * * *

They exited into the landing of the second level of the condo, an open concept room with a closet on one side, kitchen on the other, and family room in between. Shoes were stacked neatly on a rack, the countertops were clean and there, standing in front of a massive wall-mounted television, bathed in a red glow, was Dan. But it wasn't the television, it was the living Gates of Hell painting emitting powerful light. Naked, wings unfurled, eyes glowing, Dan grinned at them with pointed teeth and huge fangs. Horns jutted out of his head, a tail dangled between his hooved feet. Three-inch-long claws glistened at the ends of his fingers. His penis snaked in the air, tiny jaws desperately trying to latch on to anything nearby.

"Dan," Mike said.

"No," Dan said in a voice that wasn't his. It was deeper, seemed to rise out of the floor below them, vibrating inside their skulls.

"Then what are you?"

"No longer a man. This is my true form." He spread his wings and posed dramatically. His penis laughed, a jarring sound that seemed to scratch at their inner ears with tiny claws.

"Jesus," Southside Annie said, looking at the penis in horror. "Now *that* is something I've never seen in my time."

"That makes two of us," Frank said.

"Dan," Mike said, trying not to look at his exposed demon cock, "how about you just, you know, stop being whatever the fuck this is and we can go back to streaming. Maybe some Ocarina of Time? Final Fantasy III?"

Dan looked at Mike with a glimmer of recognition in his glowing eyes.

"That'd be fun, right?" Mike said hopefully. "We can go home, game, make fun of Joe. Just like old times."

Dan broke out laughing again, his booming voice blending with the penis's scratchy one.

"You face a marvel of evil and you talk about playing children's games?"

"Video games are for all—"

"How about you face the marvel of my gun!" Frank pushed Mike aside.

"No, don't!" Mike tried to say but Frank fired two shots right at Dan.

The demon didn't flinch. There weren't any bullet holes on his body.

"I missed? That's not like me." Frank fired again and again, emptying the whole revolver, but it was as if the bullets simply disappeared into thin air.

"Insect." Dan waved his hand. The gun flew from Frank's grip across the room. Dan lifted his other hand and Frank was pulled into the air. With a swipe of his arm, Frank was tossed across the room to the far side. He hit the wall, leaving a six-inch indent in the drywall. He fell to the floor in a stunned heap.

"Dude," Mike said. "You don't have to do this."

"Insignificant humans." Dan clapped his hands together. Mike and Joe were launched into each other with a sudden force, bouncing like pinballs, collapsing in a dazed pile. He then clenched his fist and a bookshelf fell on top of Mike, pinning him underneath a library of hardcover Stephen King novels and old Nintendo Power magazines. Dan pushed his hand down and the shelf began compressing Mike, crushing the life out of him.

"Stop, you're killing him," Joe shouted as he tried to recover from the impact.

Dan waved his hand at Joe. He grew as light as air, was picked up and dragged along by an invisible string towards the beast. Dan grabbed him by the throat and looked him in the eye. Joe could see the fires of hell within his red gaze. All the horrors of the Gates of Hell painting trapped in each glowing orb. The heat of his breath was like a four hundred and fifty degree oven.

"You will know eternal torment."

"I was actually on my way to a call, so if you'll just excuse me," Southside Annie said, backing away to the stairs.

Dan pointed at her with a clawed finger, and she started gagging. Her hands rose to her throat as she desperately tried to breathe.

"The power of Christ compels you," Father O'Hoolahan shouted. "Begone!"

The priest screamed as he ran forward and stabbed his sword into the gut of the demon. From his place in Dan's grip, Joe saw the blade aimed right for the monster's heart, but instead of piercing the skin, it disintegrated into nothing as it drove forward. The useless hilt bounced off and Father O'Hoolahan stared in shock at the handle with no blade attached.

"Foolish. Did you really think that would work?"

Father O'Hoolahan shrugged. "Kind of."

The demon penis jerked forward and drove itself into Father O'Hoolahan's stomach. He lurched in shock as blood erupted from his mouth. The penis chewed through him, spraying blood all over the floor. It raised him up into the air, putting him eye to eye with Dan.

369

"Your God is weak," Dan said.

He opened his mouth. It kept growing, enlarging to an impossible degree, stretching his skull to four times its size. He bit the head clean off Father O'Hoolahan. Blood spurted from the corpse like a fountain and the demon threw the headless husk down the hall into the bathroom.

"Fatality," Dan said.

"Mortal Kombat?" Joe said through his constricting throat. "You are in there somewhere."

"You may join him." Dan turned to look at Joe face to face.

He saw his reflection in the glowing eyes that seemed to stretch inward all the way to the world of the painting. Dan grinned, blood dripping from his teeth. The wiggling penis rose up next to Dan's face, stretching like a snake. The bloody teeth snapped.

"Feed me, pure one," Dan said. "Be the instrument of ultimate doom."

Joe knew he was going to die here, but a soft voice came from the stairs.

"Dan?"

Everyone left alive turned to see Jennifer, emaciated, stumbling down the stairs as she held the wall. She wore a long nightshirt, rubbed sleep from her eyes.

"Oh, hey, baby, sorry to wake you," Dan said in his normal voice.

Jennifer pulled her hands away and looked at the scene in front of her. It had to look like a nightmare. Dan transformed into a demon standing naked holding Joe. An unconscious old man in the corner, another one headless, leaking blood. A woman gagging for air and Mike trapped under a bookcase.

"What's going on?" she asked in confusion.

"You're still asleep," Dan said. "This is all just a dream."

"It is?" she asked groggily. "It feels so real."

"Just a combination of David Lynch and too much vanilla vodka. How about you come here and give me a big hug?"

"Oh, okay." She stumbled towards him, looking like she could barely hold herself upright.

"No, don't!" Joe tried to shout through his constricted throat.

Mike tried to push the unnatural weight of the bookshelf off him, but he could only watch in horror as Jennifer approached Dan in a daze. With each step, she seemed to lose ten pounds. Her skin pulled tight, she lost colour, her bones protruded. When she reached Dan, she was barely more than a skeleton.

"How about a kiss?" he said.

He leaned forward and their lips met. She vibrated in place, seemed to melt, then impossibly, was sucked up into his mouth as if by a vacuum. In a flash, she was gone, disappearing inside Dan's mouth. He turned and belched, vomiting out gleaming white bones in a neat pile.

"You monster!" Southside Annie shouted through his choke.

Dan wiped his mouth, contented. "My power is nearly complete."

He stared at her intently. "Nearly..."

He drew his hand forward. Annie was pulled towards him, helpless in his grip. She tried to dig her heels in, but he just kept pulling. When they were face to face, he flashed his fangs at her.

"You're not exactly pure, but you'll do."

"Hey," Frank said, crawling to his feet. "Don't talk to my

371

favourite gal like that."

Dan whipped his head to the left and the couch flew at Frank.

"Oh fuck," was all he could say before it flattened him.

Southside Annie desperately tried to pull away. Dan looked in her eyes. "You're the furthest thing from pure, a taste I've not yet experienced."

"Don't knock it," she coughed. "I age like fine wine."

The penis turned from snapping at Joe's face to hers. A forked tongue shot out and traced around her cheek, slowly down her neck, into her cleavage. Joe spotted the straight razor sticking out of Annie's pocket. He could almost reach it.

"Interesting. I can see everything deep inside of you," Dan said.

The monster was distracted for a moment. Joe reached, slowly, trying to keep him from noticing.

The tongue licked up her neck.

"Anyone ever tell you to keep that thing in your pants?"

The penis darted downward, attacking her chest, burrowing. She coughed as it ripped and tore deep into her.

Joe grabbed the handle of the razor, flicked it open and swiped hard, slashing Dan's demon penis, severing the head in a splash of blood.

Dan reared in pain, losing his grip on Joe. Annie staggered back with a shard of monster cock flailing, stuck partway in her chest. Joe looked to Dan, who danced in pain, hands between his legs

"Dude, I'm sorry I had to go full Bobbit on you but—"

With a shout, a wave of force sent Joe flying across the room, hard into the wall. He was embedded a foot deep, stuck in his own cartoon outline, groggy. He could only watch as Dan gingerly stepped over to Southside Annie, picked her up by the waist with both hands and proceeded to lift her above his head. He pulled her in half, letting a wave of blood wash over him. It absorbed into his skin and his penis began regrowing.

"Now I open the portal to hell."

"Dude, don't," Mike pleaded. "You can't let the armies of hell invade earth! They'd trash everything. Like, your complete collection of Nintendo Power magazines for instance." Mike grabbed an issue from the pile on top of him, brandishing it high as if a badly drawn image of Mario could somehow change the demon's mind.

The creature seemed taken aback.

"Invade the earth?" Dan said. "Why would I want to do that?"

"Father O'Hoolahan said—"

"You believed that idiot?" Dan said derisively. "Even if I did open a portal large enough to bring an army through, the demons that came forth would all melt in the light of the sun. The spawn of hell are not meant to live in the human realm."

"Then what are you after?" Mike asked, letting the Nintendo Power fall back to the pile. "Why are you killing everyone and sucking out their energy?"

"To return home and claim my birthright."

"I don't understand."

"I'm going home to challenge for one of the thrones of hell. Why would I want to stay here and work tech support when I could be a king of evil?"

"What?" Joe said.

Dan turned to the painting. In a flash, a fiery vortex swirled in the centre, gradually filling up the entire frame. The dark cliffs, red sky, lakes of fire and brimstone, monsters, people being tortured, flayed bodies, the screams of the tormented; all came into crystal clear focus.

Mike managed to push off the bookshelf. He saw Father O'Hoolahan's headless corpse with the holy water bandolier still on. He reached out for it.

"Dan, you don't have to do this," he said, pleading as the monster stared into the picture frame. "You can forget all this hell stuff and just go back to being a normal dude. We never did rent out your room in the apartment. Think about it. Fighting in hell or coming back to Three Gamers. Eternal damnation or minor internet celebrity. Shit, we could do a stream of all the Doom games in chronological order if you wanted to get this stuff out of your system."

"I'm infused with the powers of the damned," Dan said. "You think I want to fucking stream instead of claiming a throne and ruling as master over the tormented?"

"What about Goldeneye?" Mike said. He was within a few feet of the holy water vials now. He saw Frank stirring to life under the overturned couch, Joe trying to extract himself from the wall.

"Man, fuck Goldeneye," Dan said. "That's twenty years ago, dude. I can't keep playing that fucking game forever. This is me now, king demon shit. Just accept it."

Mike closed his hands on a vial. He met eyes with Joe, who, helpless, mutely nodded like he understood. It was up to Mike alone now.

Dan's attention was lost in the vortex of the pathway into the painting. Mike took the vial of holy water out of the bandolier and threw it at Dan like a baseball. The glass shattered on impact. The splash of clear water caused his skin to bubble and boil. The demon recoiled, shrieking in agony.

Joe dropped from the wall. Mike tossed Joe a couple of vials and the two of them faced off against their friend on the battlefield of his condo's family room.

"We were best friends," Mike said. "Together since we were little kids. First you ditch us for girls and now for a throne of hell?"

"Yeah, Dan," Joe added. "What about Magic cards, RISK on that old black and white Mac, bike rides, Slurpees, movie nights, sleepovers... Wasn't that stuff worth anything?"

They pelted the demon with the vials of holy water, lobbing their glass grenades at him in quick succession. Each blast burned him. His skin turned purple, blistering, smoking. He staggered closer to the painting vortex.

"We had so many good times, so many memories," Mike said.

His wings melted away, his monster penis retracted, the claws began shrinking as Dan lost his monster form. He screamed, his voice losing its booming edge.

Then they were out of holy water.

"Everyone has to grow up eventually." Dan leapt for the portal.

"Oh no, you don't." Mike grabbed his foot.

The beast seized the edge of the frame, pulled itself half inside the portal, dragging Mike along the floor.

"Little help here, Joe."

Joe grabbed around Mike's waist and pulled backwards. Together, they seemed to be keeping Dan from escaping, but the creature cried out in anger and began pulling them towards the swirling vortex. An inch, a foot, then another

They were so close that Joe could feel the heat of the fires, hear the cries of the tormented. Hideous faces turned to stare at them.

"Let him go, kids," Frank shouted behind them. "He wants to go home, let him."

"No!" Mike shouted. "I won't give up on him!"

* * * *

Joe saw the pillars of fire in the swirling mass, the legions of hell standing in great columns in the distance, a massive throne made of bone and black rock. He heard the cries of tortured souls as they wailed in never-ending agony at their eternal damnation. It was all there, an unspeakable afterlife he'd never truly believed in. As he held on to Mike's waist, he suddenly realized that whatever Dan was now wanted to leave. It was only a matter of time until it did and pulled them right inside the portal with him.

"Let him go!" Frank shouted.

Dan cried out, looking back at them. The effects of the holy water wore off as it evaporated from the heat that emanated from the painting. His horns regrew, his claws elongated, his fangs descended, wings unfurled.

Joe realized then that the Dan they knew was truly gone. He'd become something else that didn't want to stay in their world. All they were doing was fighting to save someone who didn't want to be saved.

"He's right, Mike," Joe said. "Let him go."

* * * *

"No," Mike said. "He's my best friend!"

He felt Frank's hand on his shoulder. "Not anymore, kid."

Mike looked up and stared into the spinning vortex of the painting. Hell. Dan's home. He wanted to go. Nothing they'd said or done had changed that. He finally realized that there could be no going back. No matter how badly he wanted everything to return to normal, that life was gone. Dan had a new path, without them.

"Let me go," Dan said, looking right at him.

His eyes glowed red, his face a twisted, misshapen thing. He had horns, wings, hoofs, a weird snake penis, but despite all that, somewhere deep inside was still his best friend.

"But all those memories…"

"You keep them." Dan roared in frustration, kicked out at Mike.

"He's got his own road to walk now, kid," Frank said.

"It's time to move on," Joe said.

Mike's grip loosened. Joe's did, too. Unencumbered, Dan flew forward into the painting. They saw his demonic form shrink away as he descended deeper into Gates of Hell. The vortex collapsed in on itself and the frame became a black nothingness, as if there'd never been a painting there in the first place.

Mike felt a tear in the corner of his eye.

"He's where he wants to be." Frank patted him on the shoulder.

"Years of friendship… gone."

"Never," Joe said. "Not as long as we remember them."

Mike looked around the room at the chaos left over. Piles of bones, the headless corpse of Father O'Hoolahan, the two halves of Southside Annie, the ruined furniture, the trashed

Nintendo Power collection.

"This is one hell of a mess," he said, picking up a torn copy of Nintendo Power number two from the wreckage.

CHAPTER FORTY-TWO:
DENOUEMENT

F rank walked down the aisle of desks, past dozens of eyes staring at him in surprise, some in confusion, others in solemn recognition. The frosted glass door at the end of the line was shut. He could see the blurred shape of the Chief sitting at his desk. The man's name was emblazoned on the door in stencilled writing. He didn't knock or wait to be let in by the secretary staring at him in wide-eyed shock, he simply walked inside. "Malone!" The little man in the suit looked up.

"Chief. We need to talk."

"I know. That's why I asked you to come here for this meeting."

"And that's why I'm here," Frank said combatively.

"Have a seat."

"I think I'll take a seat instead."

Frank slid into the empty chair opposite the Chief's desk. He fingered the paper in his coat pocket, waiting for the right moment to spring the news.

"Okay, now, first of all, I just wanted to say good work on exposing that religious cult. I don't know how you managed to stumble across it, but it's a good thing you did. If the press

379

had found out before us, I'd have the mayor on my ass."

"It was all in the statement," Frank said. "Nothing beyond simple police work."

"A murdered prostitute, human skeletons, decapitated cultists, suicides, satanic rituals, it's an incredible story, Frank."

"I didn't write it, I lived it."

"And off duty, too."

"That's what I was wanting to talk to you about, Chief. I think it's time we end this detente, don't you?"

Frank gently took out the paper from his pocket, struggling with the decision to hand it over. It would change his life forever.

"I couldn't agree more. Which is why I'm—"

Frank finally gave in and slammed down the piece of paper on the desk text side up; an official form, dated and signed, nice and legal like.

"What's this?" The Chief picked up the paper and read it over. His eyes grew three sizes as he realized what it was. "You signed it? But what about the whole lone wolf speech?" He sounded incredulous.

"I was thinking about that, Chief. You see, these past few months of forced vacation have given me lots of time to do a little soul-searching, spend time with young people. It made me realize that sometimes we need someone watching our back in case we step into shit so deep we can't get out. So deep that our brand-new boots get sucked inside and we're left in socks, and those socks were new from the package, but now they're coated in thick shit that'll never really come out, no matter how many times you wash 'em and no matter what detergent you use. You understand what I'm saying here?"

"I think so. And if what I think I'm understanding is true, then it's surprising to me, Malone."

"It was a shock to me, too, sir. But I guess sometimes, despite how it might appear to the outside world, some people can't do it all alone."

The Chief leaned back in his chair, seemingly impressed. "I think that's the first vulnerable, almost human emotion you've expressed in all my time in this job. What brought on this change of heart?"

Frank turned his chair, looking out at the fresh clean cut faces in the sea of desks, so intent on their paperwork. "Because after some time with regular young people, I came to realize just how fucked the future is going to be. This place is a glorified daycare, and you need someone like me teaching the kids what for. I can't be everywhere, but I can be here, and I can make sure that here at least, the kids will be alright."

"That makes me happy, Malone. Especially that you're the one to make the decision. I was just about ready to let you come back anyway. That cult work impressed the top brass, and they were on my ass to reinstate you even with the no-partner clause. But to have you voluntarily rescind it, that's just the cat's pyjamas."

"Uh, let me see that form for a second, it—"

The Chief slid the form into his desk before Frank could snatch it back. "It's perfectly filled out, exactly what I needed. Thanks, Frank. Now how about you meet your new partner?"

"You sure we have to do this?"

"This kid ruffled a few feathers at the academy. Solid scores, but he graduated with a note that he needed some special seasoning. They think he could be a great cop someday though."

381

Frank realized that he was stuck now, but he could still make the best of it. If this new partner really had the potential they thought, he was just the right guy to bring it out.

"Alright, Chief," Frank said, "you sold me. Even if he's the spindliest, waif-iest, most hopeless case you've got, I'll turn him into a regular Sergeant Slaughter in no time."

The Chief tapped the intercom button on his desk. "Send in Officer Hooper, please."

"Hooper, eh?" Frank said, rubbing his chin. "I guess that's a good cop name."

The door behind them opened. Frank turned to see a clean-cut, tanned, well-built man with brown eyes and a head shaved nearly to the skin. He held a Starbucks cup in one hand and a pen in the other. He seemed like solid stock, but only time would tell if he could survive on the streets of this town.

"Frank Malone, I'd like you to meet Jimmy Hooper, your new partner."

"Pleased to meet you, sir," Jimmy said, putting the pen in his shirt pocket and extending his hand.

He'd have to do.

Frank shook his hand. "Stick with me, kid, and you might pick up a few things. First thing's first, though, you need to learn what real coffee tastes like."

* * * *

The sounds of gunfire echoed in the room, the action on screen frantic and desperate, the television casting a strobing series of flashes. Joe was sweating as he strafed and took aim, desperately attempting to dodge the return fire. Goldeneye again. He looked over at the white board, the score was tied. He'd never been this close before. He'd been coming in third for so many years, but not this time. He turned the corner, saw the polygonal Xenia Onatop aiming her sniper rifle the other way. He took aim and BANG, got her point blank in the head. He saw the screen turn red as the character spun and died.

"YES!" Joe cheered as the clock ticked down and the game ended. He'd won. He'd finally won.

"Goddamn it, no way," Robin said in shock.

"That was a close one."

Robin reached forward for a chip from the bowl. "After watching this thing for so long, it was cool to finally play it."

"You sure you don't want to do something else?"

Robin grinned. She wore a dark hooded sweatshirt and silver bracelets. Her dark hair was pulled back in a ponytail. Her rounded glasses with white frames glowed with the reflection of the stage select screen.

"Sometimes yeah, but tonight, this is fun."

Joe smiled back. It felt weird to be gaming with someone else, let alone a girl, let alone someone who'd said she was a fan. They'd chatted privately for a while, and he'd decided that she seemed normal enough. Now, here she was in the flesh, Cwood4Real, AKA Robin Reynolds.

"I guess Mike worked OT today, otherwise he'd be here by now."

Joe wrote a line on his side of the whiteboard. It was strange to see the victory written in felt like that. If they'd been filming this, the forums would be as shocked as he was. He walked over to the N64 and flicked it off.

"You want to go get something to eat? Maybe some ice

cream? I know a place that does these waffle cones and—"

"That sounds nice."

Robin rose and walked over to the media shelf. "It still feels a little weird to be here, like I'm crossing some line. I never thought it would happen."

"Some lines were meant to be crossed. Is it disappointing to see in the flesh?"

She smirked at him, as if she was wondering if he was tossing out a double entendre. "Not at all."

"I will admit that I cleaned the place up before you got here. Usually there's a whole heck of a lot more pairs of Mike's underwear everywhere."

"Aww shucks, for me? Thanks."

She admired all the games and movies, lined up alphabetically, brushing her fingers along the spines, pulling out ones that interested her. Joe just watched. He had butterflies in his stomach, was nervous, but felt totally invested in the moment.

"Whatever happened to the third gamer?" Robin asked. "You guys never did make the formal announcement."

"Dan... left. He decided that he had other things he wanted to accomplish in life."

"You guys ever going to get a third member again?"

"Don't know," Joe said. "It's been fun not having to worry about keeping up a schedule, just playing... for fun."

"I was listening to this podcast the other day, MediaBoy Analyzes, and he called you guys the elder statesmen of streaming."

"Elders? What the fuck, we're not that old."

Robin laughed. "Don't worry about that guy, he's a bit of an asshole."

She slid out a copy of EVO on SNES and turned it over

curiously.

"We ever going to get that ice cream?"

Joe flicked off the television. He rolled the N64 controller cables around the handles and put them on the shelf.

"Let's go."

The door opened. Mike came in, still wearing his UPS uniform, holding the hand of a woman.

"Oh shit, sorry, man, I forgot you had a date tonight," Mike said.

Joe's mouth dropped in shock when he saw who was with Mike. A woman who had to be in her seventies, with hair like a Golden Girl, wearing a floral blouse and carrying a huge grey purse.

Mike waved to introduce her. "This is Mrs. Feldstein. She really likes the Lord of the Rings."

"And I'm a demon in the sack, too," the old woman said.

* * * *

"You treat old Betty right and she'll be there for you when you need her." Frank patted the steering wheel of the archaic cruiser he refused to allow to be retired.

Jimmy marvelled at the old radio and police band. "I didn't even know they still used radio."

"The last one left," Frank said. "And I like it that way."

"You get the calls in from here?" Jimmy asked, touching the receiver.

"Damn straight. A direct line. Keep it open in case dispatch has something good for us."

They pulled up to a red light. Frank grabbed the Fat Boy from the paper bag on the seat next to him. He took a bite and chewed, letting the smells of the meat mingle with that of the city. Buildings, alleys, shops, people...

"It feels good to be back."

"Check out the convertible," Jimmy said, pointing to a car stopped a few lengths ahead of them. "You don't see too many of those around this neighbourhood."

"No, you don't," Frank said. He squinted, trying to read the license plate. "Say, kid, run that thing for me, will ya? I've, uh, got my hands full." He held up the burger, dripping mayo down his hand.

"Sure thing, Frank."

Jimmy radioed it in and Frank stayed a few lengths back, following without following. After a few tense moments, the call came back.

"Reported stolen," Jimmy said. "You want me to put the siren on?"

"So the fly has come back to the spider's web just in time for dinner," Frank said, watching the car move over a lane.

"Is that a yes?"

"Wait till the next red, kid. I'll drop you and cut him off."

"Sounds good."

They drove a few minutes, staying one lane over and just behind the red car, making sure that the driver was oblivious to their pursuit. Then, it came: a red light. The convertible stopped at the head of the line. Jimmy hopped out. Frank peeled around the car ahead of him, gunned it in the wrong lane and swerved around to block the convertible at the light.

He saw the man's eyes pop out in shock. He made a move to back up, realized he had nowhere to go, then was about to hop out when Jimmy flashed his badge in the guy's face and hauled him to the concrete.

When it was all over, the man handcuffed in the back of old Betty, and the car being towed away, Frank smiled proudly at a job well done.

"Well, Jimmy, I'd say we're off to a good start, wouldn't you?"

THE END FOR NOW...
BUT FRANK MALONE AND JIMMY HOOPER
WILL BE BACK
WITH MORE ADVENTURES SOON!

About the Author

Author, filmmaker, martial artist, collector, gamer, dad; Winnipeg based I.D. Russell has been crafting a shared universe of books and films for the past decade and a half. Beginning with the feature films *The Killing Death* and *Cybernetic Showdown* and continuing with the *High School Hell* and *Revengist* book series, his crazy comedy/horror/action stories have found an international audience. *Demon in the Sack* is the latest project expanding the world of River City Police Officer Frank Malone. Don't worry, plenty more are on the way!

Check out *The Killing Death* and *Cybernetic Showdown* now streaming on Amazon Prime, Tubi, Vimeo, and Gumroad. Visit the YouTube pages *Ringo Jones Productions* and *Jeremy Sockman Movie Reviews* for additional content or click to www.ringojones.com to stay up to date on all upcoming work!

Follow on Facebook, Twitter, Instagram, and YouTube!

You can connect with me on:

- http://ringojones.com
- https://twitter.com/IDRussellAuthor
- https://www.facebook.com/IDRUSSELLAUTHOR
- https://www.instagram.com/idrussellauthor
- https://www.patreon.com/ringojones

Subscribe to my newsletter:

- http://ringojones.com

Also by I.D. Russell

Frank Malone also appears in:

The Killing Death
He was ready to retire but then a madman started leaving victims in pieces. Can this aging cop solve one last crime before a killer finishes his deranged pizza?

When an unhinged pizzeria owner stumbles on an ancient Egyptian ritual, he begins a spree of brutal killings that leave a city in shock. It's up to veteran detective Frank Malone and his rookie partner to piece together the clues and catch the murderer. One problem, this isn't just a simple case of catch the bad guy, it could resurrect long dead spirits of evil.

With Egyptian magic, action, gore, and an insane ending you won't believe, this comedy/horror book is a wild good time!

Under Blood Lake

Somewhere in the darkness below the surface of Lake Winnipeg, the Deep Ones are waiting.

He thought it was just a simple weekend trip to put his brother's affairs in order and lay him to rest, but when River City's toughest cop shows up in the sleepy harbour town of Lakeshore, he unwittingly steps right into a community suffering under an ancient curse. Someone is pulling the strings and suddenly he's got bigger fish to fry. Off duty, without a weapon and under orders to stay on vacation, can Frank survive when he faces up to creatures more inhuman than real?

Cursed Words
Some stories should be left unwritten…

Fifty years ago the Van Lundgren estate was the sight of unspeakable acts of evil. The truth has been long buried and forgotten. Now, the house is re-opening as a bed and breakfast and twelve souls show up for the weekend. But some crimes transcend time and when a raging thunderstorm traps them inside, the guests start dropping one by one. Soon the survivors are going to learn that some horrors can never truly be locked away.

Trapped in a nightmare, there's only one truth…

Sticks and Stones may break your bones but Cursed Words can KILL YOU!

Rock 'N' Roll Nightmare: River City Hell Book 1

High School Hell was just the beginning...

Samantha Abraham graduated, her best friend and golem boyfriend didn't. Hoping to put their deaths behind her, she's off to River City University for a fresh start. Great friends, fun parties; life in the big city was everything she'd hoped. Until she meets Scott, the mysterious, tortured lead singer of the rock band Radiant Cyanide. Their music doesn't just make the crowd go wild, it might be making them go insane...

Suddenly her dream life is turning into a ROCK 'N' ROLL NIGHTMARE

Drug Wars Part 1: Lethal Dosage

Yellow Sunshine. More addictive than opium, more potent than cocaine, more dangerous than heroin. It ruins lives, destroys communities, and threatens the very country itself. It will take the River City police force everything they have to fight the scourge from street to bloody street.

Someone's dealing the worst drug the city has ever seen. THE REVENGIST is on the case with a brand new partner and a list of broken lives he's going to avenge. But to find the source of the poison, they'll have to go so far undercover that they might never make it out alive.

Drug Wars Part 2: Blood Money

MechaMountie. The secret CSIS project in cybernetics set to revolutionize the world of law enforcement. Stronger than ten gorillas with a brain faster than twenty IBM computers, the robot is laying down the law in a city under siege!

After the death of Eddie Camponelli, River City is in chaos. Rival gangs are shooting up the streets, attempting to gain control of the drug trade. The police are powerless until the government sends in their top secret weapon.

Now THE REVENGIST is in for the fight of his life to prove that no robot can do his job better than he can. He's going to show that he's still got it, even if it kills him!

Drug Wars Part 3: Iron Curtain

Ninja. The silent assassins. Using ancient martial arts techniques passed down through the secret orders of hired killers, they stalk by night and murder without a trace. Now they've come to River City and it's not to sightsee!

He might have killed the world's biggest drug supplier in Carlos Mendoza, but that only made the real bad guys mad. Now they're after him with everything they've got. In an all out battle for the future of Canada that spans the globe, THE REVENGIST is in a fight for more than just his life!

The explosive finale to the Drug Wars trilogy!

Go-Team # 1: Bitter Rivals / African Assault

The old Go-Team is gone, long live the All-New Go-Team. Led by Jessica "Doll-face" Dawes; they're sent in to infiltrate a tiny African nation in the throes of a bloody civil war. Their mission: to try to preserve the peace in the face of a brutal warlord.

But are the supreme sniper Brutal-Suzy and the kung fu assassin Hunglo enough to take on the American's better equipped, highly public, no-so-secret commando team: Uncle Sam Squad?

It's a battle between Bitter Rivals for the right to save Baangolo in an African Assault full of action, suspense, and… spring break?

Heart of Stone (High School Hell Book 1)

It's bad enough being the most unpopular girl in school, but when a strange new exchange student shows up, Samantha Abraham discovers she may be in love with a golem.

It was love at first sight for Sam when Joshua, the dark and mysterious foreign student from Eastern Europe, walked in to class. He's dreamy, great at hockey, and she's landed the chance to be his tutor. But the more time she spends with him, the more he seems to harbour a sinister secret. It's starting to look like he's a criminal, but he might also be a monster . . .

With the help of her over-zealous, secretly- crushing BFF Duckie, and with the popular girl bullies nipping at her heels, Sam must go up against a bunch of weird science, and a hellish high school social life, before she has a remote chance of a first kiss . . . or of surviving the Halloween dance.

Heart of Clay (High School Hell Book 2)

Samantha Abraham has the power to magically control her boyfriend's every action, but now someone wants that power—and wants him dead.

After the fallout from Heart of Stone, Sam has learned the truth: that her boyfriend, Joshua, was created in a lab by a mysterious scientist known only as The Professor. A magical ruby gives her the power to control him by thought. It seems like the perfect relationship, until a gauntlet of assassins show up in River City with murder on their minds.

On a quest for the truth that takes her to Toronto and into the den of her enemies, can Sam, Duckie, and hockey-hunk Rick save Joshua's life before it all goes to hell?

Heart of Flesh (High School Hell Book 3)

Samantha Abraham lost everything when she lost Joshua—but the fight for the ruby, and what it means, isn't over yet.

Sam is back in River City and the events of Heart of Clay have left her raw. If deranged necromancers were bad, you'd think Debbie and her slugs would be small potatoes, but Sam's life has gone straight back to hell in her senior year. Even with her high level hapkido skills, and a budding relationship with hockey hunk Rick Hansen, nothing seems to fill the gaping hole that Joshua and Duckie's disappearances have left . . .

But just as suddenly as he vanished, Joshua reappears with grave tidings, and Sam must decide what lengths she'll go to prevent her life—and her boyfriend's body—from falling apart.